A TIMELESS Romance ANTHOLOGY

Kissing A Billionaire

SIX ROMANCE NOVELLAS

Kissing A Billionaire
SIX ROMANCE NOVELLAS

Taylor Hart
Heather B. Moore
Sophia Summers
Annette Lyon
Danyelle Ferguson
Sarah M. Eden

Mirror Press

Copyright © 2020 Mirror Press
Print edition
All rights reserved

No part of this book may be reproduced in any form whatsoever without prior written permission of the publisher, except in the case of brief passages embodied in critical reviews and articles. These novels are works of fiction. The characters, names, incidents, places, and dialog are products of the authors' imaginations and are not to be construed as real.

Interior Design by Cora Johnson
Edited by Kelsey Down, Kim Dubois, Lisa Leigh and Lisa Shepherd
Cover design by Rachael Anderson
Cover Photo Credit: Shutterstock #249010933

Kissing a Billionaire is a Timeless Romance Anthology® book

Timeless Romance Anthology® is a registered trademark of Mirror Press, LLC

ISBN: 978-1-947152-88-5

TABLE OF CONTENTS

The Undercover Billionaire
by Taylor Hart_____ 1

Be My Plus One
by Heather B. Moore_____ 86

To Hide and to Hold
by Sophia Summers_____ 153

Bow Tie or the Billionaire
by Annette Lyon _____ 219

How to Woo a Billionaire
by Danyelle Ferguson _____ 279

A Billionaire Abroad
by Sarah M. Eden _____ 343

More Timeless Romance Anthologies

Winter Collection
Spring Vacation Collection
Summer Wedding Collection
Autumn Collection
European Collection
Love Letter Collection
Old West Collection
Summer in New York Collection
Silver Bells Collection
All Regency Collection
Annette Lyon Collection
Sarah M. Eden British Isles Collection
Under the Mistletoe Collection
Mail Order Bride Collection
Road Trip Collection
Blind Date Collection
Valentine's Day Collection
Happily Ever After Collection
A Yuletide Regency Collection
Kissing a Billionaire Collection
Midsummer Night Collection

The Undercover Billionaire

Taylor Hart

One

"I TOLD YOU, SINCE you insisted on sending me to the backwoods of Wyoming, I'm taking some time off. I'll be out of reach for ten days, Dad. Starting now." Mia dropped her luggage on the bed in her hotel room while she talked. "It's Thursday, so don't plan on hearing from me until next Sunday. That's when I'll turn my phone back on."

"You're going into this project completely *undercover*? No one is going to know you're a Jagger?"

She scoffed. "Exactly. I want to be name free. And, just to remind you, you're the one who forced me into being on this project." Resentment coursed through her, and she thought of where she really wanted to be. Her fingers itched for a knife to cut beautiful vegetables, and her nose longed for the smell of fresh garlic.

"Sweetheart," her father said hesitantly, "is this attitude because of my feelings about cooking school?"

Mia could imagine him staring out of his New York skyline office, wrinkling his nose at thoughts of her in a kitchen, cooking. Her father was in charge of Jagger Energy Enterprises, a conglomeration of companies that dealt in all types of energy. He viewed his company as the most important thing on the planet. That company was the very reason she was on this little field trip to Casper, Wyoming.

Mia squelched down her urge to fight with him. She

would have ten days away from arguing with her father about her dream. "It's called *culinary school*, Dad. And let's not talk about *your* feelings right now. I know your feelings on *that*." She couldn't stop without one more comment. "And let me remind you: it's not like I need your approval, Dad. I am twenty-five and capable of making my own decisions."

Silence on the other end of the line. "You're my right-hand man," her father said quietly.

"*Woman*," she corrected him again.

"Pfft. I know that." She could practically see him rolling his eyes in long-suffering patience. "You know I'm not a chauvinist."

"That's exactly how you sound, Dad."

He sighed, again. "I want to keep my *daughter* at the head of my company. Tell me how that's chauvinistic."

Not wanting to point out that it wasn't really chauvinism—more controlling-ism—she opted for a different argument. "You shouldn't underestimate the guys either. I have five brothers that could *all* do my job."

"No. I need you," he said in a clipped, decided manner. "You have a sharp mind, a head for business. Look, who negotiated the Harrington deal last month? You. Without you, we wouldn't have gotten that five-hundred-million-dollar deal."

"Yeah, the rest of us are just a bunch of idiots," her brother Sam called out from the background.

Mia sucked in a breath. She hated when her father didn't tell her he was on speaker and that there were others in the room. "Dad, who else is there?"

"We're all here, Mia," Sam stated, and she heard annoyance in his voice. Sam worked so hard to gain his father's approval.

Mia had five younger brothers: Sam, Mark, Daniel, James, and Cohen. They were each a little more than a year apart, and all were employees of Jagger—some of them earned their salaries, and others were still working their way up in the company.

The rule for the Jaggers was *college first, then the company.* They could opt out, of course, but their father made it too profitable to join the family business. He was controlling, and Mia had been the first child, so she was in the deepest. Recently he'd promoted her to Vice President of Business Operations. While she could admit she was good at business and even enjoyed negotiating the deals, she didn't love it. As of late, she'd decided to go for the things she did love— cooking up culinary delights. It might sound trite to her father, but she didn't care. She just wished she really had the guts to quit the company and walk away. *Ten days,* she thought, *of the sweet freedom of mental space.*

"You fall in love with a mountain man yet?" Mark asked. Mark was the snarky brother.

She was grateful Mark had changed the topic. "Ha. Ha. You know love isn't in the cards for me." It'd been over a year, but she'd had a messy breakup with a guy she thought she would marry.

Her father chuckled. "Our girl isn't meant for a mountain man; she needs a husband who is a power player."

Testiness coursed through her. Here was another topic her father thought he could control. "I don't need a husband."

"I bet she'll be there for a week and never want to come back to the city and start riding horses or something," Daniel added with another round of laughter.

"A *cowboy,*" Cohen joined in. "She's going to marry a cowboy with a big cowboy hat." She could hear them all laughing and imagined them slapping hands.

"Right," she said flatly. She had learned a long time ago that the best way to shut them up was to ignore them.

"We will miss you, Mia," her father said. "Don't forget to check out Charm Ranch. We want to make sure it's the property we need to acquire."

"I will. But remember, Dad, I won't be talking about it until next Sunday, got it? Don't try to contact me. Give me this time! I'll talk to you next Sunday."

"Love you, sis. And be careful." This was James, the brother to whom she was the closest. He was more into the things she liked. He composed music, and they hung out even outside of family gatherings.

"I will."

"Don't get *taken* or anything." Sam cursed. "We should have chipped her."

Mia bristled. She knew he meant it.

"We should have," Mark agreed. "It's a crazy world."

"No, you shouldn't have *chipped* me," she said, scoffing. Sam was always paranoid. "I'm not a dog, and I choose what I do with my life, so don't even try to contact me. My phone is turning off. Locator turned off. I'm off grid."

"I know a guy we could fly out there to do it," Daniel chimed in. "He could keep tabs on her."

"Great idea," Sam agreed.

They still weren't kidding. Mia growled, "You'd better not, or you'll pay. Love you all. Goodbye."

"Wait!" her father called out. "Mia, you make sure to take your pepper spray with you if you don't have your phone."

"Okay, okay." Despite herself, she felt a surge of warmth fill her. Even though her dad and brothers annoyed her to no end, she loved them so much. "Goodbye again. And . . . I love you all. And yes, Daddy, that includes you!"

They laughed as she pressed END on the call. She put the phone down and then turned it off, all the way off. She would make good on her promise to disconnect this week.

Putting it down on the dresser, she abruptly didn't know what to do. The thought brought a rush of excitement—she wouldn't be chained to her phone all week, wouldn't be pestered by its interruptions. Head space. Yes, that's what she'd been yearning for.

With a sigh, she turned and let herself fall onto the hotel's king-sized bed, the pillows fluffing around her. She longed for good food, too. *Extraordinary* food. She wondered what good restaurants there were in Casper, Wyoming. It wasn't New York, but it had to have something amazing, right?

She closed her eyes, deciding she'd take a nap first. After that, she'd take a taxi out to the Charm property and go for a hike. Might as well get the work part of her trip out of the way. Then it would be time to completely relax.

Two

THE SUNRISE ALMOST MADE up for the fact that Ross had to get up at the crack of dawn every morning to get a jump on feeding the animals and moving sprinkler pipes before he met at the high school for drama camp this week.

Being a high school acting teacher was a good gig, and he wouldn't deny that it worked with his love of ranching and farming. He didn't have a huge farm; basically, he just raised feed for the cattle. Too bad he hadn't realized how hard it would be to make ends meet some years, even with the combined income of teaching and ranching. These days, it was harder than ever, as he'd been paying off medical bills since everything had happened.

His wife's face flashed across his mind, and he paused, putting a hand on the center of his chest. The thing about losing someone, he'd realized, was that no matter how much time had gone by, sometimes a memory would just hit you by surprise and take the wind out of you. He sucked in a breath, forcing himself to focus on the task at hand and not dwell on everything he'd lost. He couldn't go down that path today.

He hopped out of his Ford pickup and kicked the door shut behind him. He'd already taken care of the animals. Now he was out by the north end of his property, checking the pipe. Even though he had technology hooked up to move the pipe to water his alfalfa during the day, he always had to make sure it was working. Rushing over to the pipe, he quickly checked the digital equipment. Yep. Like clockwork, the sprinkler shot on.

He was proud of himself. It was a feat to keep up with all the changing tech with farming and ranching and stay in business. Leaning back on his heels, he surveyed the budding crops and the perfect way the sprinkler moved. Yes, it was all working out.

Ross thought about the letter from the bank that lay on his desk. He and his brother, Troy, co-owner of the ranch, were trying to figure out how to deliver on the back payments. Ross had put everything into curing his wife, even paid out huge amounts of money for nontraditional treatments, all to no avail.

He sighed and tried to think about something good, but the effort was fruitless. Thoughts of her always lurked in the back of his mind. It'd been two years since the cancer had taken her, but sometimes it still felt like yesterday. He focused on his breathing, trying to calm his heart rate. He hadn't been sleeping well lately, his mind spinning about how to pay back the huge debts he owed between the ranch and the alternative care they'd tried. His hand clenched into a fist; he hated that his brother wanted to help him. It shouldn't be Troy's responsibility, but Troy wouldn't stop trying to help.

The two brothers had inherited the land from their parents when they'd passed suddenly five years ago in a car accident. At that point, Ross had taken over and managed everything, but now Troy had come home. Troy was a doctor and still had a lot of student loans, but Ross was still grateful Troy was here.

A text showed up from his sister-in-law, Kathy. *Thanks for doing extra chores for us while we're gone. We fly out at ten tomorrow morning.*

He smiled. Troy and Kathy and their son were finally going on a family vacation, which Kathy had won on the radio. He texted Kathy back. *No problem. The least I can do for all the times you watch Kinley. Have fun in Jamaica! You deserve it.*

Bobby loves to play with her.

Ross hurried back to his truck, thinking about how Kinley and Bobby, almost the exact same age, were a bit of trouble together. He grinned, remembering the text with the smashed mud pies against their house last week. Though he hadn't been smiling when he had to help clean it up.

Suddenly, a flash of red registered in the corner of his eye. Stopping, he turned and saw what looked like someone on the ground at the edges of the tree line by his property. Who would be out here at six thirty in the morning? And who would be on his property?

He jogged toward the person, who looked like a woman. "Hey!" he called out, but as he got closer, he saw she wasn't hiding. She was just lying there, maybe asleep—then he saw the blood.

"What do you mean, she was just lying on the field in the north forty?" Troy asked, yanking on the gurney and pulling the woman into the hospital with the help of another ER worker.

Ross had acted on instinct, picking her up, rushing her to his truck, and taking off for the hospital twenty minutes away. On the way, he'd called Troy, because of course he would call his brother, the doctor. He'd told Troy to be ready to intercept them at the ER. Ross could have called 911, but that would have been a waste of time.

After that, he'd called Kathy and asked her to go to his house and get Kinley. Kinley wouldn't freak out if he wasn't home to get her, because she was used to being alone a lot, but he was thankful Kathy could go pick her up.

Ross hovered next to the gurney, feeling somehow responsible. The woman was alive—he'd felt a pulse—but there was so much blood on her head. He'd found himself praying all the way to the hospital. "I went to check the sprinkler pipe, and I caught a flash of red," he explained. "When I got closer, I found her like this."

Troy swore and pushed the gurney into the ER. "You know the cops will be coming. You're going to have to miss the drama camp today."

Now Ross swore. It was true.

"Stay there. I'll be back." Troy disappeared behind some doors in the ER.

Ross turned back to the waiting room. Reluctantly, he whipped out his phone and called Theresa Smart, the other acting teacher at the high school. She was constantly hitting on him, so he didn't like calling her.

"Ross," she answered, a bit out of breath. "I've been running. Sorry, I'm a bit breathy."

He explained the situation and asked if she would cover for him at the camp.

"If I recall," she said, a hint of irritation in her tone, "you made it clear you didn't need a partner to put on this camp. You didn't want a partner."

"Theresa." He swallowed back his own annoyance. She was right: she had offered to help, and he'd told her very adamantly that he didn't need her. "Please."

She sighed. "I don't usually give up any of my summer days. We've talked about this."

"I know."

"But I will on one condition."

Relief washed through him. "Thank you."

"You're going to owe me a date for this."

"We'll work something out. Thanks again."

He hung up as she continued talking, but he didn't feel bad. The woman would take her pound of flesh, and he would worry about that later. Now he had to focus on the police.

He pressed the number for his friend the police chief, George Harper.

"What's up, Charm?" George asked, using Ross's last name. Old football habits died hard in a small town.

"George, I have a situation . . ."

It was an excruciating three hours later when George finally showed up and brought a detective with him.

Troy emerged out of the ER doors right as George showed up, announcing, "She's stable, but she took a hard hit. I don't know when she'll wake. From the tests I'm running and the specialist out of Rapid City I'm consulting, it looks like a coma." He grunted and turned to Ross. "So you just found her?"

George exhaled. "Yes, please tell us how this woman got there."

Ross threw up his hands, frustrated. All he'd been able to do for the past three hours was pace with worry about the redhead he'd brought in and remember the last time he'd been in this ER, with his wife, Brook. "I told both of you. I was checking the sprinkler this morning on the north forty, and I saw her there on the ground. I—" His voice caught, and he said more quietly, "I was worried she was dead, to tell you the truth, with all that blood on her head."

"Head injuries bleed a lot," Troy said, nodding.

George frowned. "Was there anything on her that identifies her?"

Ross hadn't searched her; he'd just gotten here as fast as possible. "I don't know."

Troy shrugged. "The nurses found a can of pepper spray." He tugged it from his pocket and handed it to George.

"Should have taken it off her person with gloves," George said.

Troy scowled. "Been kinda busy running tests and talking with brain specialists."

George nodded, turning the can over. "Can we see her?"

"Yes, if you come with me."

George inspected the can of pepper spray. It didn't have any writing on it. "After we see the woman," he said to Ross, "can we go back to your place and check it out? I'd like to inspect it all for clues. Maybe she dropped a cell phone somewhere."

Ross nodded. "I'll take you there myself."

They followed Troy through the ER, down a long hallway to the other public part of the hospital, and up an elevator.

Ross's heart rate spiked as they walked into the woman's room. A bandage had been wrapped around her head, but the blood on her face had been cleaned up. They'd also connected her to a bunch of machines. "Dang," he said, nauseated.

Troy stared as if looking at Ross for the first time. "You okay, bro?"

"Honestly, no, I'm not okay. I . . ." He shook his head and turned away, holding the door open. "Why did this have to happen? Why am I at this freaking hospital?" His tone was quiet, but his hands felt clammy. It wasn't just that his wife had died here nearly two years ago. It was all the memories of every hospital he'd gone to with her over the course of trying to cure her.

Troy's hand was on his shoulder. "It's alright. We'll figure this out."

George circled the woman, peering closely at her. "Nothing's come through about a missing person." He pulled blue gloves out of his pocket and picked up the clothes in the bag next to her. "This is what she was wearing?"

Ross nodded.

George tucked them beneath his arm. "I'll take these back to the station with me, and we'll do some tests off the blood, see if we can find anything." He turned to Ross. "Go through the details of finding her again. What time was it?"

Ross took them through it all, hating that every time he told it, more and more worry for this woman filled him. He hated that someone had been found like this on his property, and he worried she wouldn't pull through.

After an endless amount of questions, George sighed. "Ross, do you mind if we go search your truck?"

Ross felt put on the spot. "For what?"

George shrugged. "Fellas," he said, speaking to both him and Troy, "I've seen these missing-person things go sideways, so just be prepared for the worst."

Nervous energy sucker-punched Ross in the gut. He didn't need this right now, not on top of everything going on with losing the ranch. But there was no getting out of it. "Fine, let's go."

Three

"I WANT TO GO see the woman who got hurt, Daddy," Kinley whined as she helped Ross put away the dinner dishes. It'd been a long day dealing with filling out reports and having the police come out to the ranch. Not only had they searched his truck and his property, but they'd also insisted on searching his home and Troy's home a half mile down the street.

The last thing Ross wanted to do was go back to the hospital. "Sweetheart, no. I don't think that would be a good idea."

Kinley frowned. "I want to meet her."

"She's asleep. Now go get ready for bed."

Kinley crossed her arms, sticking out her bottom lip. "She's hurt, though, right?"

He nodded, reluctant to discuss this whole situation with her again. She'd been talking about it, understandably, since the moment he'd picked her up an hour ago.

"Daddy, you always say we're supposed to help people."

Frankly, Ross was at his help limit for the day. He knew his daughter didn't understand, and it wasn't her job to understand his problems. Bending down, he dumped her over his shoulder. "I want to play airplane, so that's what we're going to do."

She giggled, but he could tell that she was trying to stay serious. "Daddy, put me down!" she yelled out, kicking her feet.

Rushing down the hallway, he made silly airplane noises, the same ones he'd always made when she was little and they would play this game. He got to her room and flipped on the light, gently zooming her to the bed and dropping her.

She bounced and giggled, "Don't! I want to see the woman!"

It made him smile that she sounded so grown-up. Diving on her, he tickled her beneath the chin. "It's bedtime, young lady."

"Stop!" She sat up, finally putting her grouchy face back on. "I really want to see the lady that got hurt."

Dang, the girl was stubborn. *Just like her momma,* he thought, but he wouldn't say it out loud. He sighed. "Kinley, Uncle Troy says he will let us know if anything changes. The hospital is on alert to let him know first."

Kinley frowned in disbelief. "But he's going on vacation. He won't know."

He put up his hands. "Dr. Frank will let us know. I promise I'll tell you when I know something."

Begrudgingly, she stood, pulled her pajamas from the drawer, and headed toward the bathroom.

"Be quick, and I'll tell you a story."

"Okay."

Ross knew that meant he was forgiven. If Kinley would beg for anything, it was a story at bedtime.

She was fast, turning off the light and jumping into bed beside him.

He laughed as she got beneath the covers and snuggled into him. "Once upon a time—"

"Is the woman going to be okay, Daddy?"

He was touched by her concern. Turning on his side, he smoothed her hair back and kissed her forehead. "I hope so, baby."

Kinley hesitated, then sat up. "What if this were me, Daddy?"

"What?" Her question surprised him.

"Isn't the lady somebody's daughter?"

Bam! The question hit the center of his chest like a ton of bricks. "I guess she is."

"Can we pray for her?"

He slipped off the bed and onto his knees, chastising himself for not having her say her prayers in the first place. "You bet. Why don't you say it?"

"Dear Lord, please bless that lady at the hospital. Please bless her family if she has a daddy, brothers and sisters, or a husband and kids. Thank you for all our blessings, our home, food, the ranch, the animals, Uncle Troy ..." She went through all the things in her life, which made it a long list. "And thank you for Daddy. Please take care of him. Amen."

"Amen."

Four

ROSS AND KINLEY SAT at the airport with Troy and his family, waiting for them to go through security. He could tell that Troy hadn't wanted to leave, protesting that he had a patient in a coma, but Kathy would hear none of it.

Ross agreed with Kathy. "There's always going to be something keeping you back," he said to Troy.

"Exactly," Kathy said, glaring at her husband.

He gave her a superior look.

She threw up a hand. "Look, I feel bad about the woman, but we've never taken a vacation. And this one is free, so we're going."

"Yeah, a free vacay!" Bobby put his fist up but kept his focus on the iPad in front of him.

Kinley stood next to Bobby, staring at Ross and looking cross.

Kathy gestured to Ross. "He'll take care of things."

Ross nodded, wanting his brother and wife to have fun. "It'll be fine."

"We haven't ever taken a vacation," Kinley said. Her fingers wiggled in his grip.

"Hush." Ross squeezed her hand, hating that she was right.

Kathy met his eyes. "I'm sorry," she said to Ross, then she bent to Kinley, lightly taking her hand. "You guys will go on the next vacation, and we'll watch your animals. Deal?" She lifted her brows, then held her arms open.

Unable to resist, because Kinley adored her, she dove into Kathy's arms. "Deal."

Ross tamped down his embarrassment that Kinley was making it so hard on them. He hadn't even thought about taking a vacation since his wife had passed away.

Kathy stood.

Ross gave her a hug. "You go. Have fun. Everything will be fine."

Kathy nodded when she pulled back. "Thank you."

Ross looked at Troy. "I mean it."

Troy sucked in a long breath and blew it out fast. "Fine, but you'll let me know when she wakes up."

Kinley piped up. "Daddy and I could check on the lady in the hospital, Uncle Troy."

"Would you?" Troy glanced at Ross, well aware that Ross wouldn't want to do it.

Ross wanted to chastise his precocious daughter, but he only sighed.

Kinley looked back at her father, her bottom lip pushing out.

"Of course." Ross cocked an eyebrow at his daughter. "No problem."

Troy grabbed him by the arm, tugging him away from the group. "I need to talk to Ross for a sec," he said to Kathy.

Ross put on an *all-is-well* smile for his brother. "Have fun, and don't worry about anything."

Troy scowled.

Ross knew it wasn't in either brother's nature to want to take a vacation. Their father had instilled "work, work, work" into them. He remembered two family vacations his family had ever taken growing up, and both were because his mother had insisted. "Try to have fun."

Troy sighed and nodded. "Look, I know we're meeting with the bank the day I get back, but I've thought a lot about it. If it comes down to it, we move into town. You get a house and teach, and I get a house and be a doctor."

Troy made it sound so simple, which only fueled Ross's anger. "Oh, right, Mr. Doctor, forget the land we grew up on. Forget the land Mom and Dad loved."

"What do you want me to do?" Troy asked, whispering loudly and backing them farther away from their families. "I've reached out to multiple people for help, and no one can swing it. I don't want to do it either. But bro, we have to face the facts: if the bank won't refinance, then the bank won't refinance. We can't pay the back payments."

Ross knew that, and he knew his brother didn't take all of this lightly. He shook his head, thinking about how he'd neglected to tell Troy about the latest letter. "That Jagger conglomerate group are wily buggers. They keep sending me letters, telling me they will buy if we give them the mineral rights straight out."

"I know. They send me the letters too. I just worry they're going to try to sneak in and buy the place out from under us if we don't cave."

Ross hated that he had no control of this situation. "I know. I would just hate to see everything Dad built turn into an oil-and-mining project."

Troy put a hand on his shoulder. "I know Mom and Dad loved the land, and we do too." He sighed. "That's part of the reason I came back here—to raise my kids on it."

Ross nodded, feeling hopeless.

"Remember, bro, sometimes all we have is two hands to rebuild whatever is taken away from us. And with the good Lord, all things are possible. We have to have faith."

Ross grunted. "Quoting Dad now?"

"You know that's what the old man would say—'go, rebuild, and build it even better than before.'"

"'Never say die,'" Ross said, quoting their father too. Thinking of his father's never-ending optimism about life actually made him feel a little better.

Troy grinned, adding the rest of the quote. "'Never quit.'"

Their father had been military, and he had been tough as nails. It had hit both Ross and Troy hard when their parents had passed in that car accident.

A second later, their flight was called. Troy hugged Ross and then headed away. "Bye."

"Have fun," Ross called out.

"Dad!" Kinley darted over, slipping her hand into his.

"Yes?" Ross squeezed her hand.

"Can we really go check on the lady?"

He nodded, although they'd need to get to the high school for his camp first. "Right after actor camp, we'll head over."

Kinley endured the drama camp well, sitting at the back of the theater for most of the camp, observing, drawing, and finally playing on Ross's phone. Later, as they headed to the hospital, she chatted happily about all the possibilities of this lady. She made Ross explain exactly what the woman looked like.

When they walked into the hospital room, Ross was stunned. The afternoon sunlight poured through the window, highlighting the woman's red hair and porcelain skin in a way that made the petite woman look unreal. Ethereal. Angelic.

Kinley rushed to her side. "She looks like a sleeping princess," she said, her voice quiet and reverent.

Ross was thinking the same thing.

"Hello." A nurse on Troy's staff, Nadine, greeted them. She was an older woman in her fifties with salt-and-pepper hair and a warm smile. "How are we doing?"

Kinley grinned at her. "Hey, Nadine."

Nadine opened her arms, and Kinley went into them easily. "I'm surprised to have visitors for this lady," Nadine said.

"Daddy promised Troy we would check on her. I think she looks like a princess."

"Oh." Nadine glanced at Ross and then back to Kinley, squatting down. "A Sleeping Beauty princess. I like it. Maybe your dad is just the one to kiss her awake?"

Ross shot Nadine a horrified look.

Kinley clapped her hands together, overjoyed. "Yes."

Nadine chuckled and stood. "Kidding." She moved to Ross, leaning in for a hug.

"Sorry," he mumbled. "Not the Prince Charming type."

Nadine grinned as she pulled back. "But you are a Charm, so there's that."

He rolled his eyes. "You never change, Nadine."

She wiggled her nose and turned back to Kinley. "I'm glad you came, because I just restocked the candy at our station. Want to come get some while we let your dad talk to Sleeping Beauty?"

Ross's heartbeat picked up speed. "Not necessary." He started to follow them out of the room.

Nadine was already pulling Kinley out the door. "Let us girls chat. We'll be right back."

Ross watched them go and listened to the two of them exchanging a million questions. Kinley adored older women. He didn't know if she gravitated to women because she'd lost her mother, but he always felt culpable, like it was his fault.

He turned to face the sleeping woman. She was beautiful. He edged closer, wondering who she could be. Why had no one come for her yet? She looked like she could wake at any moment. The heart monitor tracked her heart's rhythm, beeping repeatedly.

He studied her freckled face, grateful the blood had been cleaned up. He hadn't really looked at a woman since Brook. Not in a detailed way like this. This woman couldn't be past her mid-twenties, he thought. Could she?

All kinds of questions filled his mind. Why had she been out on his property? The investigation from the police had produced no car, no identification on her person, no phone. It was like the woman had fallen from the sky. He knew George would have called if there was news about someone looking for her.

She looked so peaceful. He hoped that she was okay, that whatever family she did have wasn't too worried, and that it would all be resolved quickly.

Hearing laughter from the hall, he could picture Nadine gathering the nurses and telling Kinley stories from the past. He loved that about living in a small community and having roots. People knew each other and loved each other.

For a time, after Kinley's mother had passed, he'd hated living here and seeing the pity in people's eyes, but that had subsided. With his brother back in Casper, he knew he never wanted to leave. He loved this town.

He sat in a chair next to the woman and studied her face, wondering what she would look like if she woke up and smiled. What in tarnation would have brought her to his property? There weren't even commercial trails out there. Nobody came out to his property unless they were there to visit.

"What are your secrets, Sleeping Beauty?" he asked quietly, hating how much he wanted to connect with this woman, that he'd actually fallen asleep worried about her the night before. It'd been a monumental effort to keep Kinley away from her. He remembered Kinley's prayer the night before, which had reminded him that this woman was alone here. No family. No husband. Where were they? Didn't someone care for her? It made him sad to think she didn't have anyone.

Before he realized what he was doing, he reached out, gently touching her hand. Her fingers were so warm and soft compared to his rough ones, which were callused from things like fixing fences. He bowed his head and muttered a prayer. "Lord, please help her. Please help her wake up and help her family to find her. Amen." He tugged his hand back and stared at her again.

Suddenly her eyes fluttered open.

Startled, he jumped to his feet. "Wh—oh my gosh."

She didn't say anything, only stared at him.

"Nadine!" he called, taking a step back. "Nadine!"

Before Nadine could come rushing in with Kinley in tow, the woman shut her eyes again.

Five

THE NEXT MORNING, ROSS stood at the front of the high school theater room, lecturing his drama students. "When you play a really great character, the trick is to get in their head," Ross said, pacing in front of the ten kids attending the camp. Today they were delving into character development. "You think about what they believe, because their beliefs always give you insight into what they want and what they can do." He grinned at his students, trying not to let his mind wander back to those piercing green eyes that he'd fallen asleep dreaming about.

The woman hadn't woken permanently, much to everyone's dismay. They'd stayed another hour at the hospital before finally heading back to get all the chores done at the ranch. Kinley had incessantly talked about the woman and made him tell her over and over again what her eyes had looked like. This morning, before coming into town, Ross had called the hospital to check on her, but she was still asleep.

"Mr. Charm?" Callie, a student from his advanced acting class who had played lead roles in many of the plays, raised her hand.

"Go ahead," he said, focusing on her.

"I get what you're saying about characters, but I find it interesting that sometimes characters do things that surprise you. In fact, sometimes the most interesting characters don't know how to do the thing they want to do."

He thought about Luke Skywalker and Obi-Wan. "True. That's the part of the character's journey we all love to see: the part when they suspend their own beliefs and do the miracles they were born for." He met each student's eyes. "Most of the time, the character thinks they want something, but usually what they *want* isn't what they really *need*. That's the trick to playing any character: knowing the answer to what a character wants and what they need."

Callie nodded. "Like in a Hallmark movie when a man thinks he wants a certain job or some material thing he's working for, but he discovers what he really needs is the love of a good woman."

The class laughed, and Ross couldn't help but chuckle too. "I think you've been watching too many Hallmark movies, but yes."

Even though the pay was less than desirable, he found so much satisfaction in teaching. At the end of the row, his eyes met Kinley's. He smiled even wider at his daughter. He'd given her his phone and thought she was playing games, but now he could see she was paying close attention.

Ross continued. "It is a privilege to play a character. To learn about them. To be able to put on their feelings and beliefs and to witness their growth. Never forget that it is a privilege, because they become real to you." He flashed them a grin. "Also, never forget that you can put on those beliefs and take them off like a jacket, slipping in and out of them. Don't get caught in someone else's beliefs, thinking that they are your own. That is important for actors to remember."

The camp ended for the day, and he said goodbye to the students before walking Kinley to his truck. He opened the door for her. "You ready to go see your grandma and grandpa?"

His wife's parents lived in Gillette, Wyoming, a little over two hours away. They were the best people and loved having Kinley come stay for a weekend every month. They would be coming to get her in just a bit.

Kinley frowned. "I don't want to go."

"What? Why?" He raced around the truck and got in, starting it.

"Because I want to be here when the lady wakes up. She might need some girl time."

His heart softened, and he took her hand. "If she wakes up, I'll make sure you get to meet her."

"Promise?"

His heart fluttered, and he felt chills wash over him. Not a premonition, no. It couldn't be. Dismissing the feeling, he said, "Promise."

Kinley sighed. "Okay, but I have a question."

"What is that, princess?"

"What does your character need?"

Later that evening, Ross sat on his back porch, doing something he rarely had time to do: sit on his porch swing and read a Vince Flynn book. It was an FBI kind of book, high action and high adventure.

Kinley's grandparents had arrived, and they'd had sandwiches together and chatted. Kinley had told them all about the woman Ross had found on the ranch and informed them she may have to come back early if the woman woke up.

Before Kinley's grandparents left, her grandmother, Sheila, had stopped inside the door, putting a hand on his forearm. "Ross."

The way she'd said his name sounded intense. "Yes?" he'd asked, wondering what was coming.

Sheila had smiled at him. "The way Kinley talks about

that woman in the hospital . . . I just want you to know if you ever decided to have a relationship again, we would be so happy for you."

It stunned Ross that Sheila would think he wasn't having a relationship because of them. He'd nodded. "I'm not interested in that, but . . . thank you."

Her words had stuck with him all afternoon as he'd moved water and fixed things around the ranch. The question of why he hadn't had a relationship plagued him. The obvious reason was that he still mourned Brook, but something else pricked at his consciousness, and he thought about the woman in the hospital. He'd found her attractive, and he hadn't felt that way in a long time. Sure, he'd been raising Kinley, but that wasn't it. Even Theresa Smart, the other acting teacher who kept asking him out, was cute, and she'd asked him out several times, but he wasn't interested. He thought of Theresa; she was a bit annoying too.

Then he thought about Kinley's question: what does your character need?

He shook his head, unable to stop Sleeping Beauty's face from appearing in his mind. He remembered the way her eyes had fluttered open and stared at him like she'd known him. Which was stupid. He tried to focus on the page he'd reread for the third time.

His phone rang, startling him. Digging it out of his pocket, he saw it was Dr. Frank. His heart raced. "Hello?"

"She's awake, and she's asking for you."

He jolted to his feet, confused. "Asking for me?"

Dr. Frank sighed. "You're the only one she remembers."

Six

THE PAIN THUDDED ACROSS her forehead like a knife jammed into her head. She didn't know anything, and she didn't like the barrage of questions they kept asking her like she was a criminal facing a firing squad. She tried to keep her eyes shut, because that was the only thing that made the pain abate.

Even though they'd all gone out into the hall, she could still hear them through the crack in the door, trying to decide what to do with her. How come nobody had come for her?

Upon waking, the only thing she remembered was a man. With his beautiful, strong face, he looked like he'd stepped out of one of those romance books in the grocery store or gas station with a cowboy hat, a strong jaw, and a button-up shirt. His cool, blue eyes had looked surprised. Then he'd yelled something, and she'd closed her eyes again.

She could remember that, but she couldn't even remember her name.

Now she was tossed in a sea of questions and uncertainties, and she was terrified. She didn't know who these people were, where she was, or even who she was. All she knew was that man's face.

"Miss," someone said. She opened her eyes and saw the man in the white coat, Dr. Frank, gesturing to another man—the man in her mind. "Is this who you wanted?"

She blinked and noted the way the man looked tentative,

as though she would strike out and scratch him. She frowned, trying to search her brain for answers. "Do I know you?"

The man held her gaze, then turned to the doctor. "She asked for me?"

The doctor nodded.

"Really?" the man asked the doctor.

"I can talk," she said.

His gaze shifted back to her.

She remembered the feel of his hand, how it had awakened her. "You touched my hand," she said softly.

"And you woke for a bit." The man took another step closer to her. "Are you okay?"

"Are you a cowboy?" she asked.

He grunted, glancing at the doctor. "Sometimes."

His response confused her. "Do we know each other?"

The man rubbed his eyebrow. "No, I found you on my property. You had fallen and bumped your head. I brought you here."

Her heart raced, and she tried to remember. "Why was I on your property?" The pain in her head grew more intense with every question she tried to solve.

"I don't know. They've been trying to find your family. Do you remember anything?"

Again, there was nothing. She thought of that annoying police chief. "I can't answer these questions. I don't want to be here anymore." She looked past the man, to the doctor. "Please, release me." She hated the smell of the place, and there was something else she hated that she couldn't put her finger on.

The doctor stepped in front of the sometimes cowboy. "Miss, we don't have anyone to release you to."

"I can take care of myself." She knew she could, even though she had this massive pain in her head. She knew she would be okay.

The doctor frowned. "I'm sorry. Until we find where you belong, it would be dangerous and risky to release you. The hospital can't take on that liability."

"I'll sign a form," she said, already tired from the legalese turn of this conversation. How did she know about legalese, she wondered? Unfortunately, she didn't know the answer to that either.

"Do you remember what your name is?" the doctor asked.

She was at a complete loss again. The pain spiked, and she cried out and leaned her head back, closing her eyes.

"You okay?"

It was his voice, the semi-cowboy's voice, but she didn't open her eyes.

"Where is the pain?" Dr. Frank asked.

"Same place. I'm okay," she said, keeping still. She didn't want to be here, but the pain was horrible.

The doctor let out a breath. "I don't think it's a good idea if you leave, miss. Not until you're better and you remember something. The hospital cannot, in good conscience, release you when you don't even know your name." Feet shuffled, and then he spoke again. "I'll give you something for the pain. Open your eyes, little lady."

She did so and looked up to see the doctor holding out a pill and a drink with a straw.

"Take this. It'll ease your pain and help you sleep."

She frowned, wanting to resist. "I don't like pills."

The doctor smiled. "I think you need to sleep."

She lifted her trembling hand, hating that she was so weak. She took the pill and let the doctor help her sip the water; then she leaned back, still staring at the cowboy.

The man stepped forward, taking the chair next to her bed and sliding it closer. "I'll sit with her, Doc, don't worry."

This man was willing to sit with her when he didn't even know her. She was touched, and the fear seeping into her receded a bit. She tried to smile at him. "Thank you."

Then it all went dark.

Seven

ROSS AWOKE WITH A start. Pain in his neck reminded him that he was still in a hospital chair. Somewhere around one in the morning, he'd fallen asleep. He remembered thinking that he should drive back to the ranch, but he didn't want to leave her. Granted, from her earlier interaction with Dr. Frank, she seemed a bit strong-minded and brash. He grinned—the temperament matched the hair color. But who would care about that joke right now? He thought about the way she'd said her soft thank you before falling instantly asleep.

It had felt like she had meant it. Again, he thought about how alone this woman was.

Picking up his almost-dead phone, he noted the time: five thirty. It was Saturday, and he didn't have drama camp, but he always had animals to take care of, and he had Troy's for the next week too.

He stood, rubbing his neck and staring at the woman, who was still asleep. The light of the hospital monitor fell across her porcelain skin. For a second, he couldn't breathe. Truly, the woman was gorgeous, and he wondered if she was married or if she had a boyfriend.

No, he thought, refocusing. It didn't matter. Somewhere out there, she had a father, and Ross knew how he would feel if his little girl were lost or missing.

That was the only reason he was here.

Later that day, Ross had just put the mushrooms and onions in the pan to cook—a nice addition he'd found to grilling hamburgers—when his phone rang.

It was Dr. Frank. Ross composed himself before answering. "Hello?"

"Ross." He sounded out of breath. "Can you come? The woman is insisting on leaving. She's gotten dressed, and the staff is trying to keep her, but the only person she says she'll talk to is you."

Turning off the stovetop, he grabbed his keys off the peg in the wall by the door. "I'll be there in a sec."

When he arrived, the first thing he noticed was the woman sitting on a bench outside of the room she'd been staying in. She was dressed in the same clothes she'd been wearing when he'd found her: hiking shoes, a T-shirt, black leggings, and a windbreaker. The hospital staff must have cleaned them.

Nadine was hovering near the nurse station, and George was there too. Both of them headed toward him, but the strange woman intercepted him first. "Mr. ... Charm? At least, that's what they told me." She didn't wait for him to respond. "I've been informed they will not release me on my own. And I cannot stay here another day, so I'm asking if I can go with you."

Shock pulsed through him, and he glanced at Nadine and George, who looked as if they'd already heard this idea. "You want to come with me?"

The woman held her chin up with a distinct air of certainty, leaving him no room to disagree. "When I do remember, I'll compensate you for your troubles. I promise."

He met her green eyes, disconcerted by the clear

attraction he felt for her. She was a couple of inches shorter than he was, roughly five ten, he thought. She was slender, and even though she obviously wasn't wearing makeup, it didn't matter. "No," he said decisively, walking around her.

"Why?" She grabbed his shirtsleeve.

The woman was stubborn. He thought of the severe stubborn streak in Brook and Kinley and wondered why all the stubborn women liked him.

Nadine and George both moved toward them, looking confused.

Ross scrambled for an answer. "Because I have a daughter, and it wouldn't be . . . appropriate to have you at my house." He gently took her hand and pulled it off of his sleeve, then dropped it.

The woman looked around. "Where is your daughter?"

He let out a light laugh at the way this woman expected her demands to be answered. He hesitated, giving George a questioning look.

George only shrugged.

"Where is your daughter?" the redhead demanded with more umph to her voice.

He turned back to this woman. Even if she was beautiful, she was irritating. "She's actually . . . gone for two days, but then she'll be back."

Without missing a beat, the redhead grinned and said, "Perfect. Then it's not *inappropriate*. I could just come with you, and then hopefully, I'll remember something soon, or someone will"—her voice broke—"have come for me by then."

"Why would you want to come with me?"

She sighed, shaking her head and looking distracted as though she hadn't heard him. "Yes, someone will come by then, so I won't be there too long, I shouldn't think."

"Why?" His pulse was racing, and he felt nervous, like he was a teenager again and about to play a football game.

"What?" The woman stared at him, confused.

"Why would you want to come home with a man you don't know?"

The woman held her ground, her face betraying nothing. "Actually, it feels like you're the only person I do know."

His heart hammered louder inside of his chest. This couldn't happen. He couldn't take a random woman home with him, even if Kinley wasn't actually there. "No."

The woman blinked and her bottom lip trembled, but she kept her head up, her eyes on his. "Please," she whispered. "I have no one else."

It was this last bit of the sentence that got him. How would he feel if Kinley were in this situation? He looked away from the woman, cursing beneath his breath.

"Please. I won't be trouble. I'll help."

"Help?" He thought this was doubtful.

She lifted a finger. "I'll cook." A small smile played at her lips. "Yes, I think I know how to do that."

Not that he wouldn't mind having someone cook, but . . . this was insane. He didn't know her at all, and wasn't there some place she could go? He turned to George and asked, "Can we talk in private?"

George nodded and moved down the hallway. "Nadine, please keep an eye on her."

Ross followed George, falling in step with him as they walked the length of the hospital floor.

George stopped, letting out a sigh. "What do you think?"

"What do you mean, what do I think? She's asking to come home with me, and that opens me up to a whole possibility of trouble, even if Kinley's not there. You know that."

George winced. "You're right." He turned and stared at Nadine and the woman.

Out of the blue, Nadine laughed, and then the redhead laughed too.

"I don't believe she's dangerous," George said. "They ran some psych tests, and she seems completely cognizant, except for the fact she doesn't remember her life."

Ross's heart rate spiked again. "Are you saying you think I should take her, George?" This couldn't be what the police chief was actually suggesting.

George let out a breath. "There was no evidence of foul play from her injury. Honestly, I think she slipped on your hillside and fell."

"Okay, but shouldn't she go to a shelter or . . ." He floundered, trying to think of where she would go. "Shouldn't she go with a woman? Not with a *rancher*?"

George nodded. "Nadine offered to have her go home with her, but she refused. She said the only person she wanted to go with was you."

"What?" Ross sputtered, caught off guard. Hyper butterflies swarmed in his stomach. "Why?"

A slight smile played at George's lips. "She said she trusts you. It appears you are Prince Charm-ing." He added the *ing* with a bit of a laugh.

Ross frowned at him. "Stop it, George." It was amazing how quickly they could revert to junior high kids all of a sudden.

George put his hands up. "Hey, I'm sorry. In all seriousness, she only wants to go with you."

"What if I were a weirdo? Would you release her to me?"

"You're not a weirdo. I've known you our whole lives. Don't worry—a social worker will be assigned to her and checking on her and the whole nine yards. I'll be checking in too."

Ross threw up a hand, panicking about having a woman alone in his home with him. "What about Kinley?"

George didn't speak for a moment. "If you don't want to do it, you don't have to." He cleared his throat. "But you did say she would be gone for two days, so you could try it out without putting your daughter at risk."

A million thoughts ran through Ross's mind. "I really can't believe you're encouraging this."

"What? You can't believe I would think good people step up and do what's right?"

Another round of irritation pulsed through Ross. "Really? This is the guilt you're laying on me?"

Surrendering, George threw his hands up. "I'm just saying the woman will have to go to a shelter, or to a home she doesn't want to go to, or she'll have to stay in the hospital if you don't take her." He rubbed his forehead, stressed out.

Ross nodded slowly. How would it look to have her stay? What would he tell Kinley? Would Kinley get too attached? He finally settled on the biggest problem. "What about her memory? Her family? Where could they be?"

"No idea. I've had an APB put out all over the place. We've been waiting for a missing-person report to be filed, but there's been nothing so far." George sighed and stopped walking. "Frankly, I would be obliged if I could release her into your custody for a few days."

It would be the right thing to do. Ross could do it. And if she ended up being a weirdo, he'd bring her back or call George, right? His mother had always talked about serving others and helping out when God put opportunities in front of you. It'd been a long time since he'd helped someone when it was really hard. He'd been so focused on his own problems, his own life. He blew out a breath. "Fine. Okay, she can come."

A tiny smile tugged at George's lips.

Ross's hackles rose, and he wanted to take the words

back. "Let me be clear: it's only because I would want someone to help my daughter if she were ever put in this situation."

George put a hand on his shoulder. "That's why I trust everything will work out."

Eight

"WHY ME AGAIN?" ROSS asked. The road was dusty as they drove onto a windy driveway, which a steel sign indicated was called Charm Ranch.

It made the woman smile, thinking that his last name was Charm. "Like a fairy-tale," she muttered, ignoring his question.

"What?" he asked, looking from the road to her.

"Charm." She pointed to the sign.

"Oh." He let out what sounded like a nervous laugh. "No, it's . . . not a fairy-tale. I'll tell you that."

It was unsettling, sitting in a truck with a man she didn't know, going to a place she wasn't sure if she would like. As the house came into view, she thought the home was quaint. Not big, not small. It wasn't old, but it wasn't new. It was a two-story with black shutters, and she could see flower boxes beneath the windows. She smiled, thinking how nice it would look when flowers bloomed in them.

Ross parked in the middle of a circular driveway. No one else must use the driveway if he could block it so casually. He cut the engine and turned to her. "I think I deserve a real answer, because I can't for the life of me think of why you would want to come with me."

She met his deep-blue eyes. They looked like a storm before it rained, before the cloud cover fully got in the way. *A bit dangerous,* she thought. He had jet-black hair beneath his cowboy hat, and a more-than-five-o'clock shadow. It surprised her to feel this attraction to him. Should she be attracted to him? She didn't know. Was she married? How old was she? For the past twenty-four hours, her mind had circled back to all of these kinds of questions, questions she felt no closer to than when she'd woken.

"Hello?" he asked, lifting a hand and waving it back and forth, clearly out of patience.

The truth was, the more he pressed for an answer, the more she didn't want to give an answer. "I . . . I don't know." She threw a hand into the air. "Why did you agree to have me come?"

He sputtered and stepped out of the truck. As he walked around the front to her door, she noted that the truck was older, and she searched for the latch to get out.

The door opened, and he waited, his hand out to help her. "Because it's the right thing to do." He flashed her a grin. "My parents always taught me to help people, so that's what I'm trying to do."

Her head still felt a bit heavy, so she took his hand to get out. "Thank you."

He stayed next to the truck, dropping her hand and narrowing his eyes. "For helping you out of the truck or for letting you stay?"

She pulled in a breath, wishing she didn't have to be at someone else's mercy, but very grateful she wasn't stuck in the hospital. "Both."

Squeezing his eyes shut for a moment, he let out a breath. Then he reached around her into the back part of the truck, taking out a bag of clothes. Nadine and the other nurses had all brought in clothes, donating them to her. She hadn't looked at the clothes yet, but it was just one more thing that overwhelmed her.

He started to the front of the house, but stopped when he realized she wasn't following. "Are you okay?"

The vulnerability she'd been feeling lessened. She nodded and continued.

He gave her a tour of the living room, the kitchen area, and the three rooms off to the side. He put down her bag of clothes in one room, explaining that this was where she would be staying.

As she took it all in, she found herself wondering more about him. She'd heard him talking with Nadine and George about his daughter, and she saw the pictures all over the walls and the purple-and-pink room that had little stuffed animals on the bed. Oddly, they hadn't mentioned his wife.

On the wall outside of her assigned room, there was a picture of him, a woman, and a little girl. The woman was blond with short, bobbed hair. It was one of those pictures that looked like the photographer captured a candid moment. Like someone had said something that had made everyone laugh.

Ross stopped next to her, but he didn't look at the picture. "I'm going to go finish my dinner. Are you hungry?"

"I saw the pictures of your wife; I'm sorry," she said softly.

Abruptly, he stopped.

"I'm sorry." She thought about how this man had been through a lot according to Nadine.

Ross let out a long breath. "I'm going to eat. Suit yourself."

Nine

Ross sat at the dinner table, finishing his hamburger. He hadn't been that hungry, but he'd needed something to do, and the process of fixing dinner and sitting to eat felt normal and helpful. He liked patterns and processes. There was something comforting about knowing the next thing that was on the schedule, whether it had to do with Kinley's activities or teaching or the ranch.

After Brook had passed, he'd found that routines were all that kept him going. He had kept going, even through the grief. Even when he felt like rolling up into a ball in bed. Even when he was sure the numbness could never be broken and he would never feel again.

So far, he hadn't stopped moving.

While he'd been growing up, his father had always said, "Work works when nothing else works." Now he could testify that his father's words were true.

The woman emerged from the hallway and walked into the kitchen area slowly, still looking at the walls and the pictures. It had unnerved him that she'd spent the past half hour staring at all the pictures in the hallways.

The only pictures he'd changed in the past two years were Kinley's school pictures. Otherwise, it was the same assortment: wedding pictures of him and Brook, pictures from around the ranch, a picture of him and Brook graduating from college, and tons of baby pictures of Kinley. Brook had loved taking pictures and putting them up.

The strange woman didn't say anything to him. She didn't turn to ask him how he was or how dinner was or give him a reason for why she'd wanted to come with him. The truth was that her being here put him on edge. He wanted to ask more, but he knew she didn't know the answers. So he waited.

Good thing Kinley was out of town. She'd be unable to stay quiet. He let out a light laugh, thinking of the hundreds of questions she could come up with.

"Is something funny, Mr. Charm?" She still stared at the pictures.

He stood, taking his dishes into the kitchen. "Nope." With practiced efficiency, he cleaned up the kitchen, putting everything away and starting in on the dishes.

She walked into the kitchen, looking around. She gestured to a wall. "If you moved the wall between the dining area and the sink, you could open up a whole bunch of space in here," she said.

He turned and noted that she was inspecting the kitchen. "Hmm."

She pointed to the counters. "You could have an island in the middle. Then you'd have a nice spot to prepare the food."

He snorted. She was already redecorating the place. "It's just me and Kinley, so we have all the space we need." He thought of the impending payments he didn't know how he was going to make on the ranch, and the meeting next week to discuss refinancing. They might not even be here much longer, he wanted to say, but he didn't want to talk about that.

"Would you mind if I opened your fridge?" she asked.

He grunted, putting a plate into the dishwasher. "Knock yourself out." He heard the fridge open, and he kept doing the dishes, not really paying attention to her. When he turned back, he found her holding an open egg carton. "You hungry?"

"Oh." Startled, she shoved the carton back inside the refrigerator. "No, thank you. I . . . Would you care if I made breakfast tomorrow?"

She had spoken of cooking. Progress! "Sure. I'm out of the house by five thirty to feed the animals, and my brother is gone on vacation."

"Your brother is Troy, right? Nadine told me he was my first doctor."

Maybe that was the reason she'd wanted to stay with him, because his brother had been her doctor. "Yep," he said.

"What time will you be back in the morning?"

"Around eight."

She nodded and turned to leave the kitchen. "I'll have breakfast at eight."

Ten

IT WAS ALMOST EIGHT, and she was almost done with the hollandaise sauce. Where in the world had she learned to make hollandaise sauce? She couldn't remember, but she'd had to improvise with a couple of ingredients. She'd searched the cupboards, hoping Ross wouldn't care. After all, he was in for a surprise. Satisfaction rolled through her as she wondered if she had been a chef in her old life. Last night it'd been so easy and innate to open the fridge and think of a million things she could make out of the ingredients in it. She yearned to feel an onion in one hand and a knife in her other. She distinctly recalled loving the feel of cutting the vegetable. Was that ridiculous?

The back door opened, and her heart leapt into her throat. Was she always this nervous when she cooked for someone? It was frustrating not to know the answers to those questions, but she pushed that negativity away and focused on the food. She felt confident in what she'd prepared.

Ross walked into the kitchen, halting abruptly. "Whoa."

She imagined how the kitchen must look to him—she'd used pretty much every pan and bowl. She couldn't help but giggle at his expression.

He met her eyes, and his face transformed with a heart-stopping smile. His eyebrows lifted. "Wow."

"Sorry," she laughed, excited and nervous. "It was like

once I started, I couldn't stop. This is eggs Benedict. I hope you like it. I mean, it's complicated to make, so I hope it's okay. I used a lot of ingredients. I'll pay you back when I know who I am." She faltered at the last part.

Ross hesitated, then laughed. "Are you kidding? This is amazing. I don't know if I've ever had eggs Benedict, but it smells wonderful."

The next moments happened so quickly. She dished him up, dished herself up, and they sat at the table she'd set. She had even folded the napkins into a shaped fan. She'd found some concentrate orange juice and made that too.

She picked up her fork, waiting for him.

He surveyed the table, then turned to her. "Thank you."

The sincerity in his voice touched her. "My pleasure."

"Do you care if I say grace?" He put his hand out.

She quickly put down her fork and took his hand. "Of course not." Did she pray? She didn't know.

He said some words, but all she could think about was the feel of his rough hand. She remembered that night in the hospital room. He finished praying, taking his hand back. Without his touch, she felt a sense of loss. It was baffling, considering he was sitting right next to her.

He picked up his fork and took a bite, pausing when he noticed she wasn't eating. "Are you okay?" His mouth was half full.

She smiled awkwardly. These were *disturbing* feelings, because she hardly knew the man and she didn't know if she was already in any kind of relationship. With some effort, she pushed those troubling thoughts away. She picked up her fork and began eating. When she tasted a fully loaded fork, the food melted in her mouth. "Mmhmm."

He watched her, his lips twitching up again. "Exactly. Girl, where did you learn to cook like this?"

"Who knows? Maybe I'm a chef from France." She paused, seeing if she knew French. "Don't know the language, though." She took another bite.

He grinned. "Would you know the language?"

She shrugged. "Didn't Goldie Hawn on *Overboard* suddenly start speaking different languages?" She frowned at him, thinking about that movie. "Wait a sec. Did you fix my closet, and I didn't pay you?"

He grunted, continuing to eat with a smile on his face. "Guess you remember a good movie, so there's that."

"Guess I do." She laughed, and it felt good to do so.

The man could put the food away; he scarfed down most everything on his plate in seconds. He left the last bite on his plate and turned to her, a bit embarrassed. "Sorry, I guess I ate rather quickly."

She was still eating, relishing every bite, tasting every spice, every burst of flavor inside her mouth. "You don't have to complain to the *chef.* There's enough for seconds if you want them."

Much to her delight, he rose quickly, heading to the kitchen. "Yes, I do."

Relaxing for what felt like the first time since she'd woken, she leaned back into her chair and stared out the back window. From here she could see a tree house, a trampoline, and a garden. Farther back, she saw a big barn and two horses. And endless fields of . . . what? She didn't know. Gratitude overwhelmed her, and annoying tears welled up. She hadn't cried at all since she'd woken up; mostly she'd been trying to figure out who she was and then seething when she couldn't. But she'd never cried.

"You okay?" he asked when he saw her dab at her eyes.

She sucked in a breath and tried to pull it together. "I'm sorry. I . . ." More tears flooded her eyes, and her throat clogged with emotion, like a torrent finally allowed to flow. She stood, knocking down the chair behind her. "I'm sorry."

Ross shot to his feet in alarm. "It's fine."

She rushed from the table, down the hall, and into the bathroom, unable to stop the sobs.

Eleven

INITIALLY, WHEN THE WOMAN had the breakdown, Ross had followed her down the hallway and waited by the bathroom door, her cries breaking his heart. He knocked, but she'd only stopped crying briefly, telling him to go away.

He'd cleaned the kitchen for her. She really had used almost every bowl, but he hadn't cared; he was too worried about her. When he'd finished the dishes, he had left a note, telling her he would be fixing things around the ranch. He'd told her to use the landline to call him if she needed him, and he left his cell number.

During the rest of the day, he'd wrestled with the decision to take her back with him. He wasn't equipped to deal with a situation like this. He'd almost called Troy, but Troy didn't need this on his vacation. Instead, Ross had called George and explained what had happened.

"Crying cleans the soul. Hang in there; you'll be fine. Hopefully someone will turn up. I gotta go." With that, George had hung up.

Now it was almost five o'clock. Ross felt bad that he'd had to work all day, but it had to be done. There had been a fence to mend, water to change, and animals to feed.

Unsure of what to expect, he opened the door slowly. He hoped there might be a mess in the kitchen again, but there was nothing. "Hello?" he called out, and he flashed back to when he and Brook were first married and they would fight something terrible. He'd come home and be afraid she'd left him.

Nothing.

"Hello!" he called out louder, walking through the house, ending in her room. She wasn't there. His adrenaline spiked. Had she left and wandered down to the road? "Great." He raced to the front of the house, rushing out the front door and looking around.

"I'm here." Her voice was quiet.

When he turned, he saw that she was sitting in the porch swing, but she wasn't looking at him. She was staring out at the field. He could tell she wasn't okay. Her eyes looked puffy. He didn't know how to handle this situation, so he just stood there, closing the door behind him but not moving to sit. They both just stared at the fields, the trees, and the mountain in the distance.

Eventually he spoke up. "I love this view. It always steadies me." He said it softly, feeling better than he had all day.

She looked to him, her green eyes even brighter with emotion. "I never told you the real reason I wanted to go with you."

His heart pounded, and he nodded in encouragement. He hated that with every passing moment, he felt more and more connected to this woman. He didn't know if she was single or married. He didn't even know her name.

"I don't know why, but you're soothing."

It wasn't the answer he'd expected, but it was an answer he liked. "Really?"

She let out a bit of a laugh. "You don't seem convinced."

Taking this opportunity to sit in a chair next to the swing, he grinned. "My wife used to tell me I drove her crazy."

Their gazes held for a moment. He chastised himself for bringing up his memories. She wouldn't know about her own past.

"Anyway," he said, standing to walk back into the house.

"I bet she had cause to feel that way."

Her response surprised him, considering all the times he'd tried to get a rise out of her. "Yeah, she did sometimes." Unable to stop himself, he turned back. "I think that's the way things go in relationships. Sometimes you tend to drive each other crazy, even on purpose. She hated when I would sneak up on her when she was in the garden, but I loved it." The memories made him laugh. "Boy, she would get me back. One time she set the hose on me right when I was coming out of the barn. And before I could respond, she took off on a horse." He slapped his knee, chuckling. "She was smart."

The woman smiled back at him. It was so nice not to see pity on her face. Whenever he spoke of Brook to anyone, they would give him that sad look. But not this woman. "It sounds like you loved her," she said. "Yet I think we should focus on my pain right now."

Her words surprised him. "What?"

A small smile played at her lips. "Well, you just seemed like you didn't want to talk about it."

It made him laugh. She was absolutely right. Respect for her washed through him. The woman was funny and smart. "Do you want to talk about it?"

She looked down at her hands, and he noticed she'd bitten her nails down. "I'll talk."

"Okay." He moved to sit next to her again.

She sucked in a slow breath. "Why hasn't anyone come for me?" She looked up and searched his eyes. "Doesn't anyone know me? Somewhere?"

Touched by her very real troubles, he leaned back. "I

don't know, but it has been almost three days since I found you."

She let out a sigh. "Okay, maybe I was wrong. You're not *that* soothing."

He smiled sadly. "Listen. I don't have answers, obviously, but I do know that when you're going through hard things, there really is always something good that comes out of it. Most of the time." His mind flashed to his wife. "Even when it's hard to see."

Her lip trembled. "I don't think there's anything good that could come out of a situation like this."

He stared at her, hoping she wouldn't cry again. Unfortunately, he didn't get his wish.

"Would I even wear a wedding ring if I was married? Why can't I remember anything?" Tears fell down her cheeks. "I'm sorry." She sniffed and put her hand over her face.

Hesitantly, he put his arm around her. Even if she was married or whatever, she was a *person in pain*. And he was a person trying to help her.

At first she froze up. Then she leaned into his shoulder, crying harder.

He held her like that for a long time.

Finally she pulled away, and he moved his arm back. "Thank you," she said, looking out into the fields.

"Eggs Benedict."

"What?" she asked.

"The something good that's come of all of this."

She grunted, then shook her head.

"What? I haven't eaten good food like that in a long time. Like . . . ever. That was amazing." He meant it.

She laughed wildly. "I can see why your wife said you drove her crazy."

Nobody had ever talked about his wife like that. This felt different, and he felt himself loosen up and laugh too.

After a bit, both of them still sat on the porch swing, but Ross didn't feel nervous or worried about this woman being in his home any longer. "You can stay however long you need to stay."

Turning to him, she frowned, then blinked.

"If you don't cry," he hastened to add.

She laughed, even though she was clearly trying not to. "Thank you."

It was the right thing to do, he thought, seeing how broken she was at this moment. "I do have a question."

"If I can answer it, I will."

He hedged, then asked, "So what should I call you?"

She let out a sigh. "I have no idea."

"That's fine. I mean, I don't have to say anything. It's not like I have other women around." This was coming out all wrong. "I mean, my daughter is coming home tomorrow, and I thought it'd be nice to have you decide on a name."

"Right, your daughter, Kinley."

"Yes." Ross sighed. "Kinley was very concerned about you. She was actually the reason I ended up at the hospital that night when you woke up."

"Really?"

He laughed and told her about how Kinley was very stubborn and then prayed for her. "She even refused her favorite pizza place if she couldn't go to the hospital first."

"Then I'll have to make her the best pizza she'll ever have," she said, smiling.

"How do you remember how to cook?"

She looked baffled. "I wish I knew."

With another nod, he leaned back. He could only imagine how frustrating it would be not to know who you were. "I could call you Red."

She frowned, then cocked an eyebrow. "How come I feel like that wouldn't be very original?"

He grunted. "Then what?"

Not answering for a moment, she leaned back, and their shoulders lightly touched. Attraction pulsed through him, and he scooted a bit away from her, self-conscious. When she met his eyes, he wondered if she felt it too.

He chastised himself for even thinking about it. No. This woman was just a guest he was helping out. He stood. "Should we go in?"

She thought for a moment, then shrugged. "Red works. Because nothing else sounds right in my mind."

"Okay, Red it is." The decision made his heart lift. Maybe meeting this woman, being here in this moment with her, might be the something good in this whole situation. Maybe he was making a friend.

She stood, and as they walked into the house, he held the door for her. The trouble was, he didn't think he wanted just another friend.

Twelve

KINLEY ARRIVED THE NEXT afternoon. Ross had prepped her and her grandparents on the phone the night before, explaining the situation as best as he could. Of course, Kinley was thrilled. When she bounced into the house the next afternoon shouting out, "Dad and Red," it made him laugh.

True to her word, Red had been in the kitchen all afternoon, making pizza dough. Since it was Sunday, Ross did minimal chores. Normally, he would have attended service, but when he'd asked Red if she wanted to go, she'd said no, so he'd stayed with her. They'd spent the afternoon playing chess and talking, and it'd felt so natural. He shared more than he had ever thought he would—about himself, growing up in Casper, working the ranch, and marrying Brook right out of high school. They'd attended the University of Wyoming in Laramie and gotten their degrees in teaching, then returned to Casper, where he'd wanted to ranch and teach. It had all worked out perfectly until she'd been diagnosed with cancer.

It was the easiest conversation he'd had since Brook, and he wasn't sure how he felt about it. Every now and then, Red would seem like she wanted to say something, then touch her head. She wasn't wearing the bandage anymore, but she would complain that her mind was a bit hazy, and she still didn't remember anything.

"Hey! Kin-bear!" Ross braced himself as his daughter ran and jumped at him.

Brook's parents followed her into the living room, and he hugged each of them.

"Where is she, Daddy?" Kinley asked.

Just then, Red walked into the living room with a warm smile on her face.

Kinley ran toward her. "Hi!"

"Kinley, stop," he said quickly.

Kinley skidded to a halt right in front of Red, who opened her arms and said, "I would love a hug."

With a squeal, Kinley hugged her.

Red's eyes met his, and in that moment, there was just another twinge of something he'd started to feel about Red. Maybe she was meant to be here. He pushed the thought away. That was . . . stupid.

He introduced Brook's parents, and they were sweet but gave him warning looks. When he walked them out later, Sheila mentioned she was worried that Kinley was already too attached.

"I know," he agreed, not knowing how to explain to them that he really wasn't that worried.

Brook's dad only patted him on the back. "Be careful."

Ross watched them leave, thinking about how he never would have imagined himself in this position.

When he went inside, he found Kinley in the kitchen, plunked on the counter, chatting away with Red as she pulled the pizza out of the oven. "I told Daddy I didn't think you should be alone in the hospital. I told him that somewhere you had a dad too." Kinley covered her mouth as he walked in. "Oops."

He wagged a finger at her. "And I told Red that you are stubborn as all get out."

They all laughed.

"Is your name Red?" Kinley asked.

Red met his eyes. "I don't know, but you can call me that."

Kinley nodded.

"Let's get ready to eat. I made this pizza for you, Kinley, because you didn't give up on me." She met his eyes, and he could tell she was holding back emotions. "I think I might still be in that hospital if I hadn't come back to your home with your father."

It hit the center of his chest hard, wondering what would have happened to Red. Would she be sitting in the hospital, just waiting? Was there someone out there who worried about her? Where were they?

They ate the delicious pizza together and heard all about Kinley's time with her grandparents, the movie they'd taken her to, and the friend she played with that lived next door. Kinley asked Red a whole bunch of questions that Red couldn't answer. Finally, Kinley asked questions about cooking, and she and Red talked and talked.

By bedtime, Ross was more than ready for Kinley to go to bed. He wanted some quiet time with Red, but he didn't want to think too much about what that meant.

"Can Red put me to bed?" Kinley asked, her teeth brushed and her pajamas on. He'd been trying to get her to this point for the past fifteen minutes.

"Uh." His eyes darted to Red's as she shuffled through some cards they'd been playing with.

"Sure." Red stood, grinning as she moved down the hallway.

Kinley hugged him quickly, then bounced down the hallway. "I want to show you my favorite book."

As she moved past him, he shrugged and put up his hands, whispering, "Sorry."

She put her hand on his shoulder and paused. "Don't be sorry. She's wonderful."

Her touch surprised him, and he put himself through another self-talk about how she was probably married or had a boyfriend. He couldn't feel things for her; he didn't really even know her. He stepped back.

"Sorry," she said, tugging her hand away.

"Red!" Kinley yelled out.

Ross's heart drummed as Red moved down the hallway, and he swallowed, unable to believe he had such strong feelings so soon. He headed toward the front door, grateful for an escape. He had to be careful. She wasn't even supposed to be here.

Chapter 13

AFTER READING *TO THE Moon and Back* and singing a lullaby to Kinley, Red walked down the hallway, thinking about that moment when she'd briefly touched Ross's shoulder and so much had passed between them. He'd definitely been caught off guard, she could tell.

The truth was that she was caught off guard, too. She shouldn't feel anything for him, right? Could she even feel anything for him? It was so frustrating not to know. Somewhere inside of her, she knew she needed to talk to him, to soothe him. Who soothed this man? From all aspects of his life that she could see, he was the rock for everyone.

Sure, from what he'd told her, Troy was an amazing brother, and Ross said he was happy he was back in Casper, but who had been watching over the ranch since college? Ross. And then his wife, Brook, died, and he was raising this amazing daughter who was also clearly precious, but maybe a bit of a handful. Not to mention that he taught school and did drama camps. He never exactly said he was feeling financial pressure, but she could tell he was. He'd mentioned that the medical bills didn't ever stop.

Walking out onto the porch, she felt the chemistry kick up between them right away. She didn't know if this was the right thing or not, but she decided everything between them had to be brought out into the open. "Look, Ross," she said, shutting the door and walking toward the swing.

It was dark, and he hadn't turned on the outside light, so there was just the soft glow of light from the living room. She sat on the porch swing next to him.

His gaze swung to meet hers, making butterflies flock in the lower pit of her gut. He had a beautiful face, a strong jaw, and the bluest eyes. Currently, he had a bit of a sexy five o'clock shadow. This man had such an effect on her.

"Listen," she said, "I know I shouldn't have put my hand on your shoulder back there, and I know there's something between us, but it's nothing for you to feel awkward about, okay?"

The edge of his lip twisted up. "I don't know what you're talking about."

"I mean . . ." She backtracked. "Not that you *did* feel anything. I was probably making it all up." Flustered, she stood up. She was probably imagining it all. "Never mind."

His hand grasped hers.

She paused, not turning back. Sparks lit inside of her. His hand was rough and strong.

"Red, sit," he said quietly.

Was it ridiculous she could swoon over a strong hand? How silly. She was embarrassed all over again.

"Red." His voice was a whisper. "I *am* feeling all these things, and you see . . ." He gently squeezed her hand. "I want to kiss you, but . . ."

Her focus was on that place of physical connection, on the way she was caught up in this man, in his life, in his daughter. She turned to face him.

"I am trying not to feel this way," he explained, "because you don't even know your name. Because it's not *right*. Because you might be married, for heaven's sake." Releasing her, he stood, raking a hand through his hair.

The loss of his hand felt too abrupt, and she wanted it back. She didn't say anything. What could she say? He was right. She might be married. Yet she didn't know how she could feel these things so deeply for him and be married. Could she be married? "Then why hasn't he come for me?" she asked, speaking louder in angry desperation. "If I have a loving husband, why isn't he looking for me? Why was I out in the middle of your ranch? Why? Why?" Her voice softened, and she spoke quietly. "Wouldn't I wear a ring?"

"I don't know," he said quietly back.

"Why?" she repeated, grabbing his shirt. They were close enough that she could feel his breath on her face.

"I don't know." The words were even quieter, and all the zing and attraction was back, rising like a lightning bolt between them.

"I don't care." She put her hands around his shoulders, pulling his head down to hers, pausing right before his lips were on hers. Every part of her was on edge, but she couldn't deny how drawn to this man she was. Unwilling tears misted into her eyes. "I don't care. Kiss me."

For a moment, he hesitated, and she thought he might kiss her. Then he put his hands over hers and took them off of his neck. "No," he said, but he didn't pull away.

"Yes," she whispered, pleading.

"I can't be that man." He moved to the edge of the porch, holding the railing.

She stayed back, sucking on a breath. While she was grateful that he wasn't *that* kind of man, she was so confused about everything she felt. "I'm sorry," she said quickly.

He stayed by the railing. "It's fine." But she could hear him sucking in long breaths. All of this was enough to drive a person mad.

She moved next to him, willing herself not to touch him. "I love it out here. I love that you can stare into the landscape forever. I don't know. It just feels like . . ." She didn't know how to end the sentence.

"What?"

Her heart hammered. "Like I belong here."

Silence reigned between them.

She felt like a fool, but she didn't care. "The doctors said my memory would come back. At least, it should in cases like mine, but I just can't help feeling that I knew this place before."

He let out a breath. "The funny thing is that I don't know if *I* belong here anymore."

This didn't make sense. "What?"

"When Brook got cancer, nothing was working, so I put a mortgage on the ranch to try experimental treatments." He was rubbing his palm like he wanted to scrape something out of it. A nervous habit. "I never caught up. My brother and I have a meeting with the bank the day after he gets back. We're asking for a refinance, but I don't know if they'll give it to us." He sighed. "And we have this giant . . . energy company that I fear will swoop in and pay the bank top dollar, and we won't be able to stop it."

Without hesitating, she took his hand. "The bank has to help you."

He stared at their joined hands. "Most things aren't ever certain."

She dropped his hand, facing the landscape. She couldn't imagine them kicking him off his land. "Isn't there something else you can do? Someone else you can go to?"

"I've learned that sometimes the only thing you can do in life"—he stared into the darkness, then turned to her—"is trust God."

She wondered if she did trust God. She let out a long breath. "Okay, if we're trusting in an all-knowing being that I'm not even sure I believe in, then I guess that's what we're doing."

A smile played at his lips. "I guess that's all we can do."

He reached out and gently moved a tendril of hair that had been in her face. "Everything's going to work out for you, Red. I know it."

Again, she wanted to kiss him, but she didn't want to make him uncomfortable. "You sure?"

"I know it."

She couldn't understand how he could say that. This man had lost his parents to a car crash, had lost his wife to cancer, and was now faced with losing the land he loved. Her heart hurt for him. "Let me get this straight—we just trust."

He nodded. "Isn't that why you wanted to come back with me? George said you said you trusted me."

His words sent warmth flooding through her. This man was kind of amazing. "You know, Ross Charm, maybe your real name should be Ross Charming."

He sputtered out a laugh. "Did George tell you how the kids used to tease us because of our last names?"

She shook her head. "No."

"Hmm."

Her lips twitched. "Did the kids tease you about being like Prince Charming?"

He sighed, his expression falling. "Yes, and I found it *annoying*, to say the least."

She laughed. "But the last name, Charm, does fit you."

"Naw. I'm not charming."

She grinned. "You can be." She grinned widely. "Plus, you're just generally kinda awesome, too. Maybe not *Prince Charming*, but . . . I kinda like you."

Fourteen

ROSS LEFT EARLY THE next morning, leaving a note saying he would see them after the actor workshops. He took care of the animals and went to the school, making an effort to calm himself before the students arrived. He'd tossed and turned all night, trying to get Red out of his mind. He tried to force himself not to think about kissing her, how easy it would have been to do so. She didn't belong with him, or even in Casper at all.

The students and their questions were a nice distraction. As he got home and headed into the house, he wondered what he would say to Red, how he would face her, and how he would stand the torture of all these feelings for a woman that he shouldn't feel them for.

Laughter rang out from inside the house. When he walked in, he found Kinley and Red in the kitchen, flour all over their faces. Kinley let out a loud yell, and before he realized what had happened, a ball of something flew through the air at him.

He dodged, but not quickly enough, and something gooey hit the side of his face.

All laughter paused.

He met Red's eyes. She was covering her face. She sputtered, and then she and Kinley were laughing even harder.

"Ohh!" He growled like a bear. "You're gonna get it!"

Red picked up some of the gooeyness—cookie dough, he realized—and threw it at him, squealing.

He found himself in the middle of a huge cookie dough fight. He grabbed a bunch in each hand and slathered it on the girls' cheeks.

More shrieks of laughter sounded through the air.

They ganged up on him, and he attempted to flee, but Kinley got a leg, and he went down in a push-up position. Not letting him escape, Red went down too. "Get him!" She smashed cookie dough in his face.

He gave up, laughing and rolling onto his back.

"Get him!" Kinley squealed. She scraped dough from her face and pushed it into his.

Red turned to leave, but he grabbed her ankle, and she tumbled beside them.

"Tickle her!" he called out to Kinley.

Kinley giggled, turning and tickling Red beneath the chin. All of them were soon laughing.

"Enough!" Red said after she'd been tickle-tortured long enough.

He laughed and pulled Kinley off, hugging her to him. "No more, bug."

Red's eyes met his.

Instant attraction pulsed into him. "That was the best," he said, grinning.

The next two days fell into an easy rhythm. He would get up, do chores, and then head to his acting camp. When he got home in the afternoons, the girls would be doing various crafts or cooking, or he'd find them wandering around the ranch. One time, Kinley took Red on the four-wheeler. He caught them laughing and going way too fast. When Red took a turn driving, it was clear that she'd never done it before. After a while, though, she looked like a natural.

Ross was amazed at how Red had changed his life. He and

Kinley didn't really know anything about her, yet it felt like they'd known her forever.

During the evenings, they indulged in spectacular dinners and games and talked or watched movies. After Kinley went to bed, he and Red would start watching something, but he always found himself muting the television and just talking with her.

He knew he was falling hard for the woman. He knew it, and he didn't want to do anything about it. It felt unstoppable.

Everything changed Thursday night when George called. Kinley and Red were in the kitchen with him as Ross answered. "Hello?" He moved out of the kitchen, through the living room, and out the front door.

"We found out who she is."

Ross's mouth went dry as he shut the front door behind him. He braced himself. "Okay."

"Apparently, they thought she was on a trip to . . . check on some business things here. Anyway, they had no idea that anything had happened to her."

He swallowed, pushing through his nausea. "Oh."

"We'll be out to your place in ten."

His pulse raced. "Minutes?"

"Yep. Gotta go."

"Okay."

The call ended. Ross stared at the phone, feeling disoriented and dizzy. How would he tell her? The center of his chest bubbled with emotion, and he stuffed it down. He'd known this wasn't real. He'd known that someone would come for her, right?

Sucking in a breath, he opened the door. Kinley and Red were standing there, holding hands, looking worried as if they already knew something was wrong.

He felt like he was facing a firing squad. He tried to smile and feel happy for Red. This was good news. "Your family found you. They're coming."

Red didn't change her expression, but Kinley started crying, covering her face. "I'm sorry. I don't want you to go."

Red tugged her into an embrace, squeezing her eyes shut.

Ross felt like his heart was being ripped out all over again. Like he'd just found out Brook had been diagnosed with cancer, and his legs suddenly couldn't bear the weight of it all.

He put his hands on Kinley's shoulders. "Kin-bug, we can't . . ." His eyes met Red's. "She doesn't belong to us." His voice cracked, and the words were a surprise to him. *To us.*

Tears streamed down Red's cheeks, and her face contorted. "I don't want to go."

Without thinking, he put his arms around both of them, and he felt tears on his own cheeks. Who was coming, and how would he and Kinley ever survive without Red now?

Red had stoically gathered her bag of odds-and-ends clothes, and now they were all waiting on the porch. George drove up in his police car, and a black SUV followed him. Five desperate-looking men jumped out of the vehicle.

"Mia!" the older gentleman getting out of the patrol car called out.

A name.

"Mia," Ross breathed out.

Mia blinked, then squeezed her eyes shut.

Ross held on to her, supporting her.

She flashed her eyes open, focusing on the man coming at her the fastest. "Dad?" she asked. Her eyes lit up, and a huge smile crossed her face. She turned to a different man. "Sam?"

One of the men moved quickly to the porch. "They said you lost your memory?"

Before Ross knew it, the guys were on the deck, clamoring around her and taking a chance to hug her one by one, saying funny things.

Mia laughed and turned back to him. "Oh my gosh, I remember!"

She looked so happy, and Ross felt bad for resenting these men, but he tried to smile. "That's great."

"We knew there must be a family behind this little lady." George let out a light laugh, nudging Ross.

All the men turned to look at them.

Ross kept a stiff upper lip. Kinley stood in front of him, glued to him, staring at the woman whose name was Mia.

One of the men threw up his hands, looking from George to Ross. "Mia told us she was disconnecting for ten days. Told us she was turning off her phone and that she didn't want us checking up on her. So you can imagine our worry when we couldn't get hold of her yesterday. Then the hotel said she hadn't been back into her room. They checked, and her phone was there with her wallet, but no one had seen her. We all flew here immediately."

Wanting this whole horrible family reunion to be over and feeling selfish about it, Ross forced a smile. "I'm glad you found her."

Mia's eyes fluttered, and she broke from her father, beaming. "I remember. When my father got out of the car, it all came back to me."

Emotion surged inside of Ross, scraping at the back of his throat. "That's great."

Kinley threw her arms around her. "Mia is a pretty name."

Mia hugged her closely, then got down and looked in her eyes. "I'm always going to remember our time together. This was the best."

Kinley nodded but stepped back, clinging to Ross's side.

Mia stared at him, and he felt the burning stares of her brothers and father upon him.

He remembered the day of his wife's funeral. Kinley had held to him that day, just like she was doing now. For days afterward, Kinley had clung to him. His eyes fluttered, and he commanded himself to keep his composure. "I'm glad you remember." He knew his face probably looked rubbery, and he hated himself for almost losing it.

Mia crossed the distance between them and hugged him.

Surprised, he held her. Wishing things were different.

She gently kissed his cheek. "Thank you. I can never repay you, Ross."

He swallowed hard, wanting to be anywhere except here. "No problem." He pulled back, telling himself to keep it together.

George seemed to sense Ross's discontent, and he cleared his throat. "Well, folks, you don't know how glad I am it turned out this way." He moved off the porch. "We should probably get going."

Everyone began moving to the stairs.

Mia stared at him and Kinley for a moment and blinked. "I'm sorry. Thank you."

"Are you married?" Kinley asked.

The question took all of them off guard, and Ross froze.

Mia let out a light laugh, then met his eyes for a second before smiling at Kinley. "Nope. Never married." She winked. "It's just my brothers and Dad and me."

Crazy electricity bolted through Ross, leaving him paralyzed.

Mia's father reached out and took her hand. "That's right, and we've missed you. Come on—we need to get back." He nodded at Ross. "Thank you. Thank you. From one father to another."

Ross nodded in return. Yes, this was why he'd done it. "You're welcome." And he meant it. Even though his heart was breaking, he was glad she'd come home with him.

"I can send a check to cover any expenses."

This took Ross off guard. "No. That won't be necessary."

They all moved to the SUV, and he saw two of the men drape their arms on each side of Mia.

"Hold up," George said, pausing next to his car. "I just have one question, Mia."

She stopped, turning to George. "Yes?"

"What were you doing out hiking on this property?"

Mia's joy crumbled into what seemed to be embarrassment, and she looked at her brothers, then to Ross and Kinley, then back to George. She broke free from her brothers and rushed up the porch stairs to Ross, throwing her arms around him. Her tears dampened his shoulder.

He held her tightly, blinking furiously and wishing she wouldn't go. She'd said she didn't have anyone except her family. Would she want him?

All eyes were on him, and he realized that he was losing her. This whole thing was over. He hugged her back tightly, relishing the feel of her body against his. "Mia . . ." Her name slid off his tongue, and he realized he loved it, and it fit her perfectly.

Tears streaked down her cheeks. "Ross, I . . ."

It was as if they were the only two people who existed. Since it was obvious she wasn't married, he did the thing he'd been wanting to do since the first day he'd gone to the hospital to check on her. He leaned down and kissed her gently on the lips.

She kissed him back.

The kiss was powerful, like it could seal fate. Fire erupted inside of him, and he didn't care that they were having their first kiss in front of her family; it might be the only kiss he got. He put his hands on her hips and pulled her closer.

Kinley moved out of the way, and he heard her giggle.

Mia pulled him closer, and he was lost in this woman. Everything that had been between them the past couple of days condensed into this moment.

"Mia!" her father called out.

Ripping away from him, Mia turned to her father. "Wait!"

Ross wanted to demand she stay, demand she be his. "Stay here. Stay with us." He kissed her again. "Please. Stay."

She took a step back, swiping at her tears. "I . . ." She squeezed his hand before squatting in front of Kinley and holding open her arms.

Kinley hugged her fiercely. "Stay, Red. Stay."

Mia hugged her for a long time, then stood. More tears trickled down her face. "I can't. I'm sorry." She looked him in the eyes. "I'm with Jagger Energy Enterprises. I was here . . ." Her voice faltered, and she clenched a hand into a fist.

Ross's heart sank, and suddenly, he knew. He knew, and it hit him like a sucker punch.

Mia let out a cry. "I'm so sorry. I was here that day . . ." she trailed.

Anger shot through him. "You were here to steal my land?"

She winced, and then she frowned.

"Let's go, Mia." Her father called out to her.

She met his eyes. "I'm sorry. I'm so sorry." With that, she turned and dashed off the porch, running to the SUV.

One of her brothers opened the door for her, and Ross watched, stunned, as they drove away.

Fifteen

MIA WOKE THE NEXT morning with a jolt, thinking that Ross would be gone and it was time to make breakfast for herself and Kinley. She breathed deeply, remembering reality.

She wasn't on the ranch.

No, she wasn't in a fairy-tale anymore. Light was barely coming into her hotel room. They'd stayed in Casper another night. She'd stayed up late, telling her father and brothers all about her experience. Her father had insisted she would go to the best doctor in New York and get her head checked out when they got back.

The trouble was that New York felt like a whole different life to her now.

Her brother James had lingered in her room after they had all left. "You have feelings for this man, don't you?"

It had stunned her that out of all of them, James would be the one to say something. She hadn't answered.

He'd pulled her in for a hug. "I saw the way you kissed him. We all did. The way you held his little girl."

She'd fallen into his hug, sinking into despair. "You know we're going to acquire their property. Dad said that the deal was still on."

James searched her eyes, and she'd remembered all the times she'd consoled him over a broken heart. "Sis, you don't have to stay with the company."

She'd blinked, thinking about what James was saying.

"You want to be a chef, and I can tell you might want something else too."

She'd let out a light laugh, remembering how she'd cooked for them. "I was a chef the past couple of days. I made eggs Benedict and pizza and cookies. Maybe I wasn't a fancy chef, but I did a lot of cooking."

James hesitated, a soft smile on his face. "You look happy about that."

"I guess I was happy." She shrugged and thought of her stubborn father. "But we're buying his property."

James laughed. "Haven't you learned anything being VP of Acquisitions?"

"What?"

"We all know you're the favorite. It's been clear since day one. Dad will do whatever you say. So talk him out of it."

Now, in the morning light, she knew she would do exactly that. Then she would go to Ross, and she would make things right.

Sixteen

ROSS SAT IN THE bank office, angry and hurt beyond anything he could have ever imagined. If it weren't for the anger, he could reasonably say that he would have fallen apart last night.

She was Mia Jagger? Mia Jagger, the *VP of Acquisitions for Jagger Energy Enterprises*? She'd been on his property that day making sure it was good enough to purchase? To *acquire*? He wanted to punch something. He wanted to . . .

Troy, sitting beside him, tapped his shoulder. "Keep it together. Lots of decisions to make."

Troy had arrived at the house the evening before, coming straight from his trip. All he'd said when he got to the door was, "George told me." They had talked until late into the night, and Ross had told him everything. About Jagger Energy Enterprises. About Mia. About falling in love with her. About how angry he was.

His brother had listened and then put a consoling hand on his shoulder. "I'm sorry, bro."

Sorry was for chumps and losers and people who clearly weren't equipped to take on Jagger Energy Enterprises. Ross hated chumps.

At noon, the banker showed up, accompanied by a woman in a pinstriped suit and three-inch heels. She'd straightened her bright red hair.

Ross's heart hammered inside his chest when she moved

into the office, sitting across from him and Troy. It was incredible, the transformation from ranch-girl Red to this Mia Jagger, VP at a billion-dollar energy conglomeration. His heart threatened to erupt inside of his chest, pulsing with a tangled mess of feelings.

The bank manager cleared his throat. "Mr. Charm and Mr. Charm, I have news for you." He hesitated.

Ross glared at Mia. "What? When do you want us off the land?"

Mia shook her head and tsked her tongue. "You're a bit of a hothead when you care about something. Do you know that?" She slipped a piece of official-looking paper across the desk.

"What is this?" Troy demanded.

The bank manager grinned. "It's the title to your property, free and clear."

Troy looked baffled. "What?"

"It's yours," Mia said, looking at Ross. "Take it."

Ross stared into Mia's green eyes. He didn't trust those eyes anymore. He stood. "No."

"Wait." Troy grabbed his arm. He turned to Ross. "Hold up, just . . . wait."

His heart raced, but Ross didn't move.

Troy looked at the piece of paper, then at Mia. "How did you do this?"

For a second, Mia didn't say anything, then she sighed. "I told my father the land should belong to you." She pointed to the deed. "There is a caveat for twenty percent of mineral rights going to Jagger Energy, but . . . the rest is yours."

Ross remembered a million memories, moments from the last week with Mia. Had anything between them been real? "I don't want charity from you." In his mind, that would be worse than actually having the land taken away.

"Stop, Ross," Troy said, standing too but staring at the piece of paper. "I think it might be okay."

"None of this is okay!" Ross bellowed out, feeling out of control.

Silence reigned, and Troy gave him a startled look, then muttered a curse beneath his breath.

"Can I have the room, please, gentlemen?" Mia asked quietly, looking at Troy and then the bank manager.

Ross noted that the woman at the table was confident and perfectly composed, so different from the Mia he'd come to know this past week—yet she was still so similar.

She nodded at Ross. "Mr. Charm and I have a few things to discuss."

Ross didn't know what to do. His gut told him not to trust her.

"Please?" Mia asked again.

Troy turned to him. "What do you want to do?"

Ross stared at her. He realized he had to know what she wanted. "Go."

Troy and the bank manager left without a word.

Mia let out a breath. "Ross—"

He put up his hand, struggling to line up his thoughts. How could he trust her? "I can't do this."

"I want to be a chef. Isn't that funny?"

He held her gaze.

"And I could hardly sleep last night, thinking about you." Her voice was soft. "And Kinley. Where is Kinley?"

His heart felt like a hammer inside of his chest. Part of him didn't want to answer her, because it felt like she'd betrayed him.

Her eyes misted.

"At her cousin's house," he said gruffly.

She nodded, then blinked. "Good. That's good."

He thought of all the time they'd spent together.

Mia sighed and let out a light laugh. "I told my father before this trip that I want to go to culinary school, and he told me no." She laughed. "I have an MBA from Yale. Can you believe that?"

Hesitating, he cocked an eyebrow. Even though he was angry and hurt, the truth was that he wanted to hear about her, to know her. Even through all of his anger last night as he'd tossed and turned before falling into a fitful sleep, dreaming of Mia . . . he couldn't stop all the questions he had about her. "Can't you be a chef and . . . whatever you are?"

Her lips pursed in a tight smile. "The funny thing is that I never wanted to marry or have kids. I mean, I had a guy who basically used me because I was a Jagger." She looked sad. "I was wrapped up in what my father wanted. In the company. In what everyone else wanted me to be." She blinked and then focused on him. "He sent me on this trip to check out your property, but the truth is that I was longing for head space. I told him—I told all of them—I needed a break. But . . ."

His heart beat out of his chest, and he wanted to ask so many questions. "But what?"

"I was also trying to be undercover."

"What?" he was confused.

"I . . . just wanted to check out the ranch and then have some time to relax. Some time *not* to be Mia Jagger for a while."

He scoffed, thinking he wanted to be angry with her, but it was pointless. "Guess you got lots of head space."

She let out a sad sigh. "Yes, I did. And I met you. I went to your ranch and cooked and played with"—her voice broke—"your beautiful little girl."

With a pang, Ross thought about how devastated Kinley had been when Mia had left last night. She'd moped around, then told him she was going to bed because she wanted to forget how sad she was. He swallowed back emotion.

"It might sound stupid and completely ridiculous, but when I remembered my dad and my brothers, it was... it was like that life was the dream and this life was the real one." A tear fell down her cheek. "You were my real life. And... I wanted the life with you."

He couldn't help but smile. "Like you were Sleeping Beauty?"

She smiled back and reached out, taking his hand across the conference table. "And you woke me up when you touched my hand, and you were my Prince Charming."

"Oh brother." He started to pull back.

She didn't let go. "Wait."

For a moment, they simply stared into each other's eyes, and time slowed down.

She released his hand. "Just stay there." She stood, moving around the table and coming to his side.

He stood too.

She took his hand again. The smell of light vanilla filled his senses, and attraction sizzled through him. His heart raced, and he could only think about how different she seemed, yet the same. "Ross."

He thought of the title to the land. He would never be Prince Charming for a woman like her. "I won't accept charity," he said.

"Just listen, please. I know it's fast. I know you might not want this, but I feel like I've lived a lifetime with you already. I trusted you since the moment I opened my eyes, since before I knew my own name."

The warmth of her words pierced his heart, and he took her other hand. "I know."

She laughed and then blinked. "I love you, Ross. I know it might be too fast. I know my father and brothers don't believe it could be this fast—well, except James." She shrugged. "We're the closest, and he's a romantic. Anyway... I love you, and I couldn't let the ranch be taken from you and Kinley. Don't you see? There was no way I could let that happen."

A myriad of thoughts ran through his mind, but he focused on the truth. "I really can't be a charity case."

With a smirk, she said, "Oh, you mean like I have been the past ten days? And you took me in, and you helped me?"

"That was different," he protested.

"How?"

Warmth rushed into his chest, and he finally relaxed, hating that this woman was so good and so brave. "It just was." He pulled her into him, not knowing what to say but unable not to hold her.

They stayed like that for a long time.

He pulled back, staring at her lips. "I love you too, by the way." He laughed. "I didn't want to. I tried to fight it."

She leaned up, pressing her lips to his.

Fire exploded through him, and he put his arms around her waist, pulling her closer.

She linked her arms around his neck and deepened the kiss.

For a moment, he was lost.

And found.

She pulled back, tears on her cheeks. "I love you. I love you. I love you."

He let out a laugh and held her. "My undercover billionaire."

She laughed, then her face got serious. "Marry me," she said simply, quietly.

Jerking back, he stared into her eyes, unbelieving. "What?"

"Marry me, Ross Charm, and make me an official princess."

He couldn't believe she was doing this. "I . . ."

"Don't let your ego get in the way. Okay? I have . . . like, billions, so you can't have an ego about any of this."

It was so hard for him to even process that. But he could process the first part. "No."

She frowned. "No?"

Sudden purpose went through him. "It's not going down like this. You're right. I'm too arrogant to let this be our story." He got down on one knee and took her hand. "I have to do this right. Will you marry me, Mia Jagger?" He lifted his brows, then sucked in a breath. "Wow, the Jagger name is a lot to get used to."

She laughed, crying even harder. "Do you mean it?"

Certainty pulsed through him. "Don't make me ask again, Red," he whispered.

She laughed. "Okay, then yes."

As they kissed, all he could think about was how he knew it wouldn't be easy, it wouldn't be a fairy-tale . . . but . . .

"It's real," she said, pulling back from him.

She seemed to read his thoughts. Satisfaction washed over him, and he took her hand into his more securely. "And real is better than any fairy-tale."

She laughed. "Yes, it is."

Epilogue

JAMES JAGGER STOOD AT his sister's wedding reception, unable to believe she'd married a cowboy from Casper, Wyoming.

Mia had insisted that the wedding would be on the ranch, and there was a huge tent and tables and pink and white lights and a country band playing in the background. There were children running around laughing and holding sparklers.

"Not a New York kind of wedding, is it?" His father stood next to him, yanking uncomfortably at his tux tie and beads of sweat falling down his face.

James grinned, part of him satisfied that his father didn't like this wedding. "Not New York at all." He pointed to the tables filled with cake. "Did you know she made her own cake?" James was proud of her.

A slight smile swept over his father's face. "It's good, too," he said a bit resentfully. "Our Mia doesn't go halfway, does she?"

James detected a sense of pride in his father's voice, even if it was a tad of annoyance too. James took a sip of his water. "She's happy, Dad; isn't that what you want for her?"

An irritated expression crossed his father's face. "No." He puffed out a breath, then laughed. "Not if *her* happiness is away from me."

James laughed too. His father was very much controlling

of his children, and Mia suddenly leaving the company had been hard for him. "It'll work out."

His father sucked in a breath, looking around. "They *do* seem happy, don't they? Almost like they know some secret the rest of us don't know."

James averted his eyes to where his father was looking and saw Mia and Ross twirling on the dance floor. Right at this moment, Mia threw her head back, laughing. The center of James's chest warmed. "I want to know that secret."

His father sighed. "I guess this place will have to do then." He shrugged, pointing to some land a couple acres out. "Maybe we can put a landing strip in for our plane."

James grinned, thinking Mia thought she would have privacy but what she didn't realize is their father would just make her more accessible to him. "So you're giving in to her living away so easily?"

His father laughed and their eyes met, because both of them knew his father didn't give in.

"Grandpa, will you dance with me?" a little voice called out, moving to his father's side.

Kinley wore a pink dress layered with chiffon. She was precocious, and she'd won all the Jagger men over instantly, especially his father.

At this moment, his father's lips turned up, and he crouched down, grinning at the little girl who, James thought, had made short work of wrapping the billionaire around her pinky. "Why, I would be honored, young lady."

She grinned and threw her arms around him. "Yay."

His father laughed and looked up at him. "I think I gave up the moment I met her."

Warmth filled James's chest.

His father pulled Kinley's arms back and stood. "Do you know the Foxtrot?"

She giggled, her little blond ponytails jiggling. "No."

"Well," his father said, "every *Jagger* girl must learn the Foxtrot."

She frowned. "But I'm a Charm, Grandpa."

His dad's face went serious, and he bent to look her in the eye. "Yes, you are. And Charm is a good name. But"—he tweaked her nose gently—"now you are a Jagger too. And I already love you."

His father's words shocked James.

"You do?" Kinley threw her arms around his neck again.

His father laughed. "I do, so let's Foxtrot." He stood, and they walked to the dance floor, Kinley partially skipping.

Unable to believe his father had softened so quickly, James fell into step with them. "You're pretty amazing, Dad."

His father winked at him. "Tell me something I don't know."

They got to the dance floor, and his father stopped, turning to James, keeping Kinley's hand inside of his. "Do you want to know the real secret to Mia and Ross's happiness?"

James yanked to a stop, and his heart raced; his father had that look he got. The look that told him what he was about to say was important. "Okay."

"No one knew she was . . . a Jagger." His father nodded at Ross. "Especially not him. It allowed them to find true love first. Not have everything get so clouded with the business or money."

"Okay, old man, now you're getting out of hand. True love?"

"Grandpa! Foxtrot!"

His father laughed. "Okay." He gave James a nudge. "You know what I wish for all of you?"

"What?"

His dad nodded at Mia. "That you could all fall in love without anyone knowing who you really were."

James didn't pay that close of attention as his father started into some Foxtrot moves and Kinley laughed.

It was a good night.

A win for the Jagger family.

Little did James know, three months later . . . he would be reading about this secret . . . in his father's last will and testament . . .

Dear Mia and boys,

If you're reading this something went wrong. Well, it was probably my heart. I knew it was going out on me. And you're probably mad I didn't tell you.

But let the old man have one last say, would you? Listen up . . . to get your shares in the company, here's what you have to do:

Mia, since you have Mr. Charm, I need you to relocate and run the company for one year. I'm sorry about this. I know you and Ross like the ranch. Tell Kinley I'm sorry, too. But maybe she'll like New York a little.

Boys—here are your instructions:

1. Leave the company for one year.

2. Leave all your belongings behind.

3. Go to some anonymous town.

4. Don't be a Jagger.

5. Fall in love.

Taylor Hart is a best-selling author of contemporary romance, sweet romance, and light suspense romance novels. Her acclaimed Last Play Romance and Bachelor Billionaire Romance Series will leave you wishing for more strong heroines and swoon-worthy men.

A little about Taylor, she has always been drawn to a good love triangle, hot chocolate and long conversations with new friends. Writing has always been a passion that has consumed her daydreams and forced her to sit in a trance for long hours, completely obsessed with people that don't really exist. Taylor would have been a country star if she could have carried a tune--maybe in the next life.

To sign up for Taylor's newsletter and receive a free book, copy and paste this link into your browser.
http://eepurl.com/45Emn

Be My Plus One

Heather B. Moore

One

Amanda Wurst.

Nope. Couldn't hide a name like that.

Five-foot-eleven.

Again. Hard to conceal. And heels had never been an option.

Childhood stutter.

Speech therapy had cured that, except in times of extreme stress.

"And I'm not stressed," Mandy said to the mirror in the nicest bathroom she'd ever be in. What did it matter that she was currently standing in the ladies' powder room on the eighteenth floor of Lodestone Capital & Holdings, where she was about to present her business plan to a roomful of venture capitalists?

Shark Tank had nothing on this group.

But the fact was, Mandy was sweating. The cream silk blouse she'd bought at 75% off was probably ruined. At least the pale-gray dress suit she wore hadn't wrinkled on the Uber ride over to the building.

Mandy rested her hands on the cool marble countertop. She should have gotten that manicure, but she'd run out of time. And it hadn't helped that she'd panicked at eleven last night and spent three hours completely revising her PowerPoint.

"You've got this," Mandy whispered, lifting her gaze from her natural nails and meeting the reflection of her hazel eyes in the mirror. She'd splurged on her favorite hair products. Her thick auburn hair was unruly and prone to frizziness in the best of times. And in the worst of times, well, Mandy wore hats.

But her hair had miraculously stayed in its sleek chignon, thanks to her roommate and forever best friend, Daisy, who was a hairdresser by day and a gamer geek by night. Daisy had tried to get Mandy to join the online world of quests and secret missions, but the pressure of the fast-action games made her jumpy.

Besides, at nearly twenty-nine, Mandy figured she should have her life on track. Her future secured. If nothing else, at least more than $908.92 in her savings account. Ironic, because Mandy was an accountant by profession, but she could never seem to save the standard six months of emergency income. She'd tried budgeting software and budgeting apps, and nothing had worked. Until now.

Mandy had spent every night for the past eight months developing an app to track spending. But it wasn't the typical budgeting app. It was an app for the busy, traveling professional; it not only sorted expenses but made recommendations based on the best prices in whichever location you lived. The app allowed you to connect with services that catered to your spending habits.

Mandy hated when she arrived in an unknown city and had no idea where to eat, where to shop, or which sites to visit first. Especially when she went to a company conference on her own, and she didn't have a group of people to travel around with. She usually ended up eating too-heavy or weirdly spiced food at the overpriced hotel restaurant.

Mandy had programmed the app to customize itself to the user. She could show up in Denver or Seattle and the app made suggestions, knowing her love for great Thai food that was under fifteen dollars a plate, or directed her to a simple breakfast of yogurt and fruit.

She had of course tested it in Boston—where Lodestone Capital & Holdings was headquartered, just a few miles from her apartment. That was why Mandy had picked this investment firm.

"Okay, one more review," Mandy said to the mirror. Then she pulled up the Lodestone company profiles on her phone. The owner of Lodestone was business mogul Richard Lode. His three sons and one daughter were also partners—apparently financing and investing ran in the family—along with two other men, Kelvan White and Logan Chase.

Mandy stared at the pictures of the Lode sons for a moment. She didn't know who was the eldest, but they all had similar looks—two of the brothers were in fact twins. The men all wore the standard power suits, their appearances classically groomed. Hollie Lode was the only female partner. Mandy wondered who might be at the meeting, and which partner might be willing to be her investor. From the research Mandy had done on the firm, each partner had their own carte blanche when it came to deals. Which meant she had to impress at least one of them enough to believe in her business plan.

Her phone alarm went off, sending a jolt of adrenaline through Mandy. Even if she spent another hour in the bathroom, she wouldn't be more ready than she was now. She just had to get in there and start, then the nerves would hopefully calm down.

She opened her laptop bag, where Daisy had put high heels—ones that Mandy had maybe worn once. Daisy had told her the heels looked better with the dress suit; Mandy's flats screamed dowdy. "Own it," Daisy had said. "Just because they're a bunch of billionaires doesn't mean they're better than you."

Mandy had in fact looked up the net worth of Lodestone, and it was indeed in the billions. She wasn't going to let herself be intimidated by the fact that the $300,000 investment she was about to ask for was probably money they moved in a single day.

"Show them you're confident," Daisy had told her. "Go in there and knock 'em dead."

"With heels?" Mandy had teased.

"The heels will be an attention-getter," Daisy said, "but your presentation will close the deal."

Mandy drew out the black heels and traded out her flats. She'd practiced walking in the heels that morning, and she hoped she wouldn't wobble in front of the panel full of investors. Next she brushed at her suit, even though there wasn't a speck of lint in sight. She picked up her laptop bag and slipped her phone into the outer pocket.

Now she was ready.

She opened the ornate bathroom door and walked to the reception desk near the glass-walled conference room. The nameplate on the receptionist's desk read *Elizabeth*. The receptionist's fake lashes lifted as she surveyed Mandy, looking up and *up*.

Mandy fought the flush threatening to break out on her cheeks. "Hi, I'm Amanda Wurst, and I have an appointment."

The receptionist held Mandy's gaze for the briefest moment, then picked up the phone on her desk. "Jeremy? Amanda Wurst is here." Without waiting for a reply, she told Mandy, "Wait in the conference room. They'll be in shortly."

Mandy nodded and tried not to feel self-conscious as she walked the few paces to the glass doors. She reached for the handle and pulled. The weight of the door surprised her, and she had to loop her laptop bag around her wrist so that she could use both hands to pull. But the bag handle snagged on the watch that Daisy had also insisted Mandy wear to look more professional.

She stuck her foot in the door before it could close all the way, and the heaviness pinched her newly donned shoe.

"Ouch," she muttered, and pulled her foot back. Her high heel fell off. Of course. She bent to grab her shoe and nearly lost her balance, but she proudly righted herself without falling against the wall or door.

Surely the giant-lashed receptionist was getting an entertaining show.

"I've got it," a deep voice said behind Mandy.

Or . . . *someone else* had just been a witness.

A man's arm came into view, and he opened the door—quite effortlessly, it turned out.

Had this man been there when she'd bent over to grab her shoe, or had he seen her wrestle with her watch and bag? She turned, aware that her face was likely bright red by now, but she had to see who had witnessed her minibattle with the door.

Still holding one high heel, she looked into blue-gray eyes that reminded her of a winter sky in Boston.

The man was tall—in fact he was at least three inches taller than she was, even with her one heel on. His dark hair was a bit unkempt—unlike his picture on the website—and his hair reached the collar of his navy business suit. This was Jeremy Lode, there was no doubt. On the website, he'd been handsome. In person, gorgeous. With his close proximity, she caught the scent of what must be his aftershave, because his jaw and cheeks looked baby smooth.

"Thank y-you," she said. *Oh no.* Was she stuttering now? *I haven't even made it through the door of the conference room.*

Mr. Lode's gray eyes remained steady on hers. "Do you want me to hold your bag so you can get your shoe back on?"

The deep tones of his voice sent an involuntary shiver through her. *Oh boy.* And ... she was still standing in the doorway holding one shoe. "No, I—I ..." *Don't stutter! Exhale, then speak slowly, deliberately.* "I've got it." She stepped past him—well, *limped*—and entered the conference room. Setting her laptop bag onto the glossy mahogany table, she breathed in. Breathed out.

With as little bending as possible, she slipped her other shoe on, then straightened. She'd fully expected to see Lodestone's gaze on her, perhaps amusement in his eyes, but he'd walked to the other end of the conference room and opened a control panel on the wall.

"Do you have a PowerPoint?" he asked without looking at her.

"Yes." Mandy was prone to stuttering her *y*'s, so she was extra proud to have said *yes* quite nicely. "Thanks again," she added.

Then he turned, and those gray eyes met hers. Why did men seem to have the longer eyelashes? This man would never have to get his lashes done like his receptionist. And his dark eyebrows were pretty much sculpted, along with the rest of his face. Mandy wasn't even going to notice his body, or how his suit looked as if it had been tailored to those broad shoulders of his. This man clearly had a life outside of this building and didn't spend all day in front of a laptop, reviewing financial spreadsheets.

"I'm Jeremy Lode," he said.

Mandy nodded. *Yes, you are.* "I'm Amanda Wurst." The response was automatic and entirely unnecessary. Of course he knew who she was; he'd been paged. And she also knew he was Jeremy Lode, because she'd memorized his photo and bio.

"The others should be here in a few minutes," Jeremy said.

"Great, thank you, Mr. Lode," she said. "Again." Mandy gave him a small, albeit nervous, smile.

"Jeremy."

"Jeremy," she repeated. "Thank you." She winced.

Another man, or person, might have found some amusement in the fact that she'd thanked him multiple times in a matter of two minutes. But there was nothing in Jeremy's gray eyes that held a speck of warmth in them. He'd been a gentleman, that was all—if *robots* could be gentlemen. Jeremy flipped a switch on the wall. With a low hum, a projector screen descended from the ceiling.

And seconds later, three others walked into the conference room.

Well, then, Mandy thought. *Here we go.*

Two

JEREMY LODE DRAGGED HIS gaze away from Amanda Wurst's legs, which went on for a mile. He prided himself in not allowing his mind to wander during business hours. That's what happy hour was for at the bar, although he'd avoided any social scenes for months now. Since his thirtieth birthday, to be exact. He was tired of the pickup scene. Tired of cocktail hours. Weekends on the yacht. Aimless conversations. Unfulfilled expectations. Women who turned into felines once they learned who he was.

Within moments of meeting a woman, he could practically see her claws come out and her teeth sharpen, along with an emerging willingness to maim the next woman in order to secure a date with one of the Lode brothers. His twin brothers found it hilarious. But they were still in their twenties.

Jeremy had been surprised when Amanda Wurst refused his help. She'd definitely blushed when he spoke to her, so he knew she wasn't completely immune to him. Or maybe she'd just been nervous in general. Yet when he'd met her gaze, those hazel green eyes of hers hadn't shied away. Their gazes had connected, and . . . there was no money-hungry gleam in her eyes.

Refreshing, he had to admit. But then again, maybe she was in a relationship with the love of her life, despite not wearing a ring that sealed the deal. Why that should even occur to him, he didn't know. He'd never see Amanda Wurst again after this hour was up.

After making sure her PowerPoint was connected, Jeremy had settled into his usual place at the farthest end of the conference table. This was their third prospective-client meeting of the week, and frankly Jeremy was burned out. His workload was intense enough without bringing on any more starry-eyed clients who thought a fifty- or a hundred-thousand dollar infusion into their company was going to put them on *Fortune* magazine's list of entrepreneurs of the year.

Such it was that Jeremy had let his brothers and sister argue amongst themselves who wanted to invest with the client who was running a bakery and hoped to open a second shop, and the client who had developed an all-natural herbal tea line—as if the world needed one more of those. Jeremy's twin brothers, Dustin and Ian, worked most of their projects together. The two were inseparable. And Hollie never strayed far from the other partner, Kelvan White.

Jeremy had suspected for some time that there might be an out-of-office relationship going on between the two of them. But it wasn't his business or his place to say anything.

Their other partner, Logan Chase, was out of town, so Kelvan was the last to join the group, and he closed the door behind him. Jeremy was officially representing his father today. Jeremy hadn't asked his dad why he wasn't coming in today, but he assumed he was probably on another golf outing; those had become more and more frequent as of late.

Jeremy had given his father some slack since the death of their mom two years before, but enough time had passed now, and Jeremy had been calling his father out on some things lately. And the conversations hadn't been pleasant. Yet Jeremy couldn't be too critical of a man who had built a billion-dollar empire and had kept most of the money in the family by insisting his children get educated and trained so they could work for Lodestone Capital.

Amanda Wurst, or Mandy, as she told everyone in the room to call her, began with an overview of her app. Jeremy guessed her to be five-ten or five-eleven, a little taller than Hollie. But those high heels of Mandy's made her over six feet tall. Even if she weren't wearing heels, the woman would be hard to miss.

That dark-red hair gave her a classic elegance, and her open gaze had an innocence or purity about it, as if she hadn't yet become jaded by life. Jeremy wondered how old she was—certainly twenty-five at the very least. Her hands had the slightest tremble. Nerves, likely. And a pink flush stole up her neck as she introduced the budgeting app she'd developed. Unfortunately, the idea was like a million others out there. In fact, Hollie rolled her eyes, and Jeremy hoped Mandy hadn't seen it.

Hollie might look sweet and talk sweet, but she was a pit bull behind the scenes. A couple of weeks ago, a client had left in tears after a few pointed words from Hollie.

Jeremy hadn't been in the meeting, or he might have tried to soften the sharpness of his sister's tongue. The client had left a multilevel-marketing firm and believed he could bring along his downline for his new vitamin product. Hollie had thrown the gauntlet down, telling him that their firm didn't work with lawbreakers. Everyone knew, or should know, that noncompete clauses prevented employees from retaining clients after quitting the company where said clients were gained.

And Dustin and Ian? They were carbon copies of each other, literally, because they were twins, and if one liked something, the other would agree. It could be maddening.

As the oldest sibling, Jeremy frequently had to be the voice of reason and remind them of the big picture. Meetings could get heated quickly, and the other two partners, Kelvan and Logan, had been caught in the middle of sibling arguments more than once.

Mandy turned to the next slide on her PowerPoint, running through the details of why she decided another app of this nature needed to be developed. Jeremy had known before Mandy showed up that he wasn't about to invest in the app market. The sales growth could take twelve to eighteen months, then peak, and ten other apps would be ready to take its place. Yet the presentation was professional and thorough, so Jeremy could appreciate that much.

He also caught the look between the twins. Dustin lifted his brows, his gaze on Ian, and Ian winked. Then Dustin nodded and leaned forward, his attention back on Mandy, a smile curving his lips.

Jeremy stared. His two brothers could be idiots, but they wouldn't dare . . .

"Excuse me, Ms. Wurst," Ian said, lifting his hand, cutting Mandy off mid-sentence. "Have you had anyone other than family and friends try the beta version of your On the Go app?"

Mandy cut her gaze to Ian. "A handful of co-workers, but I can assure you that all of the features are interfaced correctly."

Ian smirked. "Can you demonstrate the app for us?"

Mandy visibly swallowed. "Of course. I have a demo at the end of my presentation. I thought you'd want to see the financial structure first."

Bravo, Jeremy thought, even as he threw a dark glare at his brother.

"Oh, I didn't realize you had a specific order to your presentation," Ian said.

Dustin was barely holding back a laugh, and it seemed that Hollie and Kelvan were in their own whispered conversation, which probably had little to do with the current meeting.

"I'd like to see the demo before the financial statements too," Dustin said, mirth in his tone.

Jeremy had seen his brothers in action before. They were trying to throw Mandy off her game. See how well she stood up against misdirection. How well she knew her plan.

Mandy shifted her gaze from Ian and Dustin, then looked at the projector screen and advanced the slides forward at a speed that made it impossible to read anything. She stopped on an embedded YouTube video. "This is the YouTube channel that I've populated with beta tester experiences and testimonials. At the beginning of each video, there's a fifteen-second demo."

Jeremy leaned forward, slightly impressed that Mandy was using this form of media as a way to reach users.

A peppy female voice came on, decidedly not Mandy's, and in fifteen seconds explained the main features of the app. Then a young man who needed a decent haircut started in with his rather somber review of the app. Not a terrible video, but not professional either.

When the one-minute video ended, Mandy cut her gaze to Ian. "Do you want to see a couple more? Or do you have questions about this one?"

"How much capital do you need for On the Go?" Hollie suddenly asked. Apparently she was now paying attention.

Mandy's neck flushed, but she backtracked on her PowerPoint until she stopped on a slide with a comprehensive spreadsheet. "I have everything broken down and explained, but since you're in a hurry to cut to the chase, this is the grand total."

Hollie smiled, but it wasn't a warm smile. "Three hundred twenty-four thousand and eight hundred dollars? That's quite . . . specific."

"I secured multiple bids from advertisers, distributors, and event coordinators," Mandy said. "This final number reflects their quotes, plus a ten-percent cushion should rates increase or adjustments need to be made to the original launch plan. As you can see, it also includes hiring two employees and paying health benefits."

Jeremy could see more than one flaw on the expense sheet she'd put together. For instance, she hadn't accounted for the percent the app distributors would take, or how new features would be required every few months to stay competitive. But, overall, the hard numbers demonstrated a lot of thought and research behind them. Not too shabby.

"What would you say if one of us offered thirty-five-thousand?" Hollie asked.

Jeremy exhaled. His sister was lowballing, which meant she wasn't interested. And Ian and Dustin would follow suit, as they always did.

Mandy clicked on the remote and advanced to another slide. It was a rate chart comparing different loan programs and their rates. At the top of the list was a star next to Lodestone Capital & Holdings.

"I would say, Ms. Lode, that you aren't my only option, but you are my first choice."

No one in the room spoke.

"We aren't a bank," Hollie said, laughter mixed with disbelief in her tone. "You're comparing a venture capitalist to a small business loan? Do you know what services we offer?"

Mandy advanced to the next slide. "Here's why thirty-five thousand would make On the Go disappear in less than a year." On the slide were at least a dozen icons of other budgeting apps.

"So why are you reinventing the wheel?" Hollie said, her voice smug.

Mandy advanced to the next slide. On the screen several

social media apps were displayed. "There's always room for more competition, plus I plan to partner with the major social media sites. Users of my app can—"

"Impossible," Dustin said, folding his arms. "Do you know how many businesses are trying to partner with Facebook and Snapchat? You won't even get an appointment."

Mandy didn't respond for a moment, but Jeremy could see that the steadiness of her eyes had shifted into something more fiery. "Which is why, Mr. Lode," Mandy said, focusing on Dustin, "I need some brawn behind my brain. Money talks, as you most certainly know."

Dustin chuckled, but no one else in the room joined in.

In a surprising move, Mandy closed her laptop, cutting off the image on the screen. Then she unhooked her laptop from the projector. No one spoke as she loaded the laptop into her bag.

"Thank you for your time," Mandy said, her voice not quite as steady as it had been before. "I will see myself out."

Jeremy couldn't help staring at her as she walked out of the conference room. It seemed she had no trouble pushing open the heavy glass door now, and no shoes were lost in the process.

Through the glass wall, everyone watched her pass the receptionist desk, then turn in the direction of the elevators.

"She has a temper," Ian said with a scoff. "I say we dodged a bullet."

Dustin smirked. "Speak for yourself. I was ready to invest."

"No!" Ian gaped.

"Thirty-five thousand," Dustin deadpanned.

Hollie shifted in her seat. "The idea wasn't half-bad," she said. "I would have offered her the full amount if she'd stuck around."

"So you were baiting her?" Dustin said, eyes narrowing.

"*Testing* her," Hollie clarified.

Jeremy didn't want to hear any more. He rose and crossed the room. The image of Amanda Wurst, and how her eyes had been glassy just before she left the room, wouldn't leave his brain.

"Where are you going?" Ian asked.

Jeremy didn't take the time to answer, because if he did, he might miss Amanda before she left the building.

Three

MANDY LEANED AGAINST THE cool wall inside the elevator and waited for the doors to close. She would not cry, at least not until she got back to her apartment. She'd been prepared, calm, and collected, but once Hollie Lode had offered thirty-five thousand, Mandy knew it was a lost deal.

She almost wished that Jeremy Lode had said something. He had been the quietest in the room, and his gaze had been a bit unnerving, yet Mandy had known he was listening to every word and reading every line of the financial statement. From her research into the firm, she knew he was recently made president, although his father was still CEO. What she wouldn't give to have five minutes with him to get his honest assessment.

Well, that wouldn't happen now.

There were other venture capitalist firms in Boston of course, but Lodestone was the most prestigious. Their name alone as her financial backer would open doors for her and get those meetings with social media sites. And if Lodestone wasn't willing to put up three hundred thousand, then would others be?

Yet . . . she couldn't give up. She'd spent too much time on it to turn back now. But she knew, as with all things technology-related, time was of the essence. Today's brilliant idea would be tomorrow's old news.

The elevator doors slid shut, but before the elevator could descend, the doors dinged. And opened.

Mandy pushed the *Close* button before she realized someone had stepped into the elevator with her. The scent of his aftershave should have been a clue, but she had to look up and see for herself. Yep. Jeremy Lode.

The doors slid shut, and he turned to face her, those gray eyes of his more blue now.

Well. If she wasn't mortified enough, it would be even worse now that she had to ride to the bottom of the building with this man.

Jeremy slipped his hands into his pockets, his gaze still on her.

Did he never blink?

Mandy felt her lips twitch at such an inane thought. In fact, she was feeling slightly hysterical. She'd promised herself she wouldn't cry, but what if she started laughing instead? The man staring at her across the small space of the elevator was a little too intense.

If she didn't suspect sweat rings on her silk blouse, she would have slipped off her jacket. Who knew elevators were heated? Out of the corner of her eye, she saw the numbers of the descending floors flash by. Why didn't anyone need to get on the elevator right now? Of all times, and all moments, why did Mr. Jeremy Lode have to pick *this* moment?

"Are you all right?" Jeremy asked.

The question was so out of context and so unexpected, that it took Mandy a few seconds to answer. "Yes, I'm fine." And that should have been the end of the conversation, except he apparently wasn't satisfied with her curt answer.

"You left quite abruptly, and I was surprised you didn't have any questions," he said.

He was in the elevator specifically to speak to *her*? "You

followed me to see if I had questions about getting turned down?"

It was the first time she'd seen a hint of a smile on his face.

"When you put it that way, I suppose I did follow you."

The deepness of his voice rumbled through her, sending her thoughts racing in directions they shouldn't be moving. And he hadn't exactly answered her question.

She kept her gaze locked with his, because now that her pitch session was officially a bust, she wasn't about to be intimidated. He likely knew how attractive he was and the effect he had on women. And right now, when there was nothing else to look at but him in this confined space, she noticed that Jeremy Lode had a small scar on the edge of his eyebrow. It was the only imperfection in his otherwise rather perfect face.

His gray-blue eyes, which she'd thought rather distant when she first met him, weren't distant at all. In fact, he seemed to be looking right into her thoughts, past any defenses. Reading her. Studying her.

"Do you think you can look past my partners' comments and reconsider?" he said.

"*Reconsider?*" Her mind spun in another direction now. "Are *you* offering to invest thirty-five thousand, Mr. Lode?" It was hard to keep the edge out of her voice. "Because if you are, I'd have to say that I'm still not interested. But thank you for your time."

Jeremy didn't flinch or seem insulted in the very least by her brush-off.

The elevator dinged open. They'd reached the main lobby. Mandy moved to walk out, and Jeremy caught her hand. He let go almost as soon as he touched her.

"I'm not offering thirty-five thousand," he said. The elevator doors tried to shut, but he stopped it with his hand.

"I'm offering the full amount and possibly more, because I think you shortchanged your accounts payable."

If Mandy's thoughts had been racing before, now they came to a screeching halt. "You are offering to invest three hundred thousand in my company?"

His barely-there smile was back. And she wondered why she had ever thought he was unfeeling, because in his gaze she saw . . . *interest*. "What's your payment plan?"

A small furrow appeared between his brows. "Forty percent equity."

Mandy blinked. "Y-you want to be a partner?"

He didn't seem to notice her stammer. "Look, Ms. Wurst, today is fairly busy, but tomorrow let's meet here around eleven," he said. "For lunch. We can go over the terms and my ideas, then see if they mesh with yours. We'll come to all agreements before any contracts are signed."

Mandy had questions—a lot of questions. "Forty percent? That's, uh, really high—"

"I don't need your answer now," Jeremy cut in. He released the elevator doors. "Tomorrow. Eleven?"

She nodded as the elevator doors slid shut.

Mandy stood in the lobby, wondering what had just happened. When the numbness started to wear off, the excitement set in, quickly followed by worry. Giving up forty percent of the equity was very high. It would mean that Jeremy Lode would have nearly equal say in all company decisions.

She ordered an Uber to pick her up, and once the car showed, she called Daisy, even though she was probably at work.

Surprisingly enough, Daisy answered, and Mandy spilled the whole story.

After she finished, Daisy didn't say anything for a moment.

"Are you still there?" Mandy asked.

"Yep," Daisy said. "I think it's amazing, and I'm happy for you, but I do have some concerns."

Mandy sighed. "Me too."

"Is Jeremy Lode a player?"

"What do you mean?" Mandy said. "You think he'll try to steal my idea?"

"No," Daisy said with a laugh. "I mean, is he ... *interested* in you?"

It took Mandy a second to catch up. Then she laughed. "*Me?* No. We live in completely different worlds, and I'm pretty sure I'm not his type."

"*Gorgeous* isn't his type?"

"Please," Mandy said with another laugh. "You're my best friend, so I expect a pep talk from you. But we both know I'm awkward and have a million flaws. Plus, men like Jeremy Lode probably date supermodels or trust-fund women. He's a billionaire, remember?"

"Oh, I remember, sweetie. But don't sell yourself short," Daisy said. "Billionaires are still in need of genuine relationships." She called out to someone in a muffled voice before coming back on the phone. "Hey, I've got to go. Pierre is giving me the stink eye for keeping my client waiting for two precious minutes."

Mandy hung up, and as the Uber pulled alongside the curb of her apartment building, she realized that she had absolutely no idea what to wear tomorrow.

Four

"SIDNEY'S ON LINE ONE," Elizabeth said in a smooth voice. "Do you want me to take a message again?"

Jeremy sighed. This was Sidney's third call in a couple of days. He should have taken her call yesterday and let her know then that he wouldn't be playing in the charity golf event in two weeks. He'd send his dad, and his dad could use one of his brothers as a partner.

Jeremy didn't want the obligation of attending the gala fundraiser the night before and encountering the usual social scene of schmoozing, false promises, women's business cards with personal cell numbers scrawled on them, his dad's tendency to drink too much, and—

"Jeremy?" Elizabeth said.

"Uh, put her through." He might as well get this over with.

"Darling," Sidney's voice oozed. "I just spoke with your dad."

"You did?"

"I can't believe he'll be in Europe during our charity event," Sidney said with a laugh.

He will?

"So I was calling to confirm with you, dear," she said. "I'll need your golf partner and your plus-one for the gala dinner."

"I'll have Elizabeth get back to you on that," Jeremy said.

"So you don't have a date yet?" Sidney said, her voice going up an octave. "My daughter Shelby is coming into town if you need someone at the last minute."

Jeremy nearly choked. Shelby was the epitome of every type of woman he wanted to avoid. "It's all right," he said. "I've got an invitation in the works." Or he would. It was still two weeks away.

"Oh, I can't wait to meet her," Sidney cooed.

Jeremy knew the woman meant well, but he didn't want to have this conversation. With anyone. He said his goodbyes, then hung up. When he glanced at the clock, he startled. It was after eleven, and he was supposed to meet Amanda Wurst in the lobby.

He hurried out of his office, telling Elizabeth he'd be out of the office for a couple of hours. Before she could question anything, he'd continued down the hall to the elevators. Once inside the elevators he checked his phone. 11:09.

He wasn't that late, but he hated to make Mandy question anything else about his firm after the treatment she'd received yesterday. He had yet to tell his partners that he was taking Mandy on as a client. That could wait until their monthly review meeting.

As soon as the elevator doors slid open, he saw her in the lobby. She wasn't wearing a suit like she had the day before. Instead she wore tan slacks and a wraparound sweater-shirt in an olive-green color. Her hair was pulled away from her face by a barrette, and her auburn waves tumbled down her back.

Jeremy strode forward, an apology on the tip of his tongue, when she spoke first.

"I'm glad you're late, since I just walked in," she said.

"Perfect." Did she know her sweater made her eyes look more green than brown? And that she smelled of something sweet and flowery? "Are you hungry?"

Her hesitation told him enough.

"We don't have to eat," he said. "We could go to the conference room."

"Are *you* hungry?"

"I'm starving."

Her brows lifted. "Then we'd better get lunch. My mother always says that a hungry man is a horrible decision maker, and we have some negotiating to do."

"Do we?"

Her lips pressed together, but her eyes glinted with something like amusement.

She shouldered her computer bag and walked with him toward the entrance. "Where are we going?"

"Ricardo's."

Her steps slowed, and she looked up at him. "Don't you need reservations?"

"I have reservations."

She bit her lip and nodded, then continued out the door.

He wondered what was going through her mind, but he didn't have a chance to ask, because Lyle pulled up in the car just then and rolled the window down. Today he wore an orange polo shirt beneath his black blazer. Lyle never skimped on the color. He called out a greeting.

Jeremy opened the door for Mandy. "After you," he said.

She hesitated, looking inside the car. "You have a driver?"

"Yes."

She bit her lip again and slid into the seat. Jeremy decided that Mandy needed to stop drawing attention to that lip-glossed mouth of hers. He walked around the back of the car and climbed in on the other side to sit next to her.

"Ricardo's," he told Lyle.

As the car pulled away from the curb, Jeremy said, "Where are you from?" at the same time Mandy said, "What's your best email to send documents to?"

"You want to talk business first?" he asked.

Red stole its way along her neck, and he was oddly satisfied that he'd made her blush. Without flirting?

"Isn't this why we're meeting?" she asked.

"Yes," Jeremy conceded. "But I want to know my clients too."

Mandy nodded. "That makes sense, but I'm not really a small-talk person."

Jeremy felt a smile forming. "I've already decided to work with you, Ms. Wurst. I'm not grading you, or anything."

Her gaze flitted to his. "Can you call me Mandy? I'm not too fond of my last name."

"Only if you call me Jeremy like I asked you to yesterday."

"Okay, Jeremy," she said, and he quite liked hearing her say his name. "I'm not going to give you forty percent. I spent a couple of hours last night running numbers."

Jeremy did smile then. "Nice."

She paused, and it was as if she'd forgotten what she was about to say.

"We're here, Mr. Lode," Lyle said.

"Thanks, Lyle." Jeremy turned to Mandy. "Are you opposed to chivalry, or can I get your door?"

"I'm not opposed to chivalry," she said.

Jeremy opened his door and walked around the car to open Mandy's. He'd long since told Lyle that he didn't want doors opened for him. But it had always bothered Jeremy when a woman insisted on opening doors for herself. He supposed he could blame it on his mother, who'd trained him to always open doors for women, even if they didn't always appreciate it.

"Thank you." Mandy climbed out of the car, clutching her laptop bag.

"I thought you could leave your laptop in the car," Jeremy said. "We'll eat and go over some things, then we can crack out the spreadsheets another time." At her hesitation, he said, "Lyle won't touch it, if that's what you're worried about."

"I'm not worried about that." Mandy put her bag onto the seat, then moved past him, her flowery scent staying behind.

Jeremy closed the door, and together they walked to the entrance of Ricardo's. He liked this place because the music was low and the booths spacious. The waiters weren't obtrusive, and he could conduct two-hour business meetings in addition to a long lunch.

As they stepped inside, Mandy said, "Wow, this place is beautiful."

Jeremy had been here enough times that he didn't pay much attention anymore. But it was true that the elegance of the place was unparalleled by most restaurants. The marble pillars, soft leather booths, and white-linen-covered tables set with crystal and china all made for a beautiful setting.

"The food's great too," Jeremy said. "When you're hungry."

"I think I'm hungry now."

He chuckled. They sat in the booth the waiter led them to, and Jeremy ordered shrimp cocktail for an hors d'oeuvre.

"What would you like to drink?" the waiter asked.

"Water," Mandy said automatically.

"They have great wines here," Jeremy said. "Are you sure you don't want something else?"

Mandy shook her head, so Jeremy ordered his drink.

When the waiter left, Mandy said in a half whisper, "I think they gave us the dinner menu. The prices are really high."

"Lunch is on me," Jeremy said.

Mandy's gaze connected with his. "We're splitting the bill. This isn't a date."

Jeremy's brows rose. Mandy didn't mince words much.

"It's not a date," he said, "but I insist on paying. You're my client."

"Is this going to be rolled up into the investment payments?" she asked, those eyes of hers taking on the steely quality they'd had in her presentation the day before.

Jeremy set down his menu and folded his hands on top of the table. "If I'm an equity partner, there are no payments to me or the firm."

Mandy looked down, although she was definitely not focusing on her menu. "We haven't agreed to anything or signed any contracts."

"That's okay," Jeremy said. "This is a business lunch. Plain and simple. No obligation."

Finally she raised her gaze again to meet his. "The wedge salad is seventeen ninety-nine. What could possibly be on it. Caviar?"

He laughed. "No, that would be at least fifty dollars."

She smiled, and he appreciated the way it smoothed away the earnestness of her expression. "Okay, I'll get the wedge salad, and not because it's the cheapest thing on the menu."

"You can get something else too … that's like a side salad." Jeremy couldn't remember the last time he'd ever had such an in-depth discussion about menu items and their prices.

"I don't want to order something I can't finish," she said. "I can't eat a lot when I'm nervous."

This intrigued him. "What are you nervous about?"

She bit her lip again, then said, "Everything." She waved a hand, then dropped it into her lap. "Launching the app. Now that you want to invest, it makes it all the more real. Being at a fancy place for lunch. And sitting with you."

Jeremy sat back. He understood her first concern, not so much the second. Didn't most people like to eat at a nicer restaurant? But … "You're nervous about sitting with *me*?

Are you worried that your boyfriend, or maybe husband, will be bothered?"

"I don't have a boyfriend or husband," she said in that whisper of hers. "It's just that you're . . . well, you're *you*, and I'm *me*."

She was gazing at him like he should understand what she was talking about.

"Can you be more specific?" he asked.

"I've already said too much."

Five

SHE'D SAID *WAY* TOO much, Mandy knew. If Daisy were here, she'd be dying. But Mandy's biggest flaw was saying things in a blunt way, and not stopping herself in time from blurting out her thoughts. It seemed that stuttering wasn't her problem today, but she'd had no qualms telling Jeremy Lode that she had an issue over having lunch with him.

Mandy had to backtrack, and fast. So what if Jeremy was gorgeous and wealthy *and* a gentleman *and* didn't seem annoyed with her frankness *and* looked at her like he was interested? Had Daisy been right? *No,* Mandy firmly told herself.

"I'd love an explanation," Jeremy said, his voice a little firmer now. "If there are things to be worked through, then we need to have a meeting of the minds."

"I'm not really a people-person," she said. "Small talk, socializing, chatting with people outside my very small circle of friends . . . isn't really in my comfort zone."

Jeremy said nothing, just gazed at her with those beautiful gray eyes of his. He wasn't making this easy.

"I'm an accountant by day, a programmer by night," she continued. "Those professions in and of themselves should tell you that I'm more of an email-or-the-occasional-text person."

Jeremy smiled.

This was the second time she'd seen him smile, and it made parts of her flutter that she didn't know could flutter.

The waiter came and saved the day, literally. Mandy couldn't drink the ice-cold water fast enough and only stopped shy of drinking down the entire glass when she realized both Jeremy and the waiter were staring at her. Carefully, slowly, she set the water down. "I was really thirsty, I guess."

The waiter merely said, "I'll refill your glass, ma'am."

He disappeared, and Mandy picked up her cloth napkin and dabbed at her mouth.

"I'm sorry if I make you nervous," Jeremy said, his tone wry.

Mandy thought about protesting, but he'd already seen the results of her nerves.

"I'm fine with emails and texts, too," Jeremy said. "In fact, they're the most convenient way to communicate since sometimes I work late hours."

"Me too." Mandy gave him a small smile.

He nodded. "I think you're shortchanging yourself, Mandy. Even if you're not a socialite, that doesn't mean you can't expand your circle of friends and acquaintances. And I hope you'll eventually consider *us* friends. We're going to be stuck with each other for a while."

"*Friends?*" Mandy said, hoping her voice hadn't just squeaked. "You and me? Um, I think we should keep things strictly professional, if you don't mind."

Those lines appeared between his brows, but the waiter was back. With more water and the shrimp appetizer.

She hoped she hadn't insulted Jeremy. He was kind of overwhelming her senses, and once this lunch meeting was finished, she hoped things wouldn't feel so ... intimate between them. That he wouldn't gaze at her like he could see into her soul. And that her stomach would stop doing backflips.

"*Professional* is what I meant to say." Jeremy reached for one of the jumbo shrimp, dipped it into the red cocktail sauce, then ate it.

Mandy didn't feel any less fluttery, but she reached for her own jumbo shrimp. She closed her eyes for a moment to better savor the cold, tangy flavor. "Oh. This is really good."

When she opened her eyes, Jeremy was dipping a second shrimp, a half smile on his face. "I don't think I've ever seen someone enjoy their shrimp, and water, as much as you do."

"I don't get out much," Mandy said.

Jeremy laughed, and the deep rumble reached across the table and skittered along her skin.

"I'm serious," Mandy said, although she smiled at his laughter. "My roommate, Daisy, tries to drag me to all sorts of things, but I'm pretty much a homebody."

"I get it," Jeremy said. "I know other accountants and programmers. Introverts, the lot of you." His tone was warm, almost teasing.

"Exactly." Mandy began to relax. Just the smallest bit.

"Pretend like I'm your roommate Daisy and tell me about yourself," he said in that smooth, deep voice.

Jeremy Lode was one persistent man. Mandy sighed. "You are *so* not like my roommate."

"I'd hope not," he said, "especially with a name like Daisy; I can only imagine her personality."

Mandy wondered if the bubbly personality of Daisy was something Jeremy would be attracted to. "We're pretty much opposites, but it works, you know?"

Jeremy cocked an eyebrow, waiting for her to continue.

"Okay, okay," Mandy said. "I was born in Salem, grew up an only child. Parents still live there. Graduated from college in accounting. Got a job at DeMille's Accounting Firm.

Moved in with my second cousin, Daisy, who's a hairdresser. Had an idea for an app, developed it, and here I am."

"You skipped a lot."

Mandy took another shrimp because at the rate Jeremy was eating, he'd finish off the whole thing. "What about you? I read your bio on the firm's website, but that skips a lot too."

He popped another shrimp into his mouth. Chewed. Swallowed. Then drank from whatever wine he'd ordered.

"I'm from the Boston area," he said. "Two brothers and a sister, all of whom you've met. No girlfriend or wife, although my mother is probably nagging me all the way from heaven as we speak. I like numbers. And closing deals. What about thirty-five percent equity?"

Mandy laughed. The Jeremy sitting across from her was a different Jeremy than the day before. He was relaxing, opening up, bantering with her. "You haven't seen my new spreadsheets yet."

"I will soon enough."

"Have you always been so . . . confident?"

With one finger, Jeremy pushed the shrimp cocktail platter toward her. "You were about to say *arrogant*, weren't you?"

She shrugged, and he cracked a smile. Her heart flipped. Again. "You aren't in short supply of much, Jeremy Lode."

"I know I was born with a silver spoon in my mouth," he said. "But life isn't all roses, no matter which circumstances you were born into."

Mandy was curious about his statement, but before she could ask him anything more, the waiter brought their meals. She gaped at the work of art that was her wedge salad. "Wow, thank you," she told the waiter. He would probably laugh at her when he returned to the kitchen. She picked up her fork, but she didn't know if she dared eat the salad.

"Is something wrong?" Jeremy asked.

She looked at his salmon salad, another beautiful creation. "I didn't know food could be so beautiful."

Jeremy slid his plate over. "Take the curse off it."

She raised her brows.

"You know, take the first bite," he said. "See if you like the dish. Maybe next time you can order a full meal."

Mandy was about to protest, but the salmon dish looked divine. So she speared a section of the salmon and salad, dipped it in the hollandaise sauce cup, then put it into her mouth. Her eyes slipped closed as she savored the smoky, tender flavor of the salmon along with cool, crisp lettuce and the creamy tang of the sauce.

When she heard Jeremy chuckle, she opened her eyes to find him watching her. How many times could she blush at one lunch meeting? "Sorry. I'm sure you want your meal back."

"I like watching you enjoy your food," Jeremy said in a low voice.

The heat that was spreading to her neck shot through the rest of her body.

"You can have more if you want," he continued. "There's plenty."

"No." Mandy slid the plate over to him. "This wedge salad will be great." As if to prove her point, she cut into it and took her first bite. She wasn't surprised that it was the best salad she'd ever tasted.

"Good?"

Mandy's mouth was too full to speak, so she rolled her eyes heavenward to express her enjoyment of the food.

Jeremy chuckled, then started eating his meal. He ate the salmon salad much slower than he had the shrimp cocktail. "Tell me about why you decided to develop an app. Are you trying to get out of the accounting business?"

"I'd love to be my own boss," Mandy said with a shrug.

"Not that I don't love crunching numbers for other people so they can see how rich they are." She shut her mouth because she'd probably offended Jeremy in three different ways.

But he didn't look offended at all. His eyes held only amusement. "I get it. Before I was president of Lodestone, I had to take on a lot of clients I didn't care for. Now I can be more selective."

Mandy downed more ice water. "Well, I appreciate your vote of confidence in my business venture then."

Jeremy nodded and went back to eating.

"And I also must warn you that this will be our first and last lunch meeting," Mandy said.

Jeremy snapped his gaze to her.

But she had to get it all out. She waved toward the rest of the restaurant space. "I'm more comfortable with a laptop and talking numbers and ideas. The social side of things is a bit nerve-wracking. I've never been a great conversationalist."

"You're doing fine now," Jeremy pointed out.

"What I mean is, I'm not a pretty-talker."

"I've heard a lot of pretty words, as you call them," Jeremy said. "I think your bluntness is refreshing."

This she hadn't expected.

"Although we should probably discuss business a little," he said. "With your schedule, what are the most convenient times for you to meet?"

"Lunch hour, but not actually eating lunch," she said, "or after 4:30 p.m."

"Great," he said. "We'll start Monday at four-thirty. Who else is on your team?"

"Just me right now."

His brows drew together. "So you're putting in, what? Eighty-hour workweeks?"

"Pretty much."

Jeremy took another sip of his wine, as if he was thinking

some things over. "I'll have a couple other people in our Monday meeting who will be excellent at helping get the app launched."

"Not your siblings, I hope," Mandy said.

"No... Your account is my solo project."

"All right, but know there's another accountant at my firm who's interested in moonlighting," she said. "I've budgeted in her hours."

"You might want to branch out from accountants," he said. "No offense. At least wait until Monday to decide."

The business-Jeremy was back. "Is this how it's going to be?" she asked.

"What?"

"Our partnership." Mandy drank more water, then set down her glass. She was trying not to be irritated. "You make a suggestion, I come up with a solution, you railroad it—"

"Whoa." Jeremy held up a hand. "I'm not railroading you. I'm only sticking to my thirty-five percent obligations."

Mandy gazed at him and the half smile on his face. Her irritation faded, although she decided it was easier to read him when he wasn't the smiling-Jeremy. "I haven't signed a contract yet."

He held up his wine glass. "Let's toast to *almost* signing a contract."

She lifted her water glass and clinked it against his. Before taking a drink, she said, "How soon can you go over my new spreadsheets and get back to me?"

Jeremy took a sip of his wine before answering. "I'm not opposed to burning the midnight oil, so let's say later tonight."

She was both impressed and surprised, but mostly impressed. "Well, thank you."

Jeremy took out his phone, and Mandy realized she hadn't seen him use it once. This impressed her even more.

"What's your cell phone number, Mandy?" he asked.

The way he said her name in that low voice of his made the flutters return.

"I don't usually swap cell numbers with my clients," he continued, "but I think you're going to be more demanding than usual."

She narrowed her eyes. Was he teasing or serious? Both? Regardless, it made her feel a bit weightless when she thought of him texting or calling her. Which it shouldn't, at all. As far as she knew, he was a player. *Ugh* . . . she was so out of her league here.

She rattled off her number, and he typed it in. Then he sent her a text, making her phone buzz. She created a new contact from the text he'd sent over.

"Are you finished, or do you want dessert?" he asked.

Another thing to be surprised about: that he'd take time for dessert—at lunchtime no less—in the first place.

"No thanks, I'm full," she said. "Plus, if I try the cheesecake I'll probably never leave the restaurant."

"I'll order it to-go then," he said. "It's my favorite too."

Six

JEREMY RUBBED HIS EYES. He really should get those computer glasses with blue-light filtering that everyone was talking about. It was nearly one in the morning, and he'd just finished going through every line of the spreadsheets Mandy had sent over. She'd been thorough, but she didn't have a full grasp of the marketing end of things.

Launching a product was one thing, but maintaining it and keeping it competitive against copycats was another game entirely. Jeremy would need to be calling in some favors with his high-powered friends in the industry.

For another client, and another app business, he would keep the launch soft. But for Mandy... He hated to admit that he was going above and beyond his usual involvement with clients. And it was barely the third day of their acquaintance. But he felt a persistent drive to get this app well on its way as soon as possible. Certainly it had nothing to do with the refreshing person Mandy was—not to mention that she was highly attractive or that she had no scruples standing up for her company in front of a room full of investors. Perhaps warning bells should be going off in his head, but he was too tired to pay attention.

He emailed Mandy the spreadsheets with his embedded notes. She probably wouldn't be able to look at them until her lunchtime anyway, but at least it was off his plate for now.

Despite the headache pressing behind his eyes, he typed up a half-dozen emails to key players in the social media marketing space in order to start the process for the upcoming Monday meeting. Other contacts would have to be more personal and would require phone calls in the morning. He was about to log off when an email popped up. From Mandy.

She was awake?

He opened the email and read.

Better late than never.

At first, Jeremy stared. She was . . . giving him a hard time because it was past midnight? He smiled. Then he wrote back. *Technically it's still tonight since I haven't gone to bed yet.*

Her reply came seconds later. *I see you haven't stepped down from your thirty-five percent even after such a thorough review of the financials. I don't intend to stay in the poorhouse after this thing takes off.*

He scoffed. *Sixty-five percent won't keep you in the poorhouse.*

Is that the best you can do, Jeremy Lode?

Did she really just play that card? He tapped his fingers on the desk. Jeremy didn't need to pull up the spreadsheets to know the numbers. He could go to twenty-five percent and still be sitting pretty. *Thirty,* he typed. *That's my final offer. And I can't believe you're negotiating with me at one in the morning. Is it coffee?*

She typed back a smiley face. Nothing else.

He waited. Still nothing more. Finally he wrote, *Does the smiley face mean you agree to the thirty percent?*

She wrote back. *Yes.*

He laughed. Smiling, he typed. *Congratulations, Amanda Wurst. And welcome to Lodestone Capital. The contract will be in your inbox by 9:00 a.m. Not a second later.*

A half a minute later her reply came. *I'll keep an eye out for the contract. Thank you for taking this chance. Good night, Mr. Lode.*

They were back to formalities, but that didn't change the smile on his face.

Somehow Jeremy managed to catch a few hours of deep sleep before his 5:00 a.m. alarm went off. He'd learned long ago that even if he was up late the night before, he needed that 5:00 a.m. running time. It kept the stress levels at a minimum. An extra hour of sleep only made his workload loom larger.

Jeremy turned off his alarm and realized he was smiling. It was a new thing, to wake up with a smile on his face. He assumed it was because he'd effectively closed a deal at one that morning, but deep down he knew it had more to do with the person on the other side of the deal. When he'd told Mandy she was refreshing, it was the truth. Everything about her was different than any woman he'd ever been friends with or dated . . . Not that he'd ever date Mandy. She was a client. And she was . . . well, their worlds were quite far apart, as she'd so succinctly pointed out at their lunch.

But her frankness reminded him a bit of his mother's way of getting to the heart of the matter. Jeremy had never been able to fool his mom about anything. He climbed out of bed and changed into running shorts and a T-shirt. Then he queued up the music on his phone and grabbed some water from the fridge. He exited his apartment and went into the elevator that would take him to the ground level. His top-floor apartment in the city was where he'd been spending more and more of his time lately.

He owned a cottage in Martha's Vineyard and a cabin in Pine Valley, but home had always been his parents' estate outside of Boston. Maybe he'd go there this weekend, spend time with his dad, get in a golf round.

The elevator dinged open, and he stepped out.

"Hello, Mr. Lode," Raphael said.

The doorman was in his usual black suit, holding court in the lobby.

"Hi, Raphael," Jeremy said.

"It's a nice day for a run," Raphael continued, his dark eyes crinkling at the corners with his smile.

"Yes, it is," Jeremy said. They had the exact same conversation every morning. And when Jeremy returned from his runs, Raphael would update him on something about his family. His young daughter's new tooth, or his son's latest art creation in preschool.

Jeremy took his shorter, three-mile route today, so that he'd beat the traffic into Boston. He was determined to stick to the 9:00 a.m. contract deadline. It wouldn't take long to revise the boilerplate contract he always worked from, but he wouldn't put it past Mandy to find some fatal flaw that would cause her not to sign quite yet.

And for some reason, Jeremy was determined to lock the contract down today.

After his run, he showered, dressed, and was in the office by 7:00 a.m. Mornings were his favorite, especially if he could get in before the hustle of the day began.

He'd barely sat down at his desk when his cell rang. "Hi, Dad," he answered.

"I'm reading the email you sent over a few hours ago . . . at one in the morning?"

"Yeah, can I come home for the weekend?" Jeremy asked. "Or do you have other guests around?"

His dad chuckled. "Depends. Are we talking business or pleasure?"

"Downtime, that's all," Jeremy said.

"In that case, Harold and John will be here. We have a few tee times lined up."

Jeremy didn't mind his dad's friends; both men were semi-retired.

"Want to join us?" his dad continued. "We can play a four-man scramble."

"Maybe for one round," Jeremy said. "Speaking of golf, Sidney told me you've reneged on the charity tournament. I didn't know you were going to Europe."

"Ah, well, Harold talked me into following the Tour."

"Tour?" Jeremy prompted.

"You know, the Tour de France," his dad said. "Harold's been a bunch of times. Says it's good times following the race, staying in different villages every night, enjoying the French wines."

Jeremy suspected that Harold probably enjoyed the French ladies too. Jeremy couldn't care less what Harold did with his time, but now that his dad would be going too ... "You know that Harold's a ladies' man, and he's not exactly picky."

"Don't worry, son," his dad said. "Your mother can still scold me from heaven. If I do meet another woman someday, she'll speak English."

Jeremy knew he should laugh, but the thought of another woman replacing his mom was nothing to tease about. Not yet. Two years was too soon. "Well, I'll see you this weekend, then," Jeremy said, keeping the frustration out of his voice. "Book me for a golf round."

"Great," his dad said, his tone bright.

They hung up, and Jeremy busied himself with the contract for the On the Go app, and at 8:35 a.m., he officially sent it to Mandy's email.

The office outside his door was coming to life, and he heard Dustin's rather loud voice. Phones rang, doors opened and shut, and Jeremy clicked through his emails, addressing the more urgent ones first.

At 8:58, his cell rang.

Mandy.

Jeremy had assumed she'd call his office number during business hours or, like she'd said, stick to emails and texts. So a phone call on his cell sent a warning bell through him.

"Jeremy Lode," he answered, ready to hear out her negotiating terms.

"The request for monthly reporting was stated in my spreadsheets more than once," Mandy said without preamble. "Quarterly reporting is too long to wait and delays the numbers so that if new strategies need to be made, it's too late to customize to market."

Jeremy couldn't help it. The sound of her voice made him smile. Plus, her business jargon was sexy. "Did you google that?" Perhaps he'd taken his teasing a little too far.

"I googled a lot of things, Mr. Lode," she said. "But that wasn't one of them. Remember, I'm an—"

"You're an accountant," Jeremy cut in. "Yes. I know." He rose from his chair and crossed to the floor-to-ceiling windows of his corner office. Being the president had perks he never complained about. "But if you look at the notes I put in on that line, monthly reporting costs eighteen percent more than quarterly reporting."

Her phone beeped as if she had another call coming in. "My firm will offer us a discount, which I also stated in the spreadsheet."

Jeremy decided he'd rather talk to Mandy in person. Over the phone wasn't the same. "I don't think it's wise to use the same accounting firm you work for. If this thing grows and we take it public—"

Her phone beeped again.

"—we'll need the separation," he finished. "I'm looking out for the long term, Ms. Wurst."

She exhaled. "We can hire another firm then, but I still think eighteen percent would be worth it." Her phone beeped. "Sorry about that. I should have called you on the landline, but then I would have to be in my cubicle. Lots of ears around, you know."

"I can call you back in a few minutes if you need to take care of something."

Mandy scoffed. "This will take more than a few minutes. Hang on, let me send a quick text."

Jeremy slipped one hand into his pants pocket and gazed out over the Boston skyline. The morning's dawn colors had faded to a perfect blue. Not a cloud in the sky.

"Okay," Mandy said into the phone. "Sorry again. Daisy is the most persistent person I know, next to me of course."

"Is she all right?" Jeremy asked, unsure why he was taking this detour in the conversation.

"Oh, Daisy's great," Mandy said. "I forgot to throw out the invitation to my ten-year high school reunion. When she found it this morning, she asked if I was going. Which of course I'm not. It's tomorrow night, and everyone will have their spouses or significant others. Their topics of conversation will be about their adorable toddlers or second vacation homes. Daisy thinks that if *she's* my plus-one, it will make all the difference."

"You're twenty-eight?"

"Is that all you got out of what I said?" Mandy said, her tone a mixture of exasperation and amusement.

Jeremy chuckled. He wanted to see that amused gleam in her eyes. "So are you going?"

"I wasn't what you called popular in high school," Mandy said. "I was the classic geek. Five-foot-ten by the time I was a sophomore, didn't play any sports, couldn't carry a tune in choir, or play an instrument to save my life."

"I'll bet you got straight As," he mused.

"Well, yes, but what fun is that when every minute in school makes you want to throw up?" she said.

Jeremy stilled. "That bad, huh?"

She didn't answer.

Jeremy felt hot and kind of antsy. He wasn't sure what happened next, but the words just came out. "What if *I* was your plus-one? Would that make a difference?"

Seven

ALTHOUGH MANDY HAD ONE ear plugged with her finger and the other ear glued to her cell phone, she wasn't sure she'd heard Jeremy right.

"Are you still there?" Jeremy said through the phone.

"Yeah," Mandy said. "Did you just tell me that you want to come to my high school reunion?"

"I did."

Mandy turned toward the painting on the wall at the end of the hallway where she stood. The painting was some sort of mountain scene, with a dark-turquoise river snaking through the velvety-green meadow. Beyond rose a majestic violet-and-slate-gray mountain.

"Mandy?"

"I couldn't let you do that," she said. "I mean, you're . . . a beautiful man . . . and you're successful . . . and wealthy. The popular girls, who used to dump tampons into my locker so that they'd fall out when I opened it, would know something was fishy. And when they find out that we aren't really dating, they'd be all over you. You'd go home with at least a dozen phone numbers—"

"Mandy, stop." Jeremy's voice was commanding enough that she did stop talking.

Breathe. Showing up with billionaire Jeremy Lode as her plus-one at her high school reunion would be worse than staying home and sulking. She'd be laughed at because everyone would see right through her. No way would she have a boyfriend like Jeremy Lode. It would take minutes for the vixens and their dopey followers to discover that Jeremy was in fact her investor.

"They put tampons in your locker?" he asked, his voice a mixture of incredulity and steel.

"That was a good day," Mandy said. "The racoons thought my last name was the best bait for teasing, but not the right kind."

"Racoons?"

"It's how I labeled the popular girls who wore layers of makeup, since their eyeliner made them look like racoons." She squeezed her eyes shut. "We're way off track here. I'm not going to the reunion. Even if you are changing the terms of my spreadsheets, I wouldn't put you through that."

He didn't say anything for a moment, and she was about to check to make sure they were still connected when he said, "I'm the one who suggested going with you. Picture it. I'll drop the word about how amazing and successful you are. How I can't believe how lucky I am to be dating a woman like you. We arrive a little late, take some pictures, drink some cheap wine, shake some hands, then get out of there."

Mandy visualized the moment as if she were in a movie scene. She and Jeremy walking in. Him: drop-dead gorgeous. Her: dressed up as much as Daisy could help. Mandy could even wear heels because he was that much taller than her. They'd mingle. Say some fake words. Laugh. Pretend they were dating . . . *No.* Was she really considering taking Jeremy up on his offer? Then she remembered. "It's black tie."

"No problem," he said. "I have a tux."

Of course he did, and he probably looked amazing in it.

The temptation to do this with Jeremy at her side was

growing stronger. "Wait," she said. "What's this going to cost me?"

"Excuse me?"

"I mean, this is a *huge* favor," she said. "Are you going to ask for thirty-five percent again?"

She heard Jeremy exhale on the other side of the line.

"Sometimes life isn't all about the money, Mandy."

Well, that was a reprimand if she'd ever heard one. And now she felt horrible. And guilty. "You're right," she said. "I'm sorry."

"If you need a plus-one for the reunion, let me know," Jeremy said. "Otherwise, does everything else in the contract look good?"

His tone was cordial, and Mandy hated it. She wanted to hear him teasing or even arguing with her—anything but the professional-Jeremy.

"You addressed my only concern," she said. "I'll get it signed and emailed over."

They hung up, and Mandy leaned against the wall and closed her eyes.

Now what?

She called Daisy. "You can stop texting me now," she told her roommate.

"We're going?" Daisy practically squealed into the phone. "You can borrow one of my dresses, you choose first, and I'll—"

"Daisy," Mandy cut in. "Jeremy Lode offered to be my plus-one."

This time Daisy did squeal. "Wow, just *wow*. He totally has the hots for you." She squealed again.

Mandy could have predicted everything that Daisy would say about Jeremy, and she was right. After about a minute of Daisy's gushing, Mandy cut in. "I haven't decided if I'm going, but if I do, Jeremy says he already has a tux."

More squealing and gushing. From Daisy.

The more Daisy talked, the more nervous Mandy became. Her pulse was doing wild things because she was seriously considering going with Jeremy. It would feel good to maybe once have those mean girls from high school rendered speechless.

When Mandy hung up with Daisy, she knew she needed to get back to work. First she'd sign the contract though. Whether or not they went to the reunion together, she wanted to get the production on the app underway. Work was always the best way to deal with all the other things her life lacked.

By lunchtime, she'd emailed over the contract, caught up on her accounting work, and decided that the reunion was going to happen. Her stomach was in too many knots for her to eat, so she opted to take a walk along the city streets until her lunch hour was up. On the way, she could think about how to talk to Jeremy about the reunion. She could simply text him. Email might be better. Or a phone call.

As she stepped out of her building, she wondered if she should see him in person. Surely he was busy—in meetings, likely. But maybe if she saw him in person, she'd better gauge whether this whole reunion thing would work. She could hire a Uber, and . . . *No.*

Her nerves were wound too tight, and she'd say something she'd later regret. Mandy reached the end of the block and paused at the corner to wait for a traffic light. The spring air was warm today, and she relished the sun's rays on her face. The crosswalk light changed, and she stepped off the curb, walking with the other pedestrians who'd collected at the corner.

The more she walked, the more confident she felt.

She *was* successful, so to speak. She was a college-educated woman living on her own, financially independent, on the brink of more success, and she had friends: Daisy and, well, Jeremy. So what if showing up with him on her arm would be a bit of a ruse?

She paused near a café and sent a text to Jeremy. *Are you busy tomorrow night?* Then she started to walk again, heading back to her office. Before she reached the corner of the block, he'd texted back.

I have plans to go to a friend's high school reunion.

Relief buzzed through Mandy. He was back to the teasing Jeremy. *Can you be ready by 6:00?*

Yes.

Mandy's pulse drummed. *We can meet somewhere or I can pick you up.*

His reply came almost immediately. *I'll drive.*

Okay, then. Jeremy obviously had no trouble making decisions. Mandy texted: *See you tomorrow at 6:00.*

Eight

SOMEHOW MANDY MADE IT through the next twenty-four hours of anticipation. She even survived Daisy's mantra about Jeremy liking Mandy as more than a "friend." She elected to wear one of Daisy's fitted black dresses. It was shorter on Mandy than on Daisy, but that couldn't be helped. All of Daisy's dresses were short.

"Should I bring a jacket or something?" Mandy asked as she surveyed herself in the full-length mirror at the end of the hallway in their apartment. The black dress had a high neckline, but her shoulders were bare and the back cut into a low scoop.

"Jeremy will keep you plenty warm," Daisy said.

"Stop saying that kind of stuff," Mandy said. "You know this isn't a real date."

Daisy merely smiled.

Both women jolted when the doorbell rang.

"It's six already?" Mandy whispered.

"He's five minutes early," Daisy hissed.

Mandy felt light-headed. This was really going to happen—Jeremy Lode was taking her to her reunion.

"I'll get the door," Daisy said when it became apparent that Mandy was frozen in place. "We don't want to make him knock."

No . . . That wouldn't be good. Just before Daisy opened

the door, Mandy hurried into her bedroom. She didn't want to be caught staring from the hallway.

The rumble of Jeremy's voice filled the apartment, and Mandy checked her appearance one more time. Thank goodness for Daisy's help.

"Mandy..." Daisy called in her super sweet *get-in-here-right-now* voice.

Mandy exhaled. Then she left her bedroom.

Yep. Jeremy looked amazing, and Mandy decided she was proud of herself for not tripping on something as she walked toward him. She could practically feel Daisy's smirk, because, yes, Jeremy was looking at her like he was very much appreciating *her* appearance.

Oh boy.

Jeremy's dark hair was more styled than usual, and he seemed even taller in her apartment. His tux was black, as she expected, and it looked as if it had been tailored to perfectly fit his broad shoulders, then taper at his waist to the final half inch. His gray eyes were focused solely on her. And if that wasn't enough to get her heart pumping, he had brought... roses.

"Hi," Mandy said, because that was about all she could manage to say at the moment.

"Looks like you're ready." Jeremy's gaze slid down her body then back up.

The appreciation in his gray eyes made her skin hum. And... apparently she was tongue-tied.

"I hope you like roses," he said, the edges of his mouth curving.

He *knew* the effect he had on her. She had to snap out of it.

Mandy blinked and stepped forward. She took the roses and breathed in their scent. "I do. Thanks. They're beautiful. Thank you."

Jeremy's smile made her heart start racing all over again. She turned to Daisy. "Can you put these in water?"

"Sure thing," Daisy said, amusement in her voice. "Have a great time, you two."

"Thanks," Mandy said. How many times was she going to say *thanks* tonight?

Once outside, Mandy breathed a little easier. At least she didn't have to deal with Daisy listening to every word between them. But she was still plenty nervous about facing the racoons tonight.

She was so caught up in her thoughts, she didn't even notice that Jeremy had stopped in front of a silver sports car—not the same car they'd ridden in a few days ago. He opened the passenger door for her.

"Where's your driver?" she asked.

"I drive myself around mostly, if you can believe it," Jeremy said with a wink.

The soft light from the setting sun made him look like he was a painting in a Greek temple. She hadn't realized that she was staring at him, not getting into the car, until he said in a soft voice, "Are you all right, Mandy?"

She blinked. "The racoons are going to flip when they see you."

His brows lifted as if he was questioning her statement.

Mandy rested a hand on her hip. "I'm sure I don't need to tell you what effect you have on women."

Jeremy merely gazed at her, then he reached for the hand on her hip and tugged her toward him. Mandy took a step forward. She'd noticed his faint cologne scent in her apartment of course, but up closer, he smelled even better.

His warm hand encompassed hers. "Did I tell you that you look beautiful?" he said in a voice so low that it made things inside her melt. "I'm willing to bet that every racoon will be green with envy tonight because of *you*, not me."

"How much are you willing to bet?"

Jeremy chuckled and ran his thumb over the back of her hand as he studied her. "Two hundred."

Mandy scoffed. "That might be pocket change to you, but I don't have that kind of cash on me."

"How much *do* you have?"

"Thirty bucks."

"All right. My two hundred against your thirty."

Mandy was pretty sure she was blushing. Jeremy was still holding her hand. She was also pretty sure that Daisy was peeking through the blinds of their apartment window. "How will we know who the winner is?"

"A woman's envy is hard to conceal," he said, one side of his mouth lifting into a smile.

"True." Mandy sighed and pulled her hand from his, then moved past him to slide into the passenger seat. She could think better when he wasn't touching her or gazing into the depths of her soul.

Jeremy shut her door, and as he walked around the front of the car, she told herself that riding in a car that probably cost more than her parents' cozy house wasn't something to freak out over. Jeremy worked hard for his money like everyone else. He was a decent guy, and she hoped to all that was holy he wasn't a player. And holding her hand wasn't something he did on every date.

"Ready?" Jeremy said as he settled into his seat and started the engine.

She nodded, and he pulled out of the parking lot. Daisy had already sent a dozen texts along the lines of: *OMG. He's gorgeous!* And: *I'm in love with your boyfriend!* Then: *Even if he wasn't a billionaire, he'd be worth every penny in a poorhouse.* Mandy put her phone on silent and slipped it into the clutch she'd borrowed from Daisy.

The drive to the hotel where the reunion was being held

was around thirty minutes, but the time flew by as Jeremy told her about growing up with his siblings. It was plain that he'd always been the more serious, stoic brother, and his sister had been fiercely spoiled. His twin brothers sounded like troublemakers all the way around, but there was still affection in Jeremy's voice when he spoke of them.

When they turned into the circular driveway of the hotel and headed toward the valet stand, Mandy said, "You did that on purpose, didn't you?"

"What are you accusing me of now?" Jeremy said, amusement in his voice.

"You were telling stories to distract me," Mandy said.

"Did it work?" he asked as he stopped the car and rolled down the window.

It *had* worked. Mandy hadn't felt nervous for the entire drive.

"Good evening sir," the pimple-faced valet said.

"I'll be parking myself," Jeremy said. "Can you direct me to the best lot?"

The valet lifted his chin. "Certainly, sir. Just beyond the orange cones."

"Thank you," Jeremy said, then continued around the circular driveway. "I know what you're thinking," he said to Mandy. "Why doesn't the rich guy use valet parking?"

"You caught me," Mandy said. "Good thing reading my mind isn't part of our bet."

Jeremy chuckled. "I don't trust a lot of people. Especially with my car." He steered into a parking lot, then drove to the very end and parked in the last slot. When he turned off the engine, he looked over at her. "Are you okay to walk in those heels?"

"I'll manage." The air between them seemed to grow thick with . . . what, she didn't know. Although they'd been in the car together for a while, she suddenly felt very alone with him.

Thankfully he opened his door and climbed out, so Mandy took the few moments to calm her racing thoughts.

Jeremy opened her door and offered his hand to help her out. She climbed out of the car and fully expected him to release her hand, but he didn't.

"So . . . we need to talk about something," he said.

She looked up at him in the near darkness of the parking lot. The closest light was a streetlamp several car spots away. "Okay . . ."

"If the racoons are going to buy that we're a couple, then we need to act like a couple."

Heat prickled at the back of Mandy's neck. She could guess where this was going.

"We need to hold hands a lot," he continued, his gray eyes intent on hers. "And touch and . . . kiss."

The spring weather had failed her. Where was the cool wind when she needed it? "Maybe we're a couple who doesn't like PDA?"

"That's one option." Jeremy moved a step closer. "But I like my option better."

"What's that?" Mandy whispered because he was that close now.

"I think we should kiss now," he said. "Then things won't be awkward between us. It will be more natural to hold hands and other stuff . . . Because the kissing part is over."

Mandy bit her bottom lip. She was probably messing up her lip gloss by doing so, but kissing Jeremy would definitely mess up her lip gloss.

"It's a good plan in theory," she said at last. "But remember when I said I wanted to keep things professional between us?"

Jeremy didn't break his gaze. "What if I said that I think

we should keep things professional during business hours? And even if I wasn't your plus-one tonight, I'd still want to kiss you."

The melting inside of Mandy burst into flames. "You aren't playing fair, Jeremy Lode."

"I'm not playing at all, Amanda Wurst."

She swallowed. "Okay, then. Kiss me if you must."

Jeremy smiled. He lifted her hand and kissed the inside of her wrist. Then he cradled her face with both of his warm hands.

The breeze finally arrived, but Mandy didn't feel a bit of its coolness as Jeremy lowered his mouth to hers. His lips were warm, and his scent enveloped her, making her forget the very reason they were standing in this parking lot in the first place. She should have guessed that kissing a billionaire would be completely amazing. She also knew that the warmth and tingles floating through her had nothing to do with money or spreadsheets or deals. It had everything to do with the man who impressed her more every day.

When Jeremy had first suggested they kiss, she'd assumed he meant a short kiss, with a small amount of lingering. But Jeremy's mouth explored hers quite intently, and one hand moved behind her neck as his other hand trailed to her waist, pulling her closer. This was not a brief, obligatory kiss. This was . . . heaven.

"Mandy," he whispered, breaking away but not releasing his hold. "When I saw you wrestling open that conference room door, I didn't know how much my world was about to change."

Her pulse was racing so fast that it took her a second to catch her breath and reply. She gazed into his beautiful gray eyes and only saw sincerity there. "I hope it's in a good way."

His gaze moved to her mouth again. "Very good." Then he smiled before he kissed the edge of her jaw. Pulling her closer, his voice rumbled against her ear. "We'd better get in there, or not much will be stopping me from taking you home and keeping you to myself."

Mandy let her eyes drift shut as she kept her arms around him. "Mmm. I think I'm going to need to re-apply my lip gloss."

He chuckled, then he kissed her again. Briefly.

While she put on more lip gloss, he locked the car.

After she put the lip gloss into her clutch, he held out his hand. She linked her fingers with his, and together, they walked to the hotel entrance.

Nine

MANDY WAS RIGHT, JEREMY thought. Everyone was staring at them. Maybe not so much *him*, but Mandy. She was one of those women who was beautiful in an unassuming way. She was elegant, had gorgeous coloring and captivating eyes, and she carried herself with intelligence and poise.

Jeremy had predicted that heads would turn, and they did. Maybe after tonight, she'd believe his compliments more. He loved that she was doing something hard and facing the racoons head on.

Speaking of racoons . . . the women clustered near the open bar all had that similar look to them of *trying too hard.* They no longer wore mass amounts of eyeliner, but he knew they were the ones who'd bullied Mandy. And it made him furious.

The ballroom had been decorated with banners welcoming the former classmates and pronouncing the celebration of their ten-year reunion. Round tables had been set up, and it looked like a buffet was along one wall.

The music was low, and colored lights highlighted an area that must be a dance floor. No one was dancing though.

"Get your name tags here!" a petite, square woman called out to them.

Mandy's hand tightened on his as she led him to the name tag table.

The woman's tag said *Lynne*.

"Hi there," Lynne said, smiling at Mandy, then smiling wider at Jeremy. "Remind me of your names."

"I'm Mandy," she said and picked up a tag, then wrote her name in bold letters. She grabbed another one and wrote *Jeremy* on it.

Lynne scrunched her eyes. "Mandy..."

"Wurst."

"Oh, Amanda Wurst," Lynne said, her eyes still scrunched. "You've changed." Then she laughed as she looked at Jeremy. "I guess we all have. Ten years and all."

Jeremy nodded, although the interest in Lynne's eyes was practically begging him to introduce himself. He'd leave that to Mandy's discretion.

Mandy grasped his hand again, and he had to admit he liked her taking the initiative. She hadn't been shy about kissing him back either—and now... he was thinking about their kiss. *Well, kisses.* Maybe an hour in this place would be sufficient, and he could have Mandy to himself again.

A man moved toward Mandy, and she slowed. "Chris, I thought that was you."

Chris grinned, and Jeremy quickly assessed the man. Tall, lean, glasses, rather large nose.

"Jeremy, this is Chris Miller," she said. "We had like every AP class together."

Chris shook Jeremy's hand, then his gaze returned to Mandy. "It's so great to see you. I always wondered what happened to you after high school."

Mandy shrugged. "I'm an accountant; what about you?"

"Life insurance," he said with a laugh. "Do you need a plan?"

"My company's got me covered, but thanks," she said.

Chris nodded. "It was worth a try." His gaze moved to

Jeremy. "Well, I should let you guys mingle. Nice to meet you."

Mandy turned to Jeremy. "Hungry?"

He was a bit dubious about trying this hotel's food, but he didn't want to put a damper on things. "Sure."

They walked toward the buffet table, and Mandy was stopped several more times. Those speaking to her didn't seem to remember her from high school, but were making the rounds and being friendly.

They got in line at the buffet, and Mandy said, "This is so weird. It's like we're at a corporate retreat and trying to be polite to everyone in case they're a potential client."

"High school is always lame," Jeremy said.

"Did you like high school?" Mandy asked, looking up at him. Her eyes were a deeper green in this dimmer lighting.

"I survived it."

"Did you play sports?"

"A few."

Mandy smiled and rested her hand on his arm. "Of course you did. You were probably the prom king too. If I had been at your school, I would have been completely invisible to you."

Jeremy slipped an arm around her waist and pulled her close. "You're wrong." Her scent was intoxicating, and he wondered if she'd mind too much if he kissed her right now.

"Well, well," a woman's voice cut in. "I told Jean that Amanda Wurst was at the buffet table, and Jean didn't believe me."

Mandy turned, but Jeremy kept a hand at her waist. He didn't like the tone of the woman's voice.

"It *is* you," the woman said. Her name tag read *Peggy*. "Oh my gosh. I can't believe how different you look." She cast her giant-lashed eyes at Jeremy. "Is this your husband?"

He extended his hand. "I'm Jeremy."

Peggy's hand was limp and moist, and as soon as he could, he withdrew from her grasp.

"I don't see any wedding rings," Peggy continued. "Are you engaged or just dating?"

"W-we're dating," Mandy said.

Peggy must be one of the racoons.

"Well, good for *you*, Amanda . . ." Peggy's smile was so fake that Jeremy wondered if it hurt. She licked her lips, then rested her hand on her chest just above her ample cleavage she had on display. There were low-cut dresses, and then there was the dress Peggy wore. "You two bring your plates over to my table. We all want to hear what you've been up to."

"Um, okay," Mandy said.

Although she'd agreed, Jeremy heard the reluctance in her voice. "Sounds good," he said, so that Mandy knew that she'd have his support.

The tenseness of her body didn't soften, even after Peggy went back to her table.

Jeremy linked his fingers with Mandy's and moved closer. "We can leave if you want."

She exhaled and met his gaze. "No, I need to face them."

He nodded. "Okay. But after we eat, I'm dancing with you."

They filled their plates and walked over to the table, where Peggy looked as if she was a queen holding court.

Five women turned to watch as they approached, and Peggy waved enthusiastically. "Hi, Amanda and . . ." She smiled. "Jeremy." She turned to the other racoons. "Everyone, this is Amanda's *boyfriend*."

Jeremy pulled a chair out for Mandy, and she slipped into it. He sat on her right side and didn't miss how her hands trembled as she arranged the silverware at her place setting.

Peggy took over the conversation for the whole table and proceeded to introduce everyone to Jeremy. He didn't commit any of the women's names to memory. Peggy continued to rattle off the personal details of each woman as if she was reciting baseball stats. "And . . . finally, there's *me*. I'm Peggy Grayson. I'm divorced and have a little tyke at home. The most adorable towhead you've ever seen. Of course, I'm biased." She winked at Jeremy.

He draped his left arm over the back of Mandy's chair. She was picking at her food, not really eating. Jeremy had no appetite either. The women asked Mandy, rather stiffly, what she'd been doing for the past ten years. Mandy summarized her life in about three sentences; she was good at brevity.

And then it came . . . "So what do *you* do for a living, Jeremy?" Peggy asked, her gaze flitting from him to Mandy, then back again, as if she was trying to determine how serious their relationship was.

Jeremy rested his hand on Mandy's shoulder, just to be a little more possessive, and to let the five women gazing at them know that he was most definitely with her.

"I'm a venture capitalist," he said.

Three of the women's brows puckered. But Peggy was all smiles. "Wow, that's wonderful. What type of companies do you invest in?"

"Successful ones," Jeremy deadpanned.

Peggy laughed, and her racoon friends joined in, although they looked a little confused.

When Peggy stopped her laughing, she took a long swallow of her wine. Then she zeroed in on Jeremy again. "Tell me, Jeremy, if it's not *too* confidential, what is the net worth of your firm?"

Mandy stiffened, though Jeremy wasn't surprised at Peggy's question. It might be unusual for a woman to ask so directly, but men did all the time. "About eight billion."

"Billion, with a *b*?" one of the racoons asked.

Jeremy met her gaze. "Yes ma'am." He leaned toward Mandy. "The dancing's started."

He felt her exhale.

"Are you asking me to dance?" she asked.

"I am."

"In that case," she said, "I'd love to."

Jeremy didn't wait another minute. He rose from his chair and said, "It was a pleasure meeting all of you ladies. But I'm afraid I promised Mandy a dance, and she's the kind of woman men don't break promises to."

He held out his hand to Mandy, and she placed hers in his. Together they walked to the dance floor, then joined the half-dozen other couples dancing. Mandy stepped easily into his arms, and he marveled at how well she fit there. They moved slowly to the music, ignoring the faster beat. He could practically feel the gazes from the racoon table on them.

Jeremy studied Mandy's face, but the dim lighting made it hard to read her eyes. "Are you okay?" he asked.

"I'm not sure yet," Mandy said. "If not, then I will be. You pretty much saved me."

Jeremy touched the small hoop earring on her left ear. "They aren't worth thinking about anymore."

"I know." Mandy glanced toward the table of women. "They haven't changed much. It's like they're trying so desperately to hang on to the past. I've no doubt they're trying to figure out how in the world I ended up bringing a date like you."

Jeremy slipped his hand down her back, pulling her closer. "Don't shortchange yourself, Mandy."

"You tell me that a lot," she said, a faint smile lifting her lips.

"And I'll keep telling you that until you believe me."

Mandy tightened her hold on him, her body's curves pressing against him.

"You're used to being the boss, aren't you?" she whispered.

Her voice shivered through him. "Oldest child syndrome, I guess," he said in a low tone. They were so close now that it would only be a matter of leaning down a couple of inches to kiss her. So he did. He kept it brief in case she really didn't like PDA.

"You're playing your part very well," Mandy said when he lifted his head.

"I told you I'm not playing."

Mandy stared at him for a moment. "Then maybe we should get out of here."

Jeremy smiled. "I thought you'd never ask." He led her off the dance floor, winding around the couples. On their way out of the ballroom, several people tried to stop Mandy and talk to her, telling her she was going to miss the program, but she made excuses and kept walking.

The cool spring night was a welcome reprieve as they exited the hotel. They walked hand in hand, not speaking, as they headed for the far parking lot. Once they reached the final row of cars, which led to his, Jeremy noticed Mandy shiver.

He slipped off his tuxedo jacket and set it over her shoulders.

"Mmm," she murmured, pulling it closed. "It smells like you."

He stopped right there. Drew her against him and kissed her. This was not their first kiss of new exploration, or the brief kiss of the dance floor, but one of building passion. Jeremy had to force himself to break it off.

"Sorry." He released her and scrubbed a hand through his hair.

Mandy was equally breathless. "I guess you aren't playing, Jeremy Lode. Now what happens?"

Jeremy shook his head and smiled. He loved her

frankness, and he wondered if he'd ever get fully used to it. He grasped both of her hands and settled for kissing each one. "I'm taking you to eat someplace very expensive, where you can order anything you want. Then I suppose I'll have to take you back to your apartment, so that we don't get your roommate worried."

Mandy quirked a brow. "You know Daisy is our number-one fan, right?"

He chuckled. "I got that message."

"So . . . who won the bet?" Mandy said.

"Let's call it a tie." He led her to the car. "But I'll pay for dinner. Okay?"

"I get the feeling you're going to do that a lot, so I might as well stop protesting."

Jeremy unlocked and opened the passenger door for her. "You're a wise woman."

She paused next to him before climbing into the car. "Thank you for coming tonight, Jeremy," she said in a soft voice. "You were truly my knight in shining armor."

His throat felt thick. He didn't know which fates had conspired to bring this woman, quite literally, walking into his life. But he could only be grateful.

And now he didn't have to resist kissing her. So he didn't resist. One more time for the road.

Heather B. Moore is a four-time *USA Today* bestselling author. She writes historical thrillers under the pen name H.B. Moore; her latest thrillers include *The Killing Curse* and *Breaking Jess*. Under the name Heather B. Moore, she writes romance and women's fiction. Her newest releases include the historical romances *Love is Come* and *Wedding Wagers*. She's also one of the coauthors of the *USA Today* bestselling series: A Timeless Romance Anthology. Heather writes speculative fiction under the pen name Jane Redd; releases include the Solstice series and *Mistress Grim*. Heather is represented by Dystel, Goderich & Bourret.

For book updates, sign up for Heather's email list: hbmoore.com/contact
Website: HBMoore.com
Facebook: Fans of H. B. Moore
Blog: MyWritersLair.blogspot.com
Instagram: @authorhbmoore
Twitter: @HeatherBMoore

To Hide and to Hold

Sophia Summers

One

HIS DATE A POTENTIAL no-show, Chad Chamberlain unbuttoned his tux and sat next to the guys. The front room of his upper west side home had been transformed into small seating arrangements, tables for drinks, and comfortable hosting for all his parents' associates. Friends would have been a loose interpretation. These people were more networking power brokers than anything.

His oldest and best friend, Gunner, the guy who usually lived for these kinds of high-powered events, downed another drink in one gulp. "Dude, how long until we can leave?"

"They want me to meet Brilee Townsend, and then we'll see."

He groaned. "We'll see what? If we can leave? Or if she's coming with us?"

Chad rotated his shoulders, not any happier than Gunner about the situation. "Both. If she can hang with the guys, I'll invite her to come along, if not, I might have to liiiinger." He let the word roll off his tongue slowly, making it sound as distasteful as he suspected it would be.

"Is this like an arranged girlfriend or what?" His other friend, Travis, folded his napkin into what might have been a paper airplane. "If my parents tried this kind of stunt, I'd be out of here so fast…"

"Oh, back off, Travis. You know how it is." Gunner frowned and flipped hair out of his eyes. They were all kept on tight leashes by their wealthy parents threatening to cut their allowances. Gunner raised his hand for the caterers to refill his water. "I'm driving tonight."

"What? No way. That's your first water." Chad pulled out his phone. "If we don't want the parents to know where we are, we can call an Uber."

If they used the limo, their parents could track them. Most parents stopped worrying about that kind of thing once their kids were in their twenties, but when the reputation of their corporations, the feeling among stock holders, their success and livelihood rested on a responsible image and good press, parents kept closer tabs.

He had a successful relationship with his parents. They loved each other, and he respected them, for the most part. They worked together socially, and Chad understood how important networking and relationships were to the success of his business.

He wasn't surprised at all that they wanted him to meet their friend's daughter. His father had been talking for many months about a merger with Mr. Townsend. The details were almost smoothed out. What better way to seal the deal than a cozy relationship between their children? Chad was willing to meet her. Maybe she'd be a babe, and they would connect right away. Maybe not. But his guess was she'd be just as resistant to a forced set up as he was.

But the hour grew later, and their social event more boring, and everyone was losing patience. Chad and the guys, his parents, and even the Townsends all gave off signals they were ready to call it a night.

Brilee's parents spoke together in the corner. The stiff way they carried themselves, the masque on each face, the subtle tension in their jawlines. He'd seen the look before. This was the typical *I'm about to lose it* stance, and Chad guessed Brilee had bailed on the whole evening.

He stood. "I think that just about does it."

"What? Can we go?" Travis's hopeful face made Chad laugh again.

"I think we can go."

Chad's parents approached. His mom stood on tiptoe and kissed his cheeks. "Thanks for being here, honey. I just don't know about some people."

His father leaned closer and muttered through a closed-mouth smile, "Here they come. I still want this to work."

Mr. Townsend cleared his throat at he approached. "I apologize. We thought for sure she'd come."

Mrs. Townsend nodded and reached for a tissue. "I'd hoped she would. It's been a week already, and we've heard nothing."

Chad's ears perked up. "Is she missing?" Now here was something interesting. Surely she wasn't in any danger. No one was panicking.

"Not really missing, no." Mr. Townsend placed a hand around his wife's back. "She took a break, a vacation, and we haven't heard from her since she left."

"She planned to go off the grid, they say. Left her cell phone at home."

Chad leaned forward, waiting for Brilee's mother to say more. "Sounds like a refreshing break."

Her mother raised an eyebrow. "Well, I think it completely irresponsible to take off without your cell phone. How can we reach her?"

Chad held back from responding that that was surely her intent—to not be reached. He had to hand it to her. *Well played, Brilee.*

He looked from one person to another in this group of parents. "Well, since the purpose of our dinner party has not arrived, I think I'll head out and perhaps see you next time?" He pasted on his most charming smile, shook hands with Mr.

Townsend, allowed Mrs. Townsend to kiss his cheek, hugged his parents, and then scooted out of there as fast as he and his friends could respectfully walk.

Their Uber arrived within minutes and they took off to catch the rest of the Red Sox game in Chad's box seats. The game was close. The Yanks were losing. But Chad was distracted. Brilee. It took guts to not show. He hadn't had the same guts. He'd been there, had dragged the guys there, at his parents' bidding—but not Brilee. She'd gone off the grid, in the face of parental disapproval. No cellphone even. He grinned to himself.

"What are you grinning about?" Travis chugged another beer from the open bar.

"He's just sitting back and enjoying his near-miss tonight. Free again!" Gunner slugged him in the arm.

"You have to hand it to this girl though, right? That took guts."

Travis shrugged. "I guess."

"So, when we going to Tahoe?" Gunner pulled out his phone. "If we go soon, I can skip out on all the board meetings this month."

"Gunner has mastered skipping out." Chad laughed, wishing he had the same ability. "My schedule is free, for now. Let's go hike the rim."

Travis held his fist out. "I'll bring the gear. We still haven't climbed that face."

Chad's adrenaline kicked in just thinking about it. "Yes! Maybe we can make it through the pass. They're expecting snow."

"You know it. Okay, what day are we going?"

They worked it out; Chad would head up early to grab their campsite along the rim, and the others would follow two days later. "We'll use the chalet off Heavenly Valley Ski Resort and take a couple days there too."

"You know it. It's time to shred." Travis stood. "I'm gonna head. I have to finish a couple things if we're gonna peace out for the rest of the month."

They bumped fists, but Gunner stayed back. "So, this Brilee."

Chad shrugged. "I don't know. I didn't care about her until she skipped out. Maybe she's cool."

"You could find out."

"When she comes back on the grid, I guess." He called for his ride. "Maybe she'll show up next time."

Two

THE GIRL WHO DARED.

That's what she wanted to be known as. The grocery store checkout magazines glared at her with evidence she was a far cry from anything so heroic or poetic. Her picture on the covers stared back at her. "Senator Hall's Intern Staffer Quits." Image after image of her face, her mouth, wide open and smiling. "Millennial billionaire disowned." Everywhere she looked, her happy and trusting face smiled back. She adjusted her baseball cap and pushed the sunglasses further up the bridge of her nose.

The lady behind her reached for a copy. "Can you believe this?" She held it up for Brilee to see. "Quits. Family disowns her. This, this is just plain wrong."

Brilee nodded and tried to turn away.

"Look at her. She's a baby. She can't be much older than you."

Brilee laughed nervously.

"What's she gonna do with her life now? Everyone forever's gonna talk about Brilee Townsend as the girl who stepped away from billions." She clucked her tongue, turning pages. "Look at this. It says she's twenty." The woman eyed Brilee until she felt nervous she'd be recognized. "How old are you?"

She choked. "Twenty."

"Yeah, see, just about the same age. This poor thing went

up there, all starry-eyed, to work on the Hill, hoping to make a difference in the world. And then—"

"And then what?" The lady two back in the line joined in, and Brilee groaned quietly to herself. The checkout girl must have heard because she winked at her and tried to move faster.

The woman further back in line frowned. "What do you think this Senator did? Force himself on her?" She shook her head. "No, that's not what Brilee's claiming. She just up and left. Maybe she didn't like what was going on. Maybe they didn't listen to her ideas. Sounds kind of spoiled to me. Why are we blaming him?"

"No one's blaming him. You weren't listening to what I was saying."

Brilee faced the front, breathing in raspy, sporadic spurts. She clenched her fists and squeezed her eyes shut and counted as she tried to measure her breaths. As soon as a bag was filled, she snatched it and placed it in the cart.

"I just can't imagine what her parents were thinking, sending her to the thick of Capitol Hill as a young woman." She turned the pages. "And then to disown her. Why they gotta do that?"

Brilee swallowed. The checker still moved too slow. And, of course, the bar codes weren't reading. When she passed the butter across the reader for the fourth time, Brilee barely kept herself from shouting, "Just type in the numbers!" Instead, she counted in her mind.

"I heard she's living by herself now. Gotta make her way in the world like the rest of us."

The woman behind her stopped talking. She was engrossed in the article, one of the many detailed accounts of the most mortifying and hurtful experience of Brilee's life.

She piled her bags into the carriage basket of her bike. She had to tip it towards her so that she could hop on. As she biked home, exhaust fumes from the cars filled her lungs instead of the crisp smell of pine she remembered from her childhood.

Her family had been vacationing in Lake Tahoe, California, for longer than she could remember. Her great grandpa had settled part of the area, and they owned a huge piece of property by the lake and another chalet up by the ski resort. But Brilee would not be staying in either. They weren't open for her use, even though she could probably convince the staff to let her hide out there. Her parents didn't really know where she was, just that she'd taken the small camper she'd insisted on buying last year, hitched it to one of the gardener's trucks and headed west.

Her bike skid a bit on an icy patch of late snowfall. Skiers were everywhere, families come for the famous Tahoe spring skiing. She thought about getting a job as a ski instructor when her small stash of cash ran out. But for now, she was enjoying living as simply as she could and writing her story.

She biked up the last hill. This time she was going to make it to the top without having to get off her bike. It was three miles into town, where the stores were, from her spot on the national forest park land. She pumped hard, determined as she gritted her teeth. A car drove by, too close on the winding road, and sprayed slush all over her legs. It was a tan jeep. Roll bars. No doors. Music blaring through the forest. Typical.

Choking on the car's fumes, she squeezed the handlebars tighter and pushed through. She'd be happy when the spring skiers left and the mountain was quiet once again. She shook the remains of the dirty slush from her jeans while she rode and frowned. She would need to do laundry sometime soon. Why did that idiot jeep have to drive so close? There was plenty of road. And she had been the one closer to the guardrail and the thousand-foot drop-off.

At last, she stepped off her bike with trembling legs. She'd get used to the extra exertion. It was good for her. As was no cell phone. Limited Wi-Fi. And a simpler life. Every morning she meditated and focused on more ways to relieve the stressors in her life.

The negativity. The toxins. She worked to let them go, starting with all memories of Senator Hall and her time on the Hill. Those ladies at the checkout further validated her need to hide away for a while. Couldn't everyone find something more important to focus on, like their own lives?

She grinned, but not too soon. First, she had to finish her book, then they could focus on her point of view.

Bear met her as soon as she opened up the camper door. He licked her hand and wagged his tail with so much energy the egg-shaped camper rocked with the motion. He was huge. Almost too big for her small living quarters, but she couldn't leave him at home. Her parents had never appreciated the wolf she'd adopted. He wasn't really a wolf, but to her mother, a husky was almost the same thing. She put away her groceries and smiled; she wouldn't have to go back down the hill for at least a week. Breathing deeply, she grabbed her laptop and climbed into her ENO hammock, which was tied between two trees next to the camper.

What a life. The pine smell filled her with happy memories, and her seat in the hammock offered the best view she had ever seen. The blue of Lake Tahoe spread out before her, with only the tops of a pine tree or two to add to the splendor. The mountain dropped off five feet past her camper. Bear sat just below her, head down but ears perked. Now, to get in some words while she still had daylight.

She opened her screen and rested her fingers on the keys. "My time with Senator Hall was enlightening in more ways than one."

She was deep into her thoughts, typing away scene after scene of her life on the Hill as a billionaire's daughter. She'd realized that being happy wasn't about how much you had, but maybe, ironically, happiness could be measured by how little you owned. What a concept! She kept going, her teeth gently pressing into her bottom lip, the world around her silent and invisible except for the words appearing across the page almost as quickly as she thought them.

Until music blared through her campground from somewhere down around the bend in the road. Then the loud revving of an engine jarred her out of her thoughts, and the rough gravelly sound of tires spinning through rocks and then spraying to a stop. *Oh no.* The spot next to hers was now taken. So far, she'd been the only camper on this side of the mountain. Most preferred easier access to the ski slope at this time of year, she supposed.

Tan jeep, roll bars, no doors. The same one that had sprayed her with dirty slush. Music still blared until he, at last, turned off the engine.

She sighed and let out the air she'd been holding inside, relaxing the tightness in her chest.

He waved over at her, and she looked away. They were not going to be friendly, chatting neighbors. If he insisted on bothering her, she'd give up this view for a quieter spot. Nowhere on this mountain was ugly, after all. She hoped he'd quiet down and move on quickly; she loved her spot because of its closeness to the rim trail. She hiked parts of it every day. Fifty miles around the rim of Lake Tahoe. Stunning.

Her new, noisy neighbor's eyes were on her. She pretended to type on her laptop.

"Mind if I join you?" His voice—as unwelcome an intrusion as it was—tickled her insides. Deep bass. Friendly. *Mmm.*

"Actually…"

"I'll just click on right here, and I won't say another word."

Her mouth dropped. He attached his own hammock to the tree next to hers, stretched it across to another, and then plopped himself down not three feet from her. He opened up his laptop and started typing.

His chestnut hair intrigued her. It was messy, all over the place, with a slight curl to it. He had a great jawline. She had a thing for jawlines. He looked up, probably noticing her interest, and smiled one large, twinkly, white-toothed smile before going back to his work. Curse her curiosity. As intriguing as she found him, she also wanted to be annoyed at the interruption. But a break from solitude did feel nice, as long as he didn't try talking to her again.

She started typing and was soon lost in her work. Every now and then, she would register a shift in his movement, adjusting his seat in the hammock, but mostly she forgot he was there. Until he cleared his throat. Twice.

Her eyes broke reluctantly from the screen, and she finished her sentence while she looked over at the stranger beside her.

"Wow, you're still going even when you stop looking? You're totally prolific. Whatever you're writing there, it's coming out fast and strong."

She blinked.

He turned his body so that he was sitting cross-legged, facing her. Then he leaned back so that the hammock swung within inches of her and then away. "So, Neighbor."

"Hey. Yeah. Neighbor." He must be in his twenties. He looked it.

"Right. I'm Chad. Me and the guys are gonna be up here thrashing the snow and hiking the rim." He lifted his eyebrows, waiting. When she didn't respond, he added, "I think we'll hit Heavenly for a few days." The ski resort. Her favorite.

His eyes sparkled with kindness. His mouth lifted in a half smile, still waiting for her to respond.

She decided she found him charming. Part of the reason she was out here was to meet new people, to associate with the non-billionaire crowd. A super handsome guy would make everything that much more interesting, right? *Absolutely.*

"You'll love it. Have you been here before?"

His mouth lifted in a grin. "Favorite place on earth."

"Mmm. Me too." She adjusted her angle so she was facing him. "I'm out on the rim trail every day. It's clear and, so far, no bears." She didn't want to run into any bears, but had spray if she did. They were a nuisance all over Lake Tahoe, too many people leaving food out.

"Me and the guys want to complete at least half of it before we go." He waved down the mountainside. "And we brought ropes to go climbing."

She'd love to go climbing. "I want to work up to the full rim trail distance by the end of summer."

He sat forward. "You're gonna be here all summer?"

She nodded and shrugged. "For now, I am. We'll see."

His head tilted to the side. "You'll see? Like, you can just do that. Stay here, or leave, or do whatever you want?"

"It's a simple life. I don't need much."

Bear shifted beneath her.

"Oh wow, that's a beautiful dog."

"Thanks. He's awesome. Nice to have him up here with me."

"Wait. Are you all by yourself?"

Alarm bells dinged in her head.

And some portion of her feelings must have shown on her face because he held up his hands. "Sorry. None of my business. As far as I'm concerned, your huge linebacker boyfriend is on his way back and will pound me to a pulp if I try anything."

Bear growled.

Chad laughed. "If Kujo doesn't eat me first."

"It's Bear."

"Bear?"

"Yup, his name is Bear." His ears perked at the mention of his name.

"Okay then, Bear and the linebacker. You're safe."

She laughed, somewhat relaxed. "I'm trying to get a book finished."

"Oh, nice. Let me guess, a documentary on the camping habits of single males?"

Her grin widened. Somehow, knowing he was single made her happy. "Something like that."

"Ah, so perhaps I could be of assistance. A research guinea pig?"

"Maybe." She tilted her head. If only she were writing a book on gorgeous, single males. Her face heated thinking about it.

"Woah, is that a blush I see? What kind of documentary are we talking about here?"

She couldn't believe that he called her out on a blush. Already she liked this guy.

"Ho ho! Or it's not a documentary at all. You're up here writing a romance." He rubbed his hands together.

"Actually, I'm writing about some important life experiences. I've given myself the summer to figure it all out and finish the book. At least the rough draft."

He watched her, possibly waiting for more, but that's all she was willing to share at the moment.

His eyes sparked with admiration. "Fair enough. I find that impressive."

She smiled. "Thank you." She was surprised at how much his praise meant to her. Maybe having a neighbor wouldn't be such a bad turn of events.

Three

CHAD WATCHED HER HAIR try to free itself from her messy bun, and for the first time in his life, he wished his friends weren't coming to join him. It had been a long time since he'd seen a girl be completely natural and relaxed. No makeup as far as he could tell, an old, rugged flannel, hair all over the place. And more beautiful than he could remember any woman being. Her face shone with excitement while she typed. He'd give a lot to get a glimpse of what she was writing.

Her adorable resistance and pretend irritation at his presence charmed him. At first, he had been incredibly annoyed that someone had snagged his favorite campsite with a tacky eggshell camper, but now he couldn't be more thrilled.

His phone sounded an alarm. *Possible avalanche.* The local forest ranger service sent these messages to anyone in the area. "Are we expecting snow?"

She looked back up from her work, eyes wide. "I don't know." Her nose wrinkled. "Are we?"

He scrolled through the alarm and did a few searches on the web. "Hmm. I don't know how serious to take this. They have the whole area on alert. Avalanche." He sat up, and his hammock swaying at his sudden movement almost dumped him on the ground.

She snorted and put a hand to her mouth.

"Hey now, It's funny until it happens to you."

"Sorry." She made a real effort to look penitent and then gave up and laughed.

He thought about teasing her some more, but wanted to talk about the warning. "So, looks like we are in for a huge storm tonight. Many feet of snow expected." He looked up at her with concern. "Will you be alright in there?" He looked at her vehicle, and his face must have shown his lack of respect for her favorite place to live right now.

"Hey, don't knock The Bullet. This thing is amazing. It might not look like much, but it's totally state of the art."

"Oh really?" He doubted it was anything of the kind.

She raised her eyebrows, eyeing his tent. "When your living situation collapses from the weight of the snow, Bear here might let you in." Her eyes twinkled. "Really, this thing has all the bells and whistles, want a tour?"

His eyebrow raised before he could stop it. "You're inviting me in?"

She opened her mouth, flustered. "No, never mind."

He started walking toward her camper. "I'd love a tour, actually. I wasn't thinking anything, well, except how nice that sounded." He felt his own face heat.

"And now you're blushing, what kind of tour were you imagining?" She laughed and the tension eased.

"Honestly, I was wondering about your setup—if you have a comfortable place to catch a movie or anything." He cleared his throat.

"Are you asking me on a date, to *my* camper?" Her eyes teased, and he didn't know what to make of her. He couldn't tell how she felt about him.

"I was." He approached the front door. "I think. But also, and this won't sound very fun, but I was hoping you would be warm enough."

She stood up and moved past him. "Oh, come on in."

The camper felt larger inside than it looked on the

outside. The living space boasted an oversized couch, a foldable table, and a refrigerator.

"See, check this out." She pulled down a display panel with a digital control of the entire layout. "I can control all the lights, raise or lower the temperature. Turn on the outside burners for a barbecue…"

"This is amazing; what do you use for fuel?"

"Kerosene, solar energy, battery packs. Silent generators, for air conditioning or just a fan, depending. The plumbing is remarkable as well, and it has a huge water tank."

She pointed to the back of the camper. "I'll be as cozy as can be in my bed, behind that door. The mattress is equipped with heaters if I need them, but this place heats up so quickly I don't think I'll even turn them on. The floors have heaters under the floorboards as well." She paused, her expression unsure. He didn't blame her; he still didn't even know her name. "How will you manage with just your tent?"

"The guys are bringing up our camper. We have a 'bro mobile' that goes everywhere with us." Tonight he was planning to head down to the ranger station—he knew the guys down there—or to head over early to his chalet. But a daring and irresistible idea teased at him.

She laughed. "A *bro mobile*?"

His grin was crooked and teasing. "Yeah. That's right."

"Okay. Well, I don't have much, but I was going to offer a spot on the floor or on the couch, though your legs would stretch off the end…"

There was no way he would fit on that couch. He was large; his head brushing the top of the camper. But bingo! "You wouldn't mind?"

"Well, I can't let you freeze. Besides, Bear will be in here with me."

"Okay, deal. I'll bring a deck of cards and a movie."

"Wait, what?"

"Well, the guys won't be up here for a couple days yet. I wasn't expecting this storm. Don't worry, I will leave first thing in the morning."

"Okay." A grin slowly spread across her face. "So, now we're officially on a date in my camper *and* you're staying the night?"

He put his hands in his pockets. "I appreciate the offer," he said seriously. "And I'll leave you to yourself. The minute you enter that door"—he pointed to her bedroom—"you can pretend I'm not even here."

"Deal." She held out her hand. "I'm Grace."

"Happy to meet you, Grace. As I said, I'm Chad. I'll just grab a couple things and be right back. I can hear the wind picking up."

He rushed to grab everything he would need and then knocked on the door twice before stepping inside. His arms were full with a huge blanket, all manner of cords and chargers, and his laptop. "For the movie."

"Excellent. I'll let you get comfortable in here."

"Wait." He held up some microwave popcorn. "I noticed you have a microwave."

"Yes." Her smile grew. "We can warm up some soup too."

They got comfortable, and her leggings and oversized sweatshirt were even more sexy than her flannel. Who was this woman who could pull off leisurewear the way others did the big designers?

The couch pulled out from underneath to make a wider bed. It also extended in length. It was piled high with his blankets and hers, and she handed him the remote. "What movie did you bring?"

"Ooh, so much trust. You're just gonna let me pick?"

"Well, I could always boycott it, but I'm game for almost anything."

He rested his arm on the back of the couch, inviting her to scooch closer, which, to his surprise and pleasure, she did! Then he clicked play. It was a DVD with a couple chick flicks on it. He and his bros kept it around for moments just like this one. She turned to him in amazement. "You've got to be kidding."

His mouth dropped. "What?"

"You watch this stuff?"

He could feel his face heat. "Well, I mean, yeah."

She raised an eyebrow.

"When I'm with a date." His grin grew. "Otherwise, no, but this is cool."

She searched his face for a minute and then leaned back against him, cradled under his arm. "Let's watch the first one. It's actually super funny."

This night kept getting better the more he became acquainted with the lovely Grace. "Hey, what's your last name?"

She shook her head. "Oh no, we're not on a last name basis yet."

"What?"

"Shh. It's getting good." She snuggled in closer to him, and he knew better than to complain. Who was this woman who held his attention like she did? He couldn't remember a time he was so caught up in someone.

Every time she shifted, every time her fingers brushed against him, her touch tingled through him in delicious hyperawareness. Her fresh smell, peppermint maybe, calmed his mind while everything else about her woke his every sense. "Let's go climbing tomorrow," he said.

"In the snow?"

"The real storm might not hit until late morning. The inlets with the good climbing are sheltered. They won't get hit tonight. If we get out early, we can put in an hour or two before it starts to really fall." He was already trying to figure out how to get her up to the chalet with him and the guys. It would be safer there. If the storm was anywhere near as bad as the news was predicting, even her epic eggshell camper would be all but entombed at the top of the mountain.

"Okay, cool. I haven't been climbing in years."

"What? So you've been?"

"I have. There was a gym I used to go to all the time, and I have friends that took me into the mountains when I visited Utah last summer. It was more of a rappelling thing, but we climbed up the face of a rim first."

"Excellent." He reached for her hand. When her fingers laced naturally through his, and a small smile twitched at her lips, he knew he was in. He had a chance, maybe. He hoped.

The wind whipped through the trees around them, louder, and two things surprised him. He enjoyed the thought of being stranded in this tiny space with such a fascinating woman. And he hoped his friends changed their mind and delayed their trip.

Four

THE MOVIE ENDED, AND for a few minutes, neither of them spoke. She couldn't bring herself to move away from her comfortable place at his side. He lifted his hand from her shoulder and nestled his fingers in her hair. He started at the back of her neck and massaged in gentle circles. Then ran gentle trails up through her hair. A shower of tingles raced through her, along her neck and down her back. She sat as still as possible.

"Mmm, you like this," he murmured.

She felt her face heat. "I do. It's like magic." She shivered.

"Then I won't stop." His other hand joined the first, and they moved to her shoulders, gently pushing her forward as he worked out knots in her neck. "And that?"

"Yes." Her voice sounded more breathless than she would have liked. But he was too much fun, and, as much as she liked her solitude, she was lonely.

He ran his hands down her arms and back up into her hair, and she thought she might faint. Only the desperate need to continue to enjoy his attention kept her conscious. She laughed inwardly. What had become of her? All those months of resisting advances during her internship with Senator Hall, but the moment a handsome man makes an appearance in the woods she melts at his feet?

Except he wasn't simply a handsome man. He was tanned just right, had a sexy amount of scruff along his jawline, green eyes that sparkled with intelligence, kindness, and an enticing amount of interest in her and the confidence to show it. He was a full court press on her senses and desires. And what harm could it bring if she got to know someone new? He was not from her set—he'd avoided the corruption of the rich. With any luck, he was as deliciously middle class as he was handsome.

He wrapped a hand around her waist and turned her to face him. Just when she thought she would fall forward into his arms and kiss him until the morning, he placed his lips on her forehead. Their soft pressure lingered. Then he whispered against her skin. "I think I should turn in."

She felt her breath leave her in disappointment. "Okay." She leaned back. "Do you have everything you need?" When he nodded, she pointed him to the bathroom and stood, still in a daze.

"Early start tomorrow?" His eyes twinkled, as if he knew how desperately she wanted to stay right there at his side. Did he share her desire?

"Yes, I'll set my alarm for seven. Will that do?"

"Perfect. Breakfast is on me."

She wrinkled her forehead.

He winked. "Don't worry. I know my way around a kitchen."

Her sluggish feet finally responded, and she moved towards her room. Bear was already stretched across the end of her bed. "Good dog."

Chad's eyes lingered on her in an unspoken invitation until she shut the door behind her and then forced herself to silently turn the lock. "Whew, Bear. Wow. What am I doing here?"

"Having a little fun, I hope." He called from the other room.

She gasped, relieved he couldn't see the bright red flush heating her cheeks. "Goodnight."

"Night."

She woke to the smell of bacon and tea and was pleasantly surprised at the comfortable ease between her and Chad. There was none of the awkwardness she might have expected.

"Good morning, beautiful." His warm smile sent a shiver of expectation to her toes. Her body had not forgotten her response to him last night. And she couldn't blame herself one bit. He was simply delicious in the morning. His scruff along his jawline was more pronounced, his green eyes bright, his hair mussed with curls poking out—thick in some places, and flattened in others—and she hoped her quick work in front of the mirror had managed to make herself half as enticing.

He waved her over to the table. He had cleaned up all evidence of his night on the couch, folded the blankets, and set the table for breakfast. They lingered over their food, his eyes catching hers every few bites until she laughed. "What?"

"You're a pleasant sight in the morning," he said. "Is it too soon to say I was just thinking how much I would enjoy waking up to such a sight again."

She laughed, uninhibited and thrilled at his response. "As long as it's not too soon to admit I was thinking the same thing." She stopped. "Not that…I didn't mean…" Ugh. She didn't want him to think she was inviting something more than she meant.

"No worries here. I think we understand each other." His warm eyes were asking something. She wasn't sure what. But she smiled in return.

They hurried through cleaning up and bundled for the outside weather.

Once in the truck, he blasted the heat. "No snow. Not yet."

"Did the forecast estimate when it would start?"

"They pushed it back another hour. We have time for a solid climb and for rappelling back down."

"I'm excited. Do you think we can do it in the cold? Our hands, gloves?"

"It won't be windy. I'll take us to a sheltered place, and, with the clouds, it won't seem as cold."

"Okay, I trust you."

He stopped the truck in the middle of the road and turned to her, his eyes earnest. "Do you? Because I'm going to need you to trust me." He waited.

She studied his face and wanted to give a sincere response, not just a polite one. And she realized she did trust him. She must. He'd slept over in her camper last night. But it was more than that. He had a solid certainty about him, a goodness in his face that she liked. She suspected he gave good advice and that he tried to do well in the world. She lifted her chin and nodded slowly. "I do trust you."

A pleased twinkle lit his whole face. "Perfect." He stepped on the gas as he faced forward again. "This is going to be epic."

They arrived in a secluded canyon area with rock face on each side. When she squinted, evidence of climbing spikes marked vertical ascents in many places. Energy coursed through her. "I'm excited."

"Good. We have time to do a few climbs if we want."

She nodded. "I do. I think." Suddenly, she hoped she would be brave enough. She'd never climbed so high or rappelled down that far either.

His eyes held hers for a moment and energy flowed through her in a greater surge. Then he grabbed a pile of ropes, their harnesses, and a backpack out of the back and took off at a slow jog into the canyon, down a path off the side of the road.

She followed, cold at first, the wind biting into her skin, but as soon as she descended into the lower canyon area, with walls on either side, the wind stopped and the air warmed. The hurry to follow Chad warmed her, and soon she was unzipping her jacket.

When she reached his side, he stood at the base of a cliff, making knots in the ropes. "Everything's still in place. We'll both be clicked on the whole time. I'll send you up first, and you can belay for me from the top."

She nodded. "Okay, cool. I remember how to do that."

He reviewed what the ropes would look like and where she could clip in to make sure that her weight and ropes would hold him if he slipped. Then she started up the wall.

The foot and handholds were obvious, and the wall felt surprisingly warm. The world around her quieted, and she focused on each step, each reach. She had missed the exertion in her muscles. Then a voice in her ear almost made her jump. "You're stunning."

"Oh my word." She took two deep breaths, holding her still position with great concentration. Then she turned her face to his.

His eyes were inches from her face. He reached an arm around her back and grabbed a handhold on the opposite side so his body cocooned hers, his eyes still staring into her own. "Truly stunning. You're a natural at this."

His words flowed through her like a cool river across tired muscles. She wanted to lean into him, and almost did, but then jerked forward again. "Oh my gosh!"

"Don't worry. I've got you." His eyes were earnest again, urging. She adjusted her weight so that instead of clinging to the wall face, her body leaned back against his. She thrilled at his touch.

"I've got you, see."

She nodded, her mouth lifted in a small smile.

Then he moved his face closer, his gaze travelling down to her mouth. Her lips tingled in anticipation. She tilted her head, and he pressed his mouth to hers, the strength of the mountain pulsing beneath her fingers, the height below a dizzying thrill as his lips explored hers. She tipped further into him, and he put his legs up against the rock face, pulling them both away from their handholds and holding her fifty feet in the air. She clung to him, turning more to reach his mouth.

His kiss deepened and she thrilled at his touch. His hands held the ropes, and she held him. Then she shifted, laughing. "Wow. Okay." She turned to face the wall again, and he pulled tighter on the ropes so that she was once again standing with her weight on the tiny crevices for her feet and gripping the handholds with her fingers. "I'm gonna keep climbing."

He still stood behind her, his body pressed to hers, and she knew she would never forget this climb, ever. "I'll be right here." He scooted over to her right. "You go up ahead."

She nodded, swallowing. Her lips tingled. And then she began to climb again. Wow, wow, *wow*. What was she gonna do now? That had to be the best kiss of her entire life, and she didn't even know this guy—not well enough. But she didn't care. Something about him was comfortable, good. So she went with it.

And anything was better than trying to get together with a guy from her crowd. She didn't know his family; she didn't care about his connections. There were no complications, just two people who met, shared an interest in each other, spent the night in her camper, and then made out while rock climbing. She chuckled to herself.

"You laughing up there, Grace?"

"What? Not really. Well, a little bit."

"Care to share?"

"I just can't believe I made out with a hot guy while

climbing the face of a cliff." She wanted to bite her tongue, but the words were already out.

"Hot guy, huh?"

She could hear the grin in his voice.

"Oh boy."

"So, how hot is hot?"

"Typical hot."

"Now I'm typical? So all the guys you date are hot?"

"Are we dating?"

Silence. Good, she'd unsettled him a little bit too.

Then his voice, close again, "I'd like us to be."

She turned to him. His eyes were full of sincerity and adventure. He offered something so enticing that she almost didn't dare consider it.

The ledge was just above. So she nodded and then hurried up the rest of the cliff until she pulled herself up and over. Then she hurried to clamp in solid and backed up in case he needed her weight to belay. "I'm clicked in."

Twenty seconds later, his head peeked up over the top, his eyes sparkling, his grin wide. "So, how's about it, Grace with no last name? Can I see you again?"

She was in, *so* in. "Absolutely." What harm could there be in a relationship without complications, without her family and the press and everything getting in the way? When he found out who she was and everything that came along with dating her, he might already be long gone. As he cleared the top of the ridge and came to stand beside her, all six-foot-two of his nicely toned bulk, she hoped he'd stick around.

Five

WHAT A KISS. CHAD was definitely intrigued. Blown away more like.

Back in the truck, snowflakes started falling in thick, fast droves, and they hurried back to her camper. "So, we know you can kiss…"

She choked. "Pardon me?"

"Well, you're sizzling hot on a rock wall. We know that too."

Her eyebrow rose, just a little. He couldn't tell if she did it on purpose or if it was just one more adorable thing about this woman who had so completely captured his attention. "So, I'm intrigued. What makes Grace tick? Tell me about something that's important to you."

He made his windshield wipers go faster, and his phone dinged again. It had been going off for about ten minutes. He figured it was the guys' group chat, planning their arrival tomorrow.

"I want to tell my story."

"Ah, so Grace has a story."

"Everyone has a story." She turned from him.

"But you don't want to tell your story to me?"

She turned back. "Not yet. I need to get it out, type it up into a book, and then I can share it. Besides, I like what we have." She toyed with her coat sleeve. "Without bringing all that into it."

He studied the road, thoughtful. He had no idea what secrets she hid or what story she was writing, but he wanted to unravel each one. "Fair enough. I like what we have, too."

"Besides telling my story, I want to find a way to live in this world and just be *me*."

Interesting.

"What about you?"

"I want to be successful."

She snorted.

"What? What's wrong with that?"

"Nothing. But, I don't know, this is probably coming from my current place right now, but isn't everyone all about success? Driven to get more money, more prestige, more of everything, thinking it will make you happy. But, it doesn't make anyone happy." She paused. "At least, that's the way it looks to me."

So, she had a problem with the rat race. Well, didn't everyone, really? "I guess it depends how you define success. I was thinking I'd like to prove myself apart from my father's expectations."

Grace nodded. "Yes. That is exactly what I want for myself. My own thing. For once, I want to do something start to finish all on my own."

And that is exactly what he'd been missing. She understood a part of him no one else had been able to. And suddenly, he wanted this bubble to continue. He wanted a haven where he could be himself without the trappings of his name or other expectations, without his parents' social world. "So, Grace with no last name, how about I be Chad with no last name, and we'll just see where this goes?"

Her eyes lit. "Excellent. I'm game. I'll be up here for the summer."

"The whole summer?" He still couldn't believe someone could just take such a long break. He'd have to get back after this week. "Looks like I'll have to take a few more trips to Tahoe than I had planned."

They pulled into the campground, and the camper already had a couple inches on the roof. "I don't know about this storm. Let's see what the projections are."

He pulled out his phone. His friends had left fifty messages. "What..." He quickly scrolled through the first of them. Apparently Brilee hadn't shown at the party last night because she was in hiding, as he had suspected. And she was all over the press because of it.

The papers were claiming she'd been disowned. That seemed pretty harsh. When he'd last seen her parents, they had sounded like they'd expected her to have some sort of relationship with him. As he skimmed the texts, his mouth dropped open. The press had gotten wind of their parents' manipulations, and the headlines read, "Billionaire debutante goes into hiding to avoid arranged marriage." He clicked on the images, but nothing would come up. His coverage wouldn't download anything.

He groaned as he tried another with no success.

"What is it?"

His eyes whipped to hers. What a mess. Was he free to pursue anything with Grace when his life was in the headlines? He swallowed. This fun, new interest in a woman with no last name appealed all the more, if only to give him a respite from his crazy life. "Nothing."

"You're not married, are you?"

He held up his hands. "Not even close."

She breathed out. "Okay then. You tell your story when I tell mine."

He settled back in his seat, the truck heater keeping them warm. He could do that. He wasn't hiding anything as long as they both admitted they were keeping things to themselves. That seemed fair. "Deal." He scrolled some more. "Oh, man."

"What?" She laughed. "If you aren't going to tell me anything, then you are going to have to make it sound really boring. I'm dying of curiosity."

"This I can share. They've blocked the passes into Lake Tahoe. Worried about an avalanche."

Her eyes lit. "So, your friends?" A small smile tried to stay hidden, but she couldn't keep it down.

"You don't seem very concerned about my friends. They could be stuck at the side of the road for all you know."

"I guess I should be, especially if you need to go. And I do feel like I should be sad you are missing out on your guy trip…"

He reached for her hand. "They're fine. And, you know, I can't find it in me to be unhappy at all. My present company is suddenly much more preferable. Though, we are going to change up our sleeping arrangements."

He enjoyed a wicked moment as he watched her face flash through a series of reactions: planning to decline while hiding a bit of secret pleasure, a deep blush, and then her mouth opening to respond. He said, "I only mean I have a chalet booked for the week, just off Heavenly Valley Ski Resort, and the snow is gonna be epic. If we can get to it before they shut down all the roads, we'll have the resort to ourselves."

"And I bring Bear."

"Bear is also invited." He ran a thumb along the knuckles of her hand. "I have a cook who'll be living with us. And you'll have your own room."

"Wow, this sounds fancy." Her eyes narrowed just a bit, and he didn't know what to say. Did she have a problem with wealth?

He'd try not to be too obvious about his money, but the cook helped smooth over any awkward feelings about the two of them sharing a condo when they hardly knew each other.

"I'm not going to complain about ready cooked meals, especially if we become snowed in," he said.

She nodded. "Fair enough." She wrinkled her adorable forehead and then turned to him. "If you don't mind the company, I'd love to come. I'm sure I'd be trapped here in just a few hours."

They both eyed the snow and the collecting inches on top of her camper. "Let's get our things."

Soon they had everything loaded into the back of the truck. He pulled the cover flat across the back while Grace locked up the camper and put Bear in the back seat. They weren't far from Heavenly, but the snow was falling fast. He switched the truck into four-wheel drive. "Wow, it's really dumping now."

Her eyes widened with wonder. "I've never seen so much snow."

"We'll take it slow." He watched her out of the corner of his eye. So, she wasn't from around here at least.

"The trees look magical. I love to see pines with new snow caught in their branches."

"Me too, especially going up the ski lifts. I feel like it takes me to their realm or something."

"Realm? I love that."

"You gonna add it to your book?"

She laughed. "No, no, this isn't a fictional story." She shook her head, and he thought he caught her mumbled words, "If only."

"So, you're writing your story, as in, your real-life story?"

She hesitated a moment and then nodded. "I am. I want people to hear it from my own perspective."

He nodded but didn't ask more. He wanted to keep their private lives outside of their bubble for as long as possible. Who knew if she would even want to be part of his life once she knew he was all over the headlines? He gritted his teeth.

The idea that he'd be involved in an arranged marriage was absurd. What century did everyone think he was living in? He'd have to get his father working on changing the public story.

They pulled into the chalet, and Chad was glad the helicopter hangar was hidden from view. For some reason, he wanted to appear as normal as possible to Grace. The three floors of natural wood and stone, the snow melting off the roof and sidewalks from thermal heating, and the granite tile of the sidewalk would all give away the wealth he was used to.

But he didn't feel the need to apologize, he just wanted to continue to get to know her before all the outside influences crashed around them.

Soon they were unloaded, and Grace stood at the large floor-to-ceiling windows, staring out at the slope and the falling snow. He rested his hands on her shoulders, and she turned to him. "This is incredible. We might be one of the few up here. Will they keep the lift open?"

"I called, and they said yes. For all the people already up here, staying at the lodge and in the chalets, tickets will go on sale. But the roads are closed. Solidly gifting us the most epic day of skiing I've ever heard of."

She rubbed her hands together. "This is incredible. I mean, who gets to do this? Thank you."

"Thank *you*. You saved me last night. It's the least I could do. Besides I wouldn't be able to sleep, thinking of you trapped in your camper."

She nodded. "As amazing as The Bullet is, I would soon be out of supplies—water, food."

Giorgia entered from the kitchen area. "Mr.—"

He held up his hands. "No last names please, Giorgia. Let me introduce Grace. She will be staying with us, and I will just be Chad for the rest of the trip."

"Nice to meet you. She is beautiful, no?" Giorgia came forward and kissed Grace's cheeks.

"She is beautiful." He nodded. "She'll be in the back rooms. I'll take my normal set. The guys aren't coming—the roads are closed. So just dinner for two."

Giorgia wiped her hands on the front of her apron. "And some hot chocolate. I've already made it."

He looked to Grace, who nodded and said, "That would be lovely, thank you."

She carried herself well and didn't seem at all uncomfortable with the staff.

Giorgia brought out the hot chocolate and a plate full of Danishes, and winked as she returned to the kitchen.

Grace pulled out her laptop, and Chad breathed out in relief. "I have to get some work done. Maybe I could join you on the couch with this remarkable view?"

Her welcoming smile warmed him anew. Then she looked back at her screen, and her face took on the look of concentration that had attracted him at first. Her eyes widened as though the words on the page were fascinating even to her. Her lips were fuller, almost like a pout, but formed in concentration. And he could tell the world around her quieted. Then her laptop dinged, and a flood of notifications made the repetitive sound almost amusing, except that her face drained of color as she reached up to mute the computer.

"Everything alright?" He watched her, concerned.

Her expression did not clear, but she said, "Looks like I might need to respond to some of these." Her sigh was the kind that tried to expel all her worries but didn't quite manage to relieve the tension.

He pulled up his computer, and the same flood of notifications hit him. His nervous laugh sounded uncomfortable even to his ears. "Looks like I have some things to address as well. Maybe they're just concerned with the storm."

He opened the email from his dad first. After skimming it through, an uncomfortable feeling twisted in his stomach. Now that the story had leaked, Brilee's father was even more insistent that Chad at least appear with her in public, take her on dates, and give the impression that they were going to give it a try. His father reminded him how important this merger would be for both companies and for his own future.

He scrolled through the rest of his correspondence, laughing a bit at his friends' texts, They all assumed he'd found a local hottie, since he hadn't responded to them. Apparently they were all down in Reno and making the best of it until the roads cleared.

After thirty minutes of dealing with work and real-world correspondence, he began to doubt the wisdom of starting up a new thing with Grace. The more he thought about it, the more he realized a new relationship with anyone was impossible, unless her name was Brilee.

He opened his mouth to start a conversation when she said, "Oh, Chad. What are we doing?"

He scooted closer, resting his laptop beside him on the couch. "I was about to say the same thing. The real world getting in the way of our fantasy?"

She nodded. "There's so much."

"Say no more. The same thing just happened to me."

"It did?"

He took her hand. "Yes. So things are complicated for both of us. We know that, at least right now in our lives, this can't really progress, right?"

Her hand squeezed tighter in his. "Right."

"Then we're okay. We enjoy the chalet, Giorgia's cooking, the skiing, and then when the roads open, we go back to our normal lives, grateful we had this time together."

She swallowed. "It's a plan."

But even as the words left his lips, he knew he was setting

himself up for a great disappointment at the end of it all. The more time he spent with Grace, the more time he wanted to spend with her. Even though he didn't know much about her, he liked her. The person she was at rest, the woman he saw—what she allowed him to see—intrigued him, and he couldn't imagine a time when he wouldn't want more.

Six

GRACE AND CHAD WERE the first two on the lift the next morning. She swung her skis back and forth as they rode to the very top of the mountain. The world looked vibrant white through her goggles. She had to hand it to Chad, he had come up with the best equipment for her to use. "Thanks for this," she said. "I'm sure I'll be cozy warm all day."

Chad took off his glove, reached over and tapped his finger on her nose. "It suits you." Then he leaned back in the chair and watched the large snowflakes fall on his mask. He opened his mouth and caught one of them on the tip of his tongue. "So tell me about this book you're writing."

She bit her lower lip, unsure how to respond. How much should she share? Surely he had heard her story, Brilee's story. Unless he avoided all news outlets, which she doubted.

"I had an interesting experience this past summer working with a prominent senator on the Hill. We drafted a bill that would have safeguarded some really important women's rights." She cleared her throat, suddenly filled with emotion. "Not to mention, it would have protected a large group of children." She turned away, her throat too constricted to allow speech.

"Would have?" His interested and concerned eyes encouraged her to share more.

"Yeah, well, I learned really quickly who makes the rules and who really writes the laws."

To Hide and to Hold

Chad shifted in his seat. "What happened?"

She shook her head, grateful the googles hid her tears. "You'll have to read the book. But I don't think I'll ever try to work on the Hill again." Her tone didn't sound as light as she had intended.

"It could still happen," Chad said. "Sometimes these things take ten years or more. I'm impressed you tried."

The lift reached the top, and she raised the tips of her skis as she stood and exited the lift. They skidded to a stop at the top of a ridge. Steep moguls speckled the hillside in front of her. A surge of adrenaline raced through her.

"Race you to the bottom!"

She dug in her poles and jumped out over the ridge, landing at the top of the first mogul. She pushed her skis through the powder, willing herself to go faster, willing the world to speed away, to leave all her hurt from this past summer behind. She hit each bump as though it was barely there.

"Wow!" Chad whooped. His laughter carried over as she bounced down the rest of the run and raced across a steep, smooth stretch. Ten minutes later, they reached the lift line together, totally out of breath.

"That was incredible!" Chad leaned into her, the pressure from his shoulder sending comfort through her, and helping to heal a part of her heart that no amount of racing through the snow ever could. "You're amazing."

"It feels so good to be out on the mountain again. I forgot how much I love this." She pushed the goggles up onto her forehead. "Thank you. For all of it. I'm really glad I met you." Even if this were it, just this one weekend, she believed what she said. She was glad she'd met Chad.

"I would never admit this to the guys, but after watching you shred a black diamond run full of moguls, I'm happy they're stuck down there in Reno." The pink of his cheeks and shy dip of his chin was so adorable she almost kissed him right then. Chad shifted the snow from his skis. "The snow's a bit heavier than I thought it would be. But there's nothing like being the first to carve down a mountain."

They skied for three more hours, and when they stopped for lunch, she sipped her hot chocolate and asked, "So what makes *you* tick, Chad?"

"I don't know. Talking to you makes me question all of my worldly motivations. But really, my whole life I've just wanted to expand what my dad started, be successful in my own right, and use the extra to do some good in the world."

If only the wealthy set she'd known her whole life had similar motivations. "That's refreshing. I feel like everyone else I know is just trying to get ahead, no matter who they hurt in the process."

She leaned forward with her hands on the table. "It's all the wealth. It corrupts people, I'm sure of it. I don't dare share some of what I saw going down during my time in Washington. Competing special interests groups, all of it. Makes me ill. If I never see another wealthy person, I'll die a happy woman."

Chad cleared his throat. His messy curls hung over his forehead, his cheeks red from exertion, eyes bright but concerned. "They can't all be that bad, don't you think?"

"They don't know how they come across. They can't even see it. Have you ever tried to tell a truly wealthy person no? Or tried to get them to do something just for the sake of doing something good? No productivity measures and no tax breaks." She shook her head. She knew she was coming across as jaded, but she was good and tired of it. He couldn't possibly understand. She stood, pulling her goggles back down. "You ready?"

They skied the mountain until the resort closed for the night, snow falling the whole time. On their last run, they skidded to a stop outside the basement door of the chalet. The ski staff gathered their equipment and took their wet things.

They stepped into the chalet in their wool socks, and Chad hobbled up the stairs. "I don't know if my body will ever be the same. You have amazing endurance." The condo smelled of hot chicken soup. "Bless Giorgia, she's a saint." After they'd eaten their fill and cleaned up, Grace felt her eyelids close.

"Come here, you." Chad sat on the couch and indicated for her to sit on the floor in front of him. "I'll work out the knots."

She moaned with happy anticipation. "Really? Oh, yes, please. Then I'll do you."

He laughed. "If you make it that far. I've been known to put women to sleep I'm so good."

She couldn't help it. "You're that good, huh? Do they fall asleep right away or…" She turned to him, her eyebrow raised.

He let his mouth fall open and raised both eyebrows. "Is this that kind of night? Cause if we're talking about keeping women awake, I can switch gears." He ran his hand down her arms and back up, his fingers lightly tickling her skin and leaving a path of happy shivers.

"Stop, that's too fun."

His eyes widened, and he tipped his head in question. Then he trailed his fingers lightly over her skin, down her arms and ran his index finger lightly across her collarbone.

Everywhere he touched lit with yearning for more. But she wasn't sure she wanted to go down that road. "Let's start with the knots." She let her lower lip extend, just a touch. "Please?" She batted her eyelashes at him.

"Oh, boy. Turn around."

She could feel his eyes roll but soon forgot as his fingers gently and insistently pushed through her upper back, her shoulders, and her arms. All the spots that were sure to be sore tomorrow received thorough attention, and she could hardly speak with how good it felt.

"I couldn't help but notice your tears up there. What really went down when you were in Washington?"

For a second, she said nothing, but his hands lulled her into a half awake, luxurious, safe zone, and so she spilled it all. "I just really thought we could make a difference. Dad's been donating to Senator Hall's campaign for years. People always talk about how long change really takes, but I thought I'd be different. And then, one night, we were alone in the elevator. I don't even want to talk about that."

His hands stalled. "You sure? Did anything go down?"

"No, nothing physical. But I understood things might go smoother with the bill if physical interaction were a part of our relationship. I might even get to meet the president."

His silence was so solid and thick she was almost afraid to turn and see his face. When she did, his steely hard expression thrilled her at the same time it concerned her.

"It happens, I guess. I'm not the first."

His mouth was tight. "Doesn't make it right."

For the hundredth time that day, she wanted to kiss those lips. His reactions were everything she was looking for in a man but thought she'd never find. "True. So I left. In the middle of everything, I left the internship, left a pile of work on my desk unfinished. And a letter."

"Letter?"

"Yes. Sitting on his desk, with a clear message that I better see some action or I'd share my story."

"Ha!" He patted her shoulders. "Attagirl." He leaned back away, so she moved to sit next to him on the couch. He tucked a piece of her hair behind her ear. "And what's happened since?"

She shrugged. "I don't know. I went off the grid. No phone, no press. Except I think my parents publicly disowned me. I'm sure pressure from the senator had something to do with that." She huffed.

"How could they do that?"

"They don't know what happened."

"You didn't tell them? Have you told anyone?"

"Nope. Just you. I guess you're the lucky one."

He stared at her for a moment then reached for her hand. "You sure nothing else happened with this guy? Just a verbal proposition?"

She nodded. "That's what happened."

"So, what's your book about?"

"Not that. Just the work I wanted to do, my experiences with my family, and my decision to walk away from it all, go off the grid." She ran a hand over her hair, smoothing out the loose tendrils. "Of course, my parents want me to come back for their stuff—dinners and things, ugh. Otherwise, I'm disowned."

His eyes lit with some kind of realization, but all he said was, "You have to finish this book."

The strength of his confidence in her, his belief of all she said, warmed her more than anything else could. "Do you think people will want to read my story?"

"Absolutely. I'm just guessing at a lot of it, but it could be picked up all over the place." His face had a new expression, sort of pained, and she wondered what he wasn't saying. He sat forward, bouncing energy off of his toes. "How long do you need? To finish?"

"I'm almost finished with the rough draft. If I had a solid two weeks, I could get it to the point where I could send it to my friend in publishing to see what she thinks."

"Okay, done. Stay here in the chalet."

"What? How long did you rent this place?"

"Oh, um, we have it as long as you need. The guys and I were going to be up here for a month at least."

"In between jobs?"

"Something like that." He shifted then turned to her. "I mean it. Stay here, finish. I have to get back, and I'd be distracting you anyway, but I'll return when you're done. And I'd like to take you to dinner to celebrate."

"You're leaving?" Her voice sounded way more desperate than she wanted.

"I...I am. Tomorrow. I just found out a couple things I need to address back home, but I'll be back for you." He wiggled his eyebrows in a ridiculous manner. "And dinner."

She couldn't help the huge rush of disappointment that flooded her. Chad pulled her close. "You have made me feel things, taught me things, and changed me more than any other woman I've met. I don't even know you, except I feel I do."

"We started a good thing here. You sure you have to go? I could put off my book for a couple weeks..."

"No, finish."

His abrupt answer startled her, but his face was full of smiles, so she nodded, grateful he cared so much about her project. "Thank you. Bear and I will be much more comfortable here." She sat up. "But no knocking The Bullet. That thing is magical."

He held up his hands. "No one's knocking The Bullet. It saved me from near death by freezing."

She laughed, and then he pulled her back up against him. "We could watch a movie."

Her shoulders wiggled back, nuzzling against him. "Sounds perfect, as long as I can stay right here."

His hand found the remote and clicked on *The Godfather*.

"What is this?"

"Chick flicks for the first date. *The Godfather* for the second."

"Is that your method or something?"

"Worked so far."

"Oh yeah? And how many women have fallen for your charms?"

"Jury's still out."

"How many have you tried it on?"

"Just one."

She turned to him and sat up higher so their faces were inches apart.

"How am I doing?" He swallowed. "Are you falling for my charms?"

She searched his face, taking her time. "Jury's still out."

"What more do you need to know to finish your deliberations?"

"Just one more thing." She pulled herself over so she leaned across him and brushed her lips across his. "Mmm. I think I might be falling."

He wrapped his arms around her. "I'm gone already. You're killing me, woman." His lips hovered above hers for another two seconds. "I've never felt this way about anyone."

Then his mouth covered hers, and a sense of security and completion filled her. She responded slowly, fully savoring his taste, his smell of spice and vanilla. She pulled on his lips with her own, pressing and responding to his insistence, washed away in the sense of rightness between them. Whatever came of the next few weeks, wherever her book took her, whatever life brought with her family, she wanted Chad to be a part of it.

Seven

CHAD HEADED HOME ON his helicopter, but Grace didn't know he'd taken it. She didn't know who he was, and didn't know he was one of the wealthy she had defamed so completely.

But he knew who she was. Brilee Townsend. The very person his parents had wanted him to meet, from one of the wealthiest families in the world. He shook his head in wonder, not for the first time, as he thought about how that had worked out. And he didn't know what to do about it now that he knew.

He'd invited her to dinner, so they'd have the one date, that much he was sure of. He needed to bring their lives together. But he didn't know how that would go down, how she would respond, or what to do about it. Did he tell her who he was? Did he wait? He couldn't say anything last night when things were going so perfectly between them. And then when they'd said goodbye over breakfast, he couldn't ruin the sweet, mussed look on her face, the tender regard in her eyes.

He had to believe she'd still be into him once she knew he was part of everything she'd stepped away from, but they needed more time together away from that. Time they didn't have.

She must finish her book. Time was everything for her right now. She might not know how much she was the talk of the press these past few weeks, but she had to jump on that. Finish writing, offer up an interview, an exclusive, and then talk up her book.

So he'd left, planning to figure out exactly how he was going to bring their lives together.

Now that he'd tasted her lips so thoroughly, now that he'd felt so complete at her side and seen her motivations, her heart, he wasn't nearly ready to let her go. Even if it meant walking away from this coveted merger between his family and hers.

But why should he have to walk away? The way he saw it, this was exactly what both their parents had hoped for. Without any manipulation, they had met and were interested in each other. With any luck, they could all be happy.

He exhaled slowly. But he'd have to move very carefully. He sensed that the woman who took on a prominent senator and left her immense wealth behind would not be easy to sway or cross. And she wouldn't appreciate being left in the dark.

As soon as Chad left, Grace's assurance and hope fell into the pit of her stomach. His strength had held her and lifted her more than she'd realized. But she gritted her teeth. She had to do a few things she'd been putting off. First, call her mother. She used the chalet phone.

"Mom."

"Oh, Brilee. There you are. How are you doing? Wait, where are you? Do you have any idea what an embarrassment you were the other night? The Chamberlains waited and waited, and that nice boy, their son—"

She wanted to hang up, but she took a deep breath. "Mom. *MOM.* I'm calling to tell you I'm okay."

The pause lasted longer than she felt was necessary.

"Thank you. I have been worried. Who can live off the grid like that? What if something had happened to you? I don't know what to even worry about. Drowning, bears. Who knows? You aren't in any of our properties. That little camper isn't even secure—"

"Mom." She cleared her throat.

Her dad got on the line. "Honey, I need you to come home."

"I'm coming."

'What?" Both their voices in unison would have made her laugh if she wasn't dreading her return.

"I'm going to finish my project early, and then I have some meetings in New York."

"I'm so glad. You can come to dinner with us. The annual Hampton party."

"Ugh, Mom, I never go to that."

"You can go this year and meet the Chamberlains."

She closed her eyes. It would be good to start making appearances and behaving normally again, though, if she could help it, she'd never live their lifestyle. "I'll be there." She could almost see her mom's silent look of victory, and it made her want to change her mind. But instead she said, "I'll see you in a couple weeks."

He landed on the home helipad. His dad waited for him in the doorway. Not a good sign.

"Son. Pressure's on. We have to nail this deal. Buttercroft is needling their way in. They want a piece of the Townsends."

Grace's family.

"But I thought you and Mr. Townsend had all but signed." *Grace's father,* he reminded himself.

"You know it's not over until the ink's on the page."

"Okay, what do we need to do?"

"You've got to find Brilee."

"Find her?"

"Yes, bring her to that dinner in two weeks. All the families are getting together for that one. Buttercroft will also be there."

"Dad, I can't just find a woman who's gone off the grid." For some reason he couldn't tell his dad about Grace. She was not part of his negotiations. He refused to let her be.

"I don't care what it takes. Also, you can talk to her parents about it—show some interest instead of ignoring them all night and then leaving with your friends the minute you could."

"Right. Got it. Is there anything else I can do besides pimping myself out for you?"

He regretted it the minute he said it, but at least he'd spoken his mind.

"Son, that is not what's going on, and you know it. Sometimes we make sacrifices. We grow family connections. We work hard to be profitable. I'm just asking that you show the girl a bit of attention. This connection with the Townsends could solidify our place for decades to come." He nudged him in the shoulder with his fist. "Why do you think your mother and I started dating?" He winked. "You might get lucky and find she's a looker as well as comes from a good family."

His father didn't know the half of it. She was the most stunning woman Chad had ever seen, and he was on the fast track to being in love with her. But it made him ill to discuss her in such a way with his dad. "I understand, Dad. Now, if we could talk about something else?"

He kissed his mom hello. They had family dinner, and then the next morning he drowned himself in work that lasted for two days. The first day, he'd picked up his phone to text Grace no fewer than twenty times before remembering she didn't have a cell phone. Finally, after forty-eight long hours, he'd shipped a phone to her with a note: "Don't talk to anyone you don't want to. Hopefully you want to talk to me?"

She'd texted him as soon as she got it. "Thank you. Going off the grid isn't all it's cracked up to be."

He was happy she was unaware of some of the stuff being said about her. The vitriol the senator was spewing. Now that he knew the senator's posturing was in preparation to defend against a suspected accusation from Grace, he wanted to punch the guy in the face.

Two weeks went by so slowly he thought he'd aged a year. But at last, he was going to pick her up. She had finished the edits on her book, and when he saw her, she might have news from a publisher. He knew publication never happened so quickly unless you were big news. So that was a good sign the editor was anxious to talk and to move quickly.

He had opted not to tell her anything about who he was yet. And he hoped, no, he desperately counted on the hope, that she'd forgive him for being the very person she would never want to see.

The annual Hampton dinner would be much more interesting than ever before, he was sure. At least for the two of them.

Eight

SHE HEARD THE HELICOPTER coming before the text arrived. "Look up."

Her laughter escaped, unbidden, and she raced out the side door to the helipad area. She'd heard him fly away when he'd left two weeks ago. He'd snuck out, as if to take a car, but the unmistakable thumping of a helicopter so close told her it could only be him. And the pieces had started to fall together.

Who was this man? He was obviously not the working-class guy she'd assumed him to be. Whoever he was, she found her stomach alternately clenching and jumping around until, as she watched him return, the tiny dot in the sky became a loud, windy presence.

As soon as it landed, he jumped out, head down, and raced to her.

She ran to meet him, and their hug filled her with everything she'd been missing; when his mouth hungrily found hers, she laughed and responded with all the pent-up missing she'd felt over the past two weeks. "So, so good." She laughed and kissed him again. "To see you again."

"Mm." He pulled her as close as she could go, pressed up against him. "You too."

They ran inside, and then he spun her around and kissed her again. He held her. "Tell me your news."

"My friend says they want it. Just as I wrote it, with some normal editorial corrections." Her mouth hurt from smiling.

He pulled away, his face alight with joy. "That's wonderful. Congratulations!"

"Thank you. I'm thrilled. Hopefully the attention will help the children and women our bill would have protected. Hopefully it will do some good."

Did he know who she was? Had he been watching any news at all? Her parents had warned her about her face being everywhere. From what she'd seen at the grocery store, there was a good chance he knew all about her. But he didn't say anything, and his face looked the same as it always had when watching her—appreciative.

She grinned. "You always look like you want to scoop me up."

He pulled her tighter. "That's because I do." His next squeeze pushed the air out of her in a gentle nudge. "I want this day to be the first in a long line of days I spend getting to know you. I hope you aren't planning on getting sick of me any time soon?" His eyes widened with pretend insecurity, but she saw the truth of it flash through his face quickly before it was gone, hidden by the confidence he showed the world.

"Every day sounds great. Could we get together more than that, do you think?"

"Ha ha! Of course! With us, anything is possible. The way we met is nothing short of a miracle." He stopped as if he would say more, and she watched him curiously, but he didn't say anything else.

She laughed and turned in a circle. "Will this do for dinner?" He'd let her know 'dinner' required an overnight stay and a flight to New York so she dressed carefully, a pretty dress, heels, classy and beautiful.

He held her hand and made a show of looking her up and down. "You look perfect."

She spun into him, and he kissed her again. Then she said what she'd been dreading to. It was time to bring him into her world. "I was wondering if we could step out of your dinner after a bit and stop by mine?"

He held her close. "You have a dinner?" He tilted his head. "In New York?"

She shrugged. "Something my parents want me to go to."

"Of course. We'll go to both of our dinners and then take the helicopter somewhere fun."

"Is it yours?" She watched him. "For the night?"

"We can take one wherever we want."

"Then off we go." She grabbed her purse. He grabbed her luggage. And they ran for the helicopter. At the airport, they transferred to a private jet, and she knew he was so much more than he'd let on as far as his income, but they could talk about that later. First they had to get through this night.

Her shoulders tightened in dread. Apparently her parents wanted her to meet some man with the Chamberlain's company. She hadn't warned her parents, but when she met him, whoever he was, it would be on the arm of a date. Chad's arm. She also planned to tell everyone there just what she thought of the kind of people who would try to set up their children romantically to get ahead in the world.

What kind of world did they think they all lived in? What was her purpose in their eyes? She knew her purpose wasn't just to date and marry a man so that her father's business could prosper. She winced, thinking about everyone's reactions to what she planned to say.

Chad reached for her hand. "You doing okay?"

She leaned back in her seat. "Yes, I'm enjoying these comfortable travel accommodations." She raised her eyebrows, waiting for an explanation but not really expecting one. She wasn't sure she even wanted to talk about it yet.

"Good. It all suits you."

"Not just the ski gear?"

"Nope. Your bullet camper and ENO, the chalet, your work, and this private jet. It's all better because you're there."

He always said all the right things. She hoped he was for real, because the longer she knew him, the more she wanted to grab his hand and live the rest of her life holding it.

When they landed, he had his driver take them straight to his parent's house. "Dinner." He turned to her. "Would you like to sneak in the back door and freshen up before we make an appearance?"

"Wait. Where are we? Is this your house?" Her eyes narrowed before she could stop them. They were in a street in NYC that looked suspiciously like an area her parents would have frequented.

"My parents live here for part of the year. Grace, you need to know. I didn't dare tell you, but all those wealthy people you complained about. My parents." He raised a hand. "Guilty." He waited. No apology. He just respectfully gave her the opportunity to speak her mind.

"I guessed as much. Do they own the chalet too?"

"No." He toyed with her fingers. "The chalet is mine. And the jet." He looked up, an amused worry crossing his face. "Never have I been worried my wealth might turn away a woman."

She laughed. "I'm still here. For now. Let's go meet the folks."

"Whew. Okay."

The driver opened their door as if on cue, and Chad lead her up the front steps of his upper Manhattan home. Claudio opened the front door and nodded to him.

The room was full of people she knew. She froze in the entryway. Then she whipped around to him. "Is this the Hampton party?"

He nodded. And the lack of surprise, the apology on his

face, spoke betrayal more than anything else could have. "What do you know?" She stepped back. "Who are you?"

A distinguished, handsome man approached and clapped Chad on the back. "Son. Well done. I knew you could track her down." He turned to Brilee before she could say anything. "You, my dear, are a difficult person to find. But nothing gets past my Chad here." He turned to the room. "Might I introduce Chad Chamberlain, my son you might remember, and Brilee Townsend?"

The adults in the room looked overly thrilled and self-important, and suddenly Brilee found it difficult to fill her lungs. Everything was too tight. She swallowed. Then her mother came forward, and she wanted to run.

"Oh, honey. We've been so worried." Her mother pulled her into an overly long, ridiculous hug, and Grace thought she blacked out for a moment, drowned by her mother's perfume. Only the strength of a familiar voice kept her present. "Grace." Then the gentle squeezing of her hand. "Grace. Back off everyone, give her some air."

The distant gasping of a few self-important women would have made Brilee smile, except that the world was grey instead of black, and Chad's look of concern made her ill.

"You pig." Her whisper, meant only for him, was obviously heard by a few around them. "You lied. You tricked me. Brought me here?"

"No, it's not like that." He reached an arm around her to lead her away. "Let me explain."

She shrugged him off. "No, get away from me. I have nothing to say to you. Ever again."

All she wanted to do was run. Back to her bullet. Back to her solitude. She'd pick up Bear back at the chalet and hide, this time forever. Only this time, she had a publishing deal under her belt and the hopes of her own life, created by her own ingenuity. Maybe she'd change her name.

"You all should be ashamed. What century do we live in that you would use your daughter as a pawn in a business merger?"

When Chad looked like he was going to cling to her, she shoved him as hard as she could. He stepped back in shock.

"Get away from me." She didn't look back to see if he followed her out the door.

Nine

BRILEE DECIDED TO GO by Grace forever now. Even though it reminded her of Chad, even though her stomach clenched every time she heard it spoken. Even though she actually looked over her shoulder once or twice to see if he was there, she still went by her middle name.

It had been one month since she'd heard from Chad. At first he'd texted. All day, every day, but then he'd given up. His last text said, "I guess you either threw away this phone or you refuse to answer. Either way, reaching out seems to be a waste of our time. I won't cancel the phone, just in case you ever want to reach me. I can see it's upstate. I hope that's where you are. It makes me happy you are only a car drive away."

Watching her quiet street, she didn't admit it, even to herself, but she couldn't leave NY yet for that same reason. She also had meetings with her editor, and trips into NY for signings. But all that could have taken place anywhere.

A month had not yet washed away her sorrow. The ultimate betrayal of everyone she loved tortured her every time she thought about how used she'd felt. Yes, she loved Chad. She loved her parents. But none of them loved her back.

She sighed. Maybe she should write another book. This time a romance. She grimaced. Nope. Those had happy endings. This story would be a tragedy. No. Not even a tragedy. Realistic fiction. Was that a thing still? Women's fiction. She nodded. Those books always ended tragically.

She'd watched the news, scoured news sites, Wall Street mostly, to hear if their families' two companies had actually merged. And she'd heard nothing. If that had gone down, it would be the biggest merger news of the decade. So, had conversation stalled?

She tried to pretend she didn't care.

Bear's soft nose nudged her. His big eyes watched her, his leash dangling from his mouth. "Great idea, boy!"

She tied her shoes and then hooked Bear to his leash. Her body needed a good, long, hard run. She leapt off the front porch of her month-to-month rental. The small home and its cottage feel brought her a sense of comfort like fried chicken or mashed potatoes. The white picket fence surrounded the yard and met along the front at a gate she kept open.

She took off running, responding to Bear's urgent insistence for some exercise. They ran down the road, his nose to the ground, her head somewhere far away. Chad again occupied her thoughts.

If the merger hadn't gone through yet, what was he doing right now? She shouldn't care. But how could she not? She'd fallen for the man she thought Chad was. She was so consumed with analyzing how such a thing could have happened, pondering it for the millionth time, that she thought his voice was in her head. Until she heard it again.

"Grace."

Her head whipped around so fast she almost lost her balance.

Chad closed the car door of an old Camaro. The paint looked sort of new, the red still shiny but chipped in places. He stood next to it, looking better than she remembered, his blue shirt, unbuttoned at the neck and stretched just enough across his muscles, tucked into his tan pants. He took off his sunglasses and his warm eyes smiled back at her.

She found it difficult to remember his betrayal. This was

the man who had found her and wormed his way into her life at his father's request so that they could complete a business merger. At that thought, she admitted he didn't look quite so handsome.

Her expression must have given some clue to her feelings because he held up his hands. "Can we talk? Please?" He stepped forward, but Bear growled, which she found hilarious, and Chad waited.

"Okay, talk."

"I'd prefer talking in my car. But if you want to talk about this on the street…" He held up a manila folder. "I want to talk to one of the larger shareholders in the Townsend holdings, you, about a merger plan of my own."

He wanted to talk business. A part of her deflated just a bit before she rallied. A business deal. She might be interested, at least she was curious. "Come on, Bear." She led him to the Camaro. "Nice car."

He held open the back seat for Bear and then the front door for Grace. "Thank you. She's my hobby. Completely restored. Besides, I thought it spoke middle-class, normal guy more than if I'd come in the limo."

She smirked.

"Though I don't know what you have to complain about. Even if your parents disown you, you are one of the most wealthy women in the country right now."

She looked away. This was going just how she would expect of any of her parents' friends. She didn't know what hurt more, that she had been so mistaken about him or that he didn't really care about her.

"I just think it's ironic that you of all people could hold a man's wealth against him."

She didn't answer.

He cleared his throat. "Okay, the paperwork. The way I see it, we each hold significant voting power on our boards and could come up with our own merger that each would accept. Our parents seem incapable of accomplishing this on their own, especially while their children are at odds."

"That is the most ridiculous—"

"Believe me, I know."

"What? You're just as bad as they are."

"None of this was my idea. You won't let me explain. I don't know how to prove it to you. And I know it is highly suspicious that I just happened to meet you in Tahoe, but it's true—I had no idea who you were when we first met. And to at least prove my sincerity now, I told my parents we are not doing the merger. I told them I refuse to date you, and that they were utterly ridiculous to expect such a thing."

"You did?" Something about that was equal parts pleasing and sad.

"I did." He leaned closer. "Now, I'm happy to toss the merger out the window if you don't want to discuss it."

"Oh yeah, and then what?"

"And then I'll take you to breakfast." His familiar sparkle was back. "And lunch." He leaned his head forward on his steering wheel and watched her. "And dinner."

Her smile grew. "Tell me more about how you didn't know who I was?" A small flicker of hope tickled her happiness.

"There I was, an unsuspecting guy on a boys' trip. I pulled into my favorite campground in Lake Tahoe, expecting to snatch my favorite spot on the whole mountain, and this eyesore of a camper was there instead."

"What? How can you insult The Bullet like that?"

"You want the truth, don't you?"

She nodded. "That's fair. Okay, continue."

"But I'm an easygoing guy. I thought I'd get to know my new neighbor and be so incredibly intrusive and, in your face, that you'd move to another part of the campground. I kept my music loud, and when that didn't work, I made my way over to sit right next to you in my hammock."

She laughed, remembering how effective he'd almost been. She had been about to leave him to it. "I see. And then?"

"Well, then I saw you. And it became fun to pester you a bit while you were trying to work. And then I stopped pestering because it was just more fun to watch you."

She wrinkled her nose.

"Not in a creepy way. Your lips poke out while you type, and your eyes light up, and your fingers fly faster than I've ever seen a person type." He shrugged. "And I decided instead of trying to get you to move out, maybe I'd move in."

She shook her head. "And this is the truth? You really didn't know who I was? Even though my face was all over the grocery store magazines that week?"

"The truth." He watched her a moment. "You can trust me."

Her eyes welled, and tears blurred her vision before she could stop them. She remembered the first time she knew she could trust him, their moments climbing and skiing and their kisses in the chalet. She had trusted him—she'd wanted more than anything for him to be what he appeared.

"I hope so." Her whisper sounded pleading even to herself. "You're the best thing that has happened to me in a long time. At least I thought you were."

"And you mine. I was so afraid to lose you, once I found out who you were, that I've been trying to find a way to make this right. And I thought maybe me turning down the merger and offering our own version might be a good option." He tossed it in the back seat. "But I don't care about our business relationship, not really. I just want you in my life."

"Well, now, let's take a look at this merger of yours." She twisted and grabbed the envelope.

"Can we talk about it over breakfast? Or at your place? It's great, by the way, a definite upgrade from The Bullet."

"Bullet's my old friend. You saw the inside. Top of the line."

He turned the car around, and within minutes they were in front of her white picket fence. "Can I come in?" he asked

"Inviting yourself back to my place again." She laughed. "I should have known there was something sketchy about you when I first met you."

As soon as they were up on her front porch and Bear pushed through the front door into the house, Chad pulled her into his arms. "Do we have a chance?" His eyes held hope and pain.

For a moment, she let herself consider it. She felt the tingly expectation of his strong arms holding her, felt the rise of his chest against hers, felt the eager expectation of his kiss.

Then she shook her head. "I don't want that life. I really don't want to be caught up in all that. Those people. Our parents. I can't stand to be around them."

Instead of his expression falling, his hopes dashed, his eyes looked almost triumphant. "I think you need to take a look at my merger plan."

Curious now, she pulled him into the house, and they sat on the sofa while she skimmed through the papers. "This looks pretty standard."

"Keep going."

Then she got to the section about the executor and her role in the newly made company. "What is this?" The merger made her a board member, and, with the shares she owned, she would have a significant vote. But the contract also granted her honorary status, meaning she was not required at any meetings.

Her smile grew. "You gave me a get out of jail free card."

He laughed. "If that's the way you want to look at it."

"Yes."

"And we don't have to get caught up in all that. I mean, we might have to make an appearance now and then at our parent's socials; We can otherwise do what we want, but…"

"But?"

"I draw the line at The Bullet. If we travel, can we stay somewhere nice? My neck and back…"

"Next time we go to Tahoe, I'll show you my family's home."

"You have property there too?"

"On the west side of the lake. It's my favorite place in the world."

He shook his head. "That clinches it. We are perfect for each other. Please, can you give me another chance?" He got down in front of her on one knee. When the panic rose in her throat, he laughed. "This isn't a marriage proposal."

Breathing out in relief, she nudged his shoulder. "What are you doing down there?"

"I just want you to know I'm serious. I'm in this for the long haul. I'm willing to do whatever it takes."

She considered him and all that he offered. He'd given her a place in the company without having to be caught up in the mess she detested. He had been trapped in the same mess as she was, and, instead of running, he had returned to the trenches and worked out an arrangement that could work for both of them, that could give a space for them to get to know each other better.

"Chad, I don't know what to say. I'm so relieved you're not a total creep." She laughed at his indignant expression.

He stood and pulled her up to stand in front of him. "I can't tell if this is good news or bad news. Your lips are doing that pouty concentration thing." His head tilted to the side while he waited. Then he ran his fingers along the back of her neck. "Though I'm not above using other measures to influence you."

His other arm pulled her closer, and he pressed his lips to her forehead, her cheek, her neck, the side of her mouth. "I want you in my life. I love you, Grace. And I love who I am when I'm with you."

Then he pressed his lips to hers, and she melted against him. She gave in and responded with all the hope of this new man in her life—a new life she could see herself working in while being herself and moving forward with her causes, and, most importantly, loving him in return.

She nibbled his bottom lip and then pressed her mouth to his again and again, responding as his kisses lengthened and became more insistent until at length she pulled away and murmured against him, "I love you too."

The End

Sophia Summers is an award winning author who just wants to relax a little and enjoy a great beach read. She lives in a quiet southern town brimming with an extra dose of hospitality and a whole lot of charm.

She writes historical romance under a different name. You can find her on http://www.sophiasummers.com where you will be able to follow her newsletter for sales, freebies, and fun.

Bow Tie or the Billionaire

Annette Lyon

One

IF LAUREN FISHER HADN'T already decided to sell Vista Cosmetics, the company she'd founded, today's deluge of business-related emails and texts—all of which claimed to be urgent—would have convinced her. After boarding a train at the Helsinki station, Lauren put her phone on Do Not Disturb mode so no more of them would bother her and stress her out even more. Nothing short of a natural disaster would be truly urgent, and she was determined to enjoy the ride in peace.

The wheelchair she'd rented was folded and tucked out of the aisle, ready for use by Lauren's CFO, Ulla, who'd broken her leg in three places thanks to a car accident. Now Ulla was flying back after her less-than-stellar vacation in Rovaniemi, one of the northernmost cities in Finland. To help out, Lauren had rented a wheelchair and was heading to the airport to meet Ulla with it so she could go home and get around a bit easier.

As the thick pine forests slid past the train window, broken by the occasional apartment building or street, Lauren let the hum of the train relax her, washing away the stresses of running an international company. She was proud of her cosmetics and how they not only didn't exacerbate acne but healed it. The one *business* thing she was proudest of was moving her headquarters to Helsinki. Sure, the taxes were higher than in many places, but this was the hub of so much scientific discovery and so many creative people eager to work hard that it just made sense. And once she got here and had bought her own cottage on a small island off the coast, she'd fallen in love with the country and never wanted to leave.

The cottage was on an island near enough to the downtown district to be convenient, but far enough away from the bustle of the city that she could enjoy solitude and quiet as she looked out over the Baltic Sea as the sun set.

She'd even taken a liking to genuine Finnish sauna—which, she'd quickly learned, wasn't pronounced *SAW-nuh* like she'd always thought.

"The first syllable rhymes with *cow*," Ulla had informed Lauren. "It's *SOW-nah*."

"Oh, I am so sorry," Lauren had said in the washroom.

They'd been getting ready for her first authentic Finnish sauna, located inside the company's headquarters. She'd planned for a small employee gym and locker rooms, but then several people suggested she add saunas to each of the two locker rooms, one in the men's and another in the women's. When she asked why and began to learn more, she discovered that sauna was such an ingrained part of the culture that the country had more saunas than cars.

At first, she hadn't understood why saunas would make her staff happy, but that didn't matter. Her employees *did* matter, and they wanted one. If company saunas would make for a happier, and therefore more productive, work environment, then Vista Cosmetics would provide a sauna experience for its staff.

Ulla had laughed with a genuine smile. "No need to apologize. *Sauna* is the one Finnish word the world knows, and they all say it wrong."

Lauren had smiled in return and followed Ulla into the sauna, where they sat on towels and soaked in the heat. At first, Lauren was so self-conscious that she murmured, "Maybe I should have worn a swimsuit."

"No," Ulla said, eyes closed as she leaned against the wood wall. "Remember, sauna isn't about worldly things like how our bodies look or any of the lascivious things people from other places tend to associate with it."

"Oh?" Lauren asked, slowly relaxing her position from one that probably resembled a knot when she'd tried to cover herself.

"It's almost a holy place for us," Ulla said. "We've had it for centuries. Families used to build their sauna before their houses. Babies were born in them, because they were clean and warm. Many people were even brought into a sauna to die."

"Wow," Lauren said. "I had no idea."

They spent nearly an hour enjoying the sauna, going out periodically to cool off under a cold shower—an exhilarating feeling. By the time she walked out of the sauna and turned on the shower for the last time, she realized that she hadn't felt awkward or embarrassed for the last half of the sauna. Suddenly, she felt rather proud of that fact. She was absorbing the culture, bit by bit.

She relived the experience in memory on the train, thinking about how different, strange, and yet soothing that first sauna had been. How many others she'd experienced since, and how, if she ever moved back to the States, she'd have to build a sauna into her home. Sauna had helped to manage the crazy stress of the business, but it never could erase her longing to return to laboratory work.

The truth was, Lauren had never wanted to be a businesswoman. She felt most at home in the lab, where she'd created her cosmetics line. The one that had led to years spent in an office, where she was expected to crunch numbers and make executive decisions about things her doctorate in chemical engineering hadn't prepared her for.

With her phone tucked away in her purse, she'd enjoy the

quiet ride to the airport, grateful that Finns tended to be very quiet on public transportation, so she really could just relax and let her worries slip away. She'd look at the slew of "urgent" notifications later.

No doubt they were all about the upcoming merger with Carmichael Industries. She hoped that would go through without a hitch. Their reputation was one of excellence and trustworthiness, which was something important to her. But the higher-ups were oddly secretive; she couldn't find much online about the founder, Frederick Howard Carmichael III. Yet she had her bio and a headshot on Vista's website. So far, she hadn't been able to speak directly with the founder of Carmichael Industries, but everything else had clicked along smoothly. She'd meet him in person at tomorrow morning's meeting. Until then, she didn't need to get herself stressed out over things she had no control over.

If all went well—and oh, how she hoped it would—then their executives would run the day-to-day business operations of Vista Cosmetics. She'd keep a decent amount of stock and have a lot of say in how things were run, but she'd be able to leave her claustrophobic, though beautifully designed, office and get back to the lab. That's where she felt most alive: where she could create and invent and discover and do so without the constant burden of knowing that on her leadership hung the futures of two hundred employees and their families' well-being. A lot hinged on tomorrow's meeting; she'd found exactly one company she'd trust her brainchild with. Carmichael Industries had better live up to her expectations.

Needing a break from it all was one more reason she left work today to bring a wheelchair to Ulla. Everyone else would finish their work just fine without her for a couple of hours. She was just glad that Ulla had managed to get back in time for the meeting. Lauren would be lost without her.

Pushing the wheelchair before her, she stepped off the

train at the underground airport station and marveled—as she did every time—at how clean it was. Not a piece of litter in sight. No smells of exhaust or urine or anything else you might find in a big city subway like New York's. Just a clean platform surrounded by a tunnel of granite.

Lauren knew the Helsinki airport well, but she'd never needed to take an elevator with a wheelchair, so finding one on her way to meet Ulla at baggage claim took a little work. Buying herself a treat at the little candy shop next to baggage claim had become a tradition, whether or not Lauren was the one flying in. On her way there, she checked a monitor for arrivals, then glanced at her watch—still not checking her phone, which would be filled with urgent notifications—and was glad to see that the flight had just landed. Even with her elevator detour due to the wheelchair, she had time to stop at the candy shop before Ulla got here.

As Lauren entered the shop this time, she recognized the cashier, a woman who looked to be close to sixty, named Heidi—pronounced *HAY-dee*. Lauren didn't know much Finnish yet, but she'd finally learned how to tease out pronunciations.

The cashier broke into a smile and waved. "You're back!" Heidi said in heavily accented English, so *back* almost sounded like *pack*. She noticed the wheelchair, and her brow furrowed. "Oh no. You okay?"

"This is for a friend. She's flying in." Lauren plucked a 200-gram milk-chocolate bar from a stack, the one bearing the classic blue wrapper.

Heidi rang it up. "It's good to see you again," she said as she handed the bar and receipt to Lauren.

"*Hei-hei,*" Lauren said as a goodbye, then returned to baggage claim and stood between two carousels, waiting to see which would spit out Ulla's luggage. Lauren opened the blue wrapper and broke off a line of four squares of chocolate.

Then she popped one square into her mouth with her teeth. She had to consciously keep herself from moaning with enjoyment.

She must not have hidden her pleasure quite well enough, though, as a man's voice piped up a few feet to her right. "That must be an amazing chocolate bar to get that kind of reaction, I must say."

Lauren looked over, taken aback by a total stranger approaching her and talking to her without so much as an introduction. That might be normal in the States, but it certainly was *not* normal in Finland. She was what some called an extroverted introvert; she enjoyed hanging out with other people as much as anyone, but sometimes she wanted time alone for a while, time spent with herself and her thoughts. Finland was essentially an introverted nation, which fit her just fine. Quite simply, perfect strangers didn't encroach on your personal space or start talking to you—let alone loudly, like this guy.

"Um," she said, struggling to come up with something to say. She took in his appearance at a glance—slicked-back hair, an expensive suit, leather shoes, and a watch that might as well have had a neon sign pointing at it saying *Rolex*. She slipped the chocolate square into her cheek so she could speak and said, "Want some?" She held out the open end, then felt silly. She was seriously offering some rich stranger dude a piece of chocolate?

He gave her a half smile that curled just one side of his mouth. "No, but thank you. I couldn't possibly deprive you of such enjoyment."

Now she felt silly. "Okay, then."

Before she turned forward to study the suitcases circling the carousel, a guy beside the rich guy piped up. "Is that local chocolate? I've heard it's awesome. I'd love to try some." She hadn't even noticed him until she spoke.

Unsure what to think or say, Lauren glanced quickly at the rich guy and then back to the other. They seemed to be together, but the second man seemed down to earth, normal. He wore a new pair of jeans, loafers, a button-down shirt with a thin plaid pattern of red and white, and a tan blazer. Nice, but not Rolex fancy. Maybe Mr. Rolex was Mr. Blazer's boss.

She hesitated a moment, but when Blazer held out an arm across Rolex, she closed the gap by offering the chocolate again. "It's a Fazer Blue, my favorite. The Fazer factory isn't far from Helsinki. The tour is really cool. If you're into that kind of thing." She was feeling more foolish by the moment, although she was aware that a lot of the feeling came from the stare of Mr. Rolex and how, though she was plenty wealthy herself, she hadn't started that way. She didn't know how to interact with people born with trust funds and multimillion-dollar inheritances.

Blazer guy broke off a row of squares as she had, bit one off, chewed a moment, then nodded. "That *is* good. Hershey's, I never knew thee." He held out his arm again, this time to shake hands. "I'm Eric, by the way."

"Lauren," she said, shaking his hand.

"Nice to meet you, Lauren." He tilted his head toward Rolex. "And this is Mr. Carmichael. I'm his assistant."

She swallowed in surprise, and the half-melted piece of chocolate got stuck halfway down. "Oh. Hello." She should have guessed who he was. How many ultra-rich men would happen to be arriving at the airport the day before her merger meeting?

Rolex smiled wider at her and held out his hand, as if he hadn't just found her love of chocolate amusing. His smile was startlingly white and looked like something out of a movie. Would she ever get used to ultra-rich people? She constantly felt like a fish out of water around them, sure she'd say or do something dumb that would reveal her humble upbringing.

"My assistant is being too formal," he said—after having acted rather formal himself, and apparently after having flown across the Atlantic in a suit. "No need for formalities. Call me Carmichael."

"Okay. Pleased to meet you . . . Carmichael." The name felt a bit old-fashioned, like a Jane Austen heroine referring to men by their last names. So much for not using formalities. She had the urge to just call him by his first name to see what would happen. Maybe not even Frederick, but Freddy. He might have a coronary. The thought made her want to laugh, and she had to hide a smile.

They lapsed into silence as they watched the carousels. The chocolate square must have melted and made its way down, because the pressure in her chest was gone. She wanted to break off another square but didn't want to look obsessed with chocolate in front of Carmichael.

He spoke next. "Are you here on business or pleasure?"

"I live here," Lauren said. "Moved here for business."

"You're American?" he said.

"Yep," she said. "I'm at the airport to pick up a colleague. That's what the wheelchair is for."

Did she imagine Carmichael's eyebrows lifting and his posture leaning ever so slightly her direction? Before she could analyze the moment, she heard her name.

"Lauren!" The sound of Ulla's voice was as sweet as a Fazer Blue. Lauren hurried past the men and met Ulla across the way, being pushed by an airport worker in one of their wheelchairs.

"Your poor leg!" Lauren said, eying the cast.

"It doesn't hurt much anymore," Ulla said. "Thank you so much for coming to meet me."

"My pleasure," Lauren said, then helped Ulla transition from the airport chair to hers.

They returned to the carousel just as Ulla's purple

suitcase appeared. Lauren grabbed it and returned to Ulla. "Nice meeting you both," she said to Carmichael and Eric, tossing them a wave. "Maybe I'll see you around."

As hard to read as Carmichael was, she couldn't deny that he was gorgeous, and the suit certainly didn't hurt in that regard. Neither did the designer glasses. But Eric was also good looking. He had no glasses, slightly lighter hair, and an interesting, confident air about him. She would have thought that the assistant to a powerful businessman would be a bit quiet and demure, a follower in the shadows, yet Eric had taken the reins of the conversation Carmichael had dropped, and he'd gotten chocolate out of it.

If the merger went through, hopefully Eric would be the one more involved with Vista Cosmetics, not Carmichael.

She jerry-rigged a way to pull Ulla's suitcase as she pushed the wheelchair, but before heading out, she fished what remained of the chocolate bar from her jacket and held it out to Eric. "Here. Enjoy."

"Hey, thanks."

"Maybe I'll see you around." Should she have introduced herself? Would not revealing who she was bode ill for the merger? She debated quickly but decided against it. He might not even remember what she looked like—just one more blond-haired woman in a sea of them. Lauren reached for the handle of her carry-on, but before she could take another step, Carmichael spoke again.

"I don't suppose you're Lauren Fisher, are you?"

She turned to face them, eying Carmichael, then Eric, then Carmichael again. "Um, yes, I am." She glanced at her clothes—far more casual than the pantsuit she'd planned to wear to tomorrow's meeting. She would have her hair up in a French twist, her makeup fresh, and more. Instead, his first impression of her would be the sum of what he'd seen in the last few seconds: her in a graphic T-shirt under her jacket, jeans, sneakers, and a messy bun. Oh, and her obsession with chocolate. *Great.*

Carmichael stepped forward, leaning slightly toward her and smiling in a way he seemed sure would melt her insides but did nothing of the sort for her. "I believe we have a meeting in the morning?"

"Yes, of course," she said, painfully aware as they shook hands of how her voice had taken on a more refined timbre. "A pleasure to meet you, Carmichael."

Eric must have sensed her discomfort, maybe because she was smoothing back wisps that had escaped her messy bun. "Guess we'll see you soon."

"See you tomorrow," she said, and then she took the handle of Ulla's suitcase and rolled it along as she pushed the wheelchair out the doors, determined to not be stopped again. She needed to get on the next train. Hopefully Carmichael and Eric wouldn't be on the same one, or they'd get on a different car, so she wouldn't have to see him or talk to him again until morning.

Eager to return and let the stress of the impending merger melt away, she thought of her cottage. She imagined sitting on the porch and looking over the sea, the gorgeous, rocky Finnish shore all around, with its thick pine forests. Holding a mug of her favorite herbal-tea blend, warming her hands on it.

As she bought her ticket at the machine on the platform, she smiled to herself. Whenever she relaxed on the porch, she wore something close to what she was wearing now, sometimes adding a pair of fuzzy slippers into the mix. Who cared if she looked unprofessional the first time she met Carmichael? She'd built a cosmetics empire worth a fortune, and if he hoped to be the one she picked to partner with, he'd better respect her, even if she showed up tomorrow morning in pink yoga pants with a ketchup stain on one knee.

So said her intellect, but her nervous stomach wouldn't calm down until she and Ulla had boarded the train and it left the station.

A few seconds into the ride, Ulla grinned at Lauren from the wheelchair. "So that's Carmichael, eh?"

"Hush," Lauren said, holding back her own smile at how ridiculously the whole thing had played out. "Finns aren't supposed to talk on trains, remember?"

"Sure," Ulla said with a chuckle.

The rest of the ride, Lauren couldn't wait to get to her cottage after a quick trip to the *tori*, the open-air market, where she'd get fresh food before having a nice, long sauna.

Two

AT FIVE MINUTES TO ten the following morning, Lauren entered the conference room and took her spot at the head of the table. She had a feeling that a man like Carmichael would need the nonverbal reminder about who was in charge. She moved one of the padded chairs to a corner so that Ulla could sit to Lauren's left in her wheelchair, across from Carmichael.

He arrived with Eric at ten o'clock on the dot. She and Ulla greeted them and gestured toward the conference chairs on either side of the table. "Please, take a seat," she said, gesturing toward the two chairs across from Ulla, on Lauren's right. "It's good to be on the same end of the table so we can hear one another easily." She smiled politely.

Carmichael looked to Eric in surprise, and the latter just smiled. "That's perfect. You'll be able to see the notes I take on my laptop," he said to Carmichael, leading his boss into the room and along the edge of the table. He reached for the seat closest to Lauren, but Carmichael stopped him.

"I should sit next to the CEO, don't you think, Eric?" he said, scooting past his assistant. "Not only for the sake of negotiations, but also because I can't bear to be far from such a beautiful face."

Lauren exerted every effort to *not* roll her eyes and to instead keep her face inscrutable. It was that or laugh outright. Some hint of amusement must have leaked out, though, as

Eric caught her eye, grinned, and shrugged as if apologizing for his over-the-top boss. She liked Eric more all the time but needed to focus on Carmichael.

Did lines like his actually work on some women? They must, though she guessed most of the attraction was that he was rich. Maybe if she'd grown up with that kind of lifestyle she'd be attracted to him, but as things stood, she felt uneasy around him.

With Carmichael and Eric having taken their seats, Lauren rotated in her chair to look at them more head-on. "First things first, Mr. Carmichael. The values this company was founded on are very important to me."

"Naturally." Carmichael leaned his forearms against the table, drawing closer than she felt comfortable with. This was the same guy whose company had such a good reputation? He felt slimy.

She used the toe of her shoe to wheel her chair back just a bit. "I need reassurance that you will maintain the vision and mission of the company."

"Of course." He winked—actually winked—at her.

Lauren was startled into forgetting her train of thought altogether. Flustered, she glanced at Ulla, who looked both confused and amused, and then she couldn't help but notice Eric, typing away with his lips pressed together, as if he was holding back a laugh for all he was worth. The sight made *not laughing* that much harder for Lauren. "I assume you're familiar with Vista Cosmetics' products and history, but so we're clear on expectations: we donate a significant amount each year to handpicked charities, selecting organizations that benefit women and children. Each year, we earmark ten percent of profits toward causes." She slipped some stapled pages out of a folder and slid them across the table. "Here is a list of organizations we've donated to."

After a cursory glance at the papers, Carmichael passed

them to his assistant. Eric took the pages and began reading them—every word and line, from what Lauren could tell. She had a suspicion that Carmichael was an idiot and that his assistant was the one who'd done all the work to make the company what it was, with the reputation it had earned. She'd have to think long and hard about partnering with Carmichael. If she didn't have an ironclad contract and—hopefully—Eric working with Vista, she wouldn't go through with the deal.

"Your charity work is admirable, and it's smart, too—an excellent tax write-off." Carmichael clasped his hands and closed his eyes partway, like some movie star about to passionately kiss his true love. "But tell me, what will it take to close this deal? Specific numbers."

Lauren looked from Carmichael to Eric and back again. "Coming to an understanding will take a lot more than any single number."

"What are you saying?" Carmichael asked.

Eric piped up. "She wants Vista to continue its mission, which is based on specific values." He looked directly at Lauren, eyebrows raised. "Is that right?"

"Exactly." Lauren wanted to sigh with relief but kept it in, not wanting to show any weakness or reveal specific emotions to Carmichael. "I founded Vista as a way to do good." She folded her arms and leaned into her chair. "I won't do business with someone who thinks that buying mosquito nets for children at risk of malaria or providing immunizations in places where children otherwise die every day from preventable diseases is worth it only because of tax benefits. I have an entire team devoted to researching charities and working with them. Continuing that work is nonnegotiable."

He smiled at her with half of his mouth, his eyes still in that half-closed, bedroom way. "*Everything* is negotiable, Lauren."

She sat straighter, feeling her spine tighten like steel. "That's *Ms.* Fisher to you."

He nodded but smiled a little bigger. "Of course," he said with another wink.

Despite the annoyance, she continued to explain the needs of the company, the philosophy she'd developed—which was nonnegotiable—and more.

No matter what she said, Carmichael didn't seem to care about what she had to say, instead he continued to flirt with her. Two hours in, when she'd managed to steer the discussion toward Vista's history, he started talking down to her, explaining basics about both business—things she knew full well from starting her own—and the science behind the cosmetics she'd personally developed.

Just when she was about to call him out on the last bit, Eric interrupted. "Um, if I may," he said, raising a finger.

Carmichael nodded permission and leaned back, arms folded, to listen.

With the pen he was holding, Eric gestured toward Lauren. "If I'm not mistaken, Ms. Fisher has a PhD in chemical engineering."

"Really." Carmichael sounded impressed as he turned to look at Lauren.

"Really," she said flatly. "That's something you would have known if you'd spent all of thirty seconds preparing for this meeting. I also have an MBA, which I got to help me with the business side of things, but science is and always will be my passion."

When she stopped talking, she felt a bit out of breath and realized she'd probably said too much and came across as unprofessional. Why *he* could be unprofessional and successful, but others couldn't, she'd never understand. What else did Carmichael not know about her company?

Ulla leaned in. "Would you like me to get some coffee and snacks for a break?"

"Yes, please," Lauren said. "Thank you."

It was an excuse; Ulla couldn't bring in coffee and snacks while navigating her wheelchair, but she'd ask Sirkku to do it, and Lauren needed the recess. But she wouldn't break until she'd spoken more of her mind first.

She pushed her chair back from the table and stood so she could be taller than Carmichael as long as he remained sitting. "Look," she said. "I wasn't born into money. I fought my way through a male-dominated field. Every single step of the way, I had to outperform the men, just to get the lowest amount of respect. Why? Because most of my male peers were convinced that professors went easy on me because I was a *girl*, and that our professors wanted more girls in STEM fields.

"The guys didn't see me as a *woman*, mind you. I was a *girl*. I assure you, I earned every single point I was ever given on quizzes, tests, and papers. I earned every single A, and I worked ten times harder than every *boy* in my undergraduate studies as well as for my PhD. I put myself through school with hard-earned scholarships and multiple jobs. I paid for everything myself, down to my graphing calculator in college-level calculus. For my bachelor's degree, I graduated fifth in my class—a monumental achievement, considering that I didn't have blue-blood parents shoveling money to pay for it all."

"Quite impressive," he said with a nod that looked like a king acknowledging a peasant.

Frustration built ever more inside her chest. "I'm not trying to impress anyone, but I am trying to show you that I am intelligent, I am a hard worker, and I deserve the most basic respect that I suspect you'd show a man in my position. No, more than that. I *demand* the respect you'd give a man in my position. Understood?"

They eyed each other in silence for several seconds before Carmichael's mouth quirked up on one side, as if he was terribly amused. "Understood," he said, clearly understanding nothing.

Her research into Carmichael Industries had seemed so promising, but Carmichael had shown himself to be the kind of guy who had no idea of the advantages he had by birth and his family's financial situation. She'd crossed paths with plenty of his type since the company took off but thought he'd be different. Instead, he was a giant red flag warning her away from the partnership.

Ulla returned with Sirkku behind her, bearing a tray of breads and cheeses. Sirkku left and came back a moment later with another tray of coffee and mugs. As the food was served and they settled in to eat, Carmichael took a loud sip of his coffee and said, "So you're aware, I plan to relocate Vista closer to our headquarters." He lifted an eyebrow as he looked at Lauren. "You can certainly keep an office in Helsinki, but it would be a minor branch, not the main center. This is a much more expensive place to operate a company." He chuckled to himself. "But I don't need to tell you that. You're smart; you understand the basics of profits, yes?" He took another loud sip—or slurp—then set it down. "Seattle has much better coffee."

As one, Sirkku and Ulla gasped with offense. Now it was Lauren's turn to smile. "Finns take their coffee very seriously, and they drink more per capita than anywhere else in the world. It might be best to show respect to my colleagues as well as to me. And I mean about more than coffee, of course." She shot him a toothless smile that felt as fake as it must have looked.

She felt the weight of Eric's gaze on her and inadvertently glanced at him, then quickly away. He seemed rather pleased.

Almost giddily so. Did he enjoy seeing his boss get taken down a notch? She couldn't blame him.

Lauren pushed her plate away slightly and clasped her hands. "We're done here. I am sorry to have wasted your time as well as my own."

"Pardon me?" Carmichael said. "Did I offend?"

Oh, if she had no filter and could tell him what she really thought...

"Vista Cosmetics is not moving to Seattle or to anywhere else. It *will* stay in Helsinki. The company wouldn't be what it is without the people who have worked so hard right here. They are the reason we have been so successful. Aside from that, I am not about to tell one hundred ninety-two people who have become dear to me that they no longer have jobs."

"Oh, come now," Carmichael said. "I hear the economy in Finland is doing great, and the government here is good at handouts, right? I'm sure your little workers won't have any problem finding other positions."

Lauren could have sworn that steam was bursting from her ears. Yes, Finland had social safety nets to keep people alive between jobs—and the States could learn a thing or two from them on that count, and on several others, but he was missing the point.

"The people of Vista Cosmetics"—*not* her *little workers*, a term that spiked her blood pressure—"are like family to me."

No way would she be selling to Carmichael, no matter how handsome he was, no matter how flirtatious he tried to be. Character rarely changed. She'd rather do business with someone who didn't have the suave appearance of Carmichael but instead had ethics and values that mirrored hers. Someone with integrity. Someone who would do the right thing when no one was watching, who helped others without needing recognition for it. Who cared about other people over his bottom line.

Someone like Eric. Too bad I can't do business just with him—and maybe get to know him better... Her eyes widened at the unexpected thought, and she blushed. She quickly looked down at the binder where she was taking notes on the meeting. Why wasn't Ulla swooping in to bring her back to the topic? What *was* the last topic, anyway?

Lauren scanned the list she'd printed out earlier, but the text might as well have turned into hieroglyphics. She felt her eyes being drawn toward Eric, and next thing she knew, she was looking at him. Only for a second, but he seemed to sense her gaze, because he looked up too, and their eyes met across the table. He smiled warmly before Carmichael asked for an explanation about the profit and loss statement they were looking at.

I can't partner with Eric, she thought, *but maybe I can find someone like him.* Finding the right person could take a long time. Months. Maybe years.

She wanted to move forward soon, but she couldn't without knowing that the company she'd created from the ground up would be in good hands. That her employees would be taken care of, that the products would remain of the highest quality, and that the charitable efforts would continue.

Only then would she feel free to return to her lab.

What might she create when she finally got to spend every day there for weeks or months on end? She didn't know yet. An idea would come when she had the time and resources to put into it. But she knew one thing: she'd work on something that would make a difference.

Three

"Ten o'clock tomorrow morning?" Carmichael tapped the edge of a handful of papers to even them out as he stood from the conference-room table.

"See you then," Lauren said, though she would likely cancel the meeting altogether. Three hours with Carmichael had accomplished exactly one thing: convince her firmly that she could not bear to have this man come anywhere near her business.

He'd trash it, discard it, turn it into something it was never supposed to be, and he'd do it after dumping the gorgeous building she'd renovated for her headquarters and dumping nearly two hundred employees. And to what end? To increase profits by having the company based in a cheaper area.

She'd never been about cheap. Quality mattered, in products and in employees. A staff of dedicated and creative employees mattered so much more than where on the planet they were located. She knew every employee by name and considered many of them dear friends.

In contrast, Carmichael cared about little other than his bottom line. And if his behavior at the airport yesterday and again today was any indication, he believed his good looks and charm would win over any woman, no matter the situation, but especially in the business world.

What he didn't understand was that Lauren wasn't a businesswoman at heart. She was a scientist, one who'd stumbled into the business world after years in the lab. She'd conducted countless experiments, refining her products until they were so good that they practically sold themselves.

The financial windfall had been a blessing to her, and when the profits exceeded her needs by several zeros, she started making what became the company's regular donations. She never wanted to create her own charity or foundation; Vista already took too much of her time for her to take on one more thing. And she didn't make her donations automatic, either. She had a team who researched each charity, tracked its progress and responsibility and spending and how much they helped their target communities, and based on their reports, she often switched up which ones Vista donated to.

One more thing Carmichael would eliminate, given the chance. As Lauren gathered up her papers, she couldn't help but picture the woman in India who'd gotten a microcredit loan from one of Vista's donations. The woman needed a new pair of sharp scissors for her sewing business. The dull ones made her work laborious, difficult, and less precise. The new scissors enabled her to increase the output of her sewing business tenfold. She repaid the loan within a month, and a year later, she moved into a nice apartment with her three children, away from a hut made from corrugated metal. All thanks to a tiny loan and a pair of scissors.

Standing from the table, Lauren closed her laptop and set the papers on top, determined to keep Carmichael far from Vista. He tossed his head as a goodbye as he and Eric left the conference room. She waited for them to leave, setting her emotions aside and thinking ahead to how she'd partner with another company, how she needed to speak with her international lawyer about how to set things up so that any future partner would be required to continue the charitable giving.

From the lobby, she heard the elevator ding, so she waited a few seconds, until she was sure that the men had gotten on and left, before she headed out of the conference room toward her office. Ulla followed close behind in her wheelchair, though Lauren was so deep in her own thoughts that she forgot about her until she spoke.

"You don't have to find a partner, remember," Ulla said.

They'd just reached Lauren's office, and they paused at the door. "Yes, I do," Lauren said. "I'm proud of Vista, and I'm happy with how it's going and with how much good it's doing in the world, but . . ."

"But you miss the lab," Ulla said with a knowing nod.

"Yeah," Lauren said. She gestured toward her outfit. "I wasn't meant to wear business clothes. I want to wear a lab coat, wear my hair back, with goggles and gloves." She sighed. "I don't fit in the business world."

"You are good at it, though," Ulla countered. "And you're good *for* it, too."

"Maybe." Lauren leaned against the door frame. "The longer I'm in it, the more I feel like I'm dying inside."

"You'll figure out what to do," Ulla said, turning her wheelchair around to head back down the hall toward her own office.

"I hope you're right."

Ulla looked over her shoulder and grinned. "I'm a Finnish woman. I'm always right."

Lauren laughed to herself as she went into her office. She dropped into her chair and stared out the window at the skyline. She needed to create and experiment to live as surely as she needed oxygen and water. Just as art filled up the life and soul of a painter, and words and sonnets filled the soul of a poet, microscopes and beakers and the possibility of discovery filled her.

Man, she missed those things with a deep ache. She had no idea what she'd play with—rather, experiment on—next time she had an extended period in a lab, but she didn't worry about finding something. Curiosity and questions—the what-ifs of the world—always showed up when she needed them. She'd tamped down the what-ifs sparking inside her while trying to keep the company growing and thriving, but going so long without chasing down those sparks and coaxing them into a flame had left her feeling like a cave—dark and empty.

The thought reminded her of the time she'd gone on a tour of a labyrinth of caves in the Rockies, on a vacation visiting cousins who lived in Harvest Valley. She'd climbed a path with a group of relatives, then went on a tour through what had to be half a mile or more of interconnected caves with fascinating and beautiful formations. She'd never forget the moment the ranger who acted as their tour guide had turned off the light bulb that illuminated a particularly large cavern.

The darkness had been so complete that it felt like a weighted blanket draped over her. She'd looked to her left, to her right, and in front, and could see absolutely nothing, not even a hint of a darker shape of any of the people in front of her. She'd lifted her hand before her face, spread her fingers, wiggled them, turned her hand about, palm out, and was amazed that she could see absolutely nothing.

That's how she felt now—empty and dark. She needed something to light her up again, like the single light bulb that the ranger finally turned back on before clicking on his flashlight and leading them to the next area.

She could get the spark back sooner if she partnered with Carmichael, but every cell in her body protested that idea. She'd sleep on it and decide more in the morning. But today, she could have Ulla start researching more deeply into some of the other candidates they'd considered alongside Carmichael. Excited over the prospect of finding a new partner soon—and not postponing her return to the lab again—she hurried out of her office toward Ulla's.

The hall opened to the lobby and reception area, which Lauren headed across. Right then the elevator dinged, the silver door slid open, and there was Eric on the other side, leaning against the mirrored back wall, reading a book—an actual paper book.

He caught her eye and waved as he stepped out of the elevator. "Lauren!"

She swallowed what would have been a high-pitched *eep* of surprise, then tried to relax. "Eric, you're back." Her voice sounded a bit too breathy, so she cleared her throat. "Did Carmichael need something?" Why else would his assistant come back after their meeting? She peered around him as the elevator closed, expecting to see Carmichael inside.

"No, he's good," Eric said. He slipped a candy wrapper—what looked suspiciously like a Fazer Blue—into the book to mark his spot. "Do you mind if I use your locker room?"

"Sure," Lauren said. "You're welcome to use the gym and the sauna, too."

"The..."

"Sauna," she said, then realized he probably didn't recognize the term with the correct pronunciation. "The *SAW-nuh*?"

"Oh, no." He shook his head and laughed. "Don't think I'll be doing that."

After her own cultural education, Lauren was determined to pass along the knowledge to anyone she could about sauna, and that meant more than how to say the word.

"It's not some lewd, crude, gross thing," she said. "In fact, for centuries, Finns viewed the sauna as a sacred place. They'd build a sauna before a house. That's where their women gave birth and where they brought their loved ones to die."

"Really?" Eric said, looking genuinely interested.

"Really." Lauren's excitement over sharing something she loved bubbled up. "And before Christianity came here, they believed that spirits dwelt in the sauna, and people with magic could cast spells from saunas."

Eric's expression had shifted to one of curiosity. "What exactly happens in a Finnish sauna? Is there a little wizard inside?" He gave a little smile at that, knowing he was being ridiculous.

"Go inside and see. I could get Mikko from accounting to show you the ropes."

"Tempting," Eric said. "But not right now."

"Are you going to work out, or just shower, or ..." Suddenly, his need to use the company locker room seemed odd. Had Carmichael sent Eric back to spy for him? Would he reject Vista Cosmetics before Lauren could reject Carmichael Industries?

"I just need to, um, change clothes. And stuff." He looked unsure how to go on, so he didn't.

While her suspicion wasn't quelled, her curiosity was certainly piqued. "What are you going to change into? No, wait. Let me guess. At night you become a drag queen."

He rolled his eyes and laughed, but he also blushed, which only encouraged her to go on.

"Should I see if the women's locker room is empty? The lighting in there is better for makeup." Now she outright grinned with her teeth. "I should warn you that the cobblestones downtown are murder on high heels."

Eric got a glint of mischievousness in his eye. "Actually, you got part of it right."

"Wait, what?" Lauren felt one of her eyebrows go up so

high that it was probably near her hairline. Now it was her turn to blush.

He glanced at the clock on the wall behind her. "In half an hour, I'm supposed to be at the HUS children's hospital."

"You've lost me."

"I'm . . ." He licked his lips and ran a hand through his hair—something Carmichael would be incapable of with his helmet of products keeping every hair stuck in place like glue.

"You're . . . what?" Lauren took a step closer, and when he didn't retreat, she realized she'd encroached on someone else's personal space. A man's. A stranger's. But she kind of liked being this close to Eric, and he didn't seem to mind.

"I'm . . . a . . . clown." A bunch of words tumbled out of his mouth in a rush. "Would you like to come with me? I visit children's hospitals and cheer kids up."

As much as she liked the idea of spending a little more time with Eric—*not* billionaire Carmichael—she had no desire to spend time with a clown, even if that clown was Eric. She'd rather be doomed to eat Hershey's for the rest of her life. She blamed Stephen King and watching *It* a few too many times.

"I'm not a freaky clown like Pennywise," Eric said, as if he could read her mind. Her face must have registered surprise, because he added, "A lot of people are afraid of clowns because of that movie. But I swear, I'm not scary. You could watch me put on the makeup."

"I think I'll pass. Men's locker room and all . . ." She gripped her phone a bit tighter and smiled. "See you tomorrow."

She moved to step past him to reach Ulla's office, but he touched her shoulder. He didn't grab her or force her to stop and listen. It was just a touch, a light weight on her shoulder, one that felt warm and kind. Despite herself, Lauren looked at his hand, then raised her gaze to his.

"Come with me to the hospital," he said. "You can help translate so I don't get lost or make a fool out of myself because I don't know what they're saying."

"I don't know that much Finnish," she confessed. "A few words and phrases, mostly. You won't need me, though. You can always find an English speaker in Helsinki, and medical professionals *really* know their English."

"Good to know." Eric casually slipped his hands into his pockets, but the hint of disappointment in his voice didn't escape Lauren. She tried to imagine him as a scary clown bent on killing children. She couldn't do it.

Suddenly she wanted to see what he looked like as a clown cheering sick children. "Maybe I'll tag along after all. I can show you the way to the hospital."

His eyes came to life with what Lauren could only describe as a spark. The kind she missed inside herself. He was *glad* that she wanted to come. And she sincerely wanted to go.

"I'll go get ready in the locker room, then," Eric said. He pressed the elevator call button. "Meet you in the lobby?"

"Sounds good, but—" Lauren felt a tickle of a smile on the corner of her mouth. "How will I recognize you?"

"I'll be the one with the polka-dotted top hat."

"What about your makeup? You'd better look nothing like Pennywise."

"My nose gets a little blue circle, and on my cheek, I draw a big blue thing that I meant to be a dimple, but most people think is a giant comma."

"Ah." Lauren pretended soberness as she nodded. "I'll be sure to watch for the giant blue dimple comma."

"There's a little more makeup, but not much. Trust me, Stephen King would be very disappointed."

"Can't wait to see it for myself."

The elevator dinged, and he got on. As the doors closed, her mind posed two questions:

First, why was she about to go out with a literal clown, who happened to be the assistant of a man she couldn't stand?

And second, did he like her back, or was that her imagination?

Four

FOR SEVERAL SECONDS AFTER the elevator had left, Lauren stood there, staring at it, thinking of Eric. She couldn't put her finger on why and didn't want to settle on the obvious *he's really cute*. While that was true, there was something more about him.

Maybe because it was just the stark difference between him and Carmichael. But no, she couldn't believe that. Even without seeing the two men together, she would have found herself drawn to Eric.

Why? The question pinged in her mind again. He was attractive, no question. Funny. Smart. Put together, but not in a way that shouted money, status, or the need for attention. Something else tugged at her that she couldn't pin down and examine under her mental microscope.

She heard someone clear their throat, which startled her back to the present. Ulla had wheeled herself into the door of her office, where she folded her arms and grinned. Lauren blushed—hard, judging by how hot her face suddenly felt. She cleared her own throat. "I'm going out. Let me know if you hear anything from Carmichael while I'm away."

"Okay," Ulla said in a singsong voice. Then she wheeled backward into her office while throwing Lauren a knowing look.

As for herself, Lauren returned to her own office quickly to grab her purse, which she was somehow too flustered to find at first. There it was, under her desk. She got onto her knees and pulled it out, still thinking of Eric.

Something made him different. Maybe it was simply the clown thing. Never before had she met a man who sought out opportunities to make others have a better day, let alone while disguising his appearance. She idly wondered if he'd ever used her products as part of his getup. He had flawless skin, which meant he had to use a high-quality makeup, but Vista didn't produce anything a clown was likely to wear.

She took her long trench coat from the coat tree in the corner of her office, slipped her purse over her shoulder, and headed out. She stopped only long enough to talk to the receptionist, Sirkku. "Take messages if anyone calls," she said, very aware that Ulla's office was only a few steps away, and the door was open.

"Yes, Miss Fisher," Sirkku said, though it sounded more like *Fisser.* "Anything else?"

"I'll be meeting with Carmichael again tomorrow morning at ten. I'll need the conference room and breakfast brought in."

"I'll take care of everything," Sirkku said.

With a quick thanks, Lauren left through the stairway instead of by the elevator, a habit she'd picked up from being around Finns, who walked and biked even in the dead of winter. She knew a lot of people who didn't set aside time to work out, but their active lifestyles made them fitter than Lauren had been in LA even with a well-used gym membership.

After trotting down four flights to the lobby, Lauren paused at the metal door, suddenly nervous to push through and see Eric as a clown. Yet she wasn't nervous in a bad way. She trusted him when he said that his clown wasn't the Stephen King type.

Now if I see him carrying red balloons, I might run away.

Her nerves were based on what *he* might think of *her*. Shaking her head to rid herself of the thoughts, she pushed the metal bar and walked into the main lobby of the building. Eric wasn't there, so she took a seat and read a book on her phone until she heard a heavy footfall and looked up. There was Eric in full clown makeup and a clown costume. Not a crazy, out-there costume, just a loose white shirt with a colorful vest and what looked like a tie-dyed bow tie as wide as his face. The ensemble was finished off with baggy pants. No big, clomping shoes, no rubber-ball nose, and not even a wig. The floppy top hat, so colorful it might have been cut from Joseph's dream coat, was the most attention-grabbing part, and that included the white makeup around his eyes, shaped like arches, and his mouth traced in red, white, and black to look wider, with a lip that dipped downward like an innocent puppy's.

Eric, yet not Eric.

He stood and held out his hands. "Here I am."

"Yes, you are." She took him all in and found herself strangely attracted to a *clown*. "You look good, Eric."

"Oh, right now, I'm Bow Tie the Clown." He bent at the waist in a bow and then made an exaggerated show of adjusting the bow tie.

"My apologies . . . Bow Tie." Lauren looked out the big windows to the busy street outside. A tram rattled by, then several cars. Dozens of people walked along the sidewalks in both directions. Did he realize just how much he'd stick out here? As a rule, Finns didn't draw attention to themselves unless they were hammered, like on May Day, which wasn't for a few more weeks. "Do you want to walk, or would you prefer to take a bus?"

"Whatever's quickest."

"Bus it is."

They caught a bus almost as soon as they reached the stop. Once aboard, Lauren couldn't help but smile to herself at how the other passengers stared at Eric but pretended not to. Putting on his clown character, Eric waved broadly and opened his mouth as if to speak, but she grabbed his arm and tugged him down to the seat beside her.

"You don't talk loudly on public transportation here."

"You don't?" he said, loudly. When several passengers stared, he lowered his voice and tried again. "I mean, you don't? Why not?"

"For starters, it brands you as an obnoxious American."

With a totally flat expression, he gestured up and down at his getup. "I think they'll know that even if I don't say a word."

She couldn't help but laugh, but she covered her mouth to keep the volume down. He laughed—quietly—too.

A few stops later, they left the bus and walked the rest of the way to the children's hospital, part of the Helsinki University network. It had techniques and research that led the world in many areas.

Standing in the ultra-modern-looking lobby—stainless steel, white floors, wavelike lines and curved hallways—Lauren felt an ache, as if she'd come close to a home she'd missed. The smell of antiseptic, the sight of people in lab coats, signs that, even though they were in Finnish on top with Swedish on bottom, clearly had Latin roots for medical words—like the sign with the word *RÖNTGEN*. That had to refer to radiology; Wilhem Röntgen was the father of the X-ray. She was surrounded by science, but she didn't get to participate in it.

Eric had a note card he handed to a receptionist. She read it, then welcomed him in English and gave them visitor badges and directions for finding the correct wing. As they walked through the halls, Lauren worried about entering sick children's rooms and how depressing that would be. She questioned coming along but then thought of the other women and children she'd helped with financially. Shouldn't she see people who needed comfort and support, not be afraid of suffering?

Only when Eric found the first room did Lauren wonder how he planned to communicate with the children. Mimes didn't rely on words, so maybe clowns didn't either. Suddenly it dawned on her that laughter was a universal language.

They entered and found a bald child of about five. *Marja* was written on cards, on a sign, and across a white board. This bald child was a girl. Eric didn't wait to jump into his act. He showed Marja a yellow pocket square, tucked it into his fist, then opened it to reveal that the cloth had vanished. Marja giggled, and when Eric—Bow Tie—looked around, dramatically confused, she pointed to his hat, where a little corner of yellow peeked out. He nodded with understanding, took off his hat, and pulled out the cloth—as well as about twenty others in various colors, all tied together.

Marja clapped in delight and laughed some more, her face lighting up despite the gray tinge to her face and the hollows in her cheeks. Lauren watched in awe. She was witnessing something holy—this moment of pure joy and delight between two strangers. What a gift Bow Tie was to this sweet child.

They went to several other rooms, with patients of different ages and backgrounds. Most were typically Nordic white, but one little boy was an immigrant from Africa—he'd tried to explain. Lauren did her best to translate.

"His family left Africa because of a war. They heard that Finland was the best place to live, so they came here."

The boy looked at her with an even bigger grin than before. "*Puhutko Suomea?*" he asked, turning to her.

She shook her head and laughed. "*Ymmärrän parempi kuin puhun.*"

Bow Tie's eyes widened, and he pointed at Lauren, then

at his mouth, and mimed speaking, ending the acted-out question by pointing at her again.

"I understand Finnish better than I speak it," Lauren said, saying in English what she'd said to the boy in Finnish.

Bow Tie mimed applause. Lauren found herself stepping closer, drawn into the little circle of joy that included the refugee boy on the hospital bed and Bow Tie.

As they visited more rooms, Lauren acted as interpreter more often, at least when she could understand the patients. At one point, Bow Tie raised a finger and drew a circle around his face with it in the air, then, eyebrows raised, he asked a silent question of the ten-year-old girl named Varpu as he pointed at Lauren's face. Then he dug into his messenger bag, which he'd placed at the foot of each bed, and from which he pulled out magic tricks.

This time, he withdrew a makeup set in one hand and several application brushes with the other. Lauren's eyes widened, and she was about to protest, but the girl clapped and pleaded. Lauren still hesitated. She looked at Bow Tie, who clasped his hands and gave her a dramatic expression, complete with lower lip pushed out, to enhance his melodramatic plea.

"Okay, okay," she said, raising her hands in surrender.

Bow Tie guided her to sit at the foot of the bed. Lauren sat with one leg on the mattress and turned so Varpu could watch. He pulled out a variety of supplies, but when she tried to look at them, he shook his head and wagged an index finger at her. Varpu laughed every time.

He used brushes on her cheeks, forehead, and eyes. Pencils like big eyeliners traced areas all over her face, including the bridge of her nose. A big brush came near the end, and she caught enough of a look at what he held that time to know he was adding glitter to her face. He finished it off by pressing three hard things to the sides of each eye. He packed up his supplies, pulled out a hand mirror, and with a flourish, held it up.

He'd transformed her face into something of a blend between a butterfly and a fairy—blue, with pink and purple accents, the wings taking up most of her face, and delicate lines adding to the effect, along with the little plastic jewels he'd added at the end, which sparkled in the sunlight coming through the window.

"*Onpa kaunis!*" Varpu cried. "*Se on ihana!*"

Lauren gave a nod of appreciation. "*Kiitos.*" When the little girl held out her arms, Lauren gave her a hug. The thin arms wrapped around her neck, melting her heart. No wonder Eric loved this.

When they finished the rounds on the oncology floor, Lauren didn't want to leave, and she said so.

"I have an idea," Eric said as they took an elevator to the main floor. "There's something I can't do in a hospital that you might enjoy."

"What?" Lauren asked, intrigued.

The elevator doors opened, and the people standing on the other side gave Bow Tie and her blue butterfly face some odd looks.

"*Hyvää päivänjatkoa!*" Lauren said cheerfully, knowing full well that her American accent was thick as anything.

They left the hospital, stopping only to return their visitor badges. Once outside, Lauren demanded, "Okay, what are you going to show me?"

"I need an audience first."

"Silly me," Lauren said, loving that the two of them looked so out of place in a metropolitan city but not caring at all. She looked around. "There's a park a few blocks away. Would that do?"

"Especially if there are kids."

"There might be. Definitely tourists, though."

Five

SHE LED THE WAY down Micheleninkatu, one of the busiest streets in the city. When the park appeared on their right, Eric seemed to be waiting for her to head across the grass.

"A little farther," she said, until they reached the unpaved drive that led to the Sibelius Monument, which you could see from the street if you knew where to look, but it wasn't obvious until they drew a little closer. When the way opened into the parking lot, the monument stood straight ahead of them. That's when she stopped and waited for his reaction.

"Whoa," Eric said. "What's that?"

"It's one of the most-visited sites in the city, a monument in honor of the most famous composer from Finland."

"It looks like a huge set of organ pipes floating in the air. That's so cool."

Lauren grabbed his hand and pulled him onward. "I figured there would be people here, whether or not they were children." Sure enough, several small groups of people were gathered around the main monument, and others took pictures at the smaller display on the side, which featured Sibelius's likeness made of metal. A tour bus pulled in behind them, and more people got out.

She nodded toward the tourists, a group growing by the second as the tour bus unloaded. "You're on, Bow Tie."

Rubbing his palms together with excitement, Eric slipped

into character. He walked over to the rounded granite beneath the monument and hopped onto it. He waved to get everyone's attention—a cluster of Americans and the trio of Japanese women, among others—and he reached into his bag and pulled out something small and yellow.

He pulled it, stretched it from both ends, then stuck an end into his mouth—a balloon. In no time, it was filled and tied off. Eric twisted and turned the snakelike balloon, his fingers moving so fast that she hardly registered the shape when he tucked it under one arm and blew up a pink balloon. As if by clown magic, with a swift motion, he combined the two balloons and presented his creation—a flower, with yellow petals and a pink stem—to a little girl.

The boy beside her, likely her brother, looked immediately jealous. Bow Tie clearly expected as much, gesturing assurances to the boy. In no time, he'd blown up a red balloon and turned it into a sword. The boy ran off, joyfully swiping his sword back and forth like a charging knight.

Someone in the crowd pointed at Lauren and asked what her role was—understandably, as the butterfly makeup made her look like part of the act. On a whim, she hopped onto the stone and held out a hand for a balloon.

Eric gave her a blue one. They began blowing at the same time, but while his quickly filled up from one end to the other, she couldn't get the slightest bit of air into hers. Worse, the pressure made her cheeks hurt. The audience laughed, as if her failure was planned, so she went along with it and made an elaborate bow, then offered to take the bag from Eric and hand him the balloons. He happily handed it over, likely glad to not have one more thing to worry about.

She selected balloons in every color she could find so he'd have a variety to choose from. Sometimes he had a child pick which color, though sometimes she had to ask Eric which balloon was which color, because some, like blue and purple, looked awfully similar until they were blown up. Who would have thought that the very basic Finnish she'd learned, including colors, would come handy so much? They were a good team.

When at last everyone who wanted a balloon creation had one, and the crowd was thinning, Eric gestured for Lauren to come over. She zipped up the plastic bag of balloons and walked over to give him the messenger bag. When she reached him, he glanced over at the sandy parking lot and the drive from the street, as if checking to see if anyone else had come. He then nodded, indicating a spot farther into the park. Going that way required they duck under the "pipes" of the monument.

"That was so cool," she said, following him onto the grass toward a cluster of trees.

"Thanks." He reached back and took her hand, which felt both normal and electric at the same time. The feel of his hand around hers was warm and strong. He squeezed her hand gently, and she squeezed back, liking the moment far more than she should have, especially considering how she was about to reject Carmichael's offer. If he found out that she liked Eric at all, he'd probably be fired. No, she wouldn't worry about that now. She hadn't done anything wrong. What was a few hours with Eric, with balloons and children?

"I enjoy doing balloons, but I can't do them in hospitals."

"Why not?"

His answer was one word: "Latex."

Not what she expected to hear. "What's wrong with latex?"

They'd reached a grove of pines, where he stopped. She leaned against one of the trunks with branches that began above her head. Eric stepped close, which made her stomach flip deliciously.

"Allergies to latex," he said. She almost asked what he was

talking about; his nearness had chased away the thread of conversation. But he went on, clarifying. "It's not a common allergy, but it's a deadly one. So balloons are banned from most hospitals."

"Isn't there an alternative?" she asked. "Can you imagine how much sick kids would love to get a balloon dog or crown?"

"I wish," Eric said. "Typical balloons are latex. Those big silver ones are mylar."

"And those don't work."

"Right."

"What about vinyl?" Lauren couldn't let the thought go. Now that she'd seen Bow Tie in action both at the hospital and at the monument, she couldn't stop imagining him doing balloons *in* a hospital.

"There are some vinyl balloons, but they don't work either. They're the ones attached to a stick. They look more like lollipops than balloons."

"They don't have the flexibility of latex."

"Exactly."

"There's *no* latex alternative?" she asked. When he shook his head, she said, "That's crazy." Her mind drifted into that magical realm it hadn't been to in a couple of years, the one she'd missed so much: the place of wishes and daydreams and creativity. Of what-ifs.

"Um, earth to Lauren?" Eric was waving in front of her face with a bemused smile. "You okay?"

She blinked, snapping herself out of her reverie. "Yeah. Sorry." She grabbed his hand with both of hers, holding it tight in her excitement. "Why hasn't anyone invented a latex alternative for clown balloons?"

"Twisting balloons," Eric provided. He shrugged. "Maybe it can't be done."

"Or maybe no one thinks it would be profitable."

"It probably wouldn't," he admitted. "Finding a substitute just for clowns to use in hospitals wouldn't exactly be a big moneymaker."

Lauren felt a thrill go through her, one she hadn't felt since she'd found the perfect composition for Vista's concealers. "Who cares if it makes a ton of money or not? It would make children smile and laugh. It could make sick *adults* happy too. Aren't there studies that show how laughter and joy can speed up the healing process and reduce mortality rates?"

Eric looked at his hand held in her smaller ones and chuckled. "You're the scientist. You'd know better than I would."

"Think of it: a latex-alternative could help children all over the world!" In her excitement, Lauren released his hand and slapped his shirt with her open palms.

The contact with his chest made her stop breathing for a second. She froze, which meant her hands were still *on* his chest. She both wanted to tear them away and leave them there for as long as he'd let her. It had felt like such a natural action to do, as if they'd been friends for a long time. As if they knew each other much better than they did.

In a half panic, she pulled her hands back and lowered her gaze to the forest path they stood on. *What were you thinking?* she chided herself. *You don't touch anyone like that when you've barely met.* She toed the pine needles around her feet, terrified of looking up and seeing his face, dreading an expression of awkwardness, or worse, one of amusement.

He reached down and took her hand. He held it up, between them, and she couldn't help but look at their entwined fingers and watch his thumb rub the side of her finger in a gentle, warm motion. He stepped closer, pinning their hands between them. Now she could feel his chest again, separated from her hand by a little fabric. Another zip of electricity coursed through her.

He didn't speak. Lauren didn't know if she wanted him to. He didn't step away. She was *very* glad of that. He released her hand and put both of his on either side of her waist. She placed her open palms on his chest again, this time detecting a quickening in his pulse. Could he hear her racing heartbeat? It seemed to thunder in her ears.

For a moment they stood together, both somewhat breathless. The only sounds were far-off traffic and a squirrel scurrying up a tree. Eric scooted closer. The toe of his leather shoe moved pine needles with it and sent a tiny pebble skittering away. His second foot followed the first, leaving a similar trail behind it. He was much nearer to her now, so much so that she couldn't see the forest floor between them anymore.

Their bodies touched, and her elbows bent between them. She could smell his aftershave, and her insides spun and jumped. *Come even closer.* She sent the wish silently into the air.

He must have sensed her wish. While he technically didn't step closer, he closed the distance between them another way. With one hand, he touched her chin, making her look up. Suddenly their noses were touching. Her breath caught as she got lost in his coffee-brown eyes, until they closed and he tilted his head just a little. She closed her eyes too, instinctively running her palms up his chest and then wrapping her hands around his neck.

The next thing she knew, the blue fairy butterfly was being kissed—once softly, twice a little longer, and the third time, quite thoroughly—by Bow Tie the clown in the shadow of the Sibelius Monument.

Six

AFTER THE KISS ENDED, Lauren couldn't have remembered her own name, let alone the name of the company she'd founded. Or remember that she *had* a company. All that existed was the pine tree behind her, its needles below, and the toe-curling, life-altering kiss she'd just had.

Eric's brown eyes squinted slightly at the corners as he smiled. "I've never done that as Bow Tie."

When she'd kissed him, she hadn't thought about the clown makeup. He'd just been Eric, the amazing man who had a remarkable heart and happened to be employed by a jerk.

He rubbed a thumb against her lower lip; she nearly leaned in for another kiss, but he said, "I got some makeup on you. I've got some wipes from my bag to take it off."

She laughed as her hand came up and touched her lips, which still tingled. "I've never gotten makeup on myself when kissing a man."

"Another first." He zipped open a pocket and drew out a travel pack of makeup wipes.

She took it and, looking into her phone camera, worked on wiping off the smear of makeup, taking care to not ruin the blue butterfly design.

He looked around them. "Is there a restroom or something nearby? I'd like to get out of this getup."

Lauren handed the wipes back. "I've seen a building a

little down that way. I think it's a museum or something. It probably has a restroom."

Before long, they found the little building, which might have served as a house a hundred years ago. They went inside, and Lauren used one of the handful of Finnish phrases in her arsenal to ask for a restroom.

The fiftyish man inside guided them to a single door down a narrow hall. Lauren thanked him as he walked away. Eric opened the door to reveal a tiny closet of a restroom with barely enough space for a toilet and sink.

Eric looked inside and at the door. "No hook. Could you watch my bag? I'll just bring my street clothes in."

"Sure." Lauren took the bag from him and held it open as he fished out his clothes from the bottom of the bag. The plastic sack of balloons fell to the ground. Lauren reached down to pick it up, but so did Eric. They bumped into each other, which sent the bag flying from her grip and its contents spilling across the slightly warped wood floor.

"Whoops," Eric said, holding an armful of clothes as he looked at the mess, with no free hands to address it.

"No worries," Lauren said. "Go change. I'll clean it up."

"Thanks. Be right back." Before he stepped inside, though, he stared at her for a second, a gaze that sent her middle fluttering like butterflies—she pictured blue ones, like the one he'd painted on her. He leaned in for a brief kiss. Afterward, she pulled back, a grin on her face.

"Go. Change," she said, shooing him playfully. "And take off that makeup so I can kiss you without getting it on myself."

He waggled his eyebrows. "Your wish is my command."

After he slipped into the restroom, Lauren knelt to clean the mess. The bag of balloons had opened, so she gathered them up and made sure the zip enclosure was secure before plopping it into Eric's bag. She reached for his wallet next, which had fallen open. She idly wondered if his driver's license picture would be awful like most people's, or if he was even capable of being unphotogenic.

The picture was a good one. He was much cuter in person, but it wasn't the washed-out mugshot-looking thing most people had on their licenses. As she moved to close the wallet, the name beside the picture caught her eye.

Frederick Howard Carmichael III.

Her brow furrowed, and her head came up. She stared at the bathroom door, confusion spiraling around her head. She raised the wallet and read the name again. And a third time, as if she could will the name, and the horrible truth it implied, to change.

Eric was Carmichael? *He* was the billionaire trying to partner with her company? He was the one wanting to relocate it and lay off her employees? He was the one who didn't want to continue Vista's humanitarian efforts?

How. Dare. He. She snapped the wallet shut, her middle roiling as if it contained boiling oil. She shoved the wallet into the bag and then reached for his phone, which had fallen next to the wallet. Several texts had come in from someone named Mark, but without Eric's password or face to scan, she couldn't see anything but the notifications on his phone.

Rather, Carmichael's *password or face,* she thought with growing dismay. Not Eric's. Nausea washed through her.

She shoved the phone into the bag, then pulled out more of the wipes to get rid of anything that might be left on her face from the makeup—and Eric's kisses. Carmichael's kisses.

She'd kissed Carmichael. She'd wanted to explore a relationship with him. She'd pitied him for being employed by an out-of-touch billionaire.

He'd lied to her. Not once, but again and again.

What a fool she'd been.

As she tried to straighten out the past two days—meeting

him at the airport, and then that morning's hours-long meeting—the door opened.

"Hey, is my wallet out here?" Eric asked. "I think it fell out of my pocket."

"Yeah. I saw it. It's in there." She unceremoniously shoved the bag into his chest, hardly waiting for him to grab it before stalking off.

She didn't look back, and when he called her, she ignored it. At the entrance of the building, she wished the man a nice day, wrenched the door open, and walked through, then pulled it shut hard behind her.

Let Carmichael find his own way back to whatever expensive hotel he was staying in. He could find a Lyft or something. Or walk. Or he could figure out the transit system without her. One thing was for sure: she wouldn't be the one helping the two-faced, lying—

"Lauren!"

Crap. He'd followed. She didn't turn around, just continued down a path that she figured would lead her back to Micheleninkatu. From there, she could get back to busy, narrow streets and lose him quickly. She'd never have to deal with him again.

Except she did. As Carmichael, he had *all* of her information, and they had a meeting in the morning. She swore under her breath and went from power walking to running.

Unfortunately, Carmichael was in good shape and had longer legs; he could eat up distance far faster than she could. Suddenly, he was jogging at her side. "Hey, what's wrong?"

She was about to burst into a sprint, but he ran ahead and stopped right in front of her, blocking her way. "Please talk to me," he said, breathing harder.

Without a word, she went around him and kept walking. He tried to keep up, walking backward. His heel caught a tree root, and he nearly biffed it. He caught himself and turned around, now walking fast at her side. "Did you get some bad news? What's wrong? You can tell me."

At that, she stopped dead in her tracks. He did too, looking stupidly hopeful.

"I can tell you? Really?" Lauren said, arms folded. She couldn't believe the irony. "That's such a relief, *Frederick*."

Eric's mouth opened as if to try to convince her, but he remained silent.

"Do you deny lying to me?" She waited a couple of seconds for an answer, but he seemed at a loss as to what to say. He also looked in pain, and her heart twinged the slightest bit. She put up the wall again. "*Are* you really Carmichael?"

"Well, yes, but—"

"Yeah," she said. "I thought so." Disgusted, she spun around and once more headed toward Mechelininkatu, which buzzed with traffic. Fury blazed through her.

"I can explain!" he called after her.

She yelled back to him over her shoulder. "Explain to my lawyer. I don't do business with liars."

I don't date them, either.

A bus was just arriving at a nearby stop. She hopped aboard without checking where it was headed. It didn't matter; eventually, all busses went to the train station. From there it was a short walk to her office. The look on the driver's face when she boarded reminded her of the blue makeup she wore, and she blushed.

She took a window seat, glad that the local culture made it unlikely that anyone would sit beside her, then rummaged through her purse for a wet wipe, which she tore open and scrubbed over her face. Then, with her forehead against the cool pane, she closed her eyes, wishing away the ache of disappointment and embarrassment seeping into her bones.

She'd been so stupid to fall for a con man. To think she'd

wished, even for a moment, that she could partner with Eric, who turned out to be the real Carmichael.

No, she wouldn't go back to the office tonight. She had to get away from work. She hopped off the bus near a metro station and rode it to the market square, where she bought new potatoes and fresh fish at the open-air market and rye bread from the old market hall. With her purchases in tow, she headed for Katajanokka, the island where her cottage awaited. As soon as she stepped onto the bridge, she took a deep breath and let it out. She was almost home.

She'd definitely be taking an extra-long sauna tonight.

Seven

THE FOLLOWING MORNING, LAUREN woke up with a raging headache left over from the previous night's angry cry. The long sauna had helped, but it hadn't been able to release the tangle of emotions in her chest. Only time could do that. And copious amounts of Fazer Blue.

But as she ate her breakfast of muesli with blueberry yogurt and stared out into the ocean, a ferry sounded, heading toward Suomenlinna, that historic island fortress. The sight and sound reminded her of the strength of the Finns she'd come to live among—their *sisu*, a word that had no good English equivalent.

It meant strength, fortitude, grit, courage, and sheer stubbornness. Finns had used their sisu throughout the generations to maintain their identity, culture, and language when ruled by outside forces, one century after another. She'd heard more recent stories of what the Finns faced and conquered during World War II, and if she hadn't heard the stories firsthand, she might not have believed them.

She'd already called the office to cancel the morning's meeting with Carmichael, so she could stay home. But wallowing would show a lack of sisu. Staying home today would mean that after lying to her, he'd won. She wouldn't let him win. Mustering her inner sisu, she showered, put on her most professional-looking clothes, and headed for work—later than usual, but she was going. And that was a victory.

As usual, she took the back stairs up to her floor. The door from the stairwell opened right to her office. She'd picked that spot deliberately, wanting an easy way to get in and out without being stopped by a hundred people wanting her attention. Her heels clicked on the polished pine floor only a few times before she stepped into her office, where a red rug with gold symbols from the *Kalevala* epic around the edge. Just as she took off her coat, she heard a familiar American voice. A *male* voice. Her step came up short.

"Please. I need to talk to her, just for a few minutes."

Eric. Had he heard her footsteps? Her stomach clenched.

"I am sorry, but Ms. Fisher isn't in right now," Sirkku said, saving the day. Lauren let out a sigh of relief. "You'll have to leave a message."

"But we were supposed to have a meeting at ten this morning. It's after ten. She's *got* to be here."

Lauren licked her lips and pressed them together as she waited, listening.

Sirkku went on. "Miss Fisher left a message last night saying that the meeting had been canceled. I called your assistant. Did you not receive the message?"

At that, Lauren turned her head, eager to hear Eric's reply. Was he here to save a lucrative business deal?

"This isn't about that," Eric said. "I just need to talk to her. To apologize. Please."

Eyebrows raised in surprise, Lauren leaned out of her office door into the corridor. She couldn't quite see Eric from that vantage point but wanted to. She kicked off her heels into the thick rug, quietly set her bag on the chair by the door, then drew closer. Her rational self argued that this was stupid, that she knew what kind of man Eric Carmichael was—a liar.

But something deeper pushed her forward and brought back flashes from the day before: Eric interacting with sick children and making balloon creatures for the park's visitors.

He'd done it all without pretense. He might be a liar about his name, but he'd shown that there was more to him than the lie about who he was.

Did he really want to cut the annual donations, as she'd been made to believe by Carmichael? Or, uh, by whatever the other guy's name really was.

Silently, she took one step and then another, hugging the wall, until she was at the opening of the lobby, where Sirkku held a phone in her hand as if ready to call security. Across the desk from her stood two men: Eric and the guy formerly known as Carmichael.

Eric's hair looked as if he'd spent the night running his hands through it, and his bloodshot eyes didn't look much better. He wore clothes similar to what he'd worn the day before. His pants were wrinkled, and his rumpled shirt was untucked.

The former Carmichael noticed her first, barely visible behind the corner. He pointed. "There she is!"

Eric's head popped up, and their eyes met. Lauren nearly swore. Now what? Tell Sirkku to call security? She opened her mouth to do just that, but his frantic, sleep-deprived look—and the knowledge that he wanted to apologize, even if the deal was off—pricked her conscience.

"Miss Fisher," Sirkku said, indicating her phone. "Should I—"

"No, it's fine," Lauren said coolly. "Gentlemen, I have a busy day, but if you'd like, I can give you five minutes."

Lauren walked past them straight into the conference room. She was aware of the men following her, and then of the fact that she wasn't wearing any shoes. *So much for looking extra professional today.*

She took her seat at the head of the table and turned to the door. Eric entered alone and closed the door behind him, leaving his associate in the hall, visible through the narrow floor-to-ceiling window by the door. She gestured toward the chair at her right. "Please. Have a seat."

He nodded and sat down, his hands clasped on the table. He looked miserable and tired.

Good. She wasn't going to make him comfortable by opening the conversation. He'd come here to apologize. Let him apologize.

"Five minutes," she said. To emphasize the point, she looked at the clock on the wall before rotating her chair slightly to face him, brows lifted in expectation.

Eric glanced over his shoulder at the clock and nodded, as if acknowledging that she was serious about the limit. "Mark always pretends to be me during initial negotiations."

"Is that an apology?"

"No, you're right. It's not." He took a deep breath. "I'm sorry I lied to you. So sorry. You have no idea."

She waited for him to make excuses to explain away his lie, but he didn't. After what felt like a long silence, she asked, "Why do you and—Mark, is it?—do that? I thought I could trust Carmichael Industries, but this . . ." She shook her head and found her eyes threatening to water.

"I've had a lot of people try to take advantage of me."

"You mean your money?"

"Yeah. My business. My money. And, in some cases, women have tried to, well . . ." His voice trailed off. He cleared his throat uneasily and went on. "A couple of years ago, I decided I need to see future partners as they really are, when they don't know who I am."

Darn it all, he was making sense. How could she hold a white lie against a man who had to protect himself against all kinds of things? Her heart melted a little, and when he leaned a little closer across the corner of the table, she found herself doing the same. Her heart sped up slightly.

"But you know what?" he asked.

"What?" Her mind was spinning, and so were her emotions. She thought back to their kiss and wanted to experience it again.

Eric reached out gently as if he was about to lay a hand over hers, but then rested it on the table. "The truth is, I'd already done plenty of research into Vista . . . into you. I knew I could trust you weeks ago. But I still went ahead with the charade. I shouldn't have. That was wrong."

Lauren eyed him, feeling torn. "What about how Car—I mean, your friend—wanted to get rid of the charities?"

"Part of the plan."

"What, like a test?" Lauren wasn't sure whether to be impressed or to be incensed at another lie.

"In a way, yeah."

"And his come-ons?"

"His flirting?"

Lauren rolled her eyes and laughed. "Is *that* what he was doing?"

"It's worked on a lot of women."

"Not on this one." She shuddered at the memory.

Eric leaned closer, his gaze penetrating and calm. "I can't tell you how glad that makes me." His voice was low, almost a whisper, but their faces were so close that she could hear him just fine. He was so near, and she'd drawn even nearer. The memory of kissing him washed over her, and her cheeks went hot.

She broke eye contact and looked at the pattern in the juniper table, then returned to the topic at hand. "This ruse of yours. Is that why I couldn't find any pictures of you online?"

"That, and I prefer to be able to walk around without getting recognized."

She should have been happy to have passed his tests, but the idea that every second she'd spent with him had been a facade—it weighed heavily in her middle. *Remember your sisu. You founded a cosmetics empire, for Pete's sake.* She lifted her face to his. "I'm glad you're being honest now, but that doesn't change my mind."

"About the partnership."

"Yeah."

"That's fair." He reached out again, hesitantly at first, but when she didn't pull away, he touched her hand. "I've never run into this kind of situation before. I never meant to hurt you. And I am so sorry that I did. I want to make it up somehow, if you'll let me—I'd love to donate to some of your charities." He removed his hand. "And I promise I'll leave you alone. I won't bother you again. I just . . . I feel awful and want to do something to make things right."

This wasn't a man without morals or ethics after all. Was he for real? A tiny spark lit inside her.

Instead of responding directly to what he said, she posed a test of her own. "What's your real name?"

"Eric." He grinned in a goofy way that melted the edges of her heart even as confusion filled her. "Short for Frederick. But I hear that only formal situations, or when my mom gets upset with me. Although she adds my middle name, Howard."

"Your mother still middle-names you?"

"I'll always be her little boy."

Man, she wanted to kiss that uneven smile.

"You know, I might be willing to reopen negotiations."

"Really?" He seemed genuinely surprised.

"Yeah. You're the kind of partner I've been looking for." She paused, trying to straighten out her thoughts while her attraction roared back and muddled her thinking. "I miss the lab. I want to create, to experiment and fail and eventually come up with a new product that will solve a problem no one else has figured out."

Eric cocked his head. "You look like someone who already has an idea for that product."

"I do have an idea, and it has nothing to do with makeup. It would mean starting another company, in another industry, and I can't do it all only to get burned out again."

"What's your idea?"

This wasn't something she would have considered telling him twenty minutes ago, but now she had a desire to partner with him in her new endeavor, something she knew he'd care about and support. Maybe, just maybe, their partnership could be multifaceted.

"Balloons," she finally said, leaning across the table again.

He did the same, only this time, their forearms touched, and their faces nearly did. "What about balloons?" he asked.

"I'm going to invent a latex alternative so people like Bow Tie can make balloon creations for those children in hospitals."

A flash of pleasure crossed his face. "I wondered if that's what you were thinking yesterday. But . . . are you sure? Bans on latex in hospitals mean that patients still get balloons, just in mylar or vinyl. You'd probably lose a lot of money."

"What's the point of having money if it's not doing anything good?" Lauren asked. "I saw the joy you brought to those children and how excited the visitors at the monument were your—sorry, with *Bow Tie's*—creations. I can't help but think how many sick children's spirits would be lifted all over the world if they could have their own balloon dog or giraffe or flower or sword . . ."

He looked surprised. And impressed. "You're serious."

"Absolutely. Thanks to Vista, I have enough money to live on for the rest of my life. I'd like to do something meaningful with it."

Eric reached for her hand, and she happily gave it to him. His wrapped around hers, and warmth coursed into her body. "I'd like to be part-owner in that venture. And maybe . . ." He lifted one shoulder in a shrug.

"Maybe?" Her heart was beating crazier than a drum line.

"Maybe it could be based here, in Helsinki, and maybe... I could be too." He stroked the top of her hand with his thumb, a delicious sensation.

"Yeah. Maybe ..." A thrill of happiness rolled over Lauren, one she wouldn't have believed possible that morning. "You'd have to learn some Finnish," she warned. "And learn to deal with dark, cold winters. It would be a huge change from California."

"I know." He took her other hand too. "But I hear the summers are lighter than I can even imagine, and warm and beautiful."

"They are."

"I aced Spanish in high school. Finnish can't be that hard, right?"

At that, a giggle burst from Lauren. "Hardly." She grew more serious. "But don't worry about the language."

"Why not?" he asked, drawing so close that she could feel his breath on her cheek.

"Because..." Her voice was barely audible. "I don't want anything to keep you away."

"Maybe we could explore another kind of partnership as well?" he asked.

She gave a tiny nod and smiled. "Sure. Maybe."

Eric leaned in and kissed her. They'd figure out the logistics of how their businesses would merge. For now, all Lauren cared about as she kissed him back was that he was the man she'd always dreamed of—and she'd never dreamed of a rich man.

Whooping and clapping sounded, and Mark burst through the door. He must have been watching through the narrow slit of a glass. Lauren and Eric pulled apart to see Mark, Sirkku, and several other employees clapping and cheering. Very un-Finn-like.

Lauren blushed. "Let's get out of here."

"Yes, please," Eric said, blushing too, which made him even more attractive.

She took his hand as she stood. "I'll take you to the Fazer cafe."

"Is that the brand of chocolate you gave me at the airport?"

"Yep." She waggled her eyebrows.

"Be still my heart."

Hand in hand, she led him past their cheering section to her office. She retrieved her things, and then they went through the door into the stairwell. When the metal clanged shut behind them, Lauren stopped and turned around.

Eric looked back, as if she was waiting for something. She stepped nearer and said, "No one's looking now."

This time, *she* kissed *him,* Frederick Howard Carmichael III. His full name sounded like money, and money didn't matter to either of them.

To her, only one thing mattered: his heart.

She'd seen who he was, what truly lay inside him. Whether he went by Frederick or Eric or Bow Tie, the heart was the same.

This time, she wouldn't have to wipe off any clown makeup, so she quite happily indulged in a very long, very satisfying kiss.

*In memory of the original Bow Tie the Clown,
Uncle Howard Luthy, 1946–2019.*

Annette Lyon is a *USA Today* bestselling author, a four-time recipient of Utah's Best of State medal for fiction, a Whitney Award winner, and a five-time publication award winner from the League of Utah Writers. She's the author of more than a dozen novels, even more novellas, and several nonfiction books. When she's not writing, knitting, or eating chocolate, she can be found mothering and avoiding housework. Annette is a member of the Women's Fiction Writers Association and is represented by Heather Karpas at ICM Partners.

Find Annette online:
Blog: http://blog.AnnetteLyon.com
Twitter: @AnnetteLyon
Facebook: http://Facebook.com/AnnetteLyon
Instagram: https://www.instagram.com/annette.lyon/
Pinterest: http://Pinterest.com/AnnetteLyon
Newsletter: http://bit.ly/1n3I87y

How to Woo a Billionaire

Danyelle Ferguson

One

Day One

PENNY LEANED FORWARD IN the desk chair, her pale-blond hair falling over her shoulder as she focused on the income-and-expenses report for the new Bahamas resort. Her lips curled into a satisfied smile. The successful opening of her first international resort was sure to put her in the running for a seat on the Wessex Resorts board.

"Penelope Elizabeth Stewart." Her grandmother's sharp voice came from the office doorway. "I thought you came to Daytona Beach for some downtime. The last time I checked, the pool wasn't located in the business office."

Penny started, then guiltily scooted away from the laptop. "Does anyone have truly get-away-from-it-all vacations anymore? Aren't there always elements of work? Emails to answer, reports to review?"

Mimi crossed the small room, put her beautifully manicured fingertip on the back of the laptop, then pushed the screen forward until it clicked shut. "You need to socialize more. Go out with friends to the movies and flirt with handsome young men." She said the latter while shifting her eyebrows up and down, as if Penny hadn't endured several dozen other hints about her lack of a romantic life over the past few months.

Penny did what she always did: deflected the not-so-subtle nudge with laughter. "You just want me to get married and pop out some great-grandchildren."

Mimi let out a drawn-out sigh as she sank into the leather chair on her side of the desk. "I want you to be surrounded by people you love and who love you. Is that such a bad thing?"

"No, but until Mr. Right comes along, I need to create my own satisfying life. Besides, I have you and Papa. You're all the family I need."

"While I love how close we are, dear, I do believe that you're missing the point. What could be more rewarding than a scrumptious husband to snuggle up with at night?"

Penny shook her head. Her grandmother was from an entirely conventional generation. Ladies grew up, married, raised children, and supported their husbands. They may have worked when they were single, but the real goal was to start a family. "Things are different now, Mimi. Women do more than take care of babies. Besides, I'm not ready for that yet. I have a lot more work to do to earn my spot on the resort board."

Mimi held out her hand, examining the shine on her manicure. "What if I were to share that your name has recently been brought up to be considered for a new division seat on the board?"

Penny straightened. Mimi had her full attention now.

"Of course, it needs your papa's and my endorsement first." Mimi's gray-blue eyes lifted from her nails to confront Penny. It was eerie how similar their eyes were. "Quite frankly, my dear, neither of us is sure that having you delve further into the family business is the right choice." She lifted a finger, cutting off any of Penny's protests. "We would think the same of any other person we considered to be a part of the Wessex Resorts leadership. We are in the business of alleviating the stress and humdrum of everyday life by promoting relaxation, exploring new adventures, and renewing relationships. It is essential that the company's leaders not only understand the business side of running resorts, but that they also represent all that Wessex_Resorts stands for. And yes, that means disconnecting from work and truly going on vacation. It means getting out of your comfort zone and trying out the local attractions the concierge recommends, connecting with people—not because they're our clients, but because they have the potential to become friends and influence your life. Until we see you develop those qualities, your name is never going to move off the short list."

Penny sat in stunned silence. Sure, she knew the board members took long weekends away from work once or twice a month, with a few longer vacations scattered throughout the year. But she always saw it as a perk they enjoyed while working for a high-end destination resort, not something that enhanced their abilities to do their jobs. Wasn't that what their college degrees and years of experience were for? Did this mean that everything she had been doing, all her late nights and the weekends she spent working, had actually made her less appealing as a board candidate? The concept was perplexing, overwhelming her as she made a mental list of all the goals she needed to reconsider.

"I would like to offer a proposition," Mimi said.

Penny swiveled the chair to face her grandmother. She knew that look on Mimi's face. Not only had her grandmother caught Penny working, but she had some kind of scheme to inflict on her only granddaughter as well. "I'm listening," she replied cautiously.

"There are ten days left of the two weeks you planned to spend in Florida. If you can leave work behind and take a real, honest-to-goodness vacation, then we'll approve your name to be considered for the board position."

Penny wanted to squee with delight. She could sort

through her to-be-read list of books and lie around the pool for seven days. Then the position she had been working her butt off for would be within her reach. She visualized her new office, the gleaming wooden desk, and the spreadsheets! The organization goddess within her did a happy dance. "I'll do it," she blurted gleefully.

"Fantastic," Mimi said, a delightful smile making her eyes twinkle. "I look forward to reading the report about your excursions, the people you met, and your thoughts on how we can improve our destination-vacation resorts."

Penny felt like a bounce house whose air pump had malfunctioned, the big sheets of mesh and fabric folding in to bury her. "The what?"

"Like I said before, my dear, we are in the business of relaxation, discovering new adventures, and connecting with others. You didn't think we were going to let you work on your suntan for a week, did you?" Mimi chuckled as she stood to leave. "Your papa and I expect you to visit the resort concierge for a list of local attractions and eateries. You also need to attend some resort social activities and make a real effort to connect with others. I would consider it a bonus if at least one of the new friends is of the single male variety. In fact, let's say that two of those activities need to be considered an actual date." Her grandmother winked as she moved to the office doorway. "At the end of the week, you will write a report to be delivered to us. Then we'll discuss your potential future with Wessex Resorts. Enjoy your vacation, my dear," she said, then turned and disappeared down the hall.

Well, dang. Penny should have known better than to agree to anything Mimi schemed up.

It didn't sound too bad, though. She could check out the local shops, attend a resort crafting event, and talk to some random people. The dating aspect of it, though . . . That was trickier. She rubbed her forehead, wondering how to meet someone date-worthy. Then the brilliance of the entire situation struck her. It was only for ten days! The guy didn't have to be someone amazing whom she wanted to eventually marry. He simply needed to be nice and fun to be around. If he was reasonably attractive, that would be a bonus. Even better, her potential dating pool was right here at the resort.

She swished the office chair around in a circle, feeling carefree as her brilliant plan came together. *Watch out, Mimi. You haven't outsmarted me yet!*

Two

Day Two

MAC HAMMOND PEERED OUT of the Lincoln Navigator's tinted passenger window as it pulled up to the Wessex resort. The creamy stucco, wide archways, and red-tile roof gave the luxury resort a Spanish flair he appreciated. Rather than the strip of towering resorts he and his friends had passed, the Wessex resort was situated on several acres of private beach with a grouping of smaller two-story haciendas. The overall effect on the resort website was one of privacy and luxury. A resort representative came out to greet the new arrivals, and the guys climbed out of the car.

Mac was grateful for a break from Graydon's pro-hockey friends. Between them bragging about their latest purchases and debating about hockey-team lineups, it was obvious Mac was more than the odd guy out on this trip.

He walked away from the group to an archway that led out to the beach. Beautiful white-capped waves crashed onto the sandy beach. The foam rushed up to some little kids' toes, making them dance with glee as the foam lingered for a whisper of a moment before being pulled back into the blue depths of the ocean. It was a little piece of paradise, yet all he wanted to do was get on the next plane back to Crystal Creek, Kansas. The list of responsibilities waiting at home pulled tight at the knots of stress that had been his constant companion for the past two years.

A heavy hand settled onto his shoulder. Mac shifted slightly to see that Graydon had joined him.

"It's quite different from the mix of city and wheat fields, isn't it?" Graydon asked.

Mac jerked his head in a nod. "Looks like a good place for a bachelor party."

Graydon forced back a grimace before settling into an expression of resignation. "It's been a long time since my early retirement from hockey. I can honestly say there are parts I don't miss," he said, referring to his hockey friends' antics. "I'm glad I had enough foresight to convince you to come along."

Mac shifted, eyes squinting as he looked back to see Shawn, Chris, and Brighton already flirting with some ladies. "I think you overestimated my ability to help."

"The guys are in show-off mode right now, but I promise, they've stayed my friends for good reasons. Just keep a level head and be the voice of reason, and we'll all be fine." Graydon slapped him on the back. "Let's go grab our luggage and find our rooms."

The check-in process went smoothly, and soon Mac was settled into his own one-bedroom suite with an ocean-view balcony. Graydon, Shawn, Chris, and Brighton had rooms down the hall. They were supposed to meet up at the pool in a half hour. Mac unpacked, set up his laptop and phone-charging stations, then logged into his bank account.

A commission check from the restaurant-supply store had not cleared yet. He was hoping it would hit the account sometime today, as the nearly one thousand dollar auto-payment for his bank loan was due to be withdrawn the next day. *Only twelve more payments,* he reminded himself. Then he would be debt-free and able to move past the shadows of a failed business venture. He had studied in a culinary program, but while the college had taught plenty about creating delicious food and restaurant safety, it failed to provide business training. During the first year his restaurant was open, Mac made some unfortunate mistakes that cost him greatly. It was difficult to see his dream become a massive failure.

Along with failure came a bevy of well-meaning advice—everything from a pat on the head for trying, to opinions on how to fix his financial burdens. He smiled, endured, and sought out productive advice from successful businessmen. He had learned a lot from Graydon about managing his family's restaurant, Brisket and Noodles. In the meantime, Mac kept working his full-time job selling restaurant supplies, as well as taking any odd jobs he could scrounge up.

The most successful venture he had fallen into was selling gourmet ice cream at the local farmers' markets and to catering businesses. Over the past year, Mac had attended workshops and fine-tuned a plan to open a gourmet ice cream food truck. He loved the social aspect of the farmers' market. There were the regular customers who became good friends, but even more fun were the newbies searching for something to spice up their routine meals. His vision for the business combined the year-round income of working with catering companies and restaurants and the boosted summer sales the ice cream truck would provide.

To achieve those goals, he needed to finish up this next year's worth of loan payments. From his estimation, he was about two—maybe three—years away from ice cream becoming his full-time gig.

But for the moment, he needed to focus on his present predicament. Graydon's hockey buddies had been insistent on one last guys' trip before the wedding next month. Mac checked his watch. He had better get changed and head down to the pool to meet up with the group. Who knew what the Three Amigos had planned next?

Three

"YOU HAVE GOT TO be kidding me," Penny said, reviewing the resort activity list. "Where's the ceramics painting? Or the ice-cream social?"

Zandra, the activities director, cleared her throat, obviously trying not to laugh while Penny glared. "That's on da family activity calendar," Zandra said, her thick Jamaican accent making the words sound pretty, even though Penny dreaded what she was about to hear next. "Mrs. Wessex contacted me to make sure you received da Singles Meet and Greet activities."

Foiled again! She needed to give her grandmother more credit in the conniving department. Instead of the nice, safe family activities she had envisioned, Penny was now stuck with choosing from some rather socially awkward experiences. Spreadsheets were her friend. Making small talk was not. "Why do some of these already have stars drawn next to them?"

Zandra's smile grew wider, the white of her teeth contrasting against her beautiful creamy-brown skin. "Well, now, your grandmama suggested you choose from those."

Penny traced her finger down the list, reviewing the items marked, and grimaced.

"Now, not to go against your grandmama, but I'd stay away from the pool volleyball tournament. It gets rather raucous. Not only that, but it's really a bunch of grown men enjoying the benefits of watching the women jump out of the water to return the beach ball." She moved her hands to her bust level.

Penny covered her face with her hands and shook her head from side to side. She'd suggest rethinking that activity when she submitted her report. "Which activities do you recommend?"

Zandra used a red sharpie to circle a few items. "You'll meet some wonderful people at da Random Acts of Kindness activity, and it's an opportunity to do some local community service. The selfie scavenger hunt is actually quite fun, especially if you choose da right people to be in your group."

"Duly noted. I'm definitely skipping the beach cricket and reggae dancing."

"Oh, but da dancing is so much fun," Zandra countered, her hips moving in a sexy, slow, circular motion as she swayed from side to side.

"Yeah, my hips don't do that," Penny said.

"They will after a session with me." Zandra winked, making Penny laugh.

"I bet you could work some magic, but I think I'll pass all the same."

Zandra pulled out a map from behind the concierge desk. "Let me show you some of da nearby attractions."

Zandra educated Penny on the best places to go eat, the biggest flea markets, some historical sites, and fun outdoorsy adventures. Penny ended up with a list long enough to fill an entire month's worth of sightseeing. "Well, this should do it," she said, slipping the map and papers into her pool bag. She took a deep breath, then plopped her wide-brimmed beach hat on her head. "It's time to dangle the bait."

Zandra blinked in confusion. "What's da bait?"

Penny flung her arms out to each side. "I am, of course!"

She spun in a slow circle, showing off her cute pool cover-up and chunky sandals. "If I'm going to fulfill the dating requirements of this vacation, then I need to send out the availability vibes. It's all about how you market the package."

Zandra expression was skeptical. "I'm not sure if your business classes apply in dis scenario."

"Watch and take notes." Penny winked before crossing the lobby to the sliding doors that led to the beach. She skirted around the family play area, to the adults-only section of the resort's pool complex. Palm trees and potted plants made the lounging area a mini tropical paradise. A lazy river weaved around the lounge and bar area.

She chose a quiet sunbathing area on the other side of the lazy river, away from the busy bar. It was perfectly situated, allowing her to observe those around her without being obvious about vying for attention.

She set her floppy hat on the side table beside her lounge chair, leaving her sunglasses in place to protect against the bright Florida sun. Then she untied the silk ribbons of her cover-up, allowing the fabric to part, then slip off her shoulders and glide down her arms, before draping it beside her hat.

She paused for a moment in her bikini. It wasn't one of those skimpy, barely-there suits. Oh no. It was retro style with high-waisted bottoms and a super cute matching halter top. The navy-blue fabric with tiny white dots looked amazing against her honey-toned skin. The contrast of her pale-blond pigtail braids gave the look an overall tone of playful maturity.

She draped a large beach towel over the lounge chair before situating herself on it. For a blissful moment, her eyes closed, and she allowed the warmth of the sun to soak through to her core. She drew in a deep breath, reveling in the mixture of the ocean's saltiness and the scents of cocoa butter, coconut, and aloe. She tuned out the soft music and chatter coming from the bar and focused on the crash of the waves as they rushed up onto the shore and the screech of seagulls playing in the wind.

This wasn't just another Wessex resort. It was home.

Her shoulders relaxed as the first bit of stress eased away. She pulled out the latest mystery bestseller. Under the guise of reading, she peered over the top of the book to scope out possible date-worthy men.

Three men were goofing around in the lazy river. They shoved at each other, boasting the way teenage boys do when they hope to get a girl's attention. What they didn't realize was that the breeze carried over snippets of their conversation, which centered around the women they were scoping out. She hid a smirk, finding their comments and antics amusing. Her arrival at the pool had not gone unnoticed, and one of them now had another in a headlock as they argued over who should come over to say hello. They were quite good-looking, but they were not the type of guys she enjoyed spending time with.

She shifted her attention to another man sitting at the bar, eating nachos and talking with the bartender. He was cute, with brown hair and a palm-tree Hawaiian shirt. A friend joined him, and the two shared a fist bump and laughed about a comment from the bartender. Her attention brought her back to the first guy. He had a rather nice smile. Perhaps there was some potential there. He shifted his attention and looked across the deck to where she was sitting. Even with her sunglasses on, she felt like they connected. He tilted his head, sending her a nod. Heat flushed into her cheeks, and her fingertips covered a giddy smile. Oh goodness! He totally caught her checking him out.

Her curiosity was interrupted when a shadow fell across the book. She glanced up, then just about swallowed her tongue.

One of the most gorgeous men she had ever seen in real life stood before her, clad in nothing but swim trunks. Droplets of water dripped from his deeply bronzed skin. Her mouth went dry as her eyes traveled up the washboard abs, muscled arms, and broad shoulders to meet the smug face of one of the men she had noticed goofing around. He was *H-O-T* hot, and he knew it.

She hoped the large sunglasses hid some of her initial surprise as she gathered her wits back together.

"Hey there. I'm Shawn," he said, reaching up to muss his hair. Water droplets flew, landing on her legs, arms, and book. The demi-god didn't seem to notice though. "Is your name Angela?" he asked. "Because you look like an angel from heaven."

Did men seriously still use the same cheesy pickup lines from her college days? She rolled her eyes and replied before he could continue to schmooze. "Do you know what else is divine, Shawn? Donuts."

"Donuts?" He cocked his head to the side, as if trying to figure out how the conversation went off track.

"Or really anything with sugar, but my go-to addiction is donuts. Especially those powdered ones with the fluffy chocolate filling. It's a little piece of heaven on earth."

"Okay," he said, drawing out the word.

"I only mention it because all of this," she said, motioning to his ripped body, "just about burns a girl's eyes out. You need a little softening around all those sharp edges. You know, come down a few notches so you're more appealing to the average woman, like me."

Shawn's eyes widened as he took a few steps back. "Say what?"

Penny tapped her chin with her pointer finger, striking a contemplative pose. "Maybe a shirt would help until you get fattened up a bit. One of those loose ones to hide all those embarrassing curves."

"You're crazy." He rushed back to his friends in the lazy river.

"Wait a minute," she called after him. "I'm your angel from heaven, remember? We need to finish our discussion. How about dinner tonight?"

"No way!" Shawn jumped into the lazy river, where his friends razzed him for his failure.

Laughter bubbled up, and Penny couldn't hold it back. She pushed up her sunglasses to swipe at her watering eyes, and she connected again with the man sitting at the bar. He had a broad smile on his face and lifted his drink in a toast to her. She nodded her head in acknowledgment before settling the sunglasses back in place and picking up her book to read for real this time.

She'd had enough of the male species for the moment, but perhaps her bait had worked in a roundabout way. She considered the guy at the bar. She'd give him thirty minutes to approach her. Otherwise she'd mosey over his way under the guise of quenching her thirst.

Four

"THAT WAS ONE OF the most perfect kiss-offs I've ever witnessed," the bartender said, making Mac and Graydon laugh.

"She's a fast thinker, that's for sure. Witty, too, from what I could hear," Mac said in agreement.

"Oh, but definitely not the worst I've seen." Graydon shifted as the Three Amigos joined them at the bar, still dripping wet despite the towels slung over their shoulders. "Hey, Brighton, remember that time you tried to pick up that woman at the hotel bar?"

The red-headed freckled guy grimaced. "Never tell a woman that if she were a potato, she'd be a sweet one. Apparently comparing her to carbs will get you fried."

"More like tasered," Shawn guffawed, making a zapping sound, then jerking as if he were being electrocuted.

"Yeah, well, at least a woman didn't reject me for her love of sugar," Brighton zinged right back.

"That was the best," Chris said, claiming a seat at the bar.

"Man, no way was that chick in her right mind." Shawn made a circle motion next to his head with a finger.

Mac's spine stiffened. He didn't know why, but he felt compelled to defend her. "Or maybe she has more education and class than the rink bunnies you're accustomed to."

"Whoa," Chris said. "Them be fighting words."

Shawn's eyes narrowed. "As if someone like that would have anything to do with a custard boy like you."

"Obviously she likes a little sugar," Mac replied, a rush of heat swelling through him.

"Okay, guys," Graydon said, breaking in. "That's enough. Let's not get the week started off on the wrong foot."

Shawn ignored the warning and persisted. "You think you can do better than this?" He motioned to his body.

Mac simply raised an eyebrow. "Obviously all of that isn't appealing to someone with maturity and brains."

Shawn leaned forward, invading Mac's space. "I dare you to ask the ice queen over there out on a date. In fact, I'm so sure she's going to burn your sorry butt, that I'll even put five hundred dollars behind it. No way will she say yes to a guy like you."

A guy like him.

What he meant was a guy who was neither rich nor built.

While Shawn's opinion of him didn't mean squat, five hundred dollars was half a month's payment on his loan. He hated himself for thinking about the money, but he couldn't deny that it was appealing.

"So if she says yes and we go out, then you'll pay me five hundred dollars. What if she says no?"

Shawn sneered. "*When* she says no, then I get to mock you ceaselessly for the rest of the week."

"Is one date really enough to prove that she prefers average guys versus a fine specimen like Shawn?" Graydon asked, breaking into the discussion. "The only way to prove the point would be for Mac to take her out on multiple dates. He can initiate the first, but she needs to be the one to ask him out on a second date. Then we'll see where it leads from there during our stay."

"There's no way that's going to happen," Shawn sneered.

"It's good you think that, because to make it interesting,

I propose you pay him $500 for each successful date. Consider it part of my bachelor-party entertainment package." Graydon folded his arms, looking between the two of them.

Mac locked eyes with Shawn. The guy was so cocky, it would be nice to knock him down a few notches. But Mac had something to prove. If she said yes, he would prove his point that women preferred respect over muscles, and he'd enjoy the bonus of a little extra cash. If she said no, well, he was already dealing with the Three Amigos and their stupidity for the week. After the wedding, he'd never have to see them again.

"Deal." He stuck out his hand.

"I am going to enjoy watching you crash and burn," Shawn said, taking Mac's hand in a viselike grip. "Let's go check out the hot tub, guys."

Graydon shook his head as the Three Amigos sauntered away. "Well, this is certainly going to make our week interesting."

Mac groaned. "I don't get how they're your friends. And seriously, why are we on this trip with them?"

"We were all on the same college team, working our butts off and praying to get drafted. I hate to say it, but when I went pro, I let the money and fame go to my head for a while. Then I got a lot of sense knocked into me when my last injury ended up needing multiple surgeries, impairing my ability to play. It was a huge wake-up call. I took an early retirement and changed my life around. It sucked at the time, but it all brought me to Rachel, and I can't imagine living life without her. But looking at Shawn, Chris, and Brighton, I can easily see the life I could be living had things not turned that direction."

"If your lives are so different, why are we wasting our time putting up with them?"

Mac wheezed when Graydon slapped him on the back. Man, that guy was strong.

"Nothing scares an athlete more than seeing a buddy injured and stuck in a hospital bed. A lot of my teammates sent text messages but stayed away. We were all scattered across the country on different teams, but those three guys flew in and made sure I was doing physical therapy, kicking my butt as needed. When people show up during your darkest days, that makes them your friends for life—no matter how differently we choose to live it."

Mac cringed. "Well, dang. I guess I have to like them now too."

"Nah, the rivalry is kind of fun from my perspective. And seriously, Shawn has a big mouth. I sure hope your wooing powers are up for the challenge."

Mac tapped his fingers on the shiny bar. He shifted his attention to the woman on the lounge chair. What would be the best way to approach her?

The bartender snapped his towel against his leg. "Well, mate. You can never go wrong with offering a lady a refreshing beverage."

"What do you have that's non-alcoholic?"

"I can whip up a smoothie, flavored sodas or lemonades, or make a virgin strawberry daiquiri or pina colada."

"How about strawberry lemonade? Something classic for a classy lady," Mac decided.

"Coming right up, mate. Here's a pen and paper, if you'd like to send a note along."

Mac twirled the pen through his fingers. "What to say?"

"It can't be cheesy. She saw right through Shawn's pickup lines," Graydon reminded him.

"Something sincere then." Something the opposite of Shawn. And just like that, Mac knew what to write. If it didn't appeal to her, well, then he'd deal with Shawn's jubilee. He scrawled his note on the scrap of paper, then passed it over to the bartender. The lemonade and note both went on the tray, then off to be delivered. Mac forced his eyes away, but every few seconds, he glanced over, hoping to catch her reaction.

"G'day, miss."

Penny looked up, blinking to transition from the tense murder-mystery scene to the Aussie waiter standing beside her with a drink on his tray. She smiled and greeted him kindly. "I'm sorry, I haven't ordered anything."

"This strawberry lemonade is from the gentleman seated at the bar."

"Oh, goodness!" She set her book aside to accept the frosty drink, a napkin, and a folded piece of paper. "Please send my thanks to the gentleman."

The waiter nodded before taking his leave. She took a sip of the cool, sweet lemonade, realizing that she was quite parched. She had been caught up in the detective's search for clues and had forgotten to drink the water she brought with her. She fingered the folded note, then flipped it open to see tiny chicken-scratch handwriting.

I hope this builds some good will for men in general. We're not all dunderheads.

Penny smiled and sipped the strawberry lemonade. He got bonus points for the non-alcoholic beverage and for the use of the word *dunderheads*. She caught his attention and motioned for him to join her.

As the mystery man crossed the pool deck, she realized he was quite dashing and much taller than she had imagined. His smile was kind as he approached.

"Is it okay if I join?" He motioned to the lounge chair next to hers.

"Of course," she replied. He sat on the side so he was

facing her. She shifted into a position to chat with him. "Thanks for the lemonade."

"You're welcome. It was the least I could do after witnessing that unfortunate encounter. By the way, I'm Mac."

She accepted his handshake, her soft skin sliding across his rough palms, sending a delightful shiver through her. "Penny," she said, holding his hand a few more seconds before their clasp slid apart. She was intrigued by his light-brown eyes and the copper flecks in them. He was fit, but not overly buff. His dark-brown hair was cropped short on the sides with wavy curls on the top that made her fingers itch to sink into it. "So, not all men are dunderheads, you say?"

"I have to admit, those particular dunderheads are here to celebrate a mutual friend's bachelor party. I hadn't met them before today, but the sole reason I was invited was to keep them out of trouble. I thought that was going to entail nixing any unsavory ventures. I didn't expect it to extend to a simple outing at the pool. I promise, the rest of us are quite nice."

Penny swirled the straw around in her drink, making the ice clink against the sides. "I'm not sure I would have been brave enough to take on that responsibility."

He held up his hands in defense. "Believe me, had I fully understood what I was signing up for, I might've stayed home."

She tilted her head, curious about this man who seemed quite genuine. "Where is home?"

"Crystal Creek, Kansas. It's a small suburb on the outside edges of where Kansas City meets country."

She could picture him in fitted jeans and cowboy boots. In fact, the imagery made her feel a bit warmer than she could give the sunshine credit for. "Are you more cowboy or city boy?"

"I'm more of a mix of a suburbs and a country kind of

guy. I love all the conveniences the burbs offer, and my work is there. But I spend my spare time at farmers' markets, hiking, canoeing, that kind of stuff. How about you? Country or city?"

"Beach," she replied. "I work for Wessex Resorts, mostly in accounting and reports, but I do get to travel to the resorts from time to time."

"Is that what brought you to Florida?"

"I actually grew up near here," she said. Very near, as her family villa was on the same property. "I've been gone, doing business training and the like for a new resort that opened a few months ago. Now I'm here to take a break and visit family."

"Does staying at one of the resorts make it difficult to separate work from down time?"

He got right to the crux of her current situation. "It definitely blurs the lines. This trip is murkier than others. I'm supposed to be checking out the resort activities and local recommended hot spots so I can send a report back to the main office. They're considering me for a new position."

"That's exciting. Are any restaurants on that list? Perhaps I could buy you dinner, and you can check off one of the items on your to-do list."

She flushed. Even though this was exactly what she hoped for, she hadn't expected the giddy fluttering in her chest as well. "I'd like that."

They settled on a time to meet the next evening, then Mac went back to his group. With her mission accomplished, she gathered her items. Perhaps she'd treat herself to a massage at the resort spa. She couldn't stop the smile of satisfaction. Things were going according to plan.

Five

Day Three

"SWEET HOME ALABAMA" PLAYED in the background as Mac took in the surroundings of the Bubba Gump Shrimp Company. Fisherman's wharf decor competed with prominently displayed *Forrest Gump* movie memorabilia. The restaurant had an overall cheerful flair, which was also reflected in his dinner companion. He had been nervous about meeting Penny for dinner. First dates tended to be awkward in the best of circumstances. Thankfully, Penny turned out to be one of those rare people whom he connected with easily. After they ordered, their conversation turned to their favorite childhood television shows and movies.

"Your food will be here in a minute, folks," Tracy, the waitress, said when she stopped at their table. "But first, a little trivia. Who thinks they know the movie better?"

"It's a total chick flick. So, I'm sure I'll kick his butt," Penny said as she pushed her pale-blond hair over her shoulder. "No offense, Mac."

"None taken," he said, relaxing back into the cushioned booth. He folded his arms across his chest. While Fred Savage had a grandpa who read him *The Princess Bride* when he was sick, Mac's mom always put on *Forrest Gump*. She considered it to be both educational and entertaining.

The waitress rubbed her hands together. "Alright, let's get started off with an easy question. What city and state was Forrest from?"

"Greenbow, Alabama," Penny answered right away.

Mac cocked an eyebrow. "Of course, that's an easy one since it's right there," he said, pointing to the *Run, Forrest, Run* license plate on their table.

She leaned forward, smiling confidently. "A point is a point, which means I have one and you have none."

"For the moment," he said, liking her self-confidence. He nodded in the waitress's direction for the next question.

"What did Forrest name all of his shrimp boats?"

"Jenny," he said, before the waitress could finish the sentence.

"No fair! She wasn't done asking the question." Penny narrowed her stormy blue eyes. "Are you a cheater, Mac?"

"Are you a sore loser, Penny?" he countered.

She leaned forward, thumping her hand on the table. "I'm not a loser yet."

The waitress looked relieved to see the food coming. "We have enough time for one last question. What was the name of Forrest's dog: Lucky, Buddy, or Rocky?"

"Buddy," Penny said confidently.

The waitress bit her lip. "It wasn't Buddy."

Penny's eyebrows scrunched together. "Then it must have been Lucky."

"That's not it either."

"Well, that's not fair. Now you know the answer," Penny complained.

The waitress turned to Mac. He sat back, relaxed and confident. "Of course I know the answer. Forrest didn't have a dog."

The waitress smiled and nodded. "It was a trick question. You win," she said, serving their meals. "If you need anything, flip the license plate over to *Stop, Forrest, Stop*, and someone will grab me. Enjoy!"

Mac squeezed a slice of lemon over the shrimp as Penny scowled at him. He nodded at her dinner. "A taste of that might wipe the sour expression off your face."

Penny tapped a straw on the table to break through the wrapper. He tried to dodge when she blew on the end, but the wrapper nailed him in the center of his chest. Her laugh was light, bringing the carefree mood back to their date. Carefree. That was something he hadn't felt in a long time.

"Now I feel better," she said, then took a bite of her entree. Her eyelids drifted closed, and the most sensual *mmm* hummed from her. "This lobster sauce is amazing."

Her eyes were all soft and dreamy as they met his. He imagined that was what she'd look like after being thoroughly kissed. The thought of evoking that kind of emotion sent a warm zing through his chest.

"How's your shrimp po' boy?" she asked, breaking through his rush of emotions.

Instead of responding and risk sounding like a twitterpated schoolboy, he took a big bite of the flaky baguette. He concentrated on the flavors and combined textures of the breaded-shrimp sandwich.

"I've never had anything like it," he said. A feeling of calm returned as he focused on the food. "The shrimp has the potential to really dry out the sandwich or make it gummy, but it's very crispy and crunchy. The added lettuce, tomato, and squeeze of lemon give it a really nice, fresh flavor."

"You sound like a food critic." She tilted her head, observing his reaction. "You're pretty cute when you blush."

He cleared his throat, not wanting to let his voice crack and embarrass him further. "I actually attended culinary school, so I'm a bit of a food nut."

"Really? That's fascinating! Do you work at a restaurant?"

"Not right now." He pushed at his fries before selecting one and swirling it in some ketchup. He didn't want to go into his past failures. "I actually have a small ice-cream business. I create high-end twists on flavors and sell them to catering companies and restaurants, and at the local farmers' market. Eventually I'd like to open an ice-cream shop."

Her eyes were bright and intrigued. "What are some of your popular flavors?"

"It changes with the seasons. Right now, the Crystal Creek community is ready for spring to make a permanent appearance. I've been getting a lot of requests for anything with lavender, rose, or coconut."

"I'm surprised chocolate isn't on the list." Penny shifted on her side of the booth, reaching for her soda.

"You can buy chocolate ice cream anywhere. I like to focus on fresh new flavor combinations you can't find in the grocery store aisle."

"You don't do chocolate at all?"

"I took two special requests for weddings last year. One was a dark chocolate with ribbons of orange marmalade. The other had swirls of dark, milk, and white chocolate combined together."

She pressed her fingers to her mouth as she finished swallowing a bite. "You just totally ruined dessert. No way does anything on their menu look good now." She smiled, then shifted the conversation in a new direction. "What did you and your friends do today?"

"We drove down to Orlando and checked out Universal."

"Ooh, the wonders of Hogwarts. Did you buy a wand?"

"I got some *Harry Potter* stuff for my nieces and nephews, but we spent most of our time around the Hulk, Spiderman, and Kong rides."

"No Dr. Seuss?"

Mac laughed heartily. "Ah man, can you imagine a bunch of grown men on the kiddy rides? That would have been epic. No, we walked through on our way to other attractions, but that was it. How about you? What were you up to?"

"Well, while you were screaming like a little kid on roller coasters, I attended the resort's Random Acts of Kindness activity."

"My niece's school has a Random Acts of Kindness club. They meet every week and do all sorts of projects. What did your group do?"

He loved how Penny's hands became animated as she described the old church turned into a food pantry for the community. She talked about sorting through a dozen pallets filled with bulk boxes of frozen food, then repackaging them into family-sized portions. "It took less than three hours, and our group of eighteen people filled food orders for almost fifty families."

"Isn't it amazing how a small group can make such a big impact?"

"It is," she replied, turning her glass in circles on the table. "What are your plans for the next few days?"

"We're going into Daytona tomorrow. We're spending the day with Kyle Larson's crew for some race-car driving lessons."

"Seriously?" Penny asked, her voice doing that high-pitched thing that only females seemed able to master. "It's practically impossible to make those kinds of arrangements."

He flushed, embarrassed once again. He should have said they were going to tour the museum or something. He was an idiot. "When more than half the guys in your group are pro athletes, they tend to have connections that only the rich and famous are capable of securing. It's kind of surreal spending time with them, you know?"

"In what way?" she asked.

"They don't get what it's like to be normal, like me and you. People with day jobs and bills and responsibilities. They have unrealistic expectations because they're used to their current lifestyle." He rubbed the back of his neck. "Well, Graydon is the exception, but the rest of the group is full of rich-people drama."

Penny propped her elbow on the table and rested her chin on her hand. "I guess I hadn't thought about it too much. That can be frustrating. What else do you have planned? More big stuff?"

"Thankfully the rest of the trip is pretty typical guy-vacation stuff. We're planning to hit the Slingshot on the boardwalk, do the canoe run at Juniper Springs, and maybe drive down to Cocoa Beach and hit the Kennedy Space Center."

"Juniper Springs is on my list too, as well as St. Augustine and the local flea market. I heard there's an amazing vendor there called the Pickle Man. He's supposed to have thirty different flavors you can sample."

"Ah man, pickles. That would be awesome," he said, fishing for an invitation.

And she totally came through. "You should come with me. If you can get away, that is."

"I would love to! I'm not really into the whole NASCAR thing. I could go for the morning session, then slip out during lunch."

"Are you sure? I hate to have you miss a once-in-a-lifetime experience like that," she said.

"I'm pretty sure I'll be ready for a break from the Three Amigos," he assured her.

"The Three Amigos, eh? Well, if it works, here's my number. Shoot me a text, and I'll send you directions to the flea market. We can meet there."

He paid the bill, then they walked along the boardwalk on their way back to the resort. While it had been warm during the day, the wind coming off the ocean gave the evening a chilly undertone.

Mac helped Penny loop her arms into the cozy knit cardigan she had brought along. They chatted lightly but mostly enjoyed each other's company while soaking in the sounds of the surf. He was obsessed with her smile and the way she continually tried to tame her long, pale hair as the wind pushed it this way and that. Laughter from the beach drifted over the sound of the surf, and he pointed out a few adventurous families with lanterns set up on the beach.

"Thanks for dinner," she said when they arrived back at the resort.

"Thanks for the invite to the flea market tomorrow. I'm looking forward to it."

She tucked her hair behind her ear, a shy smile curving her lips. "Me too."

Mac couldn't wait to see Shawn's expression when he reported that not only had they had a great time at dinner, but she had already asked him out for the second date.

One point for the good guys.

Six

Day Four

PENNY LEANED AGAINST THE hood of her Buick Encore, her face tilted up to the warmth of the sun. It had rained overnight, making the day quite chilly. She wrapped the sides of her navy cardigan around her slim build, savoring the knit wool's extra-soft warmth. When her phone vibrated, she pulled it out of her back pocket and saw Mac's name on the screen. It was bizarre how someone she had just met could elicit the fluttering tingle surging through her.

She swiped to accept the incoming call. "Hey, Mac! Where are you?"

"I think I might be lost. This road looks like a dead end."

"Keep going. The flea market is on your left. Do you see all the metal buildings?" she asked.

"You mean the huge, derelict sheds?"

"You have arrived," she said in a monotone GPS-type voice. "Turn left onto the gravel road. Be careful; there are some big, muddy potholes." She rocked up onto her tippy-toes in her leather boots, and she saw a black SUV bumping along the road.

"Whoa! You weren't kidding about the potholes," he said.

"Come straight back to the third section of the parking lot. I'm parked near the lawn ornaments shed."

"Got it. See you soon."

Penny pulled her leather crossbody bag out of the car, clicked the lock button on the car fob, then added her keys and phone inside the purse before slinging it across her shoulder. The crunch of the gravel under her boots and the bounce of her braids as she walked made her feel young and carefree.

When Mac stepped out onto the road, walking towards her, giddiness bubbled up. She skipped over to meet him, loving how it made him laugh. "Are you ready to explore the best flea market in the county?"

An eyebrow arched over his beautiful light-brown eyes. The copper flecks sparkled with merriment. "Are you sure it's worthy of that title?"

She threaded her arm through his. "Let's go find out. Onward!"

Forget cardigans! His deep, rumbling laugh thoroughly warmed her up.

"What has you in such a good mood this afternoon?" He shifted to dodge a puddle and led them into a crazy assortment of lawn ornaments and funky metal sculptures.

"Yesterday I was rather cranky about my work assignment, but checking out Bubba Gump's with you was fun. I decided I needed an attitude adjustment. And look, Florida provided more adventure for us with all these puddles." She slipped her arm out of his, then jumped over a puddle, spinning around to face him.

She tilted off balance, and Mac caught her by the upper arms, steadying her. The scent of cedar, citrus, and pure man drifted to her, sending her senses into overdrive.

"You okay?" he asked.

She'd be just fine if she could sink in closer and take in a deep breath, but that seemed stalkerish. "Maybe I should bring it down a few notches before I break something."

His eyes were genuine as he replied. "I think you're perfect exactly as you are."

Her cheeks hurt from smiling. "How was your morning with the Three Amigos?" She ran her finger across a metal wind chime, enjoying the pretty sound it made as the dolphin and sea-turtle cutouts clinked against each other.

"They were actually pretty decent. Of course, they were occupied drooling over the race cars. The driving-crew guys were down to earth and fun. We worked with the simulators and had a run around the track in one of the training cars." Mac held a door open for her as they entered the first shed.

With his hand on her lower back, they weaved through a mishmash of vendors selling everything from vinyl records, funky vintage cameras, and DVDs to novelty socks, wallets, and clothing. It was easy to get lost in the maze of booths, which was evidenced when a small pair of arms wrapped around Mac's legs while he was browsing through a T-shirt booth.

"Got you, Daddy," the little voice chirped.

The surprised look on Mac's face was nothing compared to the little girl, whose eyes went round when she realized the leg wasn't her daddy's.

"Hey, there," Mac said with a gentle voice. "Did you lose your dad?"

Tears welled in the little girl's eyes as her arms dropped to her sides and her head darted back and forth. Penny knelt beside the little girl.

"It's okay. We can help you find him," Penny reassured her. "What's your name?"

"Sarah," she said, wiping at her face. Penny comforted the little girl while Mac turned in a circle, looking for the parent or a security officer.

"Are you looking for someone?" Mac called to someone a few booths down.

"My little girl, Sarah," the other man called back.

Mac waved for him to come in their direction.

Sarah's face brightened when she saw her dad. The two embraced, and the dad thanked them for their help.

"How did you spot him?" Penny asked as they continued through the flea market.

Mac shrugged. "He looked frantic, like he'd lost the most important thing in the world. I figured that's how I'd feel if it was my child."

Penny took his hand, weaving her fingers through his, feeling something click into place inside. Something told her to pay attention, or she was going to miss someone very important to her life. Was it possible to know you'd met The One so soon?

They worked their way to the produce and food vendors. It was fascinating to see Mac in his element, sampling, commenting on flavor combinations, and making purchases.

Penny sampled a jalapeno-cilantro lime. One bite, and beads of sweat broke out along her forehead.

"Oh my gosh. Holy hotness!" She took several quick breaths, trying to tame the fire.

"Here, take a bite of a mild dip." Mac dipped a pretzel stick into the sweet onion and chive, then held it out. She bit into it, chewing quickly, the dip taking the edge off of her tongue's traumatic experience.

Mac cupped the side of her cheek, wiping away a stray tear. His smile was sweet and gentle, not mocking in any way. "Spicy stuff isn't your thing, huh?"

"I prefer it when my food tastes good instead of trying to melt my tongue off. Let me guess: you love it?"

He shrugged. "It doesn't bother me."

Mac sampled all the way through to the ghost pepper dip. She had no idea how he handled all that heat without his tongue falling off. They each picked four of their favorites, and

Mac purchased them, even though she insisted she could buy her own. They sampled sweet-and-salty kettle corns and homemade fudges.

At Steve's Pickle Place, wooden barrels filled with sliced pickles and brine lined the booth. She loved the Horsey Bites, which were sweet with a horseradish kick at the end. Mac went with two pickles to take back to the guys. Penny was turned off by odd flavor combinations, but Mac found them the most interesting.

Mac looked up and down the rows of fresh fruits and vegetables. "It's all making me itch to cook."

And that gave her a great idea. "If I could reserve an evening in the resort kitchen, would you like to use it?"

"Would you be my assistant?"

His fingers brushed over hers, sending delightful shivers up her arm. "As long as you'll be patient with my not-so-awesome kitchen skills."

"Deal."

Seven

Day Five

"Mimi, Papa!" Penny called as she hung up her sweater in the foyer of her grandparents' villa.

"In the library, dear." Mimi's voice echoed from down the hall.

Penny's sandals clicked against the hardwood floors until she stepped onto the plush carpet in the library. She gave Mimi and Papa each a kiss on the cheek before curling up on the buttery-soft leather loveseat. Papa was in a matching recliner with a blanket across his lap and the newest issue of *National Geographic* in his hands, while Mimi had the couch all to herself. On the side table were her crossword puzzles, word-search books, and Mimi's guilty pleasure—cheesy romance novels.

"How is your vacation, dear?" Mimi asked, her tone a mite too innocent.

"Oh, it's okay," Penny said, thinking of the time she had spent with Mac at the flea market the previous day. Today he was in Orlando, hitting another amusement park. She missed him. She honestly couldn't remember feeling that way about someone other than her family.

"From the smile on your face, I'd say that young man you've been spending time with is more than okay." Mimi donned her reading glasses and glanced up over the rim as she flipped to the bookmarked page of the puzzle book. "Want to tell us more about him?"

"His name is Mac Hammond." Penny pulled her knees up and wrapped her arms around them. "He's from Crystal Creek, which is in the Kansas City area."

"Really?" Papa interjected. "I've been there before. Very nice people."

"Well, Mac is quite nice, so that's a fitting description. He's funny and well-mannered, and he studied at a culinary school. In fact, he's cooking dinner for us tomorrow night in the resort kitchen."

"And?" Mimi pressed.

Penny shrugged. "And being around him makes me happy." Warmth flooded her cheeks as she tried to not to reveal her developing feelings. "I thought this whole vacation thing was going to be torturous. Instead I met Mac, and now everything is, well, not torturous."

"Better watch out, my dear," Papa said. "You sound rather smitten."

Penny hugged her knees closer, resting her chin on top. "Smitten," she murmured. "That sounds rather adolescent. How do you know if what you're feeling is childish infatuation or real?"

Mimi and Papa exchanged amused looks. "Love starts off with a lovely twitterpation. It makes you feel young and vibrant, like a high better than any drug you could ever buy," Papa said.

"But real love, lasting love," Mimi said. "That's when you realize the person who gives you that zing is also the person you want to talk to first thing in the morning and last thing at night and share everything else in between with as well. He becomes your very best friend. It takes time to discover if a particular person is the one for you."

Time. That was something she and Mac had in limited quantities. Maybe he was a passing fling. Someone to give her hope for future possibilities. A heaviness settled in her chest at the thought of Mac leaving. She couldn't help but admit that she didn't want their time together to end. Three days. That was all the time that was left for them.

Papa broke into her thoughts. "When I met your grandmother at that veterans' dance, I knew right away that she would be someone special in my life. We only dated for a few weeks before I shipped out. Sometimes that's all the time you need. Trust your instincts, my Penny girl."

Eight

Day Six

PENNY PUSHED THROUGH THE swinging kitchen doors and discovered a round table draped with white linens, perfectly set with beautiful china.

"What's all this?" she asked.

Mac smiled as he came around the prep station counters to meet her. He looked oh so handsome in black slacks, a white dress shirt, and a turquoise-striped tie. Penny smoothed her hands over the material of the long sundress.

"Welcome to your evening dinner, mademoiselle," Mac said, pulling out a chair.

"But I thought we were cooking together," she replied. Pale-pink peonies and tiny red roses arranged in a short wooden box sat in the middle of the table, flanked on each side by mason jars with flickering candles inside. The strains of Yo-Yo Ma's cello softened the atmosphere of the kitchen. The setting was beautiful and surprisingly romantic.

"You look beautiful." He placed a kiss on the back of her hand.

"Th-thank you," she stuttered as warmth flooded through her. With such a simple gesture, he made her feel special, like a princess.

"I asked if you'd be my assistant, and you agreed. Don't worry, I'll need plenty of assistance when it's time for cleanup." He winked, lightening the mood. He squeezed her hand before releasing it.

"I see how it is. Woo me with some food, then send me to the back to clean the dishes."

Mac's eyes widened, and he put his hand to his chest. "You mean that's not the norm for courtships?"

Penny laughed to cover up her glee over his mention of courtship. Could he be as interested in her as she was in him? She didn't have time to dwell on it, as Mac came out with a tray and stand. He set out a basket of bread, bottles of oil, and balsamic vinegar, then bowls of soup.

Penny leaned slightly forward, inhaling the tangy scent wafting from the soup bowl. "This smells divine."

"I have prepared three courses for you to enjoy this evening."

"For our first course, we're starting with a lobster-tomato bisque, paired with roasted baguette bread with a blend of extra-virgin olive oil and balsamic vinegar to dip it in."

Penny started with a spoonful of the bisque. First the tang of the tomatoes came through, followed by sensuous cream. Small bits of lobster brought it all together into one luxurious experience. Mac poured some oil and vinegar onto a small plate, then moved it to the center of the table for them to share. Penny broke a chunk of bread off the baguette, then she swirled it in the blend and popped it into her mouth, again savoring the flavors, this time of the baguette's yeasty crunchiness.

"If you cook like this, you must have women lining up for you back in Crystal Creek," Penny teased, spooning up some soup.

"Not really. Most of my dating stays casual. I've had a few serious relationships, but they've always ended mostly amicably. I tend to be the guy who's more friend than boyfriend."

She tilted her head, taking in his half smile and the

affection reflected in his eyes. How could someone not find his sincerity and genuine kindness sexy? "I don't understand how someone could pass up a guy like you."

"A guy like me?"

"An honest-to-goodness good guy." Before he could interject, she went on. "You have to understand, I work in the vacation industry. I am constantly surrounded by either vacationers wanting to be pampered or entertained or by rich executives who are more interested in their flashy new gadgets, expensive cars, designer clothes, or whatever will have the spotlight shining on them. Compared to my norm, you are like fresh air."

He chuckled, looking uncomfortable. "I'm not that good."

"Would you have pawned off the lost little girl as someone else's problem to solve?"

"Of course not."

"Well, the people in my tiny part of the world are sometimes like that."

"It sounds like you need to find a new place to settle," he said.

She paused, considering his suggestion. "Maybe I do," she responded.

Quiet settled between them, only broken by one of Yo-Yo Ma's haunting melodies.

"I didn't mean to turn things so serious," Penny said.

"No worries," Mac said. He was about to say something else, but an alarm went off on his phone. "The main entree is ready to be served. May I clear away your dishes?"

She agreed, moving her hands to her lap as he cleared away the first course. He returned with prime-rib steaks, shrimp and crab meat drizzled with garlic-butter sauce, and garlic mashed potatoes with a side of béarnaise sauce. The small portions were artfully displayed on the square white plate.

Penny shared her exploration of the Castillo de San Marcos, the seventeenth-century fortress in St. Augustine. He told her about the guys' adventures on the boardwalk, including the crazy Slingshot.

"I'll be the first to admit it scared the socks off me, but I'm not going to lie. The best part of the day was listening to Shawn scream like a baby when it was his turn."

"Oh man, I would have loved to have seen that," Penny said, trying to imagine the macho guy's reaction.

"Oh, don't worry. I bought the video and already downloaded it to my phone."

She laughed so hard at the video, she had to wipe tears from her eyes.

Finally it was time for Mac's homemade ice-cream dessert.

"Grapefruit and tarragon ice cream on a meringue nest, topped with candied lemon peel," he said, serving the dessert with a flourish.

Penny felt the weight of his gaze as she dipped her spoon into the dessert. While the entire meal was a celebration of deliciousness, it was this final concoction that was his signature. As the ice cream melted on her tongue, she first noted its silky texture, then the burst of grapefruit that was tempered by the tarragon and cream. The only thing she could imagine would be more divine was kissing Mac Hammond.

"I think we should get married, then you can make ice cream for me each and every night."

Mac's eyes shone with delight as he laughed.

"Seriously, this is white-dress-and-vows-of-forever-worthy," she said, scooping up another spoonful to savor.

"I might quote you on that for my website."

When they finished the meal, Penny helped Mac clean

up. When the final dish was loaded and the dishwasher set to clean, Penny leaned against the stainless-steel counter.

"Thank you for dinner. Saying it was amazing would be an understatement," she said.

Mac rested his hip against the counter so he could face her. "You can have five-star food served to you, but it only truly tastes its best when you have excellent company. And tonight's meal was certainly shared with the best of the best."

Penny shifted, bringing him close enough to feel the warmth flowing between the two of them. She smoothed his tie with one hand, the corners of her mouth lifting as she felt the hard thumps against his chest.

"Penny, I was wondering. That is, I mean, could I?" Mac started, then fumbled over his words. A sweet pinkness flooded his cheeks.

"Mac," she said, lifting herself onto her toes, bringing her mouth inches from his. "Would you just kiss me already?"

"Thank you," he murmured before sealing his lips to hers.

The kiss was slow and tentative, the kindling having been prepared before the match was struck. Their lips barely broke contact, their breaths mingling together.

His melting brown eyes sought hers as he cupped her face with one hand, the rough pad of his thumb brushing her cheek. Then their lips found each other again, only this time there was no tentativeness. First it was like a campfire, and Penny wanted to soak up all the warmth. Mac wrapped an arm around her waist to pull her closer, and she went eagerly. As she wrapped her arms around his neck, the kiss deepened, and they fed the flames until they became a bonfire.

It was the most perfect kiss of his life.

This rush of feeling, the sense of rightness of having Penny in his arms, it was indescribable. And completely unexpected. He wanted to savor every single moment, to figure out how to make their time together extend past the two days he had left in Florida.

Because somehow over the past four days he had bungee jumped off a cliff and fallen hard for Penny Stewart. As impossible as that sounded, it was the truth.

The kitchen doors swooshed open as a woman called out. "Is Miss Stewart in here?"

Penny yelped, and their kiss ended abruptly. Her face flushed almost as bright as a Pink Lady apple. "Yes, Zandra, I'll be right there."

"I'm sorry," Zandra said, and she spun around with her back to them.

Penny took a second to smooth her dress and took a few deep breaths.

Mac leaned close, whispering so only she could hear. "Busted."

She half snorted, then whacked his arm before taking his hand, leading him over to Zandra. "Good evening, Zandra. What do you need?" Penny asked.

Zandra faced them with a serious expression. "I have an urgent fax for you."

Penny took the papers Zandra handed her. "Oh no," Penny said as she scanned the first page, flipping quickly to the next, then the next. "Have my grandparents been informed?"

"Yes, ma'am. Mr. and Mrs. Wessex will be contacting you shortly."

Penny nodded, tapping the papers in her hands. "Have the concierge contact my pilot and ask for the earliest departure time for the Bahamas tomorrow morning. No later than six a.m., please. Also, arrange for a car to pick me up at my villa an hour beforehand. You can text me the details. Thank you, Zandra."

"Yes, ma'am. Please let me know if there's anything else I can do," Zandra replied before leaving the two in the kitchen.

Mac's mind spun on overload.

Her pilot? A car to pick her up at *her* villa?

Penny wasn't talking like an office worker or an accountant. Who did the employee say her grandparents were? And then it all clicked into place.

No.

She couldn't be.

Could she?

"I'm sorry, Mac." Penny grabbed a pen from the counter and started jotting down notes on the fax sheet. She didn't notice that he hadn't followed her as she continued rambling. "There was a major accident at the Bahamas resort I recently opened up. Some kids running around and not staying out of a clearly posted area where the carpets had been shampooed. Then as the manager and another staff member were heading up the stairs to direct them out of the area, the kids apparently decided to run down the stairs. Slick shoes and marble stairs are the perfect combination for an accident. This one took out the kids, my manager, and the staff member. They've all been sent to the hospital, but it looks like the manager has some severe injuries. The poor assistant manager is freaking out."

Mac felt frozen in place as she continued talking.

The resort she had opened. *Her* manager. More facts that supported the crazy conclusion he'd come to.

"Penny," he interrupted her.

"Hmm?" she asked, glancing up distractedly.

"Who are your grandparents?"

The clink of the pen dropping to the counter was more impactful than it should have been. Everything between them fell still, her blank face more telling than she realized. But there it was, and he just knew.

She straightened, stepping towards him with the papers clutched in her hand. "I was going to tell you."

"The Mr. and Mrs. Wessex the resort employee spoke of—"

"Are my grandparents, yes," Penny said, nodding her head.

"And they are what to Wessex Resorts?" Mac hoped she'd say the groundskeepers or some distant relatives to the original Wessex of Wessex Resorts.

"They are the founders," Penny admitted.

Mac took a step back. "You aren't an accountant?"

"Technically, no, but—"

"You said you were vacationing to write some reports to be considered for a promotion. Was that a lie too?"

Her eyes widened. "No, Mac. I stretched the truth about my job."

"What promotion?" he asked. When she looked at him blankly, he repeated. "What's the promotion you're being considered for?"

Resolve settled into her eyes. "To take my family seat on the Wessex Resorts Board of Directors."

Mac paused for a moment, letting all of it sink in. Her family was as rich as rich could be. They owned resorts all over the world. He couldn't believe he had fallen for the one girl he couldn't possibly have. He rocked back on his heels, letting the finality sink in. "Well," he said calmly. "I hope you get it."

He turned, pushing through the kitchen doors into the empty dining room.

"Wait a minute," Penny said, coming after him. "That's it?"

"What else do you want?" Mac asked, continuing to walk away, only stopping when she grabbed his arm.

"You're walking away?"

"Yes," he said.

Her blue eyes were dark as a thunderstorm. He stood, waiting for lightning to strike him down.

"You're walking away because I happen to be the granddaughter of the founders of this resort."

"Penny, your world." Mac shook his head. How could she not understand how not right they were for each other? "You just ordered a private jet to be ready to take you to the Bahamas tomorrow morning. I can't even imagine your world. I'm not even a blip on the radar of your social circle. Listen, I really enjoyed getting to know you, but—"

Her eyes went wide. "Are you breaking up with me?" Her voice squeaked as she said the last word.

Mac scrubbed his hand over his face, hating the knot twisting up in his gut as he saw her eyes water. "It was four days, Penny. Were we even a thing?"

Her sharp intake of breath was like a knife stabbing him right through the heart. Her head bobbed up and down as she averted her eyes to the dining-room windows overlooking the lamppost-lit ocean boardwalk. "You're right. It was only four days. Take care, Mac."

She brushed past him, and he let her go.

He let the woman he loved walk out of his life, and it wasn't about the money. It wasn't about the lie. Or at least not her inconsequential one.

It was because of his.

Nine

Day Seven

MAC PROPPED HIS ELBOWS onto the bar and dropped his head into his hands, twisting his fingers in his hair and pulling slightly. Why had he let them bait him? His role was to keep things level-headed, and what had he done on the first day? Allowed the god-complex hockey players to push his buttons and made stupid choices. Now his heart felt like a chunk of steak, beat and battered up by a mallet, ready to be thrown on the grill and left to burn.

To make the situation worse, he was still stuck with the Three Amigos.

"Dude, I can't believe her family owns the resort," Brighton said, accepting the cold beer from the old guy tending the bar. His tag said his name was Fred. He was nice, but rather quiet. "How much money do you think she has? At least as much as us, right?"

"It doesn't matter," Mac mumbled, wishing he could get them to shut their traps. The razzing had been going on for at least fifteen minutes with no end in sight.

"A couple mil at least," Chris said, picking up his phone. "Let me ask Siri."

"It doesn't matter," Mac said again, firmer this time.

Chris swore under his breath. "I need to invest in the hotel business. Dang. Four billion."

"No way," Brighton said, grabbing for the phone.

Shawn slipped off his stool, looked over Brighton's shoulder, and shook his head. Then he sauntered over to where Mac and Graydon sat at the end of the bar and tossed down several hundred-dollar bills. "Looks like you won that bet. Three dates, fifteen hundred dollars."

The crisp bills fanned across the bar, like an insult slapping Mac in the face. He stacked them into a pile, not even bothering to count it as he folded the stack neatly in half.

Fifteen hundred dollars. What once represented freedom was now a choker pulled tight around his neck.

He swiveled around on the stool, then slid the money into Shawn's shirt pocket. "No thanks."

Shawn cocked his head to the side, looking Mac over, then shrugged his shoulders and turned back to Chris and Brighton. "Come on, guys. Let's go spend Mac's money. Graydon, you coming?"

"You guys go ahead. I'll catch up later."

The Three Amigos vacated the bar and headed to the boardwalk.

"Hopefully they'll stay out of trouble." Graydon signaled to the bartender for another sweet tea.

"I totally screwed up." Mac ran his finger up and down the condensation of his Coke glass.

"Yeah, I wouldn't have given that money back," Graydon said.

"Seriously, the bet wasn't about the money. It was about the fact that a beautiful woman would rather go out with a nice guy instead of a rich jerk."

"Did she?" The bartender asked, setting the sweet tea in front of Graydon. His eyes met Mac's. "Did she prefer your company?"

Mac straightened out of his slouch. "I think so."

Fred simply arched an eyebrow. "Ladies of privilege rarely waste their time. How many dates did you go out on?"

"Three dates over the past four days."

"From what your friends said about her portfolio, she wouldn't have said yes to a second date had the first one not been appealing," Fred said.

Mac smiled, remembering their dinner at the Bubba Gump Shrimp Company. "Ah man," he said, shaking his head, still blown away that Penny was a billionaire. Why was she spending time with a guy like him?

"Did I ever tell you how Rachel and I met?" Graydon asked. When Mac shook his head, he continued. "She was on a date at Brisket and Noodles. I was running things while my parents were out of town. Her date went terribly wrong, and she ended up in my office, asking me why men lie while she waited for her cab." Graydon cracked a smile, shaking his head. "The next time we met was about a week later when she dropped her nephew off at my hockey camp. She thought I was there to do the catering. She had no idea I was a hockey player. I didn't bother to correct her either. I liked how flustered she got by Graydon the catering guy, instead of DG the rich guy. But man, when she found out who I really was." Graydon chuckled, leaning towards Fred. "She's a redhead, mind you. She stayed all poised as she accused me of taking one too many hits to the head to be able to properly remember my own identity, then she smashed a full plate of cheesecake into my hand. Mind you, I was at my cousin's wedding, and she really was the caterer. My entire family and all their closest friends had the privilege of witnessing my rejection."

"The feisty ones make the best wives. Congratulations." Fred shot Graydon a wink. "Back to Mac. So she's rich. What's the big deal? Can't handle a woman with more heft than you?"

"It was all a deception."

"She didn't tell you—"

Mac cut him off. "Not her. Me. That first date, yeah, it was about the good guys winning for a change, but there was also an element of it being about the money, too. I figured maybe she'd go out with me once. If I was lucky, a second time, and I'd have the added satisfaction of lightening Shawn's wallet a bit. I just didn't expect, well, *her*."

Fred's eyes narrowed, then he nodded his head slightly up and down. "You didn't expect to fall in love."

Mac's shoulders slumped, and he clasped the cold drink between his hands. Defeat filled his soul. "No, I didn't."

Fred pushed off the bar counter, then wiped down the gleaming wood with a soft towel. "Well, son, moping at a bar isn't going to help you one bit. Talking is the only chance you have to resolve the issue."

"She'll hate me."

"Maybe." Fred shrugged his shoulders before moving away to help a new customer.

Did he dare talk to Penny? Would she even want to listen to anything he had to say after how he had acted last night? There was only one way to find out.

Penny tossed her briefcase on the couch before going to the kitchen to pour a cold glass of water. It had been a horrific day, from the turbulent flights and organizing staff meetings to the hospital and injury reports and comforting three upset families. Her brain was on overload even before Mimi's irate phone call about Mac and the bet he had made with his friends.

She had shoved Mac and the entire situation out of her mind until the return flight to Daytona. Why return home when the Bahamas resort gave her a variety of reasons to avoid the topsy-turvy emotions she'd have to deal with in Florida?

But Mimi wanted her home, most likely to keep an eye on her granddaughter's emotional state.

Penny sipped the cool water, not finding any pleasure as it soothed her dry throat. She wanted the day to be over. To change out of her nasty traveled-in clothes, pull on some cozy pajamas, then crawl into bed and pull the cover over her head to hibernate from the world.

A soft knock sounded at her door. Penny glanced at the clock. It couldn't be Mimi, not at eleven o'clock at night. She went to the security monitor beside the door, finding a very tired-looking Mac on the other side. She placed her hand on the knob, tempted to turn it, to let him inside. But she couldn't face him.

"What is it, Mac?" she asked through the door.

"I'd really like to talk. Can I come in?"

The sincerity in his eyes made her yearn to say yes, but she beat it back. "I'm tired. Talking right now isn't a good idea."

"I wanted to apologize and to explain about the other night," he said.

Bubbly anger pushed past the tired cracks in the walls she had tried to build throughout the day. "Do you mean, explain about the bet you and your buddies made?"

His head jerked in surprise. "How did you—"

"There isn't much gossip that makes its way around the resort without my grandmother eventually finding out."

"Penny, can you open the door?"

She ignored the request. "Did you get a bonus for scoring a kiss with the rich girl?"

"It wasn't like that, I promise. It was a stupid bet I made to prove that you'd rather spend time with me instead of someone like Shawn."

She leaned her forehead against the door, moving it from side to side. Her laugh was short and rough. "Had someone asked me whom I preferred yesterday afternoon, I would have agreed. It turns out, I'm the single billionaire chick who was stupid enough to be duped by a bunch of immature boys. Well, enjoy your bragging rights. You earned them."

The monitor showed Mac placing the palm of his hand on the door, his head tilted towards the door too. "I didn't take the money, Penny. Can we talk, please?"

Ironically, if the door magically disappeared, they would be leaning against each other for support. But there wasn't any magic that could fix this.

"I can't, Mac. Please, just go."

They were both still for a moment. She watched him on the monitor, his head bent and his hand pressed to the door. "I'm checking out tomorrow morning. If you decide you want to talk, call or send me a message."

Penny pushed away from the door. "Goodbye, Mac."

She ignored the monitor, not wanting to see his expression or to see him walk away. Instead she turned out the lights as she went to her bedroom. She didn't bother to change clothes. She pulled off her shoes and climbed right into her bed, ready for the exhaustion to take over and hoping for the emptiness of a dreamless night.

Ten

Day Eight

PENNY'S PHONE RANG, JOLTING her out of sleep. She pulled the pillow off her head, blinking at the bright light shining through the slits in the window's blinds. She fumbled before her hand connected with her phone, swiping to accept the call from her papa.

"Hello?" she asked, her voice crackly.

"Morning, sunshine! I'm at your door with fresh orange juice and bagels."

"Oh, Papa, I'm not even out of bed yet."

"Which is why I'm here with breakfast. Now come open the door for an old man."

"I'll be right there," Penny said, pulling herself out of bed. Ugh. She was a disgusting mess. Wrinkled clothes from the day before and hair sticking up every which way. She tried to smooth the worst of the tangles before she opened the door to greet her papa.

He tsked at her appearance, brushing past her to the kitchen. "I've seen drunken sailors in a better state than you, my dear. Why don't you go take a quick shower, then join me for breakfast?"

She scrunched her eyebrows together, confused. First he got her out of bed for breakfast, but now he wanted her to take a shower first? What in the world?

"Papa, is everything okay?"

"Of course. I just don't want to share breakfast with your dirty laundry. Off you go. Be quick!"

With that, he sat down on the couch, took out his favorite newspaper, and opened it up to the business section. Penny shook her head a bit, confused by his odd behavior, but decided a shower wouldn't be such a bad thing. "I'll be right back."

After taking a quick shower and donning clean clothes, Penny returned to greet her papa. She gave him a quick peck on the cheek. "Let's have breakfast on the veranda, Papa. It will be nice to have some fresh air, and my hair will dry faster that way too."

The sunshine and salty air helped soothe her dampened spirits. It was just her and Papa, sitting in comfortable chairs at the patio table. She was spreading cream cheese on her chocolate-chip bagel and giving him an update on the previous day's events in the Bahamas when he interrupted her.

"Never mind all that. What are you doing about this boy?"

"The boys who caused the accident?"

"No, the boy you've been dating. Your Mimi said she thought he was playing you. Was he?"

"Oh, Papa. I don't want to talk about it."

He thumped his newspaper down, making Penny jump in her seat. "Well, I do. Your grandmother gave you a dare, a bet if you will, to get out and socialize, especially with a man. That's what led to this on your side, isn't it?"

Penny was at a loss for words. Papa was usually the calm one of her two grandparents. What had him riled up?

"Well, wasn't it?" he pressed.

"Yes, I suppose so."

"You suppose? You're telling me that without your grandmother's bet, you would have gone out to the pool to relax and would have accepted the young man's invitation."

She sighed. "You know I would have been in the office, doing whatever needed done instead. There. Satisfied?"

He grunted. "Not yet. You said yes because of a bet with your grandmother. Oh, don't try to make it sound pretty," he said when she tried to interject. "You want that seat on the board, and your grandmother dangled it in front of you with a little incentive to start dating."

She sat back in her chair, chastised. "And your point is?"

"Why are you punishing that boy for doing something similar?"

She shook her head. "You don't understand, Papa."

"Try me."

"It's just—" She cut off, averting her eyes to look out at the ocean waves crashing against the shore. Wishing she could blame her watery eyes on the bright sunlight rather than the swell of regret weighing her down.

"He hurt your feelings," he said kindly.

Penny nodded, swiping at the tear that fell onto her cheek.

"Mac's hurting too."

That caught her attention. "How would you know how he's feeling?" Her eyes widened. "Papa, what did you do?"

Her grandfather waved his hand through the air, as if the revelation that he knew Mac was of little consequence. "Nothing more than served the man a few drinks."

"You got him drunk?"

"Of course not. I simply took a shift at the pool bar, and your young man happened to be there with his friends. I'm still questioning his choice of friends, mind you. Only one of them seemed to have a decent head on his shoulders. The other three were quite disagreeable."

"Don't try to get in the middle of this, Papa. It was only a few days. It's no big deal."

"Then why are you both moping around this morning like the world has ended?"

"Mac has a life to get back to in Crystal Creek. I have a life to take care of here."

"Or do you two have lives that need to be melded together? Now listen to your papa for a few more minutes, okay?" He reached across the table and took her hand. "I want you to be happy, my Penny girl. What I see from you and Mac is that being together made you both happy. Yes, there were some misunderstandings from both sides, but despite that, you genuinely like each other, dare I say as more than friends."

He patted her hand as she felt warmth flood her cheeks. "Do you remember when we talked about love?" Penny nodded her head. "Your Mimi said that it takes time, but I also mentioned that you simply know when you've met the right one, and you need to trust your instincts. My question is, are your instincts telling you that this was a vacation fling? If so, then let's set this aside and move on with no Mac in your future."

The thought of no Mac in her future left a heavy weight in the pit of her stomach.

"Or," Papa continued, "are your instincts asking *what if?* What if you had more time? What if you could set aside the misunderstandings and focus on the realness of your friendship, your relationship? If your instincts are asking these questions and wondering if there could be more to discover with this boy, well, then, what are you going to do to give you both that opportunity? Only you can make that choice, my Penny girl."

Her eyelids fluttered, and she rubbed her hands across them, wiping away the moisture while her heart thudded against her chest. "Papa, I can't—"

"You can do anything your heart tells you is right," he interjected.

She stood on wobbly legs. "I need to go." She glanced at her watch. It was already after ten.

"He left thirty minutes ago for the airport. I had your car brought over for you."

She rushed around the table, dropped a kiss on her papa's cheek, then grabbed her purse and ran for the car.

Eleven

PENNY SLID INTO THE driver's seat and took off for the airport. It was difficult to get through the slow lights and lower speed limits of town, but once she was on the freeway, she pushed past the speed limit as much as she dared. She should be able to get there in time. Enough time to get him to leave his gate, to talk to her, to see if they could come to any kind of conclusion about this entire beautiful, crazy mess.

A siren bleeped, and lights flashed in her rearview mirror.

No.

No, no, no!

She slowed and pulled to the side. Dang it.

She went through the entire process of showing her license, explaining she was trying to get to a flight, and accepting a ticket for being thirteen miles per hour over the posted limit.

Her heart pounded the rest of the way to the airport. Could she possibly make it in time? Even for a brief conversation?

She pulled her car over to the valet curb, grabbed her phone, and dialed Mac's number. She passed off her keys and info to the valet as the phone connected, then rang once. Twice. Three times.

Voicemail.

She hung up and tried again as she entered the airport lobby.

"Hello." Mac's hesitant voice came over the line.

"Mac, it's Penny," she said, out of breath but relieved he had answered.

"I know. I saw the caller ID."

"Are you on the plane?" she asked, knowing that at any minute, their call could be cut off by a flight attendant.

"We're getting ready to board. I only have a few minutes."

"I'm here. At the airport. I got my first speeding ticket on the way. And I just, I wanted to see you."

"Penny, I need to get on the flight. Why don't you tell me why you called?"

She sucked in a deep breath, then let it all out in a whoosh. "Don't leave hating me," she said.

"Why would that matter?" he asked.

"Because I think I'm falling in love with you."

A heavy sigh came through the ear piece. "Penny—" he started, but the line crackled, so she continued.

"I know that's crazy to say, but that's how I feel. And if you leave hating me, then we'll never be able to talk things through. To see if we can be something more." She took in another deep breath, listening for Mac, but only hearing static. "Mac?" she asked.

She pulled the phone from her ear and saw that the call had disconnected. She scanned the escalators leading down from the gate area. No Mac.

She waited. Hoping.

A few minutes later, someone announced that the Kansas City flight had departed, and they were now boarding passengers for the next flight to Orlando. All she could do was grip her phone and stare at the blank screen.

He was gone.

It was over.

"Hey."

Penny whirled around. He was there. Right in front of her. Jeans, a navy polo shirt, and mussed hair she wanted to sink her fingers into.

He hadn't left.

"How did you? I was watching the escalators—" she stammered.

He motioned to the double doors to the left. "Celebrity tunnel," he said. "Did you mean it?"

She licked her suddenly dry lips. "That I think I'm falling for you?"

He nodded.

"I did."

He tangled his fingers with hers. "Good, because I'm already there."

Her eyes went wide as she realized he was telling her he loved her. Swirls of wonder filled her, bubbling tingles overflowing with joy. He rested his forehead on hers.

"Penny, I'm very sorry," he murmured, bringing their clasped hands up to rest on his chest. The beat of his heart was strong, like hers. "Can we please start fresh?"

"I would like that oh so much," she whispered, loving the faint dimple that appeared when he smiled. Then he dipped his head, his lips capturing hers in a tender kiss: a caress full of hope, happiness, and promise.

THE END

Danyelle Ferguson grew up surrounded by Pennsylvania's beautiful Allegheny Mountains, but is currently experiencing mountain-withdrawal in Kansas. She enjoys reading, writing, dancing and singing in the kitchen, and the occasional long bubble bath to relax from the everyday stress of being "Mommy."

She can be contacted at:
Danyelle@DanyelleFerguson.com
Website: www.DanyelleFerguson.com
Blog: www.QueenOfTheClan.com

A Billionaire Abroad

Sarah M. Eden

One

KEIGHLEY AINSWORTH DIDN'T USUALLY splurge on a taxi, but she wasn't about to show up to a meeting with Sterling Westcott smelling like the subway. He was a bachelor billionaire, a philanthropist, and probably the most intriguing guy she'd ever met. As an event planner, she interacted with a lot of people, so her reference pool wasn't exactly shallow. Sterling was a step above... well, everyone.

She pulled out her phone, flipping the camera to selfie, and did a quick check. Nothing in her teeth. Makeup flattering without looking like she was trying too hard. She was having a good hair day, which was lucky. She wasn't making a *first* impression, but she still wanted it to be a good one.

The taxi dropped her on Pearl Street. Traffic in the Financial District at the lunch hour was impressive, even for New York. Sterling's offices weren't far; he had likely walked. Keighley stepped inside the restaurant where he'd asked her to meet him, a Greek spot he'd mentioned before as a favorite.

She'd learned over the couple of years she'd been in New York how to act like a New Yorker. Every bit of nervousness and feeling like she didn't fit in this swanky restaurant got tucked away, hidden behind a mask and posture of confidence. She faked it.

"I'm meeting Sterling Westcott," she told the hostess.

The expected disbelief rushed over her face for just a moment, but it was tucked away quickly. She turned back and looked at the tables behind her in the busy dining room. Keighley followed her gaze.

Halfway back, Sterling rose. She heard the hostess's breath catch in exactly the moment her own did. He was always handsome, but that blue suit fit him like it was made for him.

Keighley inwardly rolled her eyes. Of course the suit was made for him. Billionaires didn't buy off the rack at Walmart.

He smiled at her and waved her over. Keighley did her best not to smirk as she crossed past the hostess and the other diners, every single one of whom took notice of Sterling's presence and her approach. She might've been an Arizona transplant barely getting by in a tiny flat in the Bronx, but Sterling Westcott was there waiting for *her*.

"Thanks for coming," he said, holding her chair out for her.

She sat. "You've talked about this place so much, I'm excited to finally try it."

He took his seat, across from her. "You've only come for the food?"

Keighley smiled. "Of course not."

That brought his smile back in full force, a lethal weapon really. It worked its magic on her, on their server, on a lot of the diners. Keighley had a little more practice at functioning under the influence of Sterling's company. Some of that practice had come that morning in front of her mirror.

Once their lunch had been ordered, she pulled out a conversation starter that had worked pretty well with imaginary Sterling while she was putting on her makeup. "The *Times* ran a piece about the cancer benefit last week. Very positive."

"I'm not surprised," he said, flashing another of his billion-dollar smiles. "The event was a tremendous success, due mostly to you."

She hoped her blush wasn't too obvious. The fundraising dinner was the biggest event she'd ever been in charge of. She'd worked herself to the bone, but happily. Teaming with Sterling on behalf of such a worthy cause had been amazing. He'd complimented her work but also *her*. He'd been involved in the planning, wanted to know the details, and had been genuinely happy at the success of the night. He cared about the cause they'd been promoting. She liked that.

"My company is looking to expand business in the European tech market," he said. "But we don't have a presence in Dublin."

"Dublin?" He had her full attention. She used to dream of going to Ireland when she was a little girl. Any mention of that country or its capital still got her heart jumping around a little.

Sterling nodded. "That city is the heart of European tech. All the major companies are headquartered there."

"I didn't know that."

He tore off a bit of pita—the appetizer he'd chosen—talking between bites. "Anyone wanting to tap tech in Europe needs connections in Dublin." He leaned a bit toward her, lowering his voice in the way he did sometimes. It made her feel like only the two of them were around, even though that had never been the case when they were together. "I am hoping to build those connections, and I think hosting an impressive event after a couple of weeks of meetings would do the trick."

An event. She held her breath.

"Could you clear a week or so off your schedule the beginning of next month?" he asked.

She tried to keep her voice steady. "I might have trouble planning an event that's taking place on a whole different continent than I'm on."

He flashed a dazzling smile, leaning back once more. "You would be planning it while in Dublin."

In Dublin. Dublin! Somehow she kept her cool. "I could probably clear my schedule."

"Perfect." He paused while their server set their meals on the table. "I'll have my travel assistant contact you to work out the details. I'm hoping we can undertake this sooner rather than later."

Dublin! "Sounds perfect." She took a calm bite of tsipoura. "May I ask why you've asked me to plan this? You could probably hire an event planner in Dublin."

It was a stupid thing to ask, considering she was being given the chance of a lifetime. If he hadn't thought of using someone local, he'd think of it now.

That smile. She almost melted.

"I've seen your work, Keighley. I know you will put on a top-notch event. I also know we work well together." He took a sip of wine. "It would be a gamble with any other planner. I can't risk this not going well."

"You trust me then?" Again she called on the New York vibe she'd learned to fake the last two years and asked the question with amusement.

"Obviously."

He spoke with a twinkle of appreciation in his eye and a shimmering smile pulling at his lips, giving it extra meaning. The memory of it kept her heart spinning all through the remainder of the meal as he explained his ideas, what the event was meant to accomplish, and a few of the companies whose heads he would be inviting. There was something personal in the interaction, something more than just business.

Sterling Westcott was inviting her to join him in the city of her dreams and be part of his efforts there. The two of them. In Ireland.

It was the chance of a lifetime.

Two

KEIGHLEY HAD NEVER FLOWN overseas before and had never even set foot in the first-class cabin of a plane. She'd now done both. Sterling could just as well have sent her economy. Flying over the Atlantic, lying down in a seat that converted into a bed, she'd thought again and again what a personal touch it was, and how thoughtful. He was spoiling her. She had worked with other wealthy clients, and none were as thoughtful as he was.

A uniformed chauffeur had met her at Dublin Airport, driving her in a luxury Mercedes-Benz toward the heart of the city. He hadn't talked much, but his few words rang with that gorgeous Irish accent she'd fallen in love with from watching movies. Was this actually real?

Her phone didn't automatically switch over to the international coverage she had enabled before leaving New York. She fiddled with it a little while as the car flew down a freeway. If Sterling called or the hotel texted information, she needed to be able to get the message. By the time she looked up and out the windows again, they were in the heart of the city. Of Dublin!

She held back a gasp of excitement. The driver probably drove all kinds of sophisticated people around. If she came off as a total noob, that would likely get back to Sterling. She didn't want to repay his generosity by embarrassing him. But inside she was kind of freaking out. Her head snapped back and forth, looking out the windows on both sides of her. Some things about the city looked really modern. Others looked like something straight out of a BBC historical drama. Was the whole city that way, or just the part she was seeing?

A million questions swam through her mind as they inched their way through the much busier part of the city. How many people lived in Dublin? What was the name of the river they crossed over? Were all the spires she could see dotting the skyline from churches? How many were there?

They passed buildings with marble columns out front, iron gates that must have been centuries old, narrow back lanes, shops that were probably older than America itself. There were so many people walking around; that part reminded her of New York. But the rest was something totally different. It was new and exciting and spoke to her heart in a way she wasn't sure she could have explained.

The car pulled up in front of a very modern building. It was at least five stories tall and looked like a glass and concrete checkerboard. The ground level was entirely glass. The walks crisscrossed over patches of grass and paving stones. It wasn't at all what she thought of when she thought of Ireland. She liked it, but it wasn't what she was expecting.

Giant silver letters above the brass-framed glass doors declared this The Marker Hotel. Her destination.

She didn't know how Sterling had managed it, but she didn't have to wait at the reception desk or explain who she was. The driver carried her luggage in and handed it to a bellhop. The man at the desk, sporting a suit and tie and the look of someone in charge, called her "Miss Ainsworth" and welcomed her before she'd even had a chance to introduce herself. She was personally accompanied to the "lift" and on to her room, all while hearing a list of impressive amenities, all spoken in a beautiful Irish accent.

Keighley had never been in such a fancy hotel suite. Her apartment looked like a dump compared to this place. And the suite was bigger. She crossed to the windows and the view of the city. A billion-dollar view. And Sterling was providing it. She could've pinched herself.

The bellhop and concierge had both left, leaving her room keys and luggage in the spacious living area. She almost felt like holding her breath.

"I'm in Ireland." Her amazed voice echoed around the room. What hotel had accommodations big enough for echoes? And this wasn't even the only room in her suite.

She peeked through the doorway to the bedroom. Gorgeous. Elegant. She'd always dreamed about visiting Ireland, but had figured she'd do it on a shoestring budget. This was luxury.

A knock sounded at the door to her suite. Housekeeping? Maybe she left something in the car? She pulled the door open and every word disappeared from her brain. Sterling. She hadn't been expecting him, but she should have known he'd drop in. He'd flown in a few days ago. He was most likely staying in this same hotel. She was here to arrange an event on his behalf, and he liked to be involved in the details. Of course he would drop by.

"You made it," he said with his trademark smile. "Does everything meet with your approval?"

Meet with her approval? How could it not? But she kept her composure. "It's great. It will be an excellent home base for the work I have to do."

"I'm glad to hear it. And your flight?"

"It was excellent. I was surprised how well I slept."

He nodded. "Good. I want to run past you some thoughts I've had since arriving, and some useful information. But, I know you've just arrived, so take the time you need to settle in."

He was going to leave? So soon? "Come in," she instructed. "I'd like to get started right away. You've been here longer than I have. I'd appreciate whatever you can tell me."

He came in, and she closed the door behind him. Turning to face the living room again took her breath away. It didn't seem to have any impact on him. What would that be like, being so used to something like this that it basically went unnoticed?

She snatched up her messenger bag and sat at the round, glass-top table. Sterling joined her there. He pulled out his phone. She opened her laptop.

"First," she said, "have you changed anything about what you'd like this event to be?"

He shook his head. "A memorable event to, basically, seal the deal with Facebook, Google, Amazon—all the big players."

She looked over her laptop at him. "They're all headquartered here?"

He nodded. "And they're not the only ones."

Dublin really was a tech hub. No wonder he'd come here. "How soon do you want to have this event? I'll need a couple of days to narrow down locations and caterers, if needed. Entertainment. That kind of thing."

"A few days will be fine. End of the week, maybe," he said. "I know you'll scout out the best places and manage your usual miracle."

She smiled broadly. It was one of the nicest things anyone had said to her since she began working as an event planner. It was one-hundred percent trust. She appreciated that.

There was a knock at the door. "Strange," she said. She wasn't expecting another visitor.

"That'll be Brogan," Sterling said, not at all surprised. He rose and made his way toward the door.

"Who?" she asked.

"Brogan Malone."

That name wasn't familiar. Sterling opened the door and motioned someone inside. Keighley eyed the doorway with curiosity and a bit of annoyance. A guy stepped inside, probably not much older than she was. While his hair wasn't truly red, it leaned that way. He was handsome—she couldn't deny that—but in a quiet way. Different from Sterling. Even people who had no idea Sterling Westcott was a billionaire with influence and importance took note of him. This Brogan Malone wasn't like that.

Brogan nodded in her direction. "Keighley Ainsworth." Definitely Irish.

She leaned back a bit in her chair, quirking her brow upward. "Have we met before?"

He shook his head, even as a bit of a lopsided smile tugged at his mouth. "Mr. Westcott told me about you."

"What, exactly, did he tell you?"

Brogan crossed to the table where she sat and, quite at ease, dropped onto a chair as well. "He told me you and I share a profession and, for the next week, we'll also share an assignment."

What? She looked immediately to Sterling. "I don't understand."

"There is a lot to get done in only a week, and you have never been here before. Someone local will speed up the effort. He knows people and venues. It'll be helpful."

Only a moment ago she'd been thinking how great it was that Sterling had total faith in her. Then this Brogan showed up, the billionaire's plan B.

She recovered her equilibrium quickly, though. Sterling apparently didn't know how capable she really was. They hadn't done enough events together. And she was unproven overseas. But that would change in the next week. He would see.

She opened her mouth to insist she didn't need Brogan

to hold her hand as she made connections and scouted locations in Dublin, but Sterling had already boarded the gratitude train, telling Brogan how glad he was to have him on board.

Keighley kept her growl of annoyance silent. Sterling had total control over this job and who worked it. She'd simply have to show him—and Brogan—that she could manage on her own. Sterling valued hard work. So did she.

Here was her chance to remind him of how good she was. And maybe, just maybe, they'd have a chance to find out how good they could be together.

Three

"So, your boss, is he wanting a fancy do or something more casual?" Brogan asked.

Keighley didn't roll her eyes, but she was tempted. "As I've explained before, he's not my boss."

"He hired you, yah?"

"Yes."

"And he's paying you to be here, yah?"

Through tight lips she answered, "Yes."

"And he calls the shots, yah?"

She pushed out a breath. "Yes."

"What you have there, Keighley, is a boss."

He was the most annoying guy. "Do you consider him your boss? Because your situation is basically the same as mine."

He laughed. He *always* laughed. "I pay for my own flat, thank you. And I'm here only as a source of information. Books don't have bosses."

"Then be informative instead of obnoxious."

Again, he laughed.

She kept her calm. "What venues could we book on such short notice that wouldn't be a complete disaster?"

"We're running at cross purposes, here. As I asked you before, is your b—is Mr. Westcott wanting a formal event or a casual one?"

"He has left those details to me." Perhaps that hard truth would finally get through to Brogan that Sterling was not her boss.

"Then what is it you're wanting?"

"At the moment?" she grumbled.

His grin was almost as grating as his laugh.

"My aim is an event that will be both impressive enough to give those in attendance confidence in the investments that are being proposed to them, but also enjoyable enough that they build a more personal connection. That is Sterling's strong suit when it comes to forging new business relationships. *He* convinces them every bit as much as his business track record."

"I'd say, then, an upscale venue but a low-key program."

As annoyed as she was with the man, that was exactly what she had in mind. "What upscale venues could we book quickly?"

"Based on the way the staff here falls all over themselves whenever your man walks in the room, I'd say he could have the ballroom here for the asking, even if it's already booked."

"He's not 'my man.'"

Brogan held his hands up in a show of innocence. "Not what I meant. If you're going to spend any amount of time in Dublin, that's a phrase you'll have to learn to understand. Speaking of 'your man' doesn't mean a man that actually belongs to you in any way. In America, you'd say something like 'you know who' or 'that dude.'"

His attempt at an American accent made her smile despite herself.

"Ah, you do know how to not look sour. Shocking."

She cocked her head to one side. "Maybe I'm only sour with you. Did you think of that?"

He nodded. "I did. But, I'm certain that's not it."

"Are you saying you think I'm just a sour person?"

A shrug. "Is there anything that makes you *not* sour?"

As a matter of fact. "I went for a walk this morning," she said. "I saw what I thought at first was a castle, but then I realized it might have been a church."

"Probably a church," he said. "We're overrun with them."

"And the air smelled like rain."

"This *is* Ireland."

She even a smiled a little. "I know it's expected, but it was a different rain smell than we get in New York. It was cleaner or wetter or something."

"New York must be filthy for it to smell worse than this dirty old town."

"It is, actually. And loud."

"We've a fair bit of noise around in Dublin."

She set her elbow on the table, leaning her head against her upturned fist. "Maybe that's why I felt kind of at home walking around this morning. It's enough like New York that it's a little familiar."

He leaned back in his chair. "Did you go inside the 'castle church' you saw?"

"Of course not."

His brows pulled down. "Why 'of course'?"

"I have a lot of work to do. There isn't time for—"

"Happiness?"

She turned her gaze back to her open laptop, choosing to ignore his sarcasm.

"Do you mean to spend all your time in Dublin just working?" he asked.

"Sterling brought me here to do a job, not to be a tourist."

"I thought the man wasn't your boss."

"And I thought you were supposed to be helpful."

Why did he always laugh? "Fair enough." He rose.

"Are you leaving?" She made certain he could tell she hoped he was.

His half smile tugged at an odd scar below his mouth. She shouldn't have found that as intriguing as she did. He was basically the enemy, getting in the way of her work, evidence that Sterling didn't think she could handle this assignment on her own.

"I meant to suggest *we* leave." He jerked his head toward the door. "And, don't worry, I have nothing the least fun in mind. Would hate to enjoy ourselves. I'll show you a few venues you might choose between."

She motioned at her laptop. "You could just give me some websites."

"Could do, but, personally, I like to see a place for myself. Do a bit of the work, you know."

Her jaw clenched. "I do a lot of work."

"Oh, sure. I'm not denying that. I'm banking on it." Again, he jerked his head toward the door. "So let's go do a bit of work."

"I've done plenty already." She rose. "And I'm not afraid to do more."

"I don't doubt you're *excited* to do more work." He pulled open the door. "Just take care you don't accidentally enjoy yourself while you're at it."

"I'm not an unhappy person." She grabbed her phone and wallet, then her jacket, and stepped out into the hallway.

"You hide your happiness really well." Even talking, he sounded like he was laughing.

"And you hide your helpfulness really well."

"Care to put a wager on that?" he asked as they stepped into the elevator.

He had her interest.

"If, by the end of the day, I haven't proven myself helpful, I'll buy you a pint at my local."

She eyed him sidelong. "I'm going to be punished if you turn out to be useless?"

"It's a fine spot. Good craic."

That stopped her in her tracks. She turned wide eyes on him. "Good *crack*?"

He laughed loud and deep. "Another phrase you'll have to learn. Craic means good conversation and company and a good bit of fun." As they stepped out onto the ground floor headed for the lobby, he shot her an over-done look of dawning understanding. "Ah, but there's the problem, yah? You might enjoy yourself at a spot like that. Best not risk it."

"Okay, here's my bet with you. If, by the end of the day, I have proven that I do enjoy myself even when I'm working, then you bow out of helping plan this event and let me do my job."

"Can't do," he said. "You didn't hire me. Westcott did."

They stepped out into the overcast, cool Dublin afternoon. The wind was blowing. She pulled on and buttoned her jacket. Out of habit, she reached for her phone to pull up her map app.

"I grew up in this city, Keighley," Brogan said. "We don't need a phone telling us where to go."

She popped her phone back in her pocket and let him lead the way.

When she'd first gone from the master-planned suburbs of Phoenix to New York City, she'd been a little overwhelmed, in a good way, by how old and historic and eclectic the city was. She'd felt like she was stepping into a history book. Dublin felt even more that way. More than just old… it was magical.

Of course, Brogan didn't need to know that. "Tell me about the venues we're going to look at."

"Always on the clock, aren't you?"

"Humor me," she said dryly.

"The first stop is a pub."

"Shocking."

Far from offended, he simply smiled. "This pub has an upper room that's big and nice. Plenty of room for putting on an impressive do but keeping the congenial feel of an evening out with friends."

That sounded ideal, actually. "Okay. You have my attention."

"I also want to drop in on a performance hall I've hired before. Nice space. It can be set up any way at all. Tables and chairs, or cocktail tables and a long bar. There's even a small stage to one end if you're looking to bring in a band or something."

She hadn't thought about a band. But a little music might be nice.

They turned a corner down a narrow but busy street, lined on both sides with an unbroken row of colorful buildings, storefronts at the street level but, likely, apartments above.

"If we go with a venue that has room for musicians, would you suggest quiet instrumental or folk music?" she asked

"It's a shame you haven't a better grasp of the language, Keighley."

She looked to him, confused. They both were speaking English.

"We don't call it folk music. It's trad. Trad music."

"Trad?" That was an odd word.

"It's short for 'traditional,'" he said. "And, yah, trad'd be a good choice. But you'll want to hire a small group so they'll not be too loud. People will want to chat."

"I once made the mistake of hiring a band that thought they were catching their big break. When everyone in the room was talking instead of listening intently, they started playing louder. So the people started talking louder. And the music got louder."

He nodded along with her retelling. "I've made that mistake."

"You'll warn me before I hire that band, won't you?"

"You have my word." He stopped their forward progress. "Now." He pointed beside them. "Is that the castle church you saw this morning?"

She looked. It was a gorgeous, old stone church. Absolutely beautiful. "That's not the same one, but it's amazing."

"Hmm."

She didn't know what that noise was supposed to mean.

They continued on, eventually winding their way to a much larger street. The city was old. No one would miss that walking down this stretch of road. They stopped at an intersection, and Brogan pointed up the road.

"Is that your castle church?"

Another church sat up that street, all of it except the steeple blocked from view by nearer buildings. "That's not it." She eyed him, curious. "You're searching for the church I thought was a castle?"

"Mostly I'm curious to know how far you walked. You never take a break from working, but you did this morning to take a jaunt. I'm dying to know how long you were away."

For just a moment, she was flattered that he had such curiosity about her. But she pushed it aside at the reminder that they had work to do. "How far away are the venues we're looking at?"

"Not far." He tucked his hands in the pockets of his pants and kept walking.

She moved faster to keep pace with him. "All the times I dreamed of coming to Ireland, I always assumed that the Irish people would be friendly."

"We are friendly," he said.

"You're grumpy."

"That's part of the Irish charm." He leaned nearer as they walked on. "We're *both*."

"Sterling manages to be charming without being grumpy," she said.

"What he manages to be is rich. The charming or the grumpy of it doesn't matter much after that."

"That's unfair," she said.

"But is it untrue?"

The tiniest moment of doubt kept her from responding immediately. But she came back to her senses. "Of course it's not true."

"You know him well, then?" Brogan asked. "Spent lots of time with him? Seen him in a lot of different circumstances?"

"Well, no, but I have gotten to know him. We put on an event together."

"Ah." That was all he said about that. He was so frustrating.

A green double-decker bus passed. A man's voice, singing a song, floated off of it, sounding like it was coming through speakers.

"Was the driver singing?" she wondered out loud.

"They do on the tours sometimes," Brogan said. "Adds a bit of color to the drive."

It was probably considered cheesy and totally touristy, but that sounded like a blast. A tour of the city while being sung to... she could get into that.

"The whole loop doesn't take long. You ought to tuck it in to your schedule in the next day or two."

Oh, it was tempting. But she shook her head. "I'm here to work, not tour."

"Don't you think Boss Charming would give you time off enough for a bus ride?"

She pulled her jacket more firmly around herself. The

wind was a little too chilly for comfort. "Why don't you like Sterling?" she asked.

"Why do you?" he tossed back.

The question set her a little off balance. Why did she like him? She just did. And if Brogan hadn't caught her off guard, she could have told him the answer in detail.

"Where are these venues we're supposed to be looking at?" She was all business again.

He just laughed. Of course he did.

Four

KEIGHLEY MET STERLING IN the lobby early the next morning. He wanted to know how plans were coming along, but had meetings all day long. She didn't mind. She liked mornings, even with the jetlag.

"We looked at two venues yesterday. Both were promising in their own way, but neither really jumped out at me as the perfect spot. Brogan said he'd send me a list of other places to check out."

Sterling nodded. "I knew you were the right one to plan this."

She needed the compliment. He offered them often, something Brogan seemed to be allergic to.

"How do you like Dublin?" Sterling asked over his coffee mug.

"I'm enjoying it. Reminds me a little of New York." She sipped her tea. "But wetter."

He smiled at her quip. He had a very charming smile. She doubted many people got to see it over a friendly breakfast chat. "And the business heads here are harder to schmooze."

She kept both hands wrapped around her teacup. She appreciated the warmth. "Is that what we're doing? Schmoozing?"

"Schmoozing. Smooching. Whatever it takes." He chuckled a little as he took another sip of coffee.

She didn't know whether to laugh, blush, or take him

entirely seriously. That she had no idea which gave her pause. Maybe she didn't really know him that well yet. Yet.

"I would like to get invitations out in the next couple of days," he said. "So try to find a location soon and get that all worked out."

"Not a problem."

"I knew it wouldn't be." It was little wonder women melted when he smiled at them.

"I will plan on having a venue selected by tomorrow morning," she assured him. "The rest of the details should fall quickly into place after that."

He rose. "You're the best, Keighley."

"Thanks." She stayed outwardly relaxed, but inside she was a little giddy. "We can touch base tomorrow."

He raised his coffee mug as he stepped away. "I look forward to it."

She watched him walk out. Which meant she also saw Brogan walk in. She ought to have been annoyed, but he'd been kind of fun to go back and forth with the day before. She looked forward to doing it again.

He walked directly to her and, smile pulling at the scar on his chin, dropped two cards on the table in front of her. She looked at him from around her teacup. "Hop-on Hop-off bus," she read aloud.

"No American can come to Dublin and not ride the green bus."

The green double-decker. That had looked like fun. But, she couldn't. "I promised Sterling I'd have a venue for his event selected by morning. I can't spend the day on a tourist bus."

"Wouldn't take all day," he said. "And we might think of another venue option while we're out."

"We? You were born here. Why would you want to ride a tourist bus?"

He picked up the tickets once more and waved her toward the door. "Because it's fun to see the city through the eyes of someone discovering her for the first time."

Keighley rose, but hesitantly. "You're going to make fun of me?"

For once, there was no laughter in his expression. "Not at all. You said yesterday you used to dream about coming to Ireland. You can't spend the next week missing everything. Give yourself the morning to do something massively touristy. You'll enjoy it."

"And you're coming too?"

He shrugged a shoulder. "It'll be fun."

"You mean it'll be 'good craic'?"

A quick laugh. "You're learning." Another motion toward the door. How she wanted to go.

"Sterling will be upset if I don't have things worked out."

Brogan eyed her doubtfully. "The same Sterling you insisted was charming and wonderful and everything amazing, and not because he's rich? That Sterling would begrudge you a morning of seeing this beautiful city?"

She didn't have a ready answer.

"Well I can see why you find him so appealing. Sounds like a keeper."

They walked along the usual narrow, winding streets. "Why does my opinion of Sterling matter to you?"

"Because the mark of a good man is that he doesn't stand silent when another man takes advantage of the undeserved loyalty of a woman who could do a whole lot better."

She didn't know whether to be flattered or offended. Probably both.

The iconic green bus pulled to the stop just as they arrived. Brogan hopped on. "Two for the loop," he said to the driver as she stepped in behind him.

"You sound too Dublin for this," the driver said.

"I've an American in tow." He nodded toward Keighley. "First time in Ireland. Hasn't seen a thing."

"We'll show her around." The driver motioned them back.

Tourists in ball caps emblazoned with "Ireland" or shamrock covered sweatshirts and sporting backpacks and fanny packs filled the benches, phones out and ready to take pictures.

"There's not a lot of room," Keighley said.

"There'll be room up top." He took the steps upward at a fast clip.

She followed, excitement bubbling. She had seen Instagram posts from the top of these busses, and it always looked amazing and fun and exactly the sort of cheesy touristy thing she'd enjoy doing.

Brogan wasn't wrong; there were plenty of empty benches on the upper deck.

"Why does no one sit up here?"

He shrugged. "Easier to get off if you're inside. Warmer in there. They're not as bright as we are." He plopped down on the back bench and leaned back, obviously ready to relax and enjoy a ride around town.

She sat next to him, not bothering to hold back her excitement. "This is kind of great."

"Isn't it, though?"

The bus pulled back into traffic and the driver's voice sounded over the speakers. He told them the things they were seeing, a little history, a joke or two. Or seven. Before too many more stops to pick up or leave off passengers, Keighley was laughing out loud, no matter that the jokes were usually really bad puns or completely ridiculous stories that couldn't possibly be true. And each time they passed a church, which happened a lot, Brogan pointed at it and said, "Is that your castle church?"

And every time, she said, "No."

After three or four no's, he asked, "Are you certain you remember this church?"

She laughed. "I'll know it when I see it."

"Just how far did you walk that first morning?"

She didn't know, exactly. "Far."

He looked at her. "Were you escaping?"

"No, I wasn't—" But then something stopped her. "Maybe a little. I was in an unfamiliar place and that room is—don't get me wrong, it's beautiful and huge, but…" She sighed.

"But it's not *you.*"

She shook her head. "I'm not fancy like that. I like it, but it's hard to feel relaxed, and that makes it hard to work."

"Well, then." Brogan motioned to the open air around them. "Take in this grand old town. It'll ease your mind and let you relax. I do some of my best thinking out on the living streets."

She filled her lungs with cool, humid air and let herself just enjoy the ride.

The driver announced Dublin Castle to the left.

"That's not my church," she stated before Brogan could ask the question she knew was on his mind.

He laughed and, for once, it didn't bother her in the least.

Mere moments later, directly in front of them she spotted it. "That's my castle church." She pointed at it. "That's it."

"Ah, Christ Church Cathedral," he said. "You did walk far that morning. She's a grand lady. I commend your taste."

The closer they got, the more beautiful it became. "You don't suppose they hire out for events, do you?" She asked with a grin.

"Blasphemy. Careful or they'll toss you in the catacombs."

That brought her full attention to him. "There are catacombs?"

"Oh, there are catacombs."

When the bus stopped at the cathedral, they got off. He showed her the cathedral, the catacombs, the Viking museum next door. They walked up to St. Patrick's Cathedral and Marsh's Library next to that enormous church. The green bus took them all around the city. They'd hop off any time something caught her fancy or whenever there was something he thought she'd enjoy.

The entire day passed that way. Fun and joyous. And, though he likely didn't realize it, it was a dream come true. She'd always wanted to see Ireland, and Dublin in particular. And she had, though the experience had convinced her there was so much more to see than she would ever have time for.

But as they returned to the hotel in the early evening, a horrible realization struck her. She was supposed to have a venue for Sterling's networking event booked and ready in time to tell him the details in the morning. She hadn't done a lick of work.

"Breathe a bit, Keighley," Brogan said. "You can sort this."

She'd faced tighter turn-arounds than this. She could manage it. And, though she'd resented the help at first, having Brogan's knowledge of the city would help.

A bit of calm settled over her again. "We can grab dinner at the hotel restaurant and toss around ideas while we eat."

It proved a bit of genius. They talked through a lot of possibilities, narrowing down their ideas until they knew better what they were aiming for: elegant and sleek, like the rooms Sterling had chosen that fit *him* so well, and something that called on the feel of the city itself, to make certain his possible business partners knew he wasn't sweeping in to change things, but to add to the strength the companies already had.

But where to find such a place?

"The Leprechaun Museum?" Brogan suggested.

She couldn't hold back the laughter at that idea. That particular stop had been a favorite: goofy and fun, but nothing at all like what they were looking for.

The server came with the bill for her to sign. Brogan kept him there a minute, though.

"Do you have any venues for hire here in the hotel other than the meeting rooms and ballrooms?"

Keighley had thought of hosting the event here, but none of those spaces made sense.

"We've the rooftop terrace," he said. "Can't say it's often hired out entirely, but now and then."

She met Brogan's eye. "Promising."

"It is."

"Let's have a look."

She was hopeful but kept herself grounded as they took the lift to the roof. It'd be a godsend to find something workable right there at the hotel.

In the end, it proved perfect. The space was sleek, modern, impressive. But all around was the city itself. The hotel could provide catering. Brogan would definitely know some two- or three-piece musical groups who could come in to provide background entertainment.

"This could work," she said, relief mixing with excitement.

"You got your job done and saw a good bit of the city. I'd call that a successful day."

It had gone well. Excellent, in fact.

But in the morning, the real work would begin. She liked her work, but she found herself wishing she could spend another day seeing the city.

With Brogan.

Five

KEIGHLEY SAT IN THE usual spot in the hotel lobby the next morning, waiting for Sterling to join her for their morning debriefing. She sipped her tea in one hand and scrolled through Instagram with her other thumb.

After a couple of stops on the Impromptu Dublin Tour the day before, she'd gotten into the spirit of being a cheesy tourist and posted shots. Brogan had even convinced her to snap a selfie on the top of the double-decker bus, photobombing her at the last moment. She scrolled back until she came to that post. It made her laugh every time she looked at it. Friends and family had commented on it, more so than any of her other posts, all saying how happy she looked and that she seemed to be having fun.

She was. She'd had fun all day. It was hard to remember the last time that happened. Even while scrambling to find a venue last night, she'd still been enjoying herself. A text had come in while she was asleep—the time difference made that happen—from her best friend, asking, "Who's the redhead?!" And another from her mom—an animated GIF of a cat saying, "Who dat?" Mom was a little obsessed with GIFs.

She'd posted shots with Sterling at the event she'd planned in New York. No one had to ask who he was. Everyone knew Sterling Westcott.

She swiped through the pictures she'd taken at Christ

Church Cathedral. At Phoenix Park. The Leprechaun Museum. She laughed at those last ones. The museum itself had been entertaining, with lots of enjoyable folktales and an interesting tour guide. But the pictures they'd taken in the gift shop were her favorite. There had been a giant plush leprechaun to pose beside, complete with leprechaun wardrobe accessories to sport. She'd said no at first, but Brogan, being Brogan, had talked her into it. She was glad he had. If nothing else, the pictures were priceless.

She looked up at the sound of purposeful footsteps. That would be Sterling.

And it was.

He sat across from her, coffee cup in hand. She'd seldom seen him without some degree of a smile on his face. It was missing this morning.

"Everything okay?" she asked.

"A long day yesterday." He took a swallow from his steaming cup. "You seem to have enjoyed yourself, though."

She was confused.

"Your posts," he said. "You forgot I follow you on Instagram, didn't you?"

"I guess I did." Was she in trouble? She wasn't a child, and like she'd told Brogan, Sterling wasn't technically her boss. But his tone hinted that she'd broken some rule of his.

"Did you book a venue for the mingle event?" he asked. Sterling was always very business minded, but he wasn't usually this gruff.

"I did."

The man actually looked surprised. Keighley pushed back her offended frustration.

"I told you I would have a venue booked, and I do." She closed out Insta and pulled up her note app. "Friday night. The rooftop terrace here at The Marker. It can easily accommodate a group the size you're planning on. The bar will be open. The hotel will cater, plenty of cocktail foods and hors d'oeuvres. I'm going to bring in a private serving staff so no one is trying to work the restaurant downstairs and your event. We're also looking into hiring a small musical group to provide some background ambiance."

He nodded. Was that approval or simply acknowledgement? He was usually more complimentary.

"Are you unhappy with the arrangements?"

"I'm sure it'll be fine," he said.

This *was* odd. "If there's something specific you'd like for the event, now is a good time to let me know, while I'm still finalizing everything."

He smiled a little. "I'm kind of in a bad mood this morning, I guess. I shouldn't worry about this event. You pulled off the last one and did great."

"That's why you brought me here." She lightened her tone so he would know she wasn't offended that he'd been grumbling.

"It is why," he said. "And I know you'll do great. Are plans solid enough that I can mention it at meetings today, or is it still up in the air?"

She shook her head. "No reason you couldn't. I'll have invitations printed up today and distributed tomorrow so it's official and professional, but you can tell people. I don't anticipate any of the big details changing."

"This is a very important event," he said, pointedly. "Striking deals here means getting a foothold in the European market. That expansion is a multi-million-dollar opportunity."

"The mingle will help with that goal," she said. "Just like you want it to."

Where was this coming from? He hadn't been directly critical, but there'd been a heavy hint of it.

"And has Brogan been doing anything to plan this?"

"Yes."

"Hmm." It was a sound of mingled surprise and doubt.

"He has. He had a good list of venues that we checked and discussed. He knew the type of music that would be most appreciated. And he's going to find and hire the band."

"He's a multi-tasker." Sterling spoke a little dryly.

"We've gotten a lot done," she said.

"Apparently." He rose, coffee cup still in his hand.

"Are you upset with me?" she asked.

He shook his head. "I just want this to go well."

"It will," she said.

"You promise?"

"I promise."

He gave a quick nod and left. Keighley pushed out a breath, but it didn't relieve the tension.

She had her phone out the next instant and texted Brogan. "DEFCON 1."

Keighley grabbed another cup of tea on her way back up to her room. She needed to make calls, finalize things. Design an invitation and find a printer. By the end of the day, the big bits needed to all be in place. She would not have another morning meeting with Sterling like the one she'd just had.

She'd laid out her bullet journal, pens, the menu the hotel had given her the night before, and the list of information she'd gotten from Sterling on her first day in Dublin. She opened her laptop. Before she could even start designing the invitation, her phone buzzed.

A text. She glanced. It was Brogan. Perfect.

She opened the text. "What's happened?"

Some of her strain eased. Brogan would jump in and help. She knew he would; and not just because he'd been hired to. "Sterling is worried the event won't be ready in time, or good enough."

She watched the three dots. This was helping, weirdly

enough. She'd only known him three days, but he'd somehow become her friend.

"What else needs to be done?" he texted.

Her deep breaths were coming easier. "Design, print, and send out invites. Finalize menu. Decor. And a band. We need a band."

"I'm working on another event this morning. But I'll have a band for Westcott's do by this afternoon. Fast enough?"

That'd work. She sent a thumbs-up emoji.

"Do you have a printer for the invites?"

"Not yet."

"I'll send you a few reliable shops. Any of them will do."

"Awesome." She leaned back in her chair and let the tension slide from her shoulders. They were making progress. Sterling hadn't seen it, but they were.

The next morning meeting would be a million times better. It had to be.

Keighley hadn't stopped working all day. She'd ordered room service and snatched bites between texts, phone calls, and emails. The invites made it out to the printer by noon. They were delivered to the hotel by two o'clock. She delivered them to all the companies that were located within walking distance of The Marker Hotel. Those further out she sent with a courier service. Sterling, she had discovered when planning the event in New York, had money enough to spend that he would rather spend more to get things done quickly and right the first time.

On her way back to The Marker after dropping off the last of the invitations, her phone buzzed. She hoped it was Sterling asking how things were going. Giving him an impressive update would have done her ego a lot of good. But it was Brogan, which was surprisingly even better.

"Do you have dinner plans?"

She texted back, "No."

He answered with a destination name and address and few brief directions. "Half six?"

She stared at that for a long while, no idea what he meant by that. Finally she answered, "Could you translate that into American?"

"6:30."

She grinned. Now and then, the people here said something that made no sense even though they were speaking English. It was kind of fun to try to figure it out.

"Sounds great. See you then."

She stopped at the concierge desk and asked about the place where Brogan was meeting her. "I don't know if I ought to change into something more formal or…?"

The man shook his head. "It's a pub. You'll fit in grand wearing just what you are."

"A pub?"

He nodded. "A great spot. Music's always bang on."

That sounded awesome. Arriving there at 6:30, she decided "awesome" was the exact right word for it. It was obviously old, but it felt totally alive. It was bright and open. It was busy without being so crowded that it was uncomfortable. Perfect.

She spotted Brogan quickly. He smiled and wove his way over to her. "You found the place."

"I had very good directions." She looked around again, still impressed. "Maybe we should have held Sterling's event here. This place is great."

"He would've hated it." Brogan spoke with unwavering conviction.

"Why do you say that?"

He walked with her back toward the table he'd been sitting at. "The day he hired me on, we met at the hotel bar. He ordered some fancy drink I'd never heard of. I ordered a Guinness. He said, and I quote, 'Hmm.'"

It was the exact "hmm" she'd heard from Sterling a couple of times the last two days. Surprise, doubt, confusion. Maybe even a little disapproval.

"Any man who looks down his nose at a Guinness isn't going to be caught with even one foot in the door of a place like this. The hotel terrace is a better spot. You chose well there."

"*We* chose well." She wasn't the only one who'd narrowed in on that location.

"Let me know what you think of the boys playing trad tonight," he said. "I think they'd be a good choice for Sterling's do. I've hired them on before. Reliable. Affordable. Talented."

"They sound perfect."

"That's the hope."

She laughed. Man, that felt good after the day she'd had.

He watched her with his brow pulled a little. "You look tired."

"I worked nonstop today," she said. "I got everything done I possibly could, and a few things that were *barely* possible." She rubbed at her tired eyes. "Maybe Sterling won't lecture me tomorrow morning."

"He lectured you?" Brogan signaled to the server, not missing a beat in their conversation. "What about?"

"I told him all the things we've figured out and finalized. He kept saying 'Really? That's done? Are you sure? You really got that done?' It was like he was convinced we hadn't accomplished anything."

"Did he do that 'Hmm' thing?"

Keighley bit back a smile.

Brogan's jaw clenched a bit. "That sound makes a person want to punch the man in the nose."

"Punching him never entered my mind," she said. "I was too caught off guard to do anything but sputter through a bunch of reassurances. It was just so frustrating. He knows I'm reliable and that I do good work. It's the whole reason he brought me here to plan this event. But he was acting like I was a total flake. It was... stupid."

"Well, Sterling Westcott may be wealthy, but he's not that bright."

The server arrived in exactly that moment, her paper pad ready to take their order.

"How ya, Mary?" Brogan greeted her.

"Well," she said.

"This here's Keighley, from New York. Her day's been a misery. I figured I'd best fill her up with good food so she doesn't tear my head off."

Mary nodded. "A fine idea." She turned a friendly smile on Keighley. "All the food's good here. And Jackie and the lads are playing tonight. That'll liven up the place."

They put in their orders, then talked, but not about Sterling or the event they were planning. She asked about Brogan's other job, the one he'd been working on that day. He asked about the events she'd planned in New York. She showed him some of the pictures she'd posted from their day of touristing, earning one of his bubbling laughs.

"A fellow doesn't often get to be a tourist in his own hometown. It was fun to pretend for a day."

"It was fun." She took a bite of the shepherd's pie Brogan had suggested she order. "Oh, this is good."

He grinned. "Did you think I was lying?"

"You did tell me yesterday that you kissed the Blarney Stone."

"That makes a person talkative, not dishonest."

"And what does shepherd's pie make a person?" she asked after another bite.

"Very, very happy."

The rest of the night went like that. Bantering and laughing. Swapping stories of events gone awry, childhood mishaps. She laughed more than she had in a very long time. It was fun and relaxing, and she still managed to get some work done. The band was perfect, and Brogan arranged with them before the night was over to play for Sterling's mingle.

She was a good event planner and a hard worker, but Brogan was teaching her something about making that work fun and making time for something other than planning other people's memorable moments.

If she didn't have her standing morning meeting with Sterling, she would have been happy to stay all night, chatting and listening to music, laughing with Brogan and the friends he introduced her to. But, she wanted her next meeting with him to go better than her last.

"I probably need to go," she said.

"Really?" He sounded genuinely disappointed. That did her a world of good.

"I have my daily meeting with Sterling in the morning. If he lectures me again and I'm exhausted, I'll probably either tell him off or cry."

Brogan smiled. "I'd enjoy watching you tell him off."

He lighted her heart. She appreciated that so much. "And cry? Would you enjoy watching that too?"

"No." He set his hand on hers where it rested on the tabletop. "Not at all."

"Then I should go." She kept her hand in his. She liked the feel of it. "The event we're planning is going to be great, and I don't want to undermine that by making Sterling think I'm an idiot."

Brogan shook his head. "If he thinks that, he's the idiot."

She kind of loved the way he said "idiot." His Irish accent turned it into something more like "idjet," and it made her smile.

"Come on, then," he said. "I'll walk you back."

"I won't say no."

They moved toward the door, still hand in hand. She couldn't remember the last time she held hands with someone. It was sweet and tender and… she loved it.

He waved to a friend they'd chatted with. "We're gonna head on."

His friend nodded. "Ah, sure. Come 'round again, Keighley."

They stepped out. Brogan made a quick check of the street then, tugging her along by the hand, crossed quickly.

"What time do you meet with Sterling tomorrow?" he asked.

"Eight o'clock."

That brought his eyes to her again. "In the morning?"

She laughed out loud. "You Irish aren't fans of the a.m., are you?"

He shook his head. "Don't believe in it."

"I'll text you tomorrow and tell you all about it—sometime after noon."

"That'd be appreciated."

The walk back to The Marker felt shorter than she knew it was. She enjoyed being with Brogan, and he seemed to enjoy her company as well.

He rode with her up the elevator. He even slipped his arm around her and tucked her in close. She could grow used to that.

At the door to her room, he leaned against the wall beside the doorframe. "Don't let Sterling talk down to you tomorrow. You're planning a great event for him; he shouldn't get to make you feel otherwise."

She looked up at him. "You're right. I've wanted him to approve of me so badly that I basically let him decide if I deserve to be approved of."

"You do, though. Every person I introduced you to tonight liked you straight off. The more I know you, the more I like you. If Sterling Westcott can't see that, he's not worth your worry."

She set her hand on his arm. "Thank you." Keighley stretched up enough to press a quick, light kiss to his lips before stepping back again.

She could tell she was blushing a little, but he grinned, clearly not offended.

"Sleep well, Keighley. Fight the good fight in the morning and tell me how it goes. But do wait until a less miserable hour."

"I will." She stood in the doorway and watched as he walked back down the hall, his hands stuffed in his pockets, whistling one of the tunes the band had played that night.

Keighley couldn't remember the last time someone had made her heart flip around like it was doing now. He was wonderful. She had spent so many weeks wondering what it would take to catch Sterling's eye and what it would be like to have him fall for her and… and maybe she was the "idjet."

Six

KEIGHLEY HEADED TO THE lobby early enough to settle in and relax before there was any chance Sterling would be there. She brought a list with her so he wouldn't catch her off guard if he asked again what she'd been spending her time on. Impressing him on a personal level didn't really matter much anymore; she simply wasn't going to let his doubts become her doubts like she had the morning before.

She set her list on the side table, on top of the receipts for all the things she'd purchased and arranged. She'd practiced in front of her mirror that morning answers to questions she anticipated him asking. This meeting would go better than the last one.

Sleep had been elusive the night before. Nervousness about the next morning. Thoughts of Brogan. Shock that she'd kissed him. She'd texted her best friend, which had ended up in hours of back and forth.

Keighley pulled out her phone. Another text had come while she was asleep. She'd read it at least a dozen times already, but she did again. "You better hide Brogan in your suitcase and bring him back with you."

If only. Sterling would be coming back to New York. It was amazing how disappointing that had become in only a few days.

He arrived just as she was finishing her tea. His

demeanor was a lot more at-ease than the day before. "Good morning," he said.

"Good morning."

He sat in his usual spot but didn't immediately launch into questions. "I was frustrated yesterday, and I'm sorry about that."

She hadn't expected to hear an apology first thing. "I noticed. But I got a lot done yesterday, so there's less for you to be worried about now." Keighley reached for her papers, but he spoke again before she could begin rattling off her list.

"I knew you would, and I shouldn't have snapped at you."

Wow. He was being more gracious than she ever would have guessed. "We finished almost all of the arrangements yesterday. I'm picking out some flowers and other decorative elements today, but otherwise, it'll just be keeping tabs on everything and checking in with anyone we don't get an RSVP from."

"We?" he asked.

"Brogan and I," she said.

"Oh." He took a sip of coffee. "I didn't realize he was still part of it."

"You didn't fire him, did you?" She hadn't heard he had.

Sterling shook his head. "I just assumed you were getting the work done."

"I *am*." Hadn't they just established that?

"He's the reason you fell behind two days ago. Is it really smart to—"

"I didn't fall behind," she said. "Everything got done on time and on schedule."

He didn't look at all convinced. "And he's been part of it?"

"That's why you hired him. He's good at what he does."

He muttered something under his breath as he drank more coffee.

"What was that?" she asked.

He shook his head, a look of obvious annoyance in his eyes. "Never mind."

Her frustration was growing. "If you have a complaint, I'd like to hear it."

"It wasn't a complaint," he said.

"No," a familiar Irish voice answered, "it was an insult."

She looked over at Brogan, listening from not far away at all. His gaze on Sterling was hard and cold.

"Why would you insult him?" she asked Sterling. "He's worked hard."

"It wasn't me he was insulting," Brogan said.

Then it was *her*.

"Keighley's been working hard," Brogan said. "And this event of yours is going to be brilliant because of her. I'd say you owe her an apology."

"She works for me," Sterling said. "And so do you. I don't apologize to employees."

"I'm not your employee." Keighley's voice and fire returned very suddenly. She'd spent her first day with Brogan insisting Sterling wasn't her boss. She wasn't going to cave on that now. "I don't require you to apologize, but I will be treated with professional respect."

Apparently no one had ever spoken to Sterling that way. He looked surprised, baffled. How had she thought this man was anyone's ideal, let alone hers?

"Your event will be a success," she said, standing up. "That is a promise I always deliver on. It's the reason my event planning services are in demand. It is the reason the last event I put on for you was so impressive that you gave me this event to plan as well."

Brogan stood, watching Sterling with firm silence, arms folded, jaw set.

"I'll email you updates as needed, but I don't think these

morning meetings are necessary." She gathered up her papers. "And I'll contact your travel secretary directly to get the details of my return flight and hotel check-out."

She walked away without giving him a chance to either defend himself or rip into her. Brogan remained behind, but she made directly for the elevator. She felt like she didn't even breathe until she was in her room, door closed, curtains pulled.

What a nightmare this job had turned into. It had seemed like the ultimate opportunity: a dream trip to Ireland, working for someone as influential as Sterling, the stupid stars she'd had in her eyes for him.

I was such an idiot.

There was a knock. So help her, if it was Sterling...

She squared her shoulders and pulled open the door. It was Brogan. Of course it was.

"You holding up?" he asked.

She sighed and motioned him in, closing the door behind him. "What was it Sterling actually said?"

He shook his head. "I'm not going to repeat it."

Keighley dropped onto the sofa and slumped down, tired and frustrated. "He always seemed so..."

"Charming?" Brogan sat next to her.

She could smile a little at that. "I did describe him that way, didn't I? How was I so blind?"

He shrugged. "I've worked for a few people like him: wealthy, used to getting whatever they want, able to *be* whatever they needed to be to get things from people. I know his type, so it was easier not to believe the lie, ya know?"

"I live in New York. I should know the type as well; we're crawling with them."

He took her hand. "Don't be ashamed of thinking well of people. It's not a failing."

"But it makes me look like an idiot."

"No, it doesn't."

She leaned against him. The jet lag hadn't been too bad, but in that moment she felt tired to her bones. "So, is he pulling me off this event?"

Brogan half-laughed, half-snorted. "He can't afford to."

"He's a billionaire," she said. "I don't think there's anything he can't afford."

"I don't mean the money. If the event falls apart, he'll be humiliated. If there's one thing these wealthy, spoiled, always-get-their-way types can't endure, it's embarrassment."

"Maybe I should sabotage the whole thing and get my revenge." She wasn't at all serious, but it felt good to make the threat.

"I have a better idea," he said. "Let's go see a few sights. You didn't get to tour Dublin Castle."

"An actual castle?" Her heart flipped a bit.

"More of a palace, really, and nothing so grand as Buckingham, but a castle."

"I would like to see a castle."

His smile sent waves of warmth over her. "I thought you might."

"But you said you had another event to work on this morning. I wasn't expecting to see you at all, and definitely not run around the city with you."

He leaned closer to her and lowered his voice. "Are you turning down the invitation?"

"No," she whispered.

"I'm glad to hear it." His breath tickled her lips.

"I'm guessing you didn't mind that I kissed you last night," she whispered.

"Oh, I didn't mind."

He closed the gap and brushed the lightest of kisses to her lips. Such a soft and fleeting touch, but it sent jolts of electricity through her.

He stood, her hand still in his, and tugged her playfully toward the door. "Let's go see a castle."

A castle. A handsome Irishman. A heart-fluttering kiss. She could get used to this.

Seven

EVERY INVITATION HAD BEEN accepted. The rooftop terrace looked amazing. The waitstaff wove around effortlessly with hors d'oeuvres and finger foods. The band played toe-tapping music without preventing mingling and conversations.

Keighley ran go-between for all the bits and pieces, checking on things and answering questions for the people behind the scenes. Brogan put out the proverbial fires, though there weren't many. They exchanged a few high-fives, tossed each other thumbs up across the way. All-in-all, the night went off without a hitch.

Even Sterling paused his schmoozing long enough to tell them, "This turned out fine." Considering he'd apparently said something *really* insulting only a few days earlier, she took that as a compliment. "When you're done here tonight, submit your invoice to my business manager."

Brogan nodded. Keighley offered an "okay" and that was it.

As Sterling walked away, Keighley said to Brogan, "That was less rude than I'd braced myself for."

"I'd guess he didn't want a scene," Brogan said.

"I wouldn't have made a scene."

He shook his head. "But he knows I might have."

She took his hand and pulled him aside where they could talk with a little privacy. "What did you say to him that morning in the lobby?"

"A few home truths is all. He knows where I stand."

She stepped closer. "And where do you stand?"

"With you." He pressed the same feather-light kiss to her lips he had once before.

A shiver slid down her spine even as her heart dropped to her toes. "I'll be standing in New York tomorrow."

"I'm doing my best not to think about that," he said. "The Atlantic's an awful big ocean, Keighley."

"I know."

The kitchen coordinator motioned to her from across the way.

"You'd best go," Brogan said. "No point ending the night with a disaster."

She hoped he was talking about the kitchen and not the confession they'd been tiptoeing toward.

In the end, she couldn't be sure. He sent her a text as everything was wrapping up, saying another event that night was short-staffed for clean-up and he needed to go help them find a solution.

"I head to the airport at 8 tomorrow," she answered. Surely she was going to get to see him one more time before she left.

"8 in the MORNING?"

She smiled. He'd said exactly that to her before. She could hear his voice in her head saying it now.

She was going to miss him.

This trip to Dublin had seemed like the perfect opportunity for getting to know Sterling better. Spending even another moment with the billionaire no longer held any appeal. But her heart was breaking at the thought of an ordinary, amazing, exactly-what-she-dreamed-of Irishman.

Fate was sometimes a total jerk.

She didn't hear from him that night or the next morning before she checked out of the hotel. She made it through security and customs and all the way to the gate where her flight to New York would be taking off. Not a word.

Maybe she'd read too much into things. They'd had fun, and they'd become friends. The kisses and hand holding, maybe that didn't mean as much in Ireland as she thought.

Then again, what could have even come of it? As Brogan had said, the Atlantic was a big ocean. It wasn't like they were going to see each other again. Cutting off everything abruptly was probably smart. It hurt now, but it would be easier in the long run. She hoped.

She pulled out her phone again, telling herself she wasn't checking for a text. She was, though. Nothing.

Her flight didn't leave for over an hour. She had almost no time left in Dublin. And she was spending it sitting alone. She should have gone more places and seen more things, instead of wasting so much time worrying about what Sterling would think about her work ethic and dedication.

She should have gone with Brogan to see all the things he'd told her about. There would have been time. And maybe the friendship between them would have grown into something more. And maybe he would have said goodbye. Maybe.

Walking around might distract her a little while she waited to board. She pulled her wheeled, under-seat bag along behind her as she began a circuit of the small terminal.

Not many steps along, she swore she heard her name. She looked around but didn't see anyone. Then she heard it again, behind her.

She turned back. Brogan was rushing toward her.

Every ounce of air rushed from her lungs, every thought fled except one: Brogan was there.

By the time he reached her, she'd found her voice. "How did you—? Why did they let you back here?" Then she spotted his carry-on slung over his shoulder. "You're flying."

He smiled that uneven smile of his and shrugged a little. "I've never been to New York."

Her heart leaped in her chest. "You're coming to New York?"

"Thought I might."

He was coming to America. "On my flight?"

"I figure we can convince someone to switch seats with one of us."

"You're coming to New York."

"It's a big ocean, Keighley," he said. "But there's something here, between the two of us. Something I'm not ready to let go of. I figure I'd rather be on the same side of that ocean as you while we sort out what it is."

Her grin only grew. "I thought, when you didn't even text this morning to say goodbye…"

"I've been working to figure out what flight you were on, and getting myself on it, and getting things together to be gone for a while, and I—" He laughed. "And it's more romantic to just show up, I figured. Maybe it's just lame."

"It's amazing." She didn't think she would ever stop smiling. "You're coming to New York."

"Honestly"—he slipped his arm around her—"I'm just coming to *you*. Wherever you're going."

She set her hand against his chest. "Let's cross an ocean, Brogan. I think that's a good start."

He bent his head toward her but paused mere inches away. "I'm not a billionaire, you know."

"That's a very good thing for you," she said, "because I have no intention of ever falling for a billionaire."

On that declaration, she kissed him, right there in the

airport, in Dublin, in the country she'd always wanted to visit, where she'd met him, and where everything had changed.

Where her dreams had finally begun to come true.

Sarah M. Eden is the author of multiple historical romances, including the two-time Whitney Award Winner *Longing for Home* and Whitney Award finalists *Seeking Persephone* and *Courting Miss Lancaster*. Combining her obsession with history and affinity for tender love stories, Sarah loves crafting witty characters and heartfelt romances. She has thrice served as the Master of Ceremonies for the LDStorymakers Writers Conference and acted as the Writer in Residence at the Northwest Writers Retreat. Sarah is represented by Pam Victorio at D4EO Literary Agency.

Visit Sarah online:
Twitter: @SarahMEden
Facebook: Author Sarah M. Eden
Website: SarahMEden.com

www.ingramcontent.com/pod-product-compliance
Lightning Source LLC
LaVergne TN
LVHW021755060526
838201LV00058B/3095